A TOUCH OF VENGEANCE

Author's Biography

Educated at Hampton Grammar School and the University of Nottingham, Graeme Roe had a marketing career working for major international companies.

He then founded and built an extremely successful advertising agency. At the age of forty he decided to take up riding and under David Nicholson's guidance gained an amateur National Hunt licence. For ten years he rode both on the flat and over hurdles and fences. His biggest success was winning the Ayr Yeomanry Cup on Dom Perignon.

He then took out a Jockey Club permit quickly followed by a full licence. Amongst his many winners were All Bright, Dom Perignon, Kitty Wren, We're In The Money, Le Grand Maitre, Fairly Sharp and Bad Bertrich.

Graeme now runs a corporate communications company. He has written two books on business, but this is his first novel.

A Touch of Vengeance

GRAEME ROE

Published by Roe Racing Ltd

© Graeme Roe 2004

First published in 2004 by
Roe Racing Ltd,
Hyde Park Farm,
Chalford,
Gloucestershire.

British Library Cataloguing-in Publication data
A catalogue record for this book is available from the British Library

ISBN 0-9547848-0-4

Printed and bound in the UK by Antony Rowe, Chippenham, Wiltshire.
Cover design by David Simons, Art Works, Cheltenham.

To Rene Roe, who taught me the love of racing.

Acknowledgements

Jean, my wife, who supported me through the many ups and downs, the falls and the diet of ten years as an amateur jockey. Her support has continued through my training days.

David Nicholson, who set me on the road in spite of my total lack of knowledge and ability when I first went to him. Rosie Lomax and Toby Balding who gave me rides, moral support and a great deal of friendship.

The many owners who supported me both as a jockey and as a trainer. It is hard to single out any one, but I must give pride of place to Harold Berlinski who was loyal, enormous fun and a pleasure to go racing with whether his horses won or came last. It is very difficult to narrow my thanks down to a few, but I have to single out John Francome, John Suthern and the late Roy Mangan, who all supported me as friends and advisers with a great deal of humour and wisdom throughout my riding career.

I cannot let this acknowledgement pass without expressing my gratitude to the many fun horses I have ridden and trained, in particular All Bright, Dom Perignon, Kitty Wren and Le Grand Maitre. Each in his or her way gave me the delight that only those closely associated with riding or training winners will ever truly understand.

I owe a huge debt of gratitude to Caroline North who has edited the text and made many positive suggestions.

Last, but not least, Sallyann Anderson, my long suffering secretary, who has waded through draft and re-draft with cheerfulness and dedication.

Author's Notes

Horseracing has been, and is still, full of amazing characters from all walks of life, many fascinating, colourful and even eccentric. They come to racing from different backgrounds, with varying hopes and aspirations. Some come for the gambling, some for the spectacle, some for the excitement or just for the association with one of nature's most beautiful and bravest animals – the thoroughbred horse.

Racing has been the forum for raging debate, fierce arguments, wonderful friendships and even passionate love affairs. It has been littered with incidents that are bizarre, exciting, tragic and indelibly printed on many race goers' minds. Horses come in all shapes, sizes and colours. There are brave and impetuous horses. There are lazy and nervous ones. There are sprinters and stayers. There are elegant ones and those who in human life would be thugs. The differences in their appearances and personalities are legion.

All this means that it is virtually impossible to write a book of fiction that is not without some characters in it that bear some resemblance to racegoers both past and present. Similarly, the fictional horses in the story will inevitably bear some resemblance to real equines that have appeared on the racecourses of today and previous decades.

However if this has happened it is entirely by coincidence. No character or horse portrayed in this book is a real one, past or present. There has been no attempt to disguise by a fictional name. Any close resemblance is purely coincidental and I trust that no hurt or offence will have been caused. This is a book of fiction and nothing else.

Chapter One

Sandown Park racecourse was bathed in the November sunshine that is a last touch of autumn before winter sets in. The large, modern grandstand overlooks the racecourse, a venue for Flat and National Hunt racing of the highest order, but perhaps most famed for staging the last major steeplechase of the year, the Whitbread Gold Cup. It is a course that has seen many of the greatest jumping stars perform in front of one of racing's most knowledgeable and appreciative audiences. Horses like Mill House, Desert Orchid and the incomparable Arkle.

On this Friday afternoon a relaxed figure was sitting outside the Barrie Cope seafood bar in the stand, studying the *Racing Post*. There was a bottle of champagne with two glasses in front of him, one full and one awaiting an expected guest.

Even in repose Jason Jessop, universally known as Jay, had the aura of both authority and athletic power. Standing at almost exactly six foot, but weighing only 10st 5lbs, he carried not an ounce of superfluous fat on his broad-shouldered, narrow-waisted, long-legged frame. If a horse was good enough he could waste another 5lbs, but it had to be something very special to justify such extreme measures of starvation and saunas.

This afternoon he was riding only in the last race, a National Hunt Flat race known as a bumper. These races, limited to horses that had never run in Flat races, had been developed in Ireland to give potential hurdlers and steeplechasers a taste of the racecourse before having to deal with obstacles in the hurly-burly of a race over jumps. Originally bumpers were ridden only by amateurs and the name came from the way the riders' bottoms bumped up and down on the saddle.

Jason was not only an amateur jockey but an extremely successful one. He had been brought up by an aunt who devoted the whole of her life to her passion for horses. When she took the nine-year-old Jason under her wing, after his parents were killed in an air crash, she imparted this fascination and affection to him too. She did everything she could to be both father and mother to the little boy but managed to stop short of spoiling him. At twelve he was already hunting and at seventeen he rode in his first point-to-point.

At Cambridge he rode in cross-country teams and local point-to-points and at weekends he would get up at the crack of dawn to drive over to Newmarket to ride out for one of the few stables there that trained National Hunt horses. In his final year he competed in his first race under Jockey Club Rules, a National Hunt Flat race at nearby Fakenham. One race and he was hooked.

When he left university he became a junior business writer on *The Times*, swiftly moving on to the *Financial Times*, before going on to build up a hugely profitable specialist publishing company in London. Hearing that a banking magazine was in difficulty, he saw an opportunity. With the help of two university friends and some financial backing, he took it over and transformed its fortunes. Later he spotted further similar opportunities with insurance, computer software and architectural magazines, shortly followed by an advertising and marketing journal. In just a few years he had a publishing empire.

This meteoric rise did not, however, deter him from spending every spare moment pursing his great love. As a dual career, publishing and raceriding was certainly an unusual combination, but this eccentric double life was about to come to an end. Having resisted countless approaches to float his company on the stock-market, he had finally sold his company to a global American network for a vast sum of money, which meant he need never work again. Until the fine details were rubber-stamped and the sale could be announced this was still a matter of great secrecy between himself, the president and the treasurer of the American buyers.

This afternoon Jason was taking a break from business and looking forward to the race and time in the company of one of his favourite owners. He saw the sprightly figure of Howard Barrack strolling towards him. At five foot eight, with long, silver hair, Howard exuded good humour, enthusiasm and energy. Seeing Jason, a broad smile lit his face and his unusually blue eyes crinkled in pleasure.

'A glass of champagne?' asked Jason as Howard sat down next to him.

'And do fish swim and how's my baby then?' Howard answered him in the same breath. Every horse Howard owned was 'his baby', whatever its age or sex, and he loved them all equally, irrespective of their ability. 'Conker' he added unnecessarily.

The Conker was a nine-year-old dark chestnut gelding, named for his coat's resemblance to a horse chestnut the moment it comes out of its shell. He was a steeplechaser Howard and Jason had bought together in Ireland five years earlier. Having initially shown no promise in his bumpers and very little over hurdles, he had proved to be a spectacular late developer. The combination of three extra years' maturity and a cat-like ability to jump fences had seen him rattle up four wins and three seconds in ten races in his first year as a novice steeplechaser. Thereafter he had developed into a top-class handicapper. In four months' time he was going to run in the four-mile amateur chase at the revered Cheltenham Festival, the National Hunt equivalent of Royal Ascot. Here, under the shadow of Cleeve Hill on the edge of the Cotswolds, the cream of hurdlers and chasers from England, Scotland, Wales and Ireland were joined every March by the stars of France and, in more recent years, America, Poland and the Czech

Republic. They would compete not only for outstanding prize money but also for the kind of prestige enjoyed by the winners of Wimbledon or an Olympic gold medal. It was the dream of every owner, trainer and jockey to see his horse under the number one in the winner's enclosure on one of the Festival's three days.

'He's in the best form I've ever seen him,' said Jason evenly, looking Howard straight in the eye. 'I rode him this morning, and I've never known him better.' Jason was not a man who made forecasts lightly for any race, and particularly not one that involved over four miles of unforgiving fences and a stamina-sapping hill from the last bend to the finishing post.

Familiar with Jason's reputation as a cautious tipster but ever the optimist, Howard chortled at this. Coming from the man who had already won the race once and been placed four times, this assessment had to be taken seriously.

He moved on to other matters. 'What about my little girl today?' His 'little girl' was a beautiful and truly elegant five-year-old grey mare aptly named Pewter Queen.

'Why don't we go and see her? I'm sure Jed will be having his usual cup of coffee by now.'

Before leaving the grandstand they deposited the best part of a bottle of champagne with the girls behind the bar, saying they would be back to polish it off later. Connie, the blonde who had been there as long as either of them could remember, put it in an ice bucket and leaned forward. 'Would you be worth a couple of pounds today?' she whispered.

'Perhaps for a place,' Jason whispered back.

It was a safe bet that Jed Larkin, Howard's trainer, would be sitting in his ancient but reliable Mercedes at the horsebox end of the car park, drinking dark brown, incredibly sweet coffee out of an enormous Thermos flask. Jason and Howard made an odd couple as they ambled past the parade ring. Jason was wearing an immaculately fitted Donegal tweed jacket with dark brown gabardine trousers and highly polished boots with side buckles. Howard was equally expensively but rather more flamboyantly dressed, in a black leather jacket so supple as it could almost have been made out of silk, pale grey worsted trousers and snakeskin shoes with more tassels than a go-go dancer's bra.

To the casual observer Jed's car often appeared to be on fire, but the actual source of the smoke billowing out of the windows was the Gauloise cigarettes he lit one after the other as he listened to his seemingly endless supply of Country and Western tapes and sipped his coffee. Jed had been Howard's trainer since the owner had bought his first racehorse eight years previously and they got on famously in spite of their contrasting rural and East End backgrounds. Jed had never had any really wealthy owners and the great prizes had eluded him, yet he had an enviable reputation for getting the best out of mediocre horses, for giving his owners honest answers, for buying shrewdly and for winning enough races, including a few good handicaps, to ensure that a horse's prize money at the end of the season was always a respectable figure.

Seeing Jason and Howard approaching he clambered out of the car, slamming the door as if he bore it a grudge. 'I expect you'll be wanting to have a look at her, then?' he greeted them. They crossed the car park to the security gate at the entrance of the large stable block. Jed showed his security pass and signed the three of them in. Ever since some suspected doping incidents a year or so earlier the already tight controls had been enforced even more rigorously.

Walking down the row of stables to the one occupied by Howard's newest pride and joy, they saw an intelligent and beautiful grey head watching their approach. Jed pulled back the top bolt, kicked open the bottom one, and the three of them went inside. The happy relationship between Jed and his charges was amply illustrated by the affectionate nuzzle with which he was welcomed by Pewter Queen. Jason appraised the horse with a seasoned eye. Howard gazed at her with a mixture of awe and pride.

'I can hardly believe it's the same horse we bought eighteen months ago,' he said to Jed.

'She's come on a treat' agreed Jed. 'And the great thing about her is she really loves her work and nothing seems to worry her.'

'She really is a fine mare,' said Jason. 'If she runs as well as she looks, you'll have a real star there.'

Howard gave Jed a questioning look. 'Well?' he asked. 'How will she run today?'

'It's a hot race. As you know, there are three winners in it, and three that are unraced but cost a lot more than she did. But to tell the truth, I think she'll do you proud.' Turning to Jason, he added: 'I know you haven't ridden her recently, but she improves every time she works. She also has a real turn of foot when you ask her to quicken. I know Sandown's a stiff two miles, but I think she'll make the trip easily.'

'So how do you want her ridden?' asked Jason.

'Have her in the middle, don't gallop her off her feet in the early stages, even if some of them go mad, and try to be third or fourth only a few lengths off the leader with two furlongs to go. Hold her up as long as you dare, because I think she will take a lot of them by surprise at the end, but I wouldn't want her really slugging it out in her first race – particularly up that hill.'

With a farewell pat from Howard, the three of them left Pewter Queen in peace and returned to the paddock area.

'Well, Howard,' said Jed, 'I've got another owner to find, but I'll see you in the saddling boxes.' He gave them both a cheery grin and strolled off, lighting up another cigarette as he went.

'I think I'll go and take it easy now, Howard,' said Jason. 'Why don't you go and finish that champagne? By the way, after the race, I'd like to have a chat with you about something, apart from this afternoon.'

'That sounds intriguing. Is it going to cost me money?' asked Howard with a grin.

'It might just do that,' Jason called back as he skipped down the steps into the winner's enclosure and disappeared through the doors of the weighing room.

Howard made for the Eclipse Bar where he found one of his old friends from the East End, 'Kipper' Fish, a man he had known for years. He was well dressed and always had a bundle of notes in his pocket, although even Howard was never quite sure how he came by them. He felt it best not to ask too many questions.

'If it isn't my old chum,' said Kipper. 'How's that horse of yours going to run today?'

'I wish I knew. First time out is anyone's guess, but I promise you she'll be trying.'

'Ah, but Jed's always do,' declared Kipper. 'At least you know you're going to get an honest run for your money on his.'

They discussed the next two or three races and Howard, normally a favourite backer, opted for a couple of slightly longer-priced horses. Four races later, he'd had one 5-4 winner, an 8-1 second which he'd only backed to win, and two that were probably still running. However, as far as he was concerned, the sixth race was the all-important one.

As the runners for the fifth left the paddock and made their way down the Rhododendron Walk on to the course, Howard walked briskly across to the saddling boxes between the paddock and the entrance to the stable block. Pewter Queen was being led round a small ring in front of the boxes by Alison, the stable girl who looked after her at home and rode her most days. Having already been taken to a race meeting by Jed and led round the paddock at the end of the afternoon, the unraced horse was not a total stranger to the experience, and she looked interested and alert but by no means nervous. As Alison guided her to her saddling box, Howard spotted Jed coming across the lawn with Jason's saddle over his arm. He followed Jed across to the saddling box where Alison had turned Pewter Queen round and was standing in front of her, holding her reins firmly.

With the easy efficiency that comes with years of experience, Jed undid the buckles of the roller that held the paddock sheet in place. He soon had the protective pad, number cloth and saddle all firmly in position. The paddock sheet, in Howard's dark green and gold colours, was put back, with another number cloth on top, and both were secured with the roller. After a reassuring pat from Howard and Jed, Pewter Queen was led out to fulfil her destiny.

Jed and Howard wandered across to the parade ring and leaned on the rails, looking at the other runners, until all the horses were in the paddock. Then they too entered the ring and stood in the middle, as is the custom for owners and trainers who always manage to look as if they are discussing something vital right up to the bell. In reality, the racing tactics had long since been decided and the jockey briefed.

Jed pointed out the three previous winners. There was a big, almost black horse with a white star called Double Bluff. He had won a race at Ludlow, but not a particularly good one, in Jed's opinion. He had made all the running and, if he repeated this tactic today, the race was likely to be a genuinely good gallop. Tango King was an athletic-looking bright bay that came from one of the biggest National Hunt yards and had already won what looked on paper a rather better race at Huntingdon. The third winner was a three-year-old filly like Pewter Queen. Bred to run on the flat, Elegant Lass had clearly been a late developer and had failed to make the racecourse as a two or three year-old. However, like Pewter Queen, she had developed into a good-looking three-year-old and had duly won her first race a few miles away at Kempton.

'She's bound to be a hot favourite,' said Jed, 'but there's a big difference between two miles at Kempton and two miles at Sandown, and I have my doubts she'll get up this hill at the sharp end of the race – particularly if that big fellow makes it a good gallop.'

'What about the rest?' asked Howard.

'Most of those who have run have done very little, but there are a couple of well-bred first times out like us, and you always have to respect Tony Tyle's and Alan Jackson's horses in races like these.'

Tyle's mare was a racy-looking chestnut called Shooting Star and Jackson's a really light bay, Tudor Queen. These two trainers had battled for the championship for the last seven years and were still going strong.

Jed nodded to a number of his trainer colleagues. Howard had eyes only for Pewter Queen and hardly noticed Jason appearing beside him.

'What news from the weighing room?' asked Jed.

'The big fellow is probably going to make it, but Tyle's horse is going to be up there too, so it's going to be a pretty breakneck pace in the early stages.'

'Well, as I said before,' instructed Jed, 'don't make too much use of her early on.' The mounting bell rang and the three of them hurried over to Pewter Queen, who had been brought to stand with her head facing the middle of the paddock. With minimum assistance from Jed, Jason was in the saddle and Alison was leading them off. One and a half circuits of the parade ring and they were on their way down the Rhododendron Walk to the entrance of the racecourse.

Howard almost galloped across the paddock, through the hall underneath the grandstand and on to the lawn in time to see Pewter Queen make her way nonchalantly past the stand to the bottom of the hill where the two-mile race was to start near the Pond Fence. The hurdles had been removed and neatly stacked inside the rails.

The starter and his assistant carefully checked girths to make sure none of the saddles would slip during the race. Horses often resist the tightening of the girth when saddles are being put on, so it is often possible to pull it in by another inch or two once they have relaxed after their canter to the start. Satisfied, the starter mounted his rostrum and the horses filed on to the track well behind the elastic tape which stretched across it. With twenty-three runners and a lot of newcomers, the officials were anxious to ensure every horse got off to an even start. On this occasion they did so without incident and with a call of 'Come on jockeys!' the starter released the tape and a small charge of the Light Brigade set off up the hill towards the grandstand in a kaleidoscope of colours. As Jed had predicted the favourite, Double Bluff, was soon at the front and set a strong gallop, but nothing was tearing away at a pace that would be unsustainable for the distance of a little over two miles.

Jason had made a good start and easily settled Pewter Queen in the middle of the pack as he and Jed had planned. As they approached the winning post for the first time he was able to gently ease the mare on to the rails to make sure she went the shortest distance round the long bend that swept up to the crest of the hill before plunging down to the long flat back straight, alongside seven steeplechase fences that were amongst the most famous in National Hunt racing.

Today Jason and his grey mount did not have to worry about these although the race was proving to be quite eventful in its own way. A number of the inexperienced horses were not keeping a particularly straight line and some of them were running in snatches. They would accelerate as another horse came alongside them, slow down as it went past, then accelerate again. Jason, keeping a steady but not too firm hold on Pewter Queen's mouth, gave her the occasional pat and sat as still as was possible on a horse travelling at around thirty miles an hour.

Turning out of the back straight the pace was already too strong for a number of the horses and the bunched formation was stringing itself out into something much closer to Indian file. From twelfth or thirteenth Jason found he moved easily into eighth place, and was probably nine or ten lengths away from Double Bluff who had now been joined by Elegant Lass. Double Bluff was third and still appeared to be going very easily. Shooting Star was prominent but looked under pressure. Alongside Jason was Hopeful Investment, an expensive mare that was also having her first run and seemed to be going just as easily as Pewter Queen. Turning towards home, with about a furlong before the finishing straight, the three horses directly in front of Jason were clearly struggling and he came out to pass them. The mare alongside stayed with him and in a mere fifty yards there were only three ahead of them.

Double Bluff was still striding strongly, but Shooting Star was in difficulties. Still lying right up there, Elegant Lass looked comfortable. Jason had to make up his mind. Should he stay on the rail and hope that a gap would allow him to run through, or ease Pewter Queen out and deliver his challenge on the outside? The decision was made for him. Double Bluff started to wander off the straight line and, sensing his tiredness, his jockey pushed him on to the rails to help keep him straight and to give him something to run against.

Jason moved out and the other mare came smoothly with him. Double Bluff was now being ridden hard but showed no signs of slowing down, while Elegant Lass fulfilled Jed's expectations. In just a few strides she had shot her bolt and had dropped away from Double Bluff. In a flash Jason realised he was going to be blocked by her slowing down and by the mare outside him, who was also beginning to feel the strain and was hanging towards him. He had to check Pewter Queen and in a split second decided to go for the gap between her and the horse on the rails. One moment it was there, the next it was closed as both the mares in front of him leaned right. With a yell at them to keep their horses straight, Jason stayed where he was and, for the first time, asked Howard's grey to quicken. Even he was surprised at the speed with which she responded to the slap on the shoulder and, bursting through the fast disappearing space, she raced into second place.

With fifty yards to go there was only Double Bluff in front. Leaning and urging her with hands and heels, Jason roared encouragement at Pewter Queen. Like an experienced campaigner she stuck to her guns and, yard by yard, gained on Double Bluff as the winning post approached all too rapidly. Double Bluff battled bravely but the twelve pounds extra he carried began to tell. Hands and heels working, Jason moved with his mare's rhythm, pressing her to follow him like a skilled ballroom dancer leading his partner. Her head reached and passed Double Bluff's saddle in two more strides and now they were truly neck and neck, both jockeys throwing the reins at them, with Jason resisting the temptation to hit her behind the saddle. Twenty yards from the winning post her head went in front, and Howard was screaming 'My baby's won!'

But Double Bluff was not beaten. With frantic driving from his jockey, he fought back and the two horses flashed past the winning post with the jockeys' boots and stirrups so close that they seemed welded together.

'Photograph! Photograph!' announced the racecourse tannoy.

Jason and Freddie Kelly, Double Bluff's likeable jockey who was the Irish champion, allowed their horses to run on and gradually ease down as they went round the bend and up the hill. Slowing down to a trot and then a walk, they turned and slowly cantered back towards the Rhododendron Walk.

Jason gave Freddie a big grin. 'I think I got you on the nod.'

Freddie smiled back ruefully. 'I don't know how you can be taking the bread out of the mouth of a poor working lad like me. And you a rich bastard, too! Ah, well. You've saved me buying the champagne. It would have been my one hundredth winner of the season.'

Alison was hopping up and down with excitement as she grabbed Pewter Queen's rein. 'Did we do it? Did we do it?' she asked.

'I think so,' said Jason giving another pat to the sleek and sweating grey neck.

They had barely got on to the peat of the Rhododendron Walk before Howard appeared like a genie from a lamp. Before he had a chance to say anything Jason gave him a tentative thumbs-up. As he did so the racecourse announcer confirmed the result: 'First number seventeen, second number one, third number eleven.' Howard, almost running to keep up with the horse, gave Alison a big hug and turned to see Jed already waiting outside the winner's enclosure. A huge beam spread over his face as he threw down his cigarette and stamped it into the grass. Alison led Pewter Queen to stand in front of the number one spot in the winner's enclosure and Jason quickly undid the girth and removed the saddle. Photographers converged in a friendly pack snapping owner, trainer, jockey and stable girl, all proudly standing in a group or in various combinations next to the fine head of the still heavily breathing Pewter Queen.

'I'll see you in the bar, Howard,' said Jason. 'We'll finish off that champagne.' He headed for the weighing room and sat down on the scales as the Clerk of the Course checked he was still the correct weight. With a nod and a 'Well done, Jay' he made the relevant notes on the official form in front of him. Handing his number cloth to the official responsible for collecting them, Jason walked into the jockeys' changing room and dropped his saddle, pads and weights on the table.

Johnny Hampshire, an ex-jockey, and now one of the professional valets who looked after the jockeys, gathered up Jason's tack and helped him off with his tight-fitting boots and breeches. 'Are you riding tomorrow Jay?' he asked.

'Not tomorrow, Johnny. If there's any change I'll let you know, but I'm pretty certain that it'll be Plumpton on Monday.' Grabbing a towel, he made his way to the showers, exchanging a few quips with the other jockeys who had ridden in the race. After a brisk shower he dressed quickly but with care. Leaving most of his gear with Johnny, he picked up his holdall and made his way across to the grandstand where Howard was waiting.

Chapter Two

Howard Barrack, having bought a few drinks and accepted the congratulations of friends and regular race goers, many of whom he hardly knew, had extracted himself and was sitting with a new bottle of champagne in front of him, enjoying a glass with Jed and Jason.

'I'll be off now,' said Jed after a while. 'We've got a long drive. That's a grand mare you've got, Howard. She'll win you a few more races, I can assure you.' He clamped his cap firmly on his head and went off to check the horses and drive back to Sussex.

'What do you think?' asked Howard when he'd gone.

Jason drew on his trademark Havana cigar. 'She could be a very good mare,' he said. 'She's still got a lot to learn, but she won that like a horse having its tenth run, not its first. She likes the game, she settled and she'll get more than two miles.'

'Just how good is she?'

'If you're sensible with her, you'll have a Cheltenham horse next year, Howard.'

'That's exactly what Jed said.'

'One or two more bumpers this season,' continued Jason. 'That'll give her one for the beginning of next season to get her back into the swing of racing, and then you can go for really decent novice hurdles.'

'What about the Cheltenham bumper?'

'Give her a bit more time to grow up.' 'She's still a baby and would be taking on more mature horses. The way she came up that hill today, I really don't think Cheltenham would be a problem. Let's wait and see after Christmas. She may well be ready, but let's not rush her.'

Howard beamed. 'So, old chum, what else is on your mind?'

Jason put down his glass and, looked Howard straight in the eye. 'What I'm going to tell you is strictly between us. I haven't mentioned it to anyone except the president and treasurer of the American corporation I'm selling my company to.'

Howard whistled. 'Wow! So what are you going to do? Are you staying with it?'

'In the short term, yes. I am going to make sure the sale goes through and my staff are well looked after. That's going to take two or three months, but then I'm out. They want me to stay on in some sort of consultative or non-executive role. I am very reluctant but I haven't definitely said no. If I agree, it will be on a very part-time basis.'

'So what brought this on?' asked Howard.

'For twelve years I've worked like a dog. Don't get me wrong; I've enjoyed every minute of it. Racing has been my hobby and my sanity, but I can't carry on doing both and doing them well. And I want to concentrate on racing.'

'Riding?'

'Not any more. Cheltenham, or possibly Aintree, will be my last race, and if I should win on The Conker at Cheltenham I'll hang up my boots a very happy man.'

'I presume you'll want to train, then?' said Howard. 'You know you'll have my support, particularly with Jed talking about retiring at the end of next season.'

'Well, yes and no. I have a plan and I would like you to be involved, but you may not want to be of course. If you don't, I'll understand.'

Howard took a generous swig of his champagne. 'Try me.'

'I would like to form a company of a select few owners. I want us to pool our resources and produce a team of winners which will become as successful in National Hunt racing as Manchester United has been in football.'

'That's going to cost a bit,' commented Howard.

'Let me tell you my plan, and then you have a think about it. I'd like between thirty and forty hand-picked horses, no rubbish, and none of them with too many miles on the clock. I'm not going to be buying horses that have already won big races. Either we wouldn't get the credit for them winning again, or we'd be ending up with horses that were already at their peak or on the way down.'

'I'd be looking for three owners prepared to put up £200,000 each for horses. That should give me a minimum of twenty horses, at an average of £30,000 a piece. There's no reason why we shouldn't get some for £8,000 or £10,000, and I certainly won't buy anything over £30,000. Then we will take shares in the real estate, equipment and so on. I'm guessing at £2 to £3 million between us. I'll put four or five horses in myself, which takes us up to, say, twenty-five.'

'Interesting,' said Howard. 'Why limit the number of owners?'

Jason smiled. 'Well, here's the bit you might think is crazy. I want it to be a glorious syndicate, not just an owning syndicate but a group of partners who run the whole show. None of us will own any of the horses; we will each have shares in the whole lot. A management committee of three will run the company and I will concentrate only on the racing and bloodstock side. The two or three biggest shareholders will run the business. One will look after the money and the administration, another the sponsorship and purchasing, gallops, equipment and so on, and the third the PR and the relationships with racing authorities and breeders.'

'But that's your game,' said Howard.

'I want out of that now. Besides, although I know most of the racing press, my real contacts are on the City and business pages and, frankly, I think if I suddenly started trying to bring my previous experience and reputation to a relationship with racing journalists it would be resented and counter - productive.'

Howard pondered this for a moment. 'I can see you've given this a lot of thought, and it is certainly an interesting concept. But there are an awful lot of details that would have to be worked out.'

'Exactly,' said Jason. 'That is why I want a management committee. And I'd very much like you to be on it.'

'Who are the others?'

'You're the first person I've approached. I know who I'd like to be responsible for the hardware, but haven't a clue about the third person yet. I've considered a lot of likely candidates, but none of them is quite right.'

'I presume you have a location in mind? Lambourn, perhaps or Newmarket?'

'Neither of those,' said Jason. 'The place I'm thinking of is very private. If we do this, security is going to be tight and we won't be dependent on anyone else. It's not an entirely new concept – it was done many years ago on Salisbury Plain with a trainer called Jack Fallon and some shrewd backers.'

'So where is it?'

'It's on an old airfield on the edge of the Cotswolds,' revealed Jason. 'Old buildings which could readily be converted into really warm loose boxes, some hangars for keeping hay and vehicles, another for an indoor school. There's even an old administrative block which would make excellent living accommodation for the stable staff. My lawyers have already made inquiries, and I'm told there should be no problem with planning permission to convert what was a small officers' mess into accommodation for me. Nobody knows I'm the interested party. Nobody even knows it's for racing, come to that. So far the lawyers have been talking to the vendors in terms of an international show jumping training centre.'

Howard took a few more sips of champagne. 'You bloody well knew I'd be interested, he said almost accusingly. 'It would give me something new to do. It's time the two boys stood on their own feet.'

The 'two boys' were Howard's son and son-in-law, each of whom ran a division of his huge wholesale business. Peter Chivers, his son-in-law, looked after the catering side, which supplied everything from instant coffee and plastic cups to industrial microwaves, pots and pans, paper napkins, cutlery and inexpensive glassware and crockery. Take any fast-food takeaway, pub restaurant or marquee at one of the big sporting events, and Howard's products were likely to be there. Andy, his son, ran the frozen-food side. From frozen peas to exotic desserts, Howard's company purchased the raw materials and processed and packaged them for other firms who sold them under their own brand names.

These businesses ran on tight margins and couldn't afford waste, and Howard's success had earned him a great deal of respect in the City. Brokers were avidly waiting for him to 'go public', but such a move was very far from Howard's mind. He wanted to keep things under his own control and not have a lot of know-all analysts and merchant banks telling him how to run his own business. From Jason's point of view, his way of working made Howard the ideal man to run a business like training, in which margins were equally tight and waste could be fatal.

'If I came in could I bet?' he asked.

'As long as it's legal and you don't ask me to do anything crooked, yes,' was Jason's immediate reply. 'But I hope you're not expecting to get your money back that way.'

'No, but I would want one big one. Big enough to hurt a particular bookmaker like hell, and it would have to be set up carefully.' Howard spoke deliberately and soberly. Whatever this was all about, it was clearly not some throw-away remark.

'How big?' Jason pressed him.

'Quarter of a million.'

Jason, not a man easily shaken, nearly dropped his glass. 'Hell, Howard; that's a tall order.'

'Not if it's done properly,' his friend countered, his smile revealing a hint of the steel that had made him as successful as he was. But in an instant he was back in jovial mood. He slapped Jason on the knee. 'Well, old friend, we can talk about that sometime in the future. If I tell you the whole story I think it will intrigue you as much as it would satisfy me.

'Come and have lunch on Sunday and we'll talk about your plan in more detail. I'd like to come on board but I've got to think about the amount of time I'd have to commit to it. I'm assuming you're going to need more than just the odd telephone call and an eye kept on the books.'

'One day a week at least,' said Jason. 'In the early stages a lot more, because I'd want you to do the negotiations with me behind the scenes.'

'What's your next step?' asked Howard.

'I'm going to see possible partner number two tonight. I shan't mention you, but I'll outline the basic plan we've been chewing over.'

'Do I know him?'

'Yes, you do.'

'Do I like him?'

'I think you both have a grudging respect for each other. It'll be a bloody terrifying team, I can tell you.' Jason stood up, gave Howard a pat on the back and started to walk away. Pausing he turned back to the slightly bemused figure at the table behind him. Smiling, he said, 'The champagne's on you. I rode you a winner!'

In the owners', trainers' and jockeys' car park he located his dark green E-type Jaguar, ancient but in mint condition with its distinctive registration number: '10DD1', or 'one odd one'.

The number plates were a little ostentatious for Jason's taste, but they were a parting gift from an old girlfriend who had reluctantly ended their relationship when he showed no sign of wanting to settle down, and they appealed to his sense of humour. They had soon become part of his image with friends and detractors alike.

Jason turned out of the car park and, with plenty of time before dinner, dawdled along towards London reflecting on the day. He always enjoyed the company of Howard and Jed. Howard really loved his horses, good, bad or indifferent, and never questioned Jed's or Jason's judgement or plans. If only all owners had the same attitude.

Jed was something special. Year after year his horses still performed well and every so often he'd win something worthwhile, particularly a valuable handicap or two. Like Howard, Jed loved his horses. 'Just remember,' he used to say, attacking the bonnet of Jason's Jaguar with a thumping fist, 'thoroughbreds are like high-performance cars – they only have so many miles in 'em, and if you rev 'em up too much you burn 'em out too soon!' Wise words, thought Jason, and he would not forget them when he started his new venture.

As he joined the heavy Friday-evening traffic moving towards Earls Court he switched his thoughts to Victor Rainsford, the man he was meeting for dinner and who, he hoped, would be the next piece in his jigsaw puzzle. Victor was an enormously successful businessman with a wide range of interests in property and building, but he was a man with a skeleton in his cupboard and a bit of a chip on his shoulder. Many years earlier, one of Victor's warehouses had burned down. At the time the industry was in the doldrums, and this rather antiquated depot was clearly not cost effective. Rumours abounded and, although charges were never brought and the insurance paid out, in some quarters Victor's reputation had never quite recovered. He failed to become a member of The Turf Club, and was never accepted in the higher social echelons of racing. His disappointment had gradually deepened into a strong resentment.

Victor had few National Hunt horses as he thought Flat racing had 'more class'. However, one of his trainers had persuaded him that a reasonable horse on the Flat might make a worthwhile hurdler. Jason was asked to school it and, although Victor desperately wanted the champion National Hunt jockey to ride the horse, his lack of availability and a sly comment from the trainer about Jason's connections in the business world saw him riding the horse with some success. Their relationship, although not as close as the friendship between Jason and Howard, was cordial, and Jason had a sneaking regard for Victor's single-mindedness.

There had, however, been a serious hiccup a few months earlier. Jason, looking for young horses in Ireland, had come across a novice hurdler who was clearly a great deal better than his form indicated. A mixture of bad luck and the wrong ground had disguised the fact that this good Flat horse was potentially a seriously high-class performer over the sticks, and two placed runs at Leopardstown just had not shown his true worth. The trainer was loath to lose him, but the owner was in financial difficulty and Jason, who had ridden him in both his races, was asked to find a quick sale.

A telephone call to Victor apparently did the trick. Three hours later, when Jason was on the plane home, the trainer received a call from Victor. But Victor offered him £5,000 less than the asking price with £2,000 in notes for him. The trainer declined his offer and rang Jason. A call from Jason to a Cotswolds trainer with serious money to spend saw the horse on his way to England two days later. Victor couldn't believe he'd lost it, and he was shattered when Jason told him the horse had been sold for the original price.

'I'll forgive you one misjudgement,' said Jason, in a tone that left Victor under no illusion that he meant it, and the incident was never mentioned again. It was an incident that could have soured their relationship, but in fact it had the opposite effect. Victor rather admired Jason for acting as he had, while Jason knew he had made his point – particularly when the horse won the Swinton Hurdle at Haydock six weeks later.

As he pulled into Hayes Mews, behind Berkeley Square, Jason pushed the button on his remote control to open his garage door and neatly reversed his Jaguar in beside the maroon Range Rover already there. Climbing the stairs to the first floor, he strolled through the drawing room and pressed the button on his answerphone. Listening to his messages, he picked up his mail, glanced at it and discarded it almost in one movement. There was nothing there or on the machine that couldn't wait until the morning.

A shower and a change of clothes, a flick to reactivate the answerphone, and he was down the stairs, out of the front door and off again. It was a clear, crisp evening. He walked briskly round the corner of Berkeley Square and up Mount Street to the Connaught to meet Victor at his usual corner table in the bar.

As always Victor exuded wealth. A small and slightly overweight man, with greying sandy hair, he had a perpetual suntan from his frequent holidays in South Africa, the south of France or the West Indies, and he looked what he was; a man of money who enjoyed displaying it. His superb tan cashmere suit and cream silk shirt were off set by an orange tie, almost glowing in its intensity. Generous shirt cuffs displayed emerald cufflinks, matching the single-stone tie-pin of which Victor had many and always wore close to the knot.

A bottle of Krug was already in an ice bucket with alongside it a bottle of Black Label whisky. Victor only ever drank scotch, but always served his guests champagne, irrespective of their own preferences. He felt it was beneath his status to offer anything less. Fortunately, Jason adored Krug, though secretly he thought it was somewhat over-priced. At home he always drank a slightly drier champagne that he bought directly from a small chateau outside Rheims.

'I see you rode a winner this afternoon,' said Victor. 'How good is it?'

'Good enough for you to want it if it was for sale, but you probably couldn't afford it,' Jason teased.

'If Howard owns it, I'm bloody sure I could afford it and its twin sister!' retorted Howard.

'If it was a twin you wouldn't want either of them,' Jason pointed out. In thoroughbreds twins are regarded as a disaster since neither foal is likely to mature, even if both survive.

'So what's new?' asked Victor. 'I hear you've sold your business. Are you going to carry on racing or lead a life of leisure?'

Jason sipped his champagne. 'That would be telling, wouldn't it?' He was alarmed and annoyed that Victor knew about the sale though, with his connections, it probably shouldn't have come as a surprise. He just hoped the word hadn't spread too far.

'Come on, Jason, you know you can trust me,' said Victor, his grey eyes twinkling with a mischievous smile.

'It really has to be strictly between us until I tell you otherwise, but I'd like to talk to you, because you're a businessman whose advice I really value.'

At the word 'business' Victor's expression immediately changed to one of intense concentration. Jason put his glass down.

'I'm hoping to start training, but my plan is going to be very different from the way in which other trainers operate.' He outlined the proposition he had put to Howard a few hours earlier, and then sat back and waited for Victor's reaction.

You could almost hear Victor Rainsford's brain moving into gear. Reaching into his inside pocket, he withdrew a silver case and took out two Monte Cristo No. 3 cigars. Using a horseshoe-shaped gold cigar-cutter, he carefully snipped one end of each, passed a cigar to Jason, and lit his own with a long wooden match. He handed the matchbox to Jason. He didn't speak until he had taken two slow pulls at his cigar.

'And you want me to be one of these owners?' he asked eventually.

'More than that. I want you to be one of the three who run the operation.'

Victor's grin reappeared. 'So you want me to do the buying, do you Jason? My sharpness might be useful after all, might it?' he drawled in a slightly sarcastic tone. 'What's in it for me?'

'You're not going to make money. At least, not in the way you would normally consider worthwhile. But then, who does make money out of National Hunt racing? The reality is that we will probably lose a lot. The trick is to ensure we only lose what we can afford to spend on what we all know is a very expensive hobby.'

Victor watched his cigar smoke climb gently towards the ceiling. 'So you are asking me to put in between a quarter and a half million, work hard, and make little or no profit. Why would I want to do that?'

Jason waited until Victor was looking at him again. 'Because, Victor, you would be associated with the most successful venture in the history of National Hunt racing. You would lead in winners at the top courses in Britain, and you'd be part of a whole new concept in the sport. It would be as significant for National Hunt as Godolphin has been for Flat racing.'

'But then horses wouldn't be running in my name and colours,' Victor pointed out.

'True, but everybody would know you were part of the syndicate. They would also know that you were the driving commercial force behind the whole operation. You would have the chance to show that your commercial skills can run rings round the traditionalists who think they know best. The people who think that things can't be improved.'

'I'll think about it. Who are the other two?'

'I'm still looking for a front man, but I know who I'd like to handle the finance.'

'I've got a pretty shrewd idea who that would be,' said Victor, 'but I guess you wouldn't tell me even if I guessed right.'

'Of course not – no more than I would discuss this conversation with anyone else until you say yes or no. And if you decline it will remain between us; if you say yes we'll let everyone know just what an important role you're going to play when we are ready to show our hand.'

'It's a bloody intriguing idea,' admitted Victor. 'Do you want some dinner?'

'I'll have some smoked salmon, a steak, one decent glass of claret and an early night,' said Jason.

'That sounds more like an ultimatum rather than an acceptance,' smiled the tycoon. 'But I suppose you're still watching your weight. Never mind. We'll have our dinner and then I think I'll see if someone will play a little serious poker with me.' Jason smiled. He knew what 'a little serious poker' with Victor could cost an unlucky or rash player. He had long since decided that watching him was more enjoyable and far less expensive than trying to play with him. Victor waved at the waiter, pointed to the remains of the bottle of champagne, and they stood up and headed for the Grill Room.

Chapter Three

By six o'clock the next morning Jason was up, dressed in a polo-necked sweater, denim riding jeans and riding boots and had tossed down a glass of orange juice followed by a cup of strong black coffee.

Opening the *Racing Post* he turned to the list of entries for the two races he was due to ride in at Plumpton that Monday, and noted that barely half of them were jockeyed up. That didn't mean that they weren't going to run, but the chances were that the fields would be small but pretty competitive. He also quickly checked the other races to see if there were any potential spare rides he could pick up. Even though he was an amateur, Jason used an agent and quite often got the opportunity to ride a really good horse if its usual jockey was injured, suspended or had to go to another meeting. Today though nothing leapt out at him so he decided he'd settle for his two booked rides in Sussex.

The dark London streets were fairly empty at this early hour, and he was soon out of the city driving west on the M4. Bypassing Lambourn, he turned down a narrow lane leading to the small but immaculate yard at Midwood Park. Twenty-four boxes formed a shallow 'U' and opposite them stood a small elegant stone bungalow. A number of horses were already being ridden round the nearby peat circuit, supervised by a diminutive yet commanding middle-aged woman – Fiona French, one of the relatively few really successful women trainers. She was dressed ready to ride out.

'Just in time Jay!' she bellowed as he got out of the car. 'Wouldn't she let go of you this morning?'

'Don't judge everyone by your own standards!' He went over and gave her a fond peck on the cheek.

'Jump on See You Sometime. I'll be with you in a moment,' said Fiona.

Striding across the yard, Jason met Matt, Fiona's perky little head man, leading out a fine-looking horse. He beamed from ear to ear as he legged Jason up. 'If you look after him on Monday, he'll earn us all our beer money,' he remarked. Jason joined the nine other horses circling round waiting for Fiona to mount the beloved hack on which she had won many point-to-points a decade earlier.

Fiona had racing blood coursing through every vein in her body. Her recently deceased father, a tyrant who had adored her, had hunted, ridden as an amateur, been in the cavalry and virtually lived and breathed horses all his life. When he left the army to run his family estate in Warwickshire he had refused to let the fact that his only child was a daughter deter him from his ambition to have a successful amateur jockey in the family. Her triumphs had thrilled him even if, being an undemonstrative type, he had seldom showed it.

Fiona and Jason rode side by side down to the gallops with Fiona's black Labrador and Jack Russell at her horse's heels. Today all the horses in the string were jumpers and were going to do a good swinging mile and a half. Afterwards three of them, including Jason's, were going to keep their eye in over the fences before they raced the following week. None were novices so, all being well, this would be a formality, but even so the prospect of travelling at over thirty miles an hour over the almost full-sized birch fences never failed to pump the adrenaline round Jason's body.

Arriving at the foot of the slightly uphill gallop, they made their way on to the all-weather strip and had a good steady hack for six furlongs. Pulling up at the top they were sorted out into pairs by Fiona before returning to the bottom. Having told them which order they were to work in, she cantered three-quarters of the way up the gallop and then stood to one side as the pairs swept past her at three-quarters racing pace. Apparently satisfied with their work, she sent off all but the three due to school for a quiet walk home.

Jason and the two other riders, one of whom was a very competent conditional jockey, walked slowly across to the part of the gallops reserved for schooling. Along one side were some telegraph poles raised on sawn-off logs and painted in black and white stripes. Close by were hurdles, the same size as those on a racecourse but tilted at a more acute angle to make them inviting to a novice and reducing the height to be jumped by a few inches. Well to the side of these were two sets of steeplechase fences. The first was half-size; the second (consisting of two jumps), a little more than three-quarters size. Beyond these three were another two full racecourse size fences.

Fiona, knowing both Jason's skill and his horse's experience, asked him to lead and the other two riders to follow him in single file.

'Just jump the first three first time,' she called. 'Then you can go home,' she told the third rider.

See You Sometime was immediately on his toes and clearly loved the game. Eight or nine strides from the first fence, he slightly shortened his stride, before lengthening again, meeting the fence perfectly, and soaring over it. The other two fences he met without Jason having to make any adjustments, and he was still pulling hard thinking he was going to go on and jump the full-sized set some fifty or sixty yards further on. But Jason eased him down to wait for the other horses. He turned round and cantered over to Fiona, sitting on her hack.

She seemed pleased. 'Once more at racing speed and you can go on and jump the last two.' To the apprentice she said, 'This time ride upside Jason and concentrate on your horse and not what he and his are doing.'

As soon as the two horses found the other upside, they were even more eager. Jason kept a firm hold on See You Sometime until about twenty yards from the fence. Sitting quietly he waited until the right moment, then, seeing the stride, he gave the horse a gentle squeeze and sailed over the obstacle. The jockey next to him came out of the fence half a length down and Jason slightly restrained See You Sometime until they were upsides again. Going into the next they both met it right, as they did the third. Jason turned as they approached the two big fences. 'Nice and steady to start with,' he said. 'Just sit and let him do it. They both know a lot more about jumping fences than we ever will.'

Without a moment's hesitation, neck and neck, they flew over the final two fences and Jason, turning to the young lad next to him, saw on his face the exhilaration that comes from successfully completing a slightly dangerous task. They walked quietly back to the yard with Fiona loosening their girths to let the horses breath more easily.

Thirty or forty yards short of the entrance they all jumped off and, allowed the horses to have a well-earned pick of the grass on a wild verge.

'What are you doing for the rest of the day?' Fiona asked Jason.

'I'm not riding but I thought I'd go to Newbury for the afternoon. Then I'm planning to have a quiet dinner somewhere this evening. I'm bound to meet a couple of friends, and as long as they don't want anything too hectic that will suit me. I'm riding out at Jed's tomorrow.'

'Why don't you have dinner with me?' said Fiona 'I've got someone coming I'd like you to meet and who really wants to meet you.'

'Someone who wants to meet me? Male or female?' he asked.

'Come to dinner and find out,' she replied.

'Can I stay the night and leave early tomorrow?'

'By all means. In fact why don't we go to Newbury together this afternoon? If I'm not going to cramp you style, that is.'

'Great idea.'

Pulling their horses' heads up, they ambled back towards the yard. Jason handed See You Sometime over to Matt and wandered into Fiona's kitchen. He found the cafetière, put in enough coffee for four strong cups and switched on the kettle. When she came in, they took the coffee into her office. While Jason reclined in a comfortable old chair, Fiona telephoned some of her owners, reporting on racing plans, the progress of the horses that weren't running and the condition of those that were injured.

Half an hour later, both showered and changed, they were in the Jaguar and on their way to Newbury. Fiona was simply but stylishly dressed. In an olive-green slim-fitting dress of fine wool with matching jacket she looked every inch the society hostess she often was. You would never have imagined she was a racehorse trainer – and not just any old trainer, either, but a very successful one he held in high regard and a friend of whom he was also extremely fond. Glancing at her amazingly well-manicured hands, adorned by a single large, emerald ring, he wondered, not for the first time, why it was not and never had been partnered by a wedding ring. He had been tempted to ask her, but he was pretty sure he knew the answer and did not want to trespass on what he felt sure she considered a very private matter. He knew she had had a string of handsome and often very powerful lovers He suspected that she had just never found a single man with the intellectual and physical attributes she demanded in a husband. Although she was a wonderful party-giver, and had a strong network of good friends, she was equally happy with her own company. It was clear that she much preferred being alone to wasting her time on anyone who wasn't worth it.

She had already confided in Jason that she was going to retire from training at the end of the season. He took the opportunity now to ask her about her plans.

Fiona thought for a moment before replying. 'Jason, I think you understand that my father always expected me to behave like the son he'd never had. I loved him dearly but he was overpowering. I have never been short of money – in fact I have always been extremely well off, but I have never had any true freedom. Now that he is dead I have both, and I intend to enjoy them.'

'Good for you.'

'The estate is superbly well managed by Harry Frank. To all intents and purposes he's already been running it for the last seven years while father was so ill, as you know. I'm perfectly happy to leave him to carry on making a thoroughly good job of it. Over the years I've made a lot of friends in racing and breeding around the world but I've never really been able to spend any time with them unless they have visited me here. My responsibilities as a trainer have always had to come first. The only real break I've ever had was more than twenty years ago when I spent several months in South Africa. I'm not complaining. I've been lucky to have had a lot of good and some extremely good horses. Most of my owners have become friends and I wouldn't have missed my riding and training experiences for anything. But the time has come for a change. I want to go on a leisurely tour visiting mates, spending time with them enjoying other equine worlds. I'm also looking forward to exploring some different scenery and wildlife and learning a bit about other ways of life – I do realise, you know, that I am a bit of a philistine. I'm going to take the pressure off myself and enjoy being a free agent with no seven-day-a-week routine and no owners to answer to.'

She paused, lit a cigarette, blew out an elegant smoke ring and turned to look at Jason intensely. 'You need a change, too. I've noticed that you don't talk about your business with the same enthusiasm as you did when we first met. You pick up the *Racing Post* before the *Financial Times* now, and at dinner parties you much prefer to talk about racing than about business.'

Jason smiled. 'My, aren't we perceptive' he remarked. 'Are you suggesting I come with you?'

'Not bloody likely!' was the reply. 'I love you dearly, but twenty-four hours a day? One of us would be had up for murder.'

Her eyes were serious again. 'Why don't you start training? In fact, why don't you take over at Midwood Park? Most of my owners would be thrilled. I know that you much prefer jumpers to Flat horses, but I am sure it would only take you a season to change the balance significantly. If you wanted to expand the yard I already have planning permission for another sixteen boxes, and I don't think it would be hard to get another ten. You know that the gallops could handle fifty or sixty horses without a problem.'

Jason thought carefully before answering her. The idea of taking over her yard had crossed his mind. He had ridden for quite a few of her owners and knew and got on well with most of the others, but the site just didn't quite fit his plan. He really didn't want to be as close as that to the great training centre of Lambourn, even though Midwood Park had its own gallops and was some way away from the sometimes claustrophobic atmosphere of central Lambourn.

'It's a hell of an offer, Fiona, but if I did start training I think I'd want to be properly by myself, away from it all. I don't fancy a lot of old-timers criticising my new-fangled ideas behind my back or having the younger ones snapping at my heels trying to find out what is happening from my staff in pubs, smiling to my face and stabbing me in the back as soon as I walk out of the door.

'I know I have a lot of good friends, and some of those older trainers have taught me all I know and have been wonderfully loyal in giving me rides, but you'll understand what I mean.'

'Dear boy,' Fiona smiled. 'I know you're right, and I'm sure you know that much of what you say is even more true of a woman trainer who is constantly accused of having got where she has, only because she was born with a silver spoon in her mouth.' She looked at him again. 'If you do decide to train, I would love to help you.'

'I really appreciate that, Fiona.'

They were soon threading their way through the slow traffic heading off the M4 and through the outskirts of Newbury.

At the entrance gate they were both recognised and waved through to the car park with a friendly smile. Jason helped Fiona out, locked the car and they walked through the owners' and trainers' entrance, picking up complimentary race cards and greeting and exchanging greetings with friends and nodding acquaintances alike.

At the Barrie Cope fish bar under the old part of the grandstand they ordered large plates of smoked salmon and half a bottle of champagne. 'If you want an afternoon off I'm quite happy to drive,' offered Fiona.

'No, I'll go easy this afternoon. But I might make a dent in a couple of bottles of whatever you're offering from that excellent wine cellar of yours this evening,' he replied. He drained his glass. 'Righto, I had better get going. I'll see you back at the car after the fifth.'

Although Jason wasn't riding, he went to the weighing room anyway to chat to some of the jockeys. He sat down next to the tough but cheerful Irish champion, Freddie Kelly, with whom he had fought out the finish at Sandown the previous day. They discussed the going and one or two particularly interesting horses racing that afternoon.

'What are your plans for Cheltenham, Jay?'

'They're very fluid. It's still early days, although I have a definite ride in the four-mile amateur chase.'

'That'll be that chestnut you're so fond of,' came the knowing reply. 'Well, can you keep yourself open for another few days? One of my Irish trainers was talking to me about you and he might just be looking for a strong fella like you, and one who'll keep his mouth shut as well.'

Jason grinned at Freddie. 'Don't expect an agent's fee from me. I'm an amateur, remember,' he teased, patting Freddie's shoulder as he got to his feet. 'I'll do that, but don't forget I owe first refusal to Jed, Fiona and the other trainers who have given me most of my rides over the last couple of seasons.'

'Of course. I'm only talking about one or two rides, although they'll be damned good ones.'

Pausing to have a brief word with one or two other jockeys, Jason made his way up to the owners' and trainers' room at the top of the stand to watch the Novice Hurdle.

It was a rather moderate affair and, although there were one or two newcomers among the field of sixteen, the favourite and second favourite duly finished in that order. The second race had a small but much higher-quality field of novice chasers, including a seven-year-old he had ridden in two bumpers the previous season. The Wexford Wanderer had already been point-to-pointing in Ireland before coming to England, so it was not unusual that he had gone straight from being placed second and third in two bumpers at Wetherby and Uttoxeter to novice chasing this season. And as he had won his first chase at Leicester very easily, it was no great surprise to see him appearing at Newbury for his second. His trainer was an ex-Irish steeplechase jockey named Liam McDermott, universally known as Molly because of his passion for mussels. He was reputed to have lived on them when struggling to do a low weight as a racerider.

The one thing you knew about any young chaser that came from Molly's yard on the border of Derbyshire and Yorkshire was that he would be schooled to perfection on Molly's cunningly positioned schooling fences. Molly had an old saying: 'If they jump well, you've got half a chance; if they don't you've got none.' Once a young horse had mastered the basic technique and gained confidence from a string of four fences in a straight line on a slight incline, it would then be presented to three fences, one slightly uphill, one at the bottom of quite a steep incline and third met almost as soon as the horse had turned a corner as if heading for the home straight. Horses learned to adjust their stride going into a fence and to be prepared for the landing side to be at a slightly different level from the take-off.

The two or three jockeys Molly used regularly had always ridden their mounts at home at racing pace before sitting on them at a racecourse. As a result of this attention to detail and their thorough schooling, Molly, rather unusually often had more winners over fences in a season than he did over hurdles. He also had an extraordinarily high success rate with first-season novices.

The £10,000 prize money today was substantial for a novice chase and had consequently attracted some very promising young horses. Apart from the Wexford Wanderer, the other seven runners were all previous winners or had been placed. Jason watched with interest. He remembered how the Wexford Wanderer had been rather outpaced in the early stages of the two bumpers in which he had ridden him, but each time he had run on very strongly at the end. Jason was pretty confident that he would be fighting it out at the front by the time they were halfway up the rising home straight at Newbury.

Jason seldom had a bet on anything other than those horses in whose preparation he had been involved but today, mainly out of sentiment, he decided to have £50 each way on the Wexford Wanderer on the Tote. To his surprise, the screens above the Tote windows showed odds on the horse of 5-1. The favourite was 6-4, and a horse that had had one run and come second had apparently attracted a great deal of popular attention because it had been tipped on Channel 4's *Morning Line*.

Jason strolled out on to the grandstand and adjusted his binoculars to watch the horses canter down to the start. The Wexford Wanderer was a sturdy 16 hand horse, a cruiser-weight rather than a heavyweight in boxing terms. The girths checked, the starter went up to his rostrum, calling to the jockeys as the tape flicked its way across the track and the race was on.

Nobody seemed particularly anxious to make the pace and it occurred to Jason that this would not suit Molly's horse at all. Almost immediately after they had jumped the second, Jack Franklin, Molly's jockey, went to the front and gradually increased the pace. All eight runners safely negotiated another fence and, almost in single file, they approached the water jump right in front of the grandstands. Again they were all foot perfect, with the exception of a bright chestnut at the back that had taken off far too soon and dropped both hind legs into the water. By the time his jockey had got him together again and regained the lost momentum the rest of the field was a good eight to ten lengths clear.

Turning the bend and heading down the back straight the Wanderer's jockey continued gradually to increase the pace. As they approached the first of the open ditches, Jack realised his horse was meeting it beautifully for a really big effort and, given an encouraging squeeze and a slap on the shoulder, the Wanderer flew over the fence and landed a good two lengths in the lead. The next three fences demonstrated how much of difference fine jumping could make. The Wexford Wanderer dealt with them all flawlessly and only the favourite could stay with him. The heavily backed second favourite was being jumped off his feet. After two minor errors he met the next all wrong, clouted it with both front legs and shot his jockey out of the saddle. Somehow the horse managed to scramble over the fence himself without falling but his inelegant execution of a the task forced the following horses to take evasive action and by the time they had all straightened up the two leaders had the race between them, bar a fall.

As they turned for home and the bell rang marking their entry into the home straight Jason was confident Wexford Wanderer would win. The favourite moved upsides and for a few moments looked threatening, but its presence only seemed to inspire the Irish horse to lengthen his stride and if anything quicken it at the same time. Jumping the last open ditch, he put three lengths between himself and his rival. All that remained was the formality of the last two fences before he sauntered up to the winning post to polite applause from a knowledgeable and appreciative crowd. It would have been rather more enthusiastic if the favourite or second favourite had been on its way to the number one spot in the winner's enclosure.

Jason meandered over to the Tote window and collected a little over £300 for his £100 stake. Pausing to put his winnings into his trouser pocket, he felt a hand brushing the pocket. His first thought, naturally, was that he'd been targeted by a pickpocket. He remembered to his relief that he had nothing in that pocket, but slid his hand into it to check. To his surprise, he found a piece of paper that he was sure had not been there before. He unfolded the crumpled ball to find a scrawled message. 'Jay – write your mobile telephone number on dead betting slip and drop it on the way to your car. I must speak to you.' The word 'must' was underlined. The note was signed 'Danny Derkin'. Jason's jaw dropped. The message itself was odd enough; the name at the end was astounding.

Danny Derkin had been a top jump jockey coming to widespread fame when he won the Grand National on a horse trained by his father from a small yard near Clonmel Racecourse. At seventeen he had been Irish amateur champion and on turning professional the next year he had been snapped up by various leading yards all eager to reap the benefit of his extraordinary skill and strength, aided by first of all his 7lb, then 5lb and finally 3lb allowance. His second season as a professional had been something of a disappointment. With his allowances gone he got fewer class rides and two bad falls sidelined him for spells of five and then three weeks. However, the next season a shrewd English trainer had Danny brought over as his second jockey and this time injuries had been to his advantage.

The Saturday before Christmas that year the stable's first jockey broke a wrist. It turned out to be a very nasty fracture. During the busy Christmas and New Year period the most sought-after jockeys were already booked and Danny got plenty of good rides. Five winners, two seconds and a third from twelve outings were enough to convince his guv'nor that this lad was no flash in the pan.

Within two years he had replaced the now recovered stable jockey as the number one choice and was loudly proclaimed as the next Johnny Francome or Richard Dunwoody. But fate dealt him a bitter blow. Three days before the Cheltenham Festival, a crashing fall broke his thigh. Danny Derkin went home to Ireland to recuperate and never returned. Various stories circulated about him. He had 'lost his nerve', he 'couldn't walk properly', he 'had a terrible illness'. Whatever the truth, he had never ridden again and seemed to have disappeared off the face of the planet.

Jason looked down and picked up a discarded betting slip from the hundreds that littered the ground. He wrote Fiona's number and his own mobile number on it, slipped it into his jacket pocket and wandered apparently aimlessly on to the lawns, where he could easily be seen. The fourth race had already finished so he walked slowly towards the parade ring to watch the runners in the fifth. This was a high-class handicap hurdle and at least four of the twelve runners were likely to appear at Cheltenham in a few weeks' time for the New Year meeting.

Before long he saw Fiona on the other side of the ring talking to one of her owners, Harry Clough, and his wife, Frances. With them, though apparently, much more interested in the horses than she was in the conversation, was a striking blonde. Jason waited until the horses left the paddock and then strolled across to where the four of them were standing, still talking. 'Ah, Jason,' said Fiona with a big smile, 'I think you know Frances and Harry Clough? This is their friend Eva Botha.' Jason politely shook hands with Frances and Harry, though not particularly warmly. Jason was under no illusions as to Harry's opinion of him. In the kitchen at Midwood Park after breakfast one morning, when Jason had been schooling two of Harry's three horses, Fiona had called Harry and suggested Jason should ride them in their forthcoming races. Booming down the telephone, Harry had declared: 'I don't want some part-time, jumped-up, nouveau riche prat riding my horses. I want a professional, not a Savile Row dummy of an amateur.' Jason had no hope of pretending he hadn't heard. Fiona had gone scarlet, but he had just grinned. As she put down the telephone, he smiled and said, 'My day will come.'

Now, as he shook hands with the blonde, Fiona said, 'Eva will be joining us for dinner.' She returned her attention to Harry. 'I'll talk to you on Monday morning about the entries. Jason and I are going to watch this race and then dash off. I want to be back in time for evening stables.' Jason, meanwhile, was looking into the only truly green eyes he had ever seen.

'I look forward to our next meeting being more leisurely,' he said.

'So do I,' she said. 'And to sampling Fiona's celebrated wine cellar. I'll see you tonight.' With that she smiled and walked away with the speed and grace of an ice dancer.

Her long, flowing stride reminded Jason of a big African cat. He became aware of Fiona's hand on his arm and the impish grin on her face. 'Don't be in too much thrall to her tonight. She actually wants to talk to you seriously.' She led him up to the lower steps of the grandstand, where they watched a thrilling hurdle race in which three of the four Cheltenham possibles battled it out with only a short head and a neck dividing first from third after a blistering two and a half miles.

As they left the course Jason fingered the screwed-up note and betting slip in his pocket. Cautiously extracting the betting slip he whispered to Fiona, 'don't look behind us all the way to the car. I'm going to drop something. I haven't become a litterbug – I'll tell you about it on the way home.' He opened the door for Fiona and went round and climbed into the driver's seat.

'What was all that about?' asked Fiona as they drove out in convoy with other race goers who were leaving promptly in an attempt to miss the worst of the traffic.

'I don't know,' said Jason truthfully. It didn't take him long to fill her in on the little he did know.

They had barely got through the front door when Fiona's telephone rang. She picked it up, acknowledged the caller and, nodding to Jason, handed him the phone.

'Is that you, Jay?' said a voice. It sounded familiar but it wasn't by any means instantly recognisable. 'It's the man you took home the night his mother died,' the caller continued, 'and who you sat and talked to until after two in the morning.'

'So it really is you, Danny. What's the problem?'

'I need to speak to you urgently. Can you meet me at the Membury service station on the M4 in forty minutes?' Jason looked at his watch. He had a good two hours before dinner. They agreed to meet in the Happy Eater.

'You may not recognise me, Jay,' added the voice. 'But I'll know you all right'.

Picking up his car keys, Jason promised Fiona he would be back in time for dinner at eight.

Chapter Four

Jason had barely got himself a cup of coffee and sat down when a short, sturdy figure appeared in his eye line. The man was casually dressed in black jeans, a black polo-neck sweater and a black anorak. Putting a glass of orange juice on the table, he sat down opposite Jason.

'Well,' he said.

Jason stared at him in disbelief. The man sitting opposite him could have been Danny Derkin's brother, or his cousin, but he wasn't Danny Derkin. The eyebrows were not as thick and straighter; the eyes were grey, not blue; the lips were fuller and a small but deep scar puckered the cheek just below his left eye. 'It really is me, Jay,' he said. 'But apart from a doctor, one surgeon, my father and two priests, you're the only person who knows it. The voice was similar but the accent was American.

'Ask me a question no-one else would know the answer to.' He held Jason's gaze. Jason thought for a moment. 'What happened the day after you won the Whitbread Gold Cup?'

A smile lit up the grey eyes. 'I had drunk a lot so you'd stolen my car keys and sent me back to Lambourn in a taxi you paid for. The next day you and Peta arrived with a bottle of champagne, a dozen oysters and a video of the previous day's race. We must have watched it a dozen times, me never quite believing I was going to win. Then you drove me to Simpson's in the Strand and I had one of the biggest helpings of roast beef I've ever eaten in my life.' He paused and smiled. 'And the waiter recognised me and gave each of us a port. Peta was driving, so you and I drank hers between us.' Peta was Jason's ex-girlfriend: the donor of the ostentatious number plates. He smiled at the recollection.

'OK, so what happened?'

Danny lit a cigarette and then began his story. After he broke his thigh, it was weeks before he was able to walk, even with crutches. He was bored to tears. He took to going down to a bar in his home town where he was something of a celebrity and people bought him drinks.

He spent quite a bit of time with one of the regulars, a man from Dublin known to one and all simply as 'the Friend' though his real name, he told Danny, was Liam. He didn't seem short of a bob or two, and was certainly very generous to Danny, but Danny couldn't quite get a handle on what line of business he was in. He was apparently one of those wide boys who had fingers in a lot of pies, some of them quite sensitive, and Danny respected his privacy. He enjoyed Liam's company, and the two of them occasionally went on from the pub to have a meal together and talk racing. On one of these evenings, after dinner, they went back to Liam's flat for a nightcap. Danny was pretty drunk and in self-pitying mood bemoaning his lot and the pain he was still in from his injury.

'You shouldn't be putting up with all that,' said Liam with concern. 'The medics should have given you something to ease it. Tell you what, I have some stuff here that will do the trick.'

Danny looked at him warily through glazed eyes.

Liam laughed. 'Don't look so worried. I'm your friend – I'm trying to do you a favour. I'm just talking about a bit of help to get you through this. That's what drugs are for. Everyone needs a lift sometimes. It's up to you but I hate to see a man suffer when there's no need for it at all. I can give you something now and a supply to take away with you if you like, then you'll have it handy just in case. What do you say?'

Danny had been too plastered and too naïve even to realise that he was standing at the top of a slippery slope, let alone that he was launching himself down it. It was only a matter of weeks before he was hooked on heroin. When he wasn't high he was drunk, his money was running out and his father was refusing to speak to him. He didn't see anything of the Friend for a while – he'd apparently told the barman in the pub he was going back to Dublin on business. When Danny did run into him his manner was considerably colder.

'Hello again, Danny,' he said. 'I want you to come with me. It's payback time.'

Danny, who was in no condition to object or even to ask what he meant, accompanied the Friend back to his flat. 'Sit down,' ordered Liam. He went to a cupboard and pulled out two crutches, handed them to Danny and took away Danny's own crutches.

'You're to go to Liverpool on the ferry tomorrow,' said the Friend. 'A taxi will pick you up and take you to a house. A man there will exchange your crutches for another pair, and then you'll come home. That's all.' Danny stared at him in amazement.

'What the hell for?'

'You're my messenger. You'll be carrying something valuable for me.'

Danny was too befuddled and frightened to refuse. Suddenly his whole life was overtaken by fear. He didn't know what scared him more, the prospect of falling foul of the Friend or the danger of getting caught in possession of heroin or whatever else it was that was hidden in the crutches. Soon he was crossing the Irish Sea on a weekly basis, sometimes by sea and sometimes by air, bound for Liverpool, Cardiff or Swansea.

Everyone knew Danny Derkin, everyone asked how he was getting on and no one questioned the purpose of his trips. Customs officers greeted him warmly and waved him through. One day, as he got off the boat at Holyhead, he saw a group of uniformed policemen standing at the bottom of the gangplank, three of them with dogs. They were stopping every passenger for the dogs to sniff their bags.

The sweat was pouring down Danny's back. There was nowhere he could go. One of the policemen saw him approaching and in a broad Irish accent announced: 'well, if it isn't Danny Derkin! Let me help you.' And putting a hand under his elbow, he led Danny on his crutches, past the dogs and across the dock to the taxi rank.

'Are you feeling all right?'

'Just a bit of a twinge, it's sore sometimes.'

'Can I get you a taxi?'

'No, it's all right, I'm being met,' Danny told him. The policeman smiled and walked away. A moment later a taxi drew up. Danny got in and was swept away.

'What was that about?' the driver asked.

Danny told him.

'Jesus! They've got the sniffer dogs, have they? We'll have to give this route a rest.'

On his return to Dublin Danny went to see the Friend. 'That's it,' he said. 'I'm not doing this any more.'

'Oh, your career as a courier isn't over yet, Danny boy. Not by a long way,' said Liam menacingly.

'I've done enough for you. Just leave me alone.'

Liam gave Danny a long chilling stare. He smiled unpleasantly. 'Suit yourself, Danny. But you'll be back. You have no choice. You're a junkie!'

Danny turned on his heel and marched out of the flat.

Within hours he was suffering a glimpse of hell as the withdrawal symptoms gripped him. Within days he was hammering desperately at the Friend's door. There was no answer. He knocked harder and started shouting, but still nobody came. He gave up and staggered towards the pub. At least he could get a drink there. Suddenly he felt an explosion in the side of his head, and then everything went black. Danny woke up feeling awful. His head throbbed and his mouth was so dry he couldn't speak. There were two men leaning over him. One looked like a priest. The other was dressed in a suit. Danny realised he was lying on a table.

He struggled. 'Steady, boy,' said the priest. 'You nearly died.' Danny looked from one to the other, utterly confused. Perhaps he was already dead. The priest introduced himself as Father Brennan. He explained that he had found him, unconscious and desperately ill, in the street. Father Brennan had worked with drug addicts and knew the signs of a massive overdose when he saw them. With the help of a taxi driver he had got Danny back to his house and telephoned his brother, David, who was a doctor.

'You nearly killed yourself,' David told the bewildered Danny sternly. 'That amount of heroin and that amount of alcohol would normally be fatal.'

'Can I sit up?'

'Yes, but take it easy.' Danny hauled himself, with difficultly, into a sitting position. Disjointed scenes from the previous day began to come back to him, and he tried to piece them together.

'I haven't taken any heroin.'

Father Brennan looked him squarely in the eye. 'Danny, you have to admit it. Denial is the biggest problem in overcoming addiction.'

'I'm not denying it. Of course I take heroin, and of course I drink, but I haven't taken any drugs for several days. I was trying to kick it, but it was too much for me. I was trying to get some gear, or at least a drink, and that's the last thing I remember.' He put his hand to his head and winced. 'I think somebody hit me.'

The priest was about to say something but David stopped him. 'Let me look at your arm.' He took hold of Danny's right arm. 'Are you right-handed?'

'Yes.'

David turned to his brother. 'He couldn't have done this. Look where the needle mark is on the right arm. He would have to have been a contortionist.'

Everything started to come into focus for Danny. 'Christ! They tried to murder me!' he shouted. 'A drug pusher was forcing me to smuggle for him,' he said more calmly. 'And I wanted out.'

Father Brennan sighed wearily. 'In that case, if you stay here you're a dead man. Are you really determined to come off the drugs?'

'I'll be a dead man if I don't.'

'Right. You can stay here, and David will prescribe you some Methadone and help you over the next two or three days. When you're better we'll get you away somewhere where nobody knows you.'

'That won't be easy,' Danny muttered to himself.

It was three weeks before Danny recovered enough of his health and strength for David to give him the go-ahead to leave. Father Brennan took him down to Dublin docks, where he was put on a small boat that was crossing to Boston. For seven days Danny sat in a tiny cabin and kept himself sane with the Methadone. The captain brought him his meals himself and was friendly but not inquisitive. It was clearly not the first time he had carried this kind of passenger.

When he arrived at Boston, somehow or other Danny was spirited away through customs and immigration with no sign of any paperwork being completed. He was in the USA, but officially he wasn't. A quiet old man met him and took him to a waiting car.

Danny gazed out of the car windows in wonder at the beautiful countryside whizzing by. Gradually they climbed into the green mountains of Vermont, eventually arriving at a high stone wall with imposing wrought-iron gates. The driver stopped and rang a bell, the gates opened and they drove in. Ahead was a simple low stone building surrounded by several outbuildings. A mediaeval-looking figure appeared in the drive, walking towards them. 'Jesus,' thought Danny. 'I'm in some kind of monastery.'

Smiling, the white-robed monk greeted him. 'Hi – we've been expecting you.' He beckoned for Danny to follow and led him to a small annexe a few yards away from the main house.

He was shown into a small but light and airy room that included a basic but spotless en-suite shower and WC. Motioning him to unpack his holdall and wait, the monk left him. Ten minutes later, an imposing silver-haired figure, dressed in similar white robe relieved by a silver crucifix, knocked on the door and entered the room.

'Welcome, Danny. I am the Prior here. I know who you are, but no one else does. I understand from Father Brennan that you want to kick your unhealthy habit? I also understand that you need a new identity.'

First of all, he explained, Danny would be detoxified. This would be painful and tough. He would be helped by the monks who would ask him nothing about his life, not even his name. His only discussions would be with the Prior. When Danny thought he was ready, he would be given plastic surgery. 'You will have a lot of time to think and read. For half an hour every evening, we will talk,' the Prior concluded.

Danny saw nothing ahead of him but torment, yet soon he felt really well again, better than he had in years, in fact. He wasn't expected to participate in the religious life of the monastery if he didn't want to, but he spent many hours helping the monks in the gardens and doing his fair share of the everyday chores that underpinned their existence. In this uncomplicated, meditative atmosphere he began to recover in mind as well as in body. His leg was almost healed and benefited enormously from the ministrations of one of the monks who was a skilled physiotherapist. Even so, he doubted it would ever be strong enough for him to raceride again.

The day came when he felt ready to discuss his change of identity. A date was fixed for his plastic surgery and it was agreed that the operation would take place in the monastery's own small but adequately equipped medical wing. The work was not dangerous and did not require a lot of specialist hardware, just a surgeon of great skill. He appeared within a couple of days in the shape of a tiny man with bright eyes, a completely bald head and a huge nose, like a small and very active bird of prey. But his hands were the hands of a musician and his smile was kind and constant. He also, it transpired, had a great sense of humour. He inspected Danny's face with a practised eye and asked him whether he wanted to look like Paul Newman or Sylvester Stallone. 'As I understand it,' he continued more seriously, 'our priority is to make you unrecognisable. That isn't difficult, and we don't have to be too dramatic in what we do. I can change your eye line, alter your lips, we'll give you new front teeth – that should be straightforward as they are already capped – and change the colour of your eyes.' Danny was clearly alarmed at the thought of his eyes being tampered with. 'It's OK, we're not going to take them out and give you new ones,' said the surgeon dryly. 'I'm just going to give you tinted contact lenses.'

'Scars, even small ones, become a focal point of the face, so we'll give you a modest scar that will alter your expression. But you'll still be a good-looking guy. You must grow your hair but don't dye it. The less we do to draw attention to your appearance, the better.'

Between procedures, for the three days all this took, Danny's face was swathed in bandages. When they were removed he could scarcely believe he was seeing himself. The scars were tiny and he was assured that within a few weeks all but the one deliberately created would disappear entirely. He was shown how to put in the tinted contact lenses, and the transformation was complete.

A few nights later the Prior summoned Danny rather earlier than usual for their talk. 'Well, Danny,' he said. 'We've done all we can for you. Now you have to get yourself an American accent. I'm going to send you to Texas, where you're going to work on a ranch. I don't expect you to turn into a cowboy, but the work will do you good. Don't force the accent, or it will sound false. If you pick up the intonation it will meld in with your Irish voice, and that should be enough for you to blend in here and for you to sound American at home.' He had handed Danny a large envelope. In it were a few hundred dollars and a passport in the name of Sean Maguire. 'A good Irish name,' commented the Prior. 'Good luck to you.'

The next six months had been wonderful for Danny. He was overjoyed to be working with horses again and he loved the life. He was made very welcome in Texas, and nobody asked any awkward questions. He grew stronger, fitter and more weatherbeaten, his leg finally stopped hurting and his voice changed significantly. He worked hard and saved up the money to go home. At the end of those six months he knew he was ready.

Sean Maguire was distinctly nervous as he presented his new passport at Kennedy airport. But not an eyebrow was raised on either side of the Atlantic. Itching to try out his new identity he cautiously went to race meetings at Clonmel, Wexford, Naas and the Curragh, keeping well away from the jockeys. Instead he mingled with the crowds, drank orange juice in the bar and watched the racing, sizing up the young horses and listening to the conversations going on around him.

To begin with he avoided Leopardstown where he knew the Friend was a regular. But as his confidence grew Sean felt he had to face the possibility that he was going to bump into him some time. He couldn't spend the rest of his life skulking in the shadows. Maybe it would be better and safer to encounter the enemy when he was prepared for it, rather than unexpectedly.

It was on his second visit to Leopardstown, turning from the bar with a cup of coffee in one hand and a ham roll in the other, that he finally found himself face to face with the Friend – a somewhat closer encounter than he'd bargained for. Their eyes met briefly and, with a supreme effort, Danny smiled and moved to one side to let the other man get to the bar. 'Thanks,' said the Friend automatically, without a flicker of recognition, and ordered himself a drink. When Danny sat down his hands were shaking and it was a good few minutes before he could pick up his coffee. Carefully he watched the Friend's reflection. He downed his whiskey and, without so much as a glance in Danny's direction, threaded his way out of the bar. It had been a harrowing test but at last Danny felt safe.

It was one of the conversations he overheard at the races that prompted Danny to come to England. Sheltering from the wind behind a small storage building in an attempt to light a cigarette, he became aware of voices coming from round the corner. He recognised one as that of Paddy O'Flynn, a bookmaker who was well known not only as a big punter but also as a dangerous man. Strange things had happened to jockeys and others involved in some of his biggest coups. Suspicions had been voiced but nothing had ever been pinned on him. Listening intently, Danny identified the other voice as that of a notorious hard man who had enjoyed more than one spell behind bars.

'They're going to try to get that Hooray Henry amateur Jay Jessop to ride it. The bloody horse is brilliant but it's too strong for most of the jockeys. It'll cost me a fortune if it wins. I want that jockey stopped, not the horse. Nobble him well before Cheltenham. I'll let you know if they put on another jockey I don't like and if necessary we'll deal with him, too.'

This pair was deadly serious and Danny knew he had to warn Jason. Within twenty four hours he was on his way to England.

'That's why I had to see you, Jay. I saw him at Newbury yesterday.

'Thank you Danny, I owe you.' He was silent for a moment, trying to take it all in. 'What are you doing at the moment? Workwise I mean?' he asked eventually.

'I'm still living on my savings and I'm having the occasional bet. I've learned a lot by keeping quiet, listening a lot and watching.'

'Danny, I've got an immediate job for you, if you want it. I might have a permanent job for you as well, but for now I've got one starting tomorrow. I'm on the look-out for some good young horses – and I need a scout. Point-to-point winners, or horses ready to go and run in bumpers. Are you interested?'

'Interested! I'd bite your hand off for it,' beamed Danny.

'Good. Look, I'm going to have to get used to calling you Sean, so let's start now. But we need to keep our new relationship as quiet as possible. People know we were friends in the old days, so we had better not take unnecessary risks. It'll suit me to have you listening and finding out what's going on without people knowing you're working for me, particularly until my new venture is off the ground.'

'What's that, then?' asked Danny.

'I'll tell you another time, but if all goes well it'll mean a real working partnership between us. Let's sort out how we handle this one first.' He drummed his fingers on the table, thinking. 'I'll get you a mobile phone to use for all our business. When you ring me, I'm going to need to be sure it's you. If you leave a message, say 'this is Sean calling on Wednesday, and then give the date of the day before, so if its Wednesday 21st, say Wednesday 20th'. If you're speaking directly to me, just start off: 'and how are you feeling on this grand 20th day of such and such a month? Or something similar.'

'In time I'll get to know your new voice, but let's not take any chances at this stage. We need to have some kind of formula to our conversations, so that we'll know immediately if something is wrong. How does this sound?'

Danny looked at him admiringly. 'I always knew you were a shrewd fella. That makes a lot of sense. And likewise, if I'm ever in trouble, I'll say to you: 'This is Sean, Mr Jessop, and how are you this fine day?' If I use your surname, you'll know I'm not alone and I've got a problem.'

'Right,' said Jason. 'I'll have the telephone in two or three days. How shall I get it to you?'

'What about that pub just off Berkeley Square, where you and I had a drink a couple of times?' suggested the Irishman.

'I seem to remember you're very well in with the landlord there.'

'Oh, The Running Footman, you mean. Good idea. I'll leave the telephone in an envelope there for you. Go in and ask for Bob Tanner and he'll see you get it. It'll be the latest model. You'll be able to get me from anywhere on it whatever country either of us are in. It'll be a digital phone so it won't be easy to hack into.'

They shook hands warmly. 'It's great to know you're alive;' said Jason quietly. We're going to have some good times together.' He paused. 'I've had another idea. I'll leave a small video camera for you, too. Send me tapes of the horses you like.'

Danny watched the departing figure with a feeling of elation. At last Sean Maguire was going to have a worthwhile role to play.

Chapter Five

Driving back to Midwood Park Jason replayed Danny's amazing story in his mind. He was more than a little concerned about the news the jockey had brought, but at least he was forewarned. As he approached Fiona's yard he thought he had better turn his attention to the evening ahead. As he parked outside the house he noticed an unfamiliar dark blue Lotus in the drive. Not his favourite car, but somehow it seemed to complement the image of the glamorous young woman with whom he was going to dine and to whom it doubtless belonged.

He found Fiona and Eva sipping a fine South African chardonnay. He kissed Fiona on the cheek and smiled at Eva, captivated anew by those green eyes. As they chatted he was impressed by her self-possession. Clearly this was no mere pretty, shallow little rich girl. There was a quiet determination about everything she did.

Fiona led them into dinner and sat Jason between herself and Eva. The first course, an avocado mousse, was already on the table. Rapidly and easily, the conversation turned to racing and Jay's hopes for the forthcoming Christmas and New Year meetings and the all-important March National Hunt Festival. He was pleasantly surprised at how much Eva knew about National Hunt racing in general and Cheltenham in particular. He assumed Fiona had filled her in on his past triumphs while they had been waiting for him. A superb Dover sole followed. This was not only one of Jay's favourites, but perfect when you were weight-watching. Fiona, as always, had thought of everything. They finished with a delicious homemade lime sorbet and retired to Fiona's cosy little study where a large cafetière was already waiting for them along with decanters of port and cognac. Jay allowed himself a small cognac but the two women stuck with the Chardonnay.

By the time they moved into the study, Jason had learned that Eva was the only daughter of the president of one of South Africa's most successful small and independent diamond merchants. The company had been started by her grandfather, who had handed it over to her father. It was in her father's hands that the business had prospered, making him fabulously wealthy. Before taking over the company he had been a student in England and had fallen deeply in love with National Hunt racing. It had always been his intention to return on his retirement and indulge himself with a few top-class jumpers, his objective being to win one of the major races at Cheltenham. In South Africa he had had the *Sporting Life*, and in later years the *Racing Post*, sent to him every day and read everything he could about National Hunt racing in the UK. Growing up with his passion, his daughter had caught the bug.

Eva's father had recently been injured in a terrible car crash and initially, although he had survived it, he knew that his days were numbered and that he would never see England again. He told Eva, his sole heir, that he had set aside a significant sum of money for realising his long-held dream and that it was sitting in a separate bank account in Zurich. He asked her to use it to achieve for herself, and in his memory, what he had always hoped to do himself. 'It would be nice if your colours included a diamond,' he had smiled. Shortly afterwards he had died peacefully and Eva had decided to come to England to fulfil his dearest wish.

Eva was staying in her late father's company flat in central London. She had made contact with Fiona, a family friend, as soon as she arrived, and had also looked up Harry Clough who had been one of her father's London agents, but apart from them she had few racing acquaintances in the country.

'I was very disappointed when I found that Fiona was not going to train any more,' Eva told him, putting down her coffee cup. 'I've known her since I was a child, and I was rather pinning my hopes on her. And having heard about you, I thought that you might help us find the horses I need and possibly ride them. Now I have to start from scratch.'

She looked so crestfallen that Jason was tempted to tell her all, but it was far too soon for that. 'Well,' he said instead. 'That's the sort of challenge that any number of people in National Hunt racing would jump at. I'll certainly help you in any way I can. Give me a few days to think about it and I'll get back to you.'

'We don't have that long do we?' she said. 'This year's Festival is too soon, and I know there is over a year between this one and the next, but unless I go and buy ready-made stars, which are going to cost a fortune, we're going to need time to find the right horses and prepare them properly. Besides, I don't want to just go and buy this year's winner of one of the big races, in the hope that it will win again next year. There's not any great achievement in that when other people have done all the real work. All I'd be doing would be using my money to buy success. It wouldn't involve me, or the team I work with, in any real skill or enterprise.'

Eva suddenly rose several notches in Jason's estimation. He was also pleased to hear her use the word 'team'.

'I couldn't agree with you more,' he said. 'Which is why I want a little more time to think about it. Is there any particular race you want to win?'

'Well, I know that the Gold Cup is the absolute height of everyone's ambition, and of course the Champion Hurdle is very special too. But strangely enough, it's the Queen Mother Champion Chase that has always appealed to me particularly. There's something about the speed of those horses, the precision of their jumping, and the fact that so often it's a thrilling tussle at the end. It's always been very special to me. Having said that, the great novice races are wonderful, too. In all honesty, I suppose I'd be satisfied with almost anything, but one of those, or perhaps the Supreme Novices Hurdle, would be the icing on the cake.'

Once again Jason was impressed by both her knowledge and her down-to-earth attitude. He was about to say so when he was interrupted by Fiona.

'Well, my children,' she said with a benevolent smile. 'I'm going to leave you with your dreams of future glory. I've got a long day ahead of me tomorrow.' Pausing to give Jason a motherly look, she reminded him, 'And you've got an early start, too.' She smiled mischievously at Eva. 'Don't keep him up too long!'

When Fiona left them the conversation continued easily. Eva told Jason that she had worked as her father's marketing manager, a role that had included handling their sponsorship of five big races, a women's international tennis tournament and the national women's swimming team. What serendipity, he marvelled to himself. Her experience would make her ideal as his third partner. Jay became more and more aware of the young woman's feline sensuality. By now she had taken off her shoes and curled herself up on the chaise-longue opposite him. Somehow she seemed both languid and vibrant at the same time. The silk dress she was wearing was clinging to her curves in a way that accentuated her sexuality rather than hiding it.

He sensed that the attraction was working both ways and he briefly wondered whether or not to make a move. It didn't take him long to decide against it. This is too good to spoil, he thought. With his good looks, charm, his success in business and the thrilling appeal of his victories in the saddle, he had never had a moment's trouble attracting women. What he was less good at was sustaining a deeper relationship when his every waking hour was spent either working or riding. The break-up with Peta, his longest-standing girlfriend, had shaken him more than he anticipated and made him cautious. It would be most unwise to complicate matters with Eva by rushing in without a thought for the consequences, especially in view of the importance of the matters they had been discussing.

Pulling himself up out of the chair, Jason stepped across the room, picked up Eva's hand and gently kissed the fingertips. 'It's been a delight to meet you,' he said with a warmth that was completely genuine. 'I really will think about what you said, and I promise you that within a week I will come back to you with some really concrete ideas. In the meantime, I'm racing at Plumpton on Monday, so if you have nothing better to do, why don't you come along? We could meet there. Just give me a ring when you know what your plans are.'

She smiled slowly at him. 'I'd love to,' she said. 'And I trust I will be applauding you in the winner's enclosure.' She got to her feet, too, and standing on tiptoe she lightly brushed her lips across his cheek. 'I've had a lovely evening, Jay,' she said. 'Or should I call you Jason?'

'Most people call me both, depending on the mood, so I'll leave it up to you.'

'I think I'll call you Jay,' she said, after a moment's consideration. Then she glided soundlessly up the stairs.

Jason put out the lights and followed her up the stairs, humming quietly to himself.

At 6.10 on Sunday morning Jason was off, having grabbed a quick cup of black coffee. As he turned right out of the yard he glanced to his left. There was no traffic at that time of the morning and the only vehicle he saw was a Mercedes parked a few hundred yards down the road. He drove quickly but carefully along the quiet but rather winding Berkshire roads. Rounding a corner, he instinctively braked as his brain registered something in his path. A motorcycle was lying on its side. A few yards away he saw a prone figure on the grass verge. He leaped out of the car and ran over to the the rider. Blood appeared to be seeping from under his helmet and down one side of his face. Jason heard the sound of a car engine and looked round. It was the Mercedes he'd seen earlier. The driver pulled up and he and his passenger got out.

'See what you can do for him while I phone for help,' said Jason, rushing towards his car. Before he knew what was happening, one of them produced a baseball bat and swung at him with some violence. He saw that the second man was similarly armed. They were moving in on him. Jason felt a numbing blow connect with his right shoulder from behind. He spun round to find the motorcyclist, now on his feet wielding a spanner. Three to one were poor odds: the element of surprise was his only hope. Without warning, he ran straight at the motorcyclist. At the last moment he side-stepped him, far more adroitly than he ever had playing rugby, made for the post-and-rail fence on the roadside and vaulted it with one hand. He looked back to see all three attackers in hot pursuit. Suddenly, one of the three attackers paused and yelled at the other two. Coming down the road was a tractor, pulling an empty trailer on which sat two men. The three of them rushed back to the car, leaving the motorbike on the ground. The Mercedes reversed with a squeal of protesting rubber and disappeared in the opposite direction of Midwood Park, but not before Jason had noted the number plate.

The tractor drew up and the driver came down from the cab, evidently puzzled by the abandoned motorcycle and Jason's somewhat dishevelled appearance. Briefly explaining what had happened, Jason dialled 999 on his mobile and gave the police the details of the car and the direction in which it was travelling. Insisting that he could not wait, despite the entreaties of the policewoman at the other end, he thanked the somewhat bemused farmworkers for their timely appearance, got back into his car and continued on his way.

It was clear that this must have been the attack that Danny – no, he had to *think* of him as Sean rather than merely calling him by the alias if this was going to work – had warned him was in the offing. Fingering his shoulder gingerly, he was relieved to find that the collarbone was still intact. The bruising probably wouldn't be any worse than it would have been from a run-of-the-mill fall.

Thank God, he breathed to himself. The New Year meeting was only a few weeks away.

By the time he reached Jed's yard, the police had called back to say they had found the Mercedes dumped in a public car park. The number plates were false so it was almost certainly a car that had recently been stolen. The motorcycle had been purchased for cash two days earlier. They said they would keep Jay informed of any developments.

Jay had then phoned Howard Barrack and outlined what had happened, promising to fill him in on the details later. His immediate concern was organising some sort of protection, for the next few months.

'Leave it to me, old lad,' said Howard. 'I'll have something sorted by the time you arrive here for lunch. You're still on for that?'

'Of course. I've had worse bangs and ridden in a race immediately afterwards, so relax. I'll ride Conker this morning and then see you as arranged.'

At Jed's, Howard's horse was already saddled and being walked round by one of the lads, along with three other horses due to be schooled after a strong gallop. Jed took the cigarette out of his mouth and grunted, 'So what kept you?' Jason told him about the attack without revealing any of the background. Jed nodded, muttered to himself and patted Jay on the back.

The Conker galloped with all his usual enthusiasm and schooled with the mixture of exuberance and precision that made him such an exciting ride, and boosting Jason's confidence that he would be a serious contender round the four miles at Cheltenham.

Jason then paid Pewter Queen a visit and watched her trot up and down the yard. He would be able to assure Howard that she was none the worse for her exertions at Sandown.

After a quick look at Howard's other two horses, he gulped down a cup of coffee and talked to Jed about his mount for Plumpton the next day. Then he set off for The Laurels, Howard's splendid home, and the warm welcome he knew he would be given there. Bubbles, Howard's small and aptly nicknamed wife – as always beautifully if somewhat brightly dressed – greeted Jason as if he were a prodigal son returning after a ten-year absence. She was a superb cook, but curbed her natural culinary ebullience when entertaining Jason in the interests of his diet restrictions. Today she served wafer-thin Parma ham and ogen melon, followed by a fish stew that would have done credit to the waterside of Marseilles. While Howard and Bubbles, who were both possessed of a fearsome sweet tooth, tucked into a homemade trifle covered with hundreds and thousands, Jason contented himself with some fresh fruit. The trifle, it was explained without any great conviction, had been prepared for their grandchildren, who were coming to tea later.

Bubbles brought the men coffee in Howard's study and went off to get ready for the grandchildren. Howard offered Jason a Monte Cristo No.3 which he always kept even though he didn't smoke himself.

'So what about that rigmarole this morning?' prompted Howard now that they were alone.

Jason cut and lit the cigar and, sitting back in his chair to ease the stiffness in his shoulder, gave Howard the full story.

'You don't need to worry about a thing,' Howard reassured him. 'I've got four serious characters arriving this afternoon who'll make it their business to see that you can go about yours without coming to any harm.' He looked at his watch. 'They should be here any time.'

He poured more coffee and leaned forward in his easy chair.

'Now let's talk about this company of yours. I've thought about it, and I want in. But do we need anyone else? I could put up the whole amount myself, you know, and then it would just be the two of us.'

Jason went over the reasons why he wanted to spread the operation between four people, including himself.

'And with only two partners, the whole concept would be different,' he pointed out. 'I think I have the second partner. The man I saw on Friday is thinking about it, as you have been, but my gut feeling is he'll want in, too. And since then I'm almost sure I've found the third as well, though I haven't discussed the proposal with her yet.'

'With her? So it's a woman?'

Jason picked up his second cup of coffee, and launched into his second story of the afternoon.

'So,' said Howard when he had, 'the reason you want this Ms Botha on board is purely that she's got real money and a real contribution to make. It wouldn't have anything to do with her feminine charms, would it?'

Jason didn't dignify this with an answer.

Howard smiled to himself and changed the subject. 'I'm very keen to see this airfield of yours.'

'Can you take the rest of the afternoon off?' asked Jason.

'I'll have to square it with Bubbles, but the truth is she rather likes having the grandchildren to herself.'

Whilst they had been talking two cars had pulled up outside. Howard walked out of the house. 'Ah!' he said. 'Jason, you had better meet your protectors.'

Stepping out of Howard's imposing front porch, Jason noticed an elderly BMW and an equally undistinguished Rover parked in the drive. In each of the cars sat two men. On seeing Howard, the four men got out and there were enthusiastic greetings all round. The newcomers were clearly in good physical condition and they looked like guys who could take care of themselves too. Later Jason was to learn that they all regularly attended a famous East End boxing club and two of them had been amateur England internationals.

'This is Benny, he's the boss,' said Howard to Jason. Benny was slightly shy of six foot with an almost shaven head and a handshake like a steel vice. 'We're going to stick to you like glue, guv'nor,' he assured Jay. He then introduced the other three, who, it turned out, were all his brothers. Harry was a nondescript-looking guy with prematurely grey hair; Robbie looked rather like James Cagney, and Angel, the youngest, had a blond mop that was responsible for his nickname.

'These boys have so many friends they could turn out an army for you if you needed it,' joked Howard. 'OK lads – we're going on a recce, and then Jason's driving straight to London. Since you're all here, why don't you all come with us, then one car can stick with the E-Type and the other can bring me back to The Laurels.'

'Right you are, boss,' said Benny cheerfully.

Jason led the way out of the drive and towards the motorway, with the Rover and the BMW following at a discreet distance.

'I'm very grateful, Howard,' said Jason in the car, eyeing the convoy behind him in the rear-view mirror. 'But don't you think this is slightly over the top?'

'Not at all. If we are going to do the job, we need to do it right. These bastards are going to get more desperate, having failed to nail you, and we need guys who can blend into the background, and that means more than one or two. They've got a fleet of cars, so not even you will always know if you're being followed. But believe me, these boys are real minders, and God help anybody who has another go at you. Just remember to keep them in touch with your movements.'

Jason cut across to the M4, and a few miles outside Swindon on the Gloucestershire-Wiltshire border they left the motorway and started to climb. County View airfield was on a raised plateau surrounded by farmland. Until recently it had been the home of a private flying club but not having enough rich members to keep it really fashionable it had lost out to some rather better-supported outfits. A high chain-link fence in surprisingly good condition protected the property. Jason got out of the car at the entrance and produced a key acquired from the estate agents. Unlocking the double gates he drove through and pulled over with a gesture to the other two cars to come in and wait. Jason and Howard set off round the perimeter road which, like the fence, was still in excellent repair. Jason pointed out the various buildings that would be used as loose boxes, hay barns, an indoor school and living accommodation for stable staff and the administration block he hoped to convert into a house and office for himself.

'Not very grand,' was Howard's comment on the latter.

'It's not meant to be. I don't expect to spend a lot of time indoors during the day, and this is going to be a seven-day-a-week project.'

Jason headed down the central runway, pointing out its virtues. If they ran an all-weather strip alongside it, it would be an excellent vantage point from which to monitor the horses' work; it would also enable them to move equipment without spoiling the grass that would become one of the main gallops.

On the far side of the site, he showed Howard how the plateau dropped away quite sharply. This piece of land would be ideal for an uphill gallop that would make the horses work even harder and help build their stamina. The country lanes beyond the fence were relatively free of traffic and offered a number of hills for roadwork on non-gallop days.

'Well, you're right, old son – it seems ideal,' said Howard. 'I think it's time we were getting back. Let's stop for a cup of tea on the way home.' A few miles from the airfield they found an attractive country house hotel. While Jason's minders busied themselves with a thermos of coffee and settled down to a football match on the radio, Jason and Howard wandered into the lounge, chose a quiet corner and ordered tea.

'I think we're going to have a lot of fun, and I think you're a winner,' said Howard. 'That's why I'm backing you. But there is also another reason.' He looked out of the window his eyes narrowing, recalling the past vividly and with obvious distaste. Jason sensed that he was about to hear the tale to which his friend had alluded at Sandown.

Chapter Six

The East End in the post war years was a tough nursery, and like many of its inhabitants, Howard Barrack had not had an easy start in life. His father had died when he was ten, and from a young age he and his sisters turned their hands to whatever work was available to help make ends meet. Howard was part of a gang – not a crooked gang, but a group of boys who had known each other all their lives and kept in contact as they grew up. They lived mainly on their wits, bringing home the bacon in a variety of ways and taking opportunities where they found them rather than pursuing a single ambition, and helping each other out whenever they could. One of Howard's jobs was working for a bookmaker.

Howard's closest friend in the gang was Freddie Johnson, son of the biggest bookie in the area, Limpy Johnson, so named because he had one leg slightly shorter than the other as a result of a motorcycle accident when he was only seventeen. As a small boy Howard often went to the Johnson's house for tea. As the lads got older they'd go out and play snooker together or go to the dogs or horse races with Limpy.

Even at ten Howard had a head for figures. It wasn't merely that he was quick at mental arithmetic. He could look at a column of figures and know if something was wrong. For him figures had a pattern, a sort of symmetry and he was never happier than when he was working with them.

At the dog tracks and racecourses, Limpy soon noticed this aptitude for figures and one day he asked Howard if he'd like to learn bookmaking. The idea appealed to him. Racecourses seemed exciting places and he had never seen a poor bookmaker. Bit by bit he became more involved, and eventually Limpy set up Frankie separately from himself as an on-course bookmaker at both the dogs and the horses, with Howard as his number two.

Howard had always got on well with people. It didn't take him long to get to know some of the folk who worked in racing, in particular several of the less successful jockeys and a few of the stable lads. He always kept his ears open, and from time to time he would be given a good tip, either that a fancied horse wasn't likely to win, or that an outsider was going to. If the information proved right, he was always generous with his friends.

One day an ex-jockey who he had known for some time took him to one side and told him that there was a chance of a big payday. He explained how a decent horse had run badly twice. The stable couldn't understand it. They were doing nothing to stop their horse and they couldn't find anything wrong with it. The vet visited the yard and asked the trainer for a quiet word. Howard's friend happened to be nearby and overheard their conversation. The vet said he thought the problem might be the oilseed rape the farmer next door had planted that year for the first time. Some horses were violently allergic to it, said the vet, and come out in lumps. Others didn't show any obvious symptoms, but suffered enough of a reaction to affect their form. It seemed highly likely that this was the case here.

The former jockey was close to the head man in the adjoining yard and very discreetly asked him whether any of his horses appeared to be similarly affected. The head man thought it was a possibility that he had two such cases. Both horses were due to run the following week and one of them, if back to its best, would be a good thing. The same, of course, was true of the horse from the first stable. It was now pretty certain that the horses would be back on form when they ran because the rape was now in seed and the harmful pollen was no longer in the air. The ex-jockey and the head man wanted to have good bets, including a double on the two horses, but they knew that as soon as either of them placed a big bet the word would be out and the odds would be wrecked. Could Howard do anything to help? Of course he agreed.

Howard explained the situation to Frankie who agreed it was a golden opportunity. He would spread the bets around. Howard dug into his savings and handed over £500 for a £200 bet on each horse individually and £100 on the first doubling up with the second. He gave Frankie another £200 from the two stable men, who were having £50 between them on each horse and a £100 double.

When the big day came the first horse romped in at 12-1 and the second just got up on the line to win in a photo finish at 5 – 1. Howard was jubilant. His total winnings amounted to about £10,000, and the other two punters were to collect over £5,000.

He dashed round to Frankie's office and burst in. 'What do you think of that!' he cried joyously.

Frankie looked at him with a blank expression. 'What do I think of what?' he asked.

'The win, of course. 'How much did you make?'

'I don't know what you're talking about.'

Howard froze. 'The big bets you said you'd put on for me – today.'

'I thought you'd changed your mind,' mumbled Frankie. 'You never gave me a slip.'

Howard pointed out that he had never needed a slip before but Frankie was adamant that he hadn't placed the bets.

Howard was furious. He asked where his stake money was. Frankie opened a desk drawer, counted out the stake money and handed it back to Howard. Seething, Howard left to go and break the bad news to the two stable men. Howard's friend couldn't believe it. He said that Frankie had stitched them up. Howard defended Frankie, arguing that Frankie would never do that to him – as they had been friends for too long. If they looked around they would find no sign of the horses being backed. Eventually, deeply disappointed and far from satisfied, the two men went away, knowing they would never have an opportunity like that again in their lives.

Over the next few weeks and months Frankie behaved as if nothing had happened, and he never mentioned the bet again. Then he moved to a bigger house, and suddenly a shiny new Jaguar appeared outside it.

Howard knew that he did all right for himself and that Limpy treated him from time to time, but this still seemed beyond his usual means. One evening, having a drink with Limpy, Howard commented on Frankie's new acquisitions. Limpy said he didn't know where he had got the money, but it certainly wasn't from him. Frankie had told him he'd had a bit of a lucky touch. Howard's blood ran cold. He asked as casually as he could what sort of touch, and Limpy replied that Frankie had been very vague, but it seemed he had pulled off a big double and managed to spread it around without anybody really knowing.

The next day Howard tackled Frankie.

'Oh that,' he said noncommittally. 'I backed some long-priced horses in the two handicaps at Doncaster, both with each-way bets, and I was dead lucky. They both won.'

Howard said no more. He couldn't prove anything, but he was now convinced that Frankie had used his information and stakes to make a killing for himself. It was obvious he could never trust the man again.

Years later, Howard ran into Janice, Frankie's first wife, at the funeral of one of Limpy's old employees. Frankie had not bothered to come and pay his respects. By this time he was living a flash lifestyle and had traded in the mother of his two children for a leggy blonde twenty years his junior who had gold digger written all over her.

At the small wake after the funeral Janice came up and chatted to Howard. She told him how she had thought he might kill Frankie one day. Howard asked her what she meant. She said she knew Frankie had cheated him over some bets and that she wouldn't have been surprised if he'd taken his revenge.

'How do you know about that?' Howard inquired.

'The night of those races Frankie had come home roaring drunk', Janice recalled. 'I'd never seen him in such a mood. He was dancing, singing and shouting and finally he told me what had happened. The next morning he realised he shouldn't have, and over breakfast he just looked at me and said that if I ever mentioned it he would make sure that my looks were ruined for life.'

'Why are you telling me all this now?' asked Howard.

'I thought you should know. And I'm curious as to whether you will ever do anything about it. I hope you do. I'm sure he thinks you've forgotten about it now, if you ever even knew. You're respectable these days, but he's the same old Frankie. He'd cheat anyone. He doesn't need the money anymore. He just loves thinking he's pulled the wool over somebody's eyes.' She smiled at Howard sadly.

In the lounge of the country-house hotel, Howard fell silent.

'That's a terrible story, Howard,' said Jason.

Howard forced a grin. 'Oh, I don't know. It made me change my career, so I suppose in a funny kind of way I owe what I have today to Frankie cheating me. What he did also taught me never to trust anyone else with my money and to make my own decisions.'

His jaw tightened. 'But there are some things you can't let go. Our little project is going to give me the chance to have my revenge on Frankie. As you will have guessed, that's the little extra I want out of our partnership. And I know you're the man who can give it to me.'

'I understand your feelings,' said Jason. 'Of course I'll help you, but you must understand that it has to be legal, as I said before. It's got to be within the rules of racing and it must never be at the expense of the opportunity to win a race.'

'Understood,' replied Howard. They shook hands.

'Right,' said Howard, back to his normal self. 'What next?'

'Can I tell the other man you're in?'

'By all means. And why don't I start negotiating for that airfield? If these other two don't come in, I don't mind funding it until we find the partners we're looking for. That is, of course, if you still insist on it being more than the two of us.'

'Yes, I do,' replied Jason with a smile. 'But I accept your kind offer. So I'd be delighted for you to start talking to the estate agents, and the local council, to make sure we can do what we plan.'

'There's a lot of construction work to be done,' said Howard. 'How are we going to handle that?'

'I hope that one of the partners will look after that side for us.'

Howard laughed, 'I think I know who you have in mind. He'd be about as sharp as me, and I'd sooner have him on my side than against me.' He held his hands up. 'No, I'm not going to ask you who it is, I wouldn't want you to break any confidences and I know you wouldn't anyway. And this South African lady sounds fascinating.'

Jason paid the bill, despite Howard's protestations, and went out into the car park. Howard went off in the Rover, and the BMW followed Jay as far as Berkeley Square. Then his mobile rang. 'Someone will be outside tonight,' said Benny. 'But not in one of these cars. Look out for an old white Ford van.'

In his flat, Jason played back the messages on his answerphone. Among the usual crop of calls about rides was a message from Eva saying how much she had enjoyed Saturday night, and asking whether it would be convenient for him to meet her at Plumpton. She had left her host's telephone number. The next message was less friendly. 'Today was just a warning,' said an Irish voice. 'You'll get hurt if you ride any Irish horses at Cheltenham – badly hurt.' Jay hesitated. Better safe than sorry, he decided. He then phoned Benny.

'We'd better watch you,' Benny said. 'They obviously mean business. Don't worry, we'll look after you.' He chuckled and added: 'Otherwise Howard will hurt us!'

He rang Eva back. His call was answered by a rather hostile Harry Clough, who put Eva on the line. Jason explained that he had to go to the races straight from the office, but would be very happy to meet her there, if that was OK with her. There was a train right to the racecourse. Maybe they could drive back together after the racing? He could drop her back at her flat, and then perhaps they could have dinner later to continue the discussion they had begun at Midwood Park. She accepted all three offers.

The next morning Jason was jogging round Hyde Park by seven o'clock. A quick shower, a cup of coffee and two bananas and he was on his way to his office on the south side of Berkeley Square. He had two short meetings and was ready to leave for the races when Hal Bancroft, the president of Pan America Hi-Tech Publishing, was shown into his office. He had his coat on. Shaking Jason's hand he said, 'I hear, young man,' – he always called Jason young man – 'that you're racing at Plumpton this afternoon. Can you get anything decent to eat there?'

'Strangely enough, you can,' replied Jason. 'It used to be dreadful, but now there's a restaurant where you can get an adequate hot meal, even if it's not exactly the Ritz.'

'Right,' said Hal. 'I don't think I've ever told you that racing is a hobby of mine. I've only ever seen your jumping game on television, so why don't I come with you? We could have lunch there and talk over some points I'd like to discuss with you, and then we can enjoy the rest of the afternoon.'

'That's a great idea,' said Jason. 'But you do realise that half an hour before the first race I'll have to disappear. So unless I find a friend there you could hook up with, you'll be on your own until we come back. What's more, I've promised to bring a lady back to London with me.'

'Well,' grinned Hal mischievously, a twinkle in his eye, 'Why don't you introduce me to her and she and I can hold hands until you're ready to take us both back to London?'

'That sounds like a good deal.'

In the car Hal and Jason chewed over some of the remaining details relating to the sale of the company. Jason was again reassured by what Hal had to say and that the man understood the sensitivities that were likely to rise to the surface when a massive American outfit took over a substantial UK firm. One of the reasons he was happy to hand over his organisation to Hal was that the American really cared about people. It wasn't just enlightened self-interest based on the necessity of keeping the key editors; he also wanted people who would stay with the new organisation because they enjoyed their work and trusted the management.

Hal sat back in his seat and lit a Lucky Strike. 'So what's next on your agenda, Jason? I know you want to spend more time racing, but surely you won't be riding more than you do already?'

Jason not only liked Hal, but he knew he could trust him. He felt it wouldn't do any harm to confide in him. 'You're right on both counts. I have some exciting plans which I'd like to talk to you about, but they have to remain a secret for the moment.'

'You have my word on it.'

Pulling off the Brighton road, they were still deep in conversation about Jason's project.

'If I understand you right,' Hal was saying, 'you also want three more small partners who'll put up some money, listen to what you've got to say, sit in the background, not expect big financial returns, but who will be happy to just be involved in a successful if not particularly profitable racing venture?'

'That's it in a nutshell.'

'I just might be able to help you there, my boy. I'm going to be spending a lot of time over here. My brother-in-law is also based in London, working for the Texas North Sea Oil Consortium. And then there's my best friend from my Yale days. A few weeks ago he bought a group of five country clubs in the UK and he'll be spending at least half of the year here developing them to the standards of the ones he has in the States. We're all about perfect from your point of view. We're too busy to want to interfere in what you're doing, we're none of us short of cash. We all like going racing and we've often talked about owning horses together. What do you say?'

Jason was not able to say anything immediately. Coming from left field, this suggestion had taken his breath away. 'It sounds terrific,' he managed in the end. 'Clearly I can't make a decision until the other two partners are in, but I'm touched, I really am. And if we can work as well in racing as we do on the publishing side, I can't see why it shouldn't work.'

'OK,' said Hal. 'My offer is on the table. Naturally, I'll have to talk to my guys too, but I can't imagine they won't be agreeable. Can I sound them out?'

'Of course,' said Jason, 'but please do it in principle without going into the details, and certainly without mentioning me.'

'When would you expect to start?'

'Assuming we get the land we're after, and I can see no reason why we shouldn't, very soon. Within the next six to eight weeks I would hope to begin collecting the horses. Although initially we'll have to use temporary accommodation, I expect to be operating on a small scale by the end of May or June and to be fully operational by August with our first runners going out in September or October.'

Hal whistled. 'That sounds like a pretty ambitious programme, but I've seen enough of you to know that you don't make rash forecasts.'

As they neared Plumpton Jason caught sight of what was obviously Benny's BMW a couple of cars behind them. He parked up and shepherded Hal towards the weighing room.

Hal was intrigued by everything. From the moment Jason emerged from the weighing room, having left his bag with Johnny Hampshire, the questions never ceased. What was the difference between a hurdle and a steeplechase? Why were jump jockeys so much bigger than flat jockeys? Why were all the male horses geldings? Was the prize money really this low? Jason answered them all easily and patiently. National Hunt racing, he told Hal, was still a sport. Nobody could expect to make money out of it. Very few maintained they did, and you could be pretty sure that most of those who claimed a profit were talking about the odd purple patch rather that a long-term gain. People who play golf, shoot, fish for salmon or have boats don't expect their hobby to make a profit. National Hunt horse-owners should have the same expectations or face disillusionment. Please stress that to your friends.

Climbing to the top of the grandstand, they took their seats in the members' restaurant. Jason had a cup of tea and a plate of smoked salmon while Hal worked his way through a very passable three-course lunch. Over the meal Jason outlined to Hal the peculiarities of the Plumpton racecourse with its downhill back stretch, sharp bends and surprisingly testing uphill run from the final bend to the winning post. It was a course that didn't suit all horses, but Jason had been fortunate enough to have one or two course specialists among the horses he rode frequently and he was the third most successful course jockey riding here today.

As they finished Jed Larkin appeared and was invited to pull up a chair. He declined food but accepted a cup of coffee and, with some caution, one of Hal's Lucky Strikes. He and Jed seemed like long-lost brothers, and Jason decided he could safely leave Jed to further Hal's education in National Hunt racing, not to mention the widening of his vocabulary. They watched the first race together and Jed commented on the action as the race unfolded.

On his way to the weighing room to get ready for his first ride Jason spotted Eva who gave him a cheery wave but made no attempt to join him. Jason breathed a sigh of relief. It was not that he was antisocial or particularly nervous before these races, but he did believe in giving every horse and every race his undivided attention. It was only fair on the animal, the owner and the trainer.

Chapter Seven

Astride Jed's novice hurdler Vintage King in the parade ring, Jason saw Eva again. He gave her a warm smile, which was reciprocated, and a discreet thumbs-up sign.

The horse had run in only one previous hurdle but Jason had schooled it and knew it was a perfectly adequate jumper. On its previous outing it had been seriously interfered with when a horse had almost fallen in front of it, and had lost so much ground it was impossible to make a fair assessment of its ability or potential. The one thing he did know was that Vintage King pulled fairly hard at home, so he had agreed with Jed to have him settled in the middle of the eleven-runner field. They started smoothly and the leading two or three horses set a sensible pace so Jay had no problem settling his mount in the middle of the pack. Passing the stands on the first circuit, he felt very comfortable. He grinned at a young jockey upsides him who was having only his tenth ride in public.

'How's it going?' he asked.

The lad smiled with real enthusiasm. 'It's great,' he said.

Going down the back straight, Jason inched Vintage King forward from seventh to fifth and, turning into the final bend, had only three horses in front of him, two having failed to handle the increased speed. The young jockey was staying with him stride for stride, almost like a Siamese twin, and his horse was going just as well as Vintage King.

The leading jockey gave his horse a slap on the shoulder as they came off the bend and the second and third horses failed to respond to the sudden injection of extra pace. Jason squeezed Vintage King and, delivering a tap to his shoulder, went past both of these as they approached the second-last hurdle. He jumped it really well and was rapidly gaining ground on the leader. Out of the corner of his eye he was aware of another horse moving up towards him, and a quick glance registered the blue-and-yellow colours of his Siamese twin.

Going into the final hurdle, Jason knew that he had the measure of the horse in front of him. Harry Tomkins, the jockey, was an old professional and was working hard, giving the horse an occasional slap, but waving his stick at him more than hitting him. Harry was one of those experienced riders who knew when a horse was trying its best, and did not knock it around and turn it sour – easy to do with a young horse.

Vintage King jumped the last perfectly adequately, but Harry's horse was getting tired and could only clamber over. Jason went smoothly into the lead, clicking his tongue. With the winning post approaching rapidly, the race was his he thought. However at that moment the blue-and-yellow colours came up on his right, and try as he might Jason could not get Vintage King to match the sudden acceleration of the other horse.

As he came up to the winning post, Jay saw the young rider sitting very still until he passed the line. Then he stood up in the stirrups and waved his whip in a Frankie Dettori gesture of triumph before sitting back down to pull the horse up and avoid disappearing too far round the bend.

Jason was soon alongside him. He leaned over to shake his hand. 'You rode him very well,' he said.

The young man was flushed with pleasure but immediately responded, 'Ah! It was the horse. He really does have a turn of foot at the end.'

'How many winners have you ridden?' asked Jay.

'That's my first,' confessed the boy.

'Well, you'll never forget it, I promise you. What's your name?'

'Paul Jenkins.'

He patted Paul on the shoulder and turned to meet the stable girl who had come out to lead Vintage King back to the winner's enclosure where the first four horses were unsaddled.

The racecourse announcer confirmed that this was the young man's first winner and a great deal of enthusiastic applause and the odd cheer greeted him as he went to the number one spot.

Jay turned to Jed and Vintage King's owners, John and Sally Anderson. 'Nothing wrong with that run,' he said. 'Your horse needs at least another half mile. He'll stay for ever, but the winner was just too quick at the end.'

John and Sally thanked him and invited him to join them for a drink. 'That's very kind,' he said, 'but I'm afraid I'm with some other people here and I've still got another ride.' They said they looked forward to him riding for them again in the near future.

Jay went into the weighing room and took off his colours to change into those for his next ride. At that moment in came Freddie Kelly who was not riding until the last two races. 'That's a nasty bruise you've got on your shoulder Jay.' he said.

'Oh, bit of a schooling fall,' said Jay dismissively. He had actually forgotten all about it. That sort of bruise was nothing new to him, and it looked much worse that it felt.

'You'll be hearing from a friend of mine in Ireland,' Freddie went on. 'His name is Pat O'Hara. He's young and has just started, but he's good and has a few good horses. He'll offer you three or four rides at the Festival, depending how you feel. There's only two worthwhile. One is Ivan's Paddy which is due to run in the Hunter Chase. It's bloody good and wouldn't be without a chance, particularly if it's on the soft side.'

'OK. What's the other one?'

'Ah, the other I know a bit about. He won a few point-to-points, but was always treated tenderly and won them as he wanted. The problem is he takes a fierce hold and, if anything, he's got harder and harder to settle. He has to front run, otherwise he fights you the whole time, but he jumps like a bloody stag. I've schooled him, and I can tell he's a really great leaper.'

'Why aren't you riding him?' asked Jay.

'Because of my retainer – my trainer intends to run two. But I'll be hard pushed to beat this one.'

'What's he called?'

'Oak Tree Mile. And I can tell you, he's as tough as the wood he's named after.'

'It's a long time to Cheltenham,' remarked Jay.

'I know,' said Freddie. 'But you know how far in advance the top jocks get booked up.'

Jay thanked Freddie for the information and sat down to watch the next race on the closed-circuit television in the jockeys' changing room, but his mind was on what Freddie had said about Oak Tree Mile. Was it worth the added work with so much at stake? The prudent decision was not to take the ride, but that would be copping out. He knew he had to go for it.

Before his next ride he went out to meet Fiona and owners Joan and Don Dalling in the parade ring. Jay was riding an old handicapper, See You Sometime, in a two-and-a-half mile chase. Fiona had arrived in time to supervise the saddling. 'I see Eva is here,' she said disingenuously.

'I know,' was Jason's enigmatic reply as he walked back into the jockeys' room.

See You Sometime was not a great horse but running at small tracks, he nearly always managed one or two wins a season plus a few places. He gave the owners a lot of fun and did not cost a great deal of money – a rarity in National Hunt racing. Jay rode him in nearly all his races, so there was no need to talk about the race. Fiona and the owners knew that he would settle the horse second or third, and if the pace wasn't strong enough he'd go out and make it. There were only five runners in the race and Jason's horse was 6 – 4 favourite.

All went according to plan. A young and very promising rider made the pace on a horse having its first year as a handicapper, having been a moderately successful novice the season before. Rapidly the two of them drew clear of the other three horses. Going down the back straight they met the fences stride for stride, and Jason realised he had a race on his hands.

As they approached the last fence down the back straight, Jay decided that now was the time to put the pressure on. He asked his mount to quicken and put in 'a long one', (take off a stride earlier rather than just popping over the fence). See You Sometime responded magnificently. The challenger tried to go with him but was taken rather by surprise. It hit the top of the fence, staggered and slipped on landing. His rider produced a spectacular acrobatic performance to stay aboard, but by the time he and the horse had got themselves together Jay was six or seven lengths ahead and the other horse had lost its momentum. Barring an accident Jason had the race won. He kept his horse up to the work, went in and measured each of the final two fences carefully. Although the other horse had made up a little ground, the experience of hitting the previous fence had slightly unnerved both him and his jockey and, taking the fences very carefully, they lost a little more ground. Jay came in an easy six-lengths winner, cheered home by a majority of the racecourse punters, who had backed either him because of his record at Plumpton or the horse because it was well tipped in the racing columns.

Don and Joan were equally delighted and this time Jay agreed to join the owners for a glass of champagne. He showered and changed and met them in the owners' and trainers' bar where he briefly relived the events of the race.

'What would you think of us running him at Cheltenham?' Joan asked.

'He'd jump round all right, but I honestly think he'd be a bit out of his depth there,' Jason told her. 'Keep him till all the best horses have run at Cheltenham and the other big Christmas and holiday meetings, and by then I'm sure we can find another easy race for him. It depends on how hard the handicapper is on him after his win today.' Fiona nodded her agreement. Jason shook hands with Joan and Don and thanked them for the ride, told Fiona he would ring her the next day and went off to find Hal whom he'd arranged to meet after the race.

He was surprised to find Hal already with Eva. She had been talking to Fiona when they'd run into Jed and Hal and introductions had been made all round.

Both congratulated him excitedly on both his rides, and both were full of questions. Jason was delighted at the level of their interest in small details.

'I've one more errand to run,' he said when he had the chance to pause for breath.

'Hal knows where my car is. I'll meet you there as soon as possible after the last race. Unless you have a long wait to collect all your winnings, that is.' He handed over his keys.

Eva laughed. 'I rarely bet, and certainly not when I know nothing about the runners,' she told him.

'I have to confess I've had a few wagers. But happily the only serious one was See You Sometime,' said Hal, clapping Jay jovially on his good shoulder.

Jay went over to the bar, bought a bottle of champagne and took it to the weighing room, where he gave it to Johnny Hampshire. 'Put that in young Paul Jenkins's bag, would you Johnny? Tell him it's from me, and that I hope he'll ride many more winners.'

He joined Hal and Eva in his car; the conversation was lively all the way back to London. His companions were buoyant from their great afternoon and Jason was relaxed safe in the knowledge that the BMW was right behind him.

Later that evening Jason was sitting opposite Eva at The Elephant on the River. They had a table by the window overlooking the Thames Embankment on the Chelsea side of the Houses of Parliament. A three-piece band played music from the charts of the last two or three decades and the atmosphere was one of relaxed opulence. They both ordered Mediterranean prawns followed by grilled tuna with leaf spinach. A bottle of champagne was already open and effervescing gently in their glasses.

Jason's mobile phone rang in his pocket. 'Blast,' he said. 'I thought I'd switched it off.' It was Victor.

'I've thought about it and I'm in,' he said without preamble. 'Let's meet for breakfast tomorrow. Simpson's in the Strand. Eight o'clock.'

'Fine,' said Jason. 'I'm clear tomorrow morning. That's two of the three, and the small investors are on board as well. Just one to go. I'll tell you about that in the morning.' He put down the phone with an expression of quiet triumph.

Eva looked at him quizzically over her glass. Jason ate another prawn. It was time to tell her what this was all about.

'Well,' said Eva, unwrapping an after-dinner mint. 'It seems to me like extremely hard work for a man who has just retired from business.' There was a note of gentle sarcasm in her tone.

'I always was a driven man,' said Jason. 'Besides, if you really want to do something, the only way to get the most out of it is to put everything into it. Would you consider joining us?'

'It sounds the perfect way to invest my father's racing fund, but are you sure I'm the right person? When it comes down to it, I know next to nothing about racing here.'

'Actually, I think you are ideal.' he said. 'The third partner will handle public relations, which is vital to getting our enterprise off the ground and running. You've got experience in this field and specifically with handling the press. You'd certainly intrigue our journalists, and you'd be a wonderful counter-balance to my two other partners. I can see them being charmed by you, but I've no doubt you'd make tough decisions and stand by your opinions when necessary.'

'Oh yes,' Eva agreed. 'I'm not my father's daughter for nothing. He certainly didn't bring me up to be a smiling little yes girl.'

'There is a down side to it for you,' said Jason. 'There'll be a good deal of jealousy and we won't be popular with many of the old school. There's a hell of a lot of bitchiness in the game as well as a host of wonderful people. We'll inevitably be seen as rich types trying to buy our way to the top of the tree, and we'll get little credit for our hard work and planning from our critics.'

'That's nothing new to me,' Eva assured him. 'I've been living with it all my life. My father wasn't very popular with the big diamond barons, and my role in the company was invariably put down to nepotism rather than to hard work or ability.'

'I don't doubt for one moment that you can handle that admirably. I wouldn't have suggested you get involved otherwise.'

'Does that mean I'm in?'

'As far as I'm concerned, yes,' said Jason cautiously. 'But the other two partners have to be happy with it as well. We've all got to complement each other, if this is going to work.'

'What are they like?' she asked.

Jason gave her potted biographies of Howard and Victor – their backgrounds, their personalities, how he had come to know them and why he felt they were so important to the enterprise.

'You've certainly gone for heavy hitters,' she commented. 'So what's in it for them?'

'Well, I think that's something you should hear from them,' said Jason, 'or not, as the case may be. There's certainly a degree of personal score-settling in both cases, but how far they take you into their confidence is their call. The one thing I can promise you is that they are both dedicated. They'll both play by the rules. But they will be hard rules at times, and neither man is one to cross.'

'I have a feeling that that could be said of you too, Jay.'

'Me?' exclaimed Jason in mock amazement. 'I'm an old softy, really.'

'If I thought that, I wouldn't be accepting your proposition.'

'Eva, are you sure you're not rushing your fences? I mean, are you certain you really want to live in England for a start? I'd be much happier if you thought about this overnight and gave me your decision in the morning.'

'What for?' she asked. 'With Father dead, Africa has no real hold on me. I'll always love it, and I'll always want to spend time there, but an opportunity like this doesn't come along more than once in a lifetime. I told you what I came here for. You know I hoped that Fiona would be involved. I'm fairly sure now that Fiona can't be, but you're going to be able to provide even more than Fiona would. You are offering me a real purpose. It's more than just looking at horses. It means being totally immersed in one of the most exciting ideas I've heard of in years. I'm in. As long as the three of you will take me.'

'Well, you couldn't put it any clearer than that,' remarked Jason.

'Enough of business for one night.' He took her hand and led her on to the dance floor.

'I only have eyes for you,' crooned the Caribbean voice of the lithe young guitarist. How very appropriate, thought Jason. The chemistry between them was startling and he had to take a deep breath and tell himself sternly to cool it. The gorgeous woman floating gently in his arms was having the same trouble. She was powerfully attracted to Jason, and she liked him enormously, too. But he was going to be a business partner, and she would be working with him on an almost daily basis. This is all happening too quickly, she told herself, and distanced herself from him very slightly as they danced.

Jason was immediately alert to the signal. He saw out the song and, when it was over, he led her back to their table.

'Let's have another cup of coffee and be on our way,' he said. 'You've got a lot to think about and I've got a breakfast meeting.' Outside Eva's flat, Jason got out of the cab and went round to open her door for her. They paused, facing each other, on the pavement and their lips met briefly. Each sensed what the other was feeling, but they both knew that now they had time on their side.

'Give me a ring tomorrow,' whispered Jason.

'I'll do that. But I've made up my mind,' she smiled.

'I know you have, but there are things we must talk about – when you meet the others, when we start.'

He waited until she was safely in the building. Getting back into the taxi, he noticed Benny's old BMW a few yards down the road and resisted a sudden urge to wave.

Chapter Eight

Only in the last few years had Simpson's in the Strand added a full English breakfast service to its traditional beef and lamb lunches and dinners. It was nearly always full at an early hour. Peter, the head waiter, knew Jay well. He greeted him with a broad smile and led him to one of the 'boxes', the tables set between high benches down one side of the wonderful oak-panelled room which allowed totally confidential conversations to take place between the many businessmen and heavy sprinkling of national journalists who used it regularly. When Victor arrived Peter brought him straight over to join Jay. Jason ordered coffee, orange juice, stewed fruit and brown toast and watched in astonishment as Victor polished off bacon, sausage, tomato, fried egg and black pudding. This he followed with three Danish pastries, to each of which he added a thick layer of strawberry jam.

Victor, as was his way, had come straight to the point. 'Now I'm in, for God's sake tell me who the others are.' As soon as Jason gave him Howard's name, Victor nodded vigorously. 'Just as I thought, and he's a shrewd old devil, he's a good choice and, between you and me, I've always liked him. I think he and I will work well together. We both know each other's strengths and we both trust you. What about the others?'

Jay told him about Hal's offer to take up the minority holdings with two of his American friends.

Victor chewed thoughtfully on his Danish pastry, took a gulp of black coffee and nodded approvingly. 'It makes sense,' he said. 'It helps us spread the burden. They're all guys who can throw in a few extra dollars if we need them, and they're not going to be counting the cents. The one thing this venture does not need is penny-pinching. If we fall out over money we've got no chance when it comes to the big issues, the horses and the races.'

Victor picked up his final Danish. 'That brings us to the third partner.'

'The third partner you won't know,' Jason told him. 'She only came into the frame last week, but her credentials are impeccable.'

Victor raised his eyebrows, but listened intently as Jason brought him up to speed.

'The money and background sound fine, but is she going to fit in with us?' he asked. 'Is she going to be a real working partner?'

'I think so, but you and Howard must make up your minds for yourselves. What I thought I'd do is set up a lunch between the three of you and leave you to it. I don't want to influence any of you.' He finished his coffee. 'I also want you to see the site, Victor. Howard will be handling the negotiations from now on, so why don't you go down with him? He's had a whistle-stop tour, but he'll need to look at it properly. I have a site plan from the agents I can send over to you beforehand.'

'Well, if we like this young lady,' said Victor, 'why don't we take her with us?'

'A splendid idea.' It was a good sign that Victor was including Eva before he'd even met her.

Victor paid the bill and parted to start work for the day. Arriving at his office, Jason's first call was to Howard to report on developments.

'Well, no time like the present,' said Howard. 'I'll get hold of Victor and fix up a lunch, today if possible. Give me Eva's number and I'll see if she can join us. Victor and I could meet for half an hour or so before she arrives.'

'That sounds sensible to me,' agreed Jason. 'Although after the breakfast I've just seen Victor eat, I don't think he'll be all that hungry.

Howard laughed. 'Why don't you come along for coffee afterwards?' He suggested. 'I know you'll be keen to find out how we've got on.'

'That would be great.'

Before getting on with his company business, Jay had the site plans and his notes on them couriered round to Victor and arranged for the video camera and mobile telephone he'd had his secretary order to be delivered to The Running Footman for Sean. Howard rang back to say that the prospective partners had arranged to meet for lunch at Victor's private dining room in his Aldwych offices, and that they were looking forward to seeing Jason there around two o'clock.

At 12.30, Jason joined Hal for a working sandwich lunch. After they had covered their agenda, Hal asked him if he was busy at the end of the day. 'I thought maybe we could have a drink at the Dorchester with my brother-in-law and my pal. They're very excited about the project and they want to meet you.'

'Great. I'll see you at half-past six. I might even have some more up-to-date information by then, too.'

The moment Jason walked into Victor's dining room he could tell the meeting had been a great success. All three of his chosen partners were relaxed and smiling. Victor leaped to his feet, came round from the other side of the table and put his arm round Jason's shoulders. 'We've had a really serious talk, Jay, and we're all agreed that we can work together brilliantly. It's you we're a bit worried about,' he said mischievously.

'You see, Jay, we feel we want somebody who really knows what he's doing – a real professional,' Howard chimed in.

Not to be outdone, Eva added: 'And of course, somebody who'll do as we tell them.'

Howard and Victor dissolved into very unbusiness-like giggles.

'Very funny,' said Jason. 'I take it that no blood has been spilled?'

'We're a real team, Jay,' said Howard, recovering his composure. 'We all understand each other, we all think that we can work with each other and we agree on our specific roles. Of course there'll be times when we differ, but we're all really excited and can't wait to get on with it.'

Victor and Eva nodded their agreement.

'And we all know we are not going to make money out of this,' Eva added.

'Right,' said Jay. 'In that case I suggest that the three of you go down to County View this afternoon and have a good look at it. Howard knows what I've got in mind; make notes on how you think we can improve on my rough outline. Then we'll need a down-to-earth architect who can advise us on the most effective way to convert the buildings. As far as the gallops are concerned, Jack Rosebury, the head groundsman at Cheltenham, is due to retire soon, and I'm sure he'd be delighted to give us advice on both the grass and the all-weather gallops. I've known him for years and I know he'd relish the challenge. He would doubtless appreciate a few extra pounds in his pocket as well.'

The four of them arranged to meet again at Victor's Holland Park house that evening, and Jay left his new partners to get ready for their site visit.

As he flagged down a taxi outside Victor's office, out of the corner of his eye he caught sight of Angel's blond head disappearing into a beaten-up Honda being driven by a character he'd not seen before. It dawned on him that he hadn't noticed any of his minders all day. He knew the boys were good, but he hadn't realised quite how good. Howard had been right. Not only did he feel physically safe and able to relax and concentrate on the business in hand, but the psychological reassurance was such that he had almost forgotten he was a marked man.

After a productive few hours in his office, Jason walked round to the Dorchester, having remembered to telephone Benny to tell him when he was leaving and where he was going. A traffic warden wandering down the street paused to look at a car's windscreen and then, with a shrug, closed his pad and, looking at his watch, put his pen away. Clearly he'd decided he'd finished his work for the day. Something about the way he moved seemed familiar to Jay. And then it came to him: Robbie, the James Cagney lookalike. There was, it seemed, no end to the boys' ingenuity.

Entering the bright and mirrored bar of the Dorchester, Jason spotted Hal and two other men seated near the piano, silent at this hour. All three rose to greet him.

'Jason, I'd like you to meet my longstanding friend, Bart Eastington, and my brother-in-law, Len Lavinger,' said Hal.

Jay shook hands with two typical examples of American businessmen who took care of themselves physically. Both were bronzed enough to indicate that they were no strangers to the golf course, tennis court or ski slope, but neither of them was so tanned you felt they had spent more time playing than working.

'We're all three agreed we'd like to do it,' Hal began, 'but the boys have got a few questions.' The inquiries that followed were penetrating and sensible. It was plain that they under-stood this was not an enterprise to be viewed as a business investment. However, not unreasonably, they wanted to know what their total investment was likely to amount to, and how much of it they would lose if everything went wrong.

Jason explained the prize-money situation in National Hunt racing, and the fact that, although they would be happy to win small races, their objective was to win some of the really good ones. This meant that horses would not run too often. It was agreed that rather than each of them being listed as shareholders, Bart, Len and Hal would put their stakes into a syndicate, managed by Hal, which would own all their shares. The syndicate would make payments when necessary and collect any prize money or other income. Jason would contact them individually whenever necessary.

'Normally that would simply be to alert you to forthcoming runners,' said Jason.

'You don't need to do that,' said Bart. 'All that information is on the web, and we all know how to use that. Just let us know if anything unusual is happening.'

'That's great,' smiled Jason. 'It'll save someone a lot of time.'

After a brief debate it was decided to call the syndicate The Big Apple in honour of its members' strong Manhattan connections.

'When will you want the money?' asked Len.

'Probably not for another three or four weeks,' replied Jay, 'but Howard will be in touch with Hal to let him know. Perhaps we could all arrange to go racing together one day? That would seem the appropriate place for you to meet the other three partners. And you're all welcome to go and see the site we've chosen.'

On his way to Holland Park, Jay called Fiona to finalise his riding out and racing commitments with her the next day. She was intrigued to know how he and Eva were getting on and he promised to bring her up to date in the morning. 'You haven't taken advantage of the poor innocent, have you?' she asked, in what Jay felt was a fierce tone.

'No I haven't,' replied Jay. 'And I'm not so sure she's all that innocent, either.'

There was a throaty chuckle at the end of the line. 'Well, I'm sure you'll find out in due course. Goodnight, Jay. See you in the morning.'

By the time he arrived at Victor's house the events of the day were beginning to tell on him. The door was opened by Victor's butler who had looked after him ever since his wife had died over ten years earlier. He had never remarried. His three partners were already sitting in Victor's glorious oak-panelled library. Howard and Eva were drinking champagne and Victor his ubiquitous Scotch. The estate agent's plan was on a table in front of them and the conversation was bubbling. Hardly anyone could get a word in edgeways as they all pointed to various parts of the chart. 'So,' said Jason, 'what do you think?'

'We think it's great, Jay,' Howard said. 'And Victor's convinced it won't take too much money and very little time to make the adjustments you're looking for. New drains are likely to be the biggest problem for the stable area, but we're sure that won't be insurmountable. And we're going to have to look at the drainage and water system for the stable staff accommodation and your house. It should be easy to convert it into a spacious place both for living and to entertain owners. The limestone subsoil makes the gallops easy to keep in the winter, but we'll put in a watering system for the summer.'

Victor got up to pour Jason a glass of champagne. 'I'm planning to go down there the day after tomorrow with my best site manager and a young architect who's responsible for some very sensible conversions of eighteenth- and nineteenth-century woollen mills into modern flats. He started off designing small factories and workshops on redeveloped industrial sites, so he doesn't have fancy ideas about costs, and he knows how to use modern materials efficiently.'

'What we were talking about when you arrived,' Eva said, 'was the perimeter fence. Obviously that needs to be effective.'

'Good point,' said Jason. 'And as well as protecting the horses, we want to deter sightseers. Once we start having some success, the serious gamblers and perhaps some of the smaller bookmakers will be trying to find out what's going on. I don't particularly want our rivals knowing which of our horses are going particularly well either, or what sort of work they're doing.'

'Right,' said Victor. 'We need to check on the fence itself, stick some razor wire around the top and put in some closed-circuit TV cameras. Do you want dogs as well?'

'I don't think that's going to be necessary for the whole perimeter,' said Jay, 'but we might want night-time guards with a dog where the stable blocks are. We don't want anyone getting at the horses. It's rare, but it does still happen occasionally.'

They went over the various plans for each building in some detail and Jason agreed to meet the others at County View that Thursday with the architect. Then they would produce working drawings for the key buildings and, once Jason had approved those, the whole project would be left in the hands of Howard and Victor to leave him free to concentrate on getting the horses.

Feeling suddenly that he'd seen enough of all of them for one day, Jason quietly excused himself. He thought he detected a look of faint surprise on Eva's face when he asked Howard if he would be kind enough to drop her off when they finished. He repaired any possible slight by whispering that he looked forward to seeing her very soon as he kissed her lightly on the cheek.

When he had locked his front door behind him, Jason left a message on Benny's answering machine telling him what time he would be leaving for Lambourn the next morning. There was a brief message from Sean on his own machine, thanking him for the video camera and mobile phone and informing Jay that he was off to Ireland in the morning. He would check in every three or four days.

Before turning in Jay telephoned Jack O'Hanlon, one of the top Irish horse vets and a long standing friend whom Jason planned to take into his confidence when everything was finalised. He explained that he was looking for a number of horses for the next season for a couple of owners he'd be riding for, and that he had an agent called Sean Maguire scouting for them in Ireland. Sean might ring him and ask him to vet them and, if he did, Jack would know that Jay would pick up his bills.

He put down the phone wearily. It had been an extremely long day.

Chapter Nine

There were now only ten days to Christmas and the host of meetings on Boxing Day, including the big Kempton Park fixture, shortly followed by the Cheltenham New Year meeting. Although Jason had a few rides booked, he was very careful to commit himself only to horses he knew were safe jumpers. There was no point in taking unnecessary chances on unknown or inexperienced horses when there was so much to be done in the days ahead.

As Howard had anticipated, there had been no problem with the planning permission for County View. The contract had gone through very quickly and JCBs were already in digging drains for the yards. As soon as the lease had been signed Jason made his application for a trainers licence to the Jockey Club licensing committee. Fortunately, there was a committee meeting the following week, and it was agreed that Jason should attend it.

Work on the gallops would have to wait a couple of weeks as Jack Rosebury was flat out at Cheltenham until after the New Year meeting, but his initial diagnosis had confirmed Jay's view that it would not take very much to set out the gallops. The all-weather track was straightforward, and a little weed-killing and good-quality top dressing was all the turf needed to make first-rate gallops. Howard had already arranged for the weed-killing to be done in the spring, and the subsequent dressing and fertilising would have the turf in good shape by the beginning of summer, by which time Jason hoped his first horses would be ready for some serious work.

During one of Jack Rosebury's visits he suggested an ideal location for a second all-weather gallop, shorter but steeper, at the other end of the airfield. Not only would this give the horses a change of scenery, he pointed out, but it would be very well sheltered from the prevailing winds by a thickly wooded ridge. This meant an extra expense, but all the partners agreed it would be worth it in the long term, and they decided to install it at the same time as the main all-weather parallel to the turf gallops.

That afternoon, on his way back to London, Jason had a call on his mobile phone from Eva. 'Have you any plans for tonight?' she inquired.

'No. I was going to ask you to have dinner with me.'

'In that case, I'll ask you. You've been treating me for weeks and weeks now, and it's my turn. What time would you like me to pick you up?'

'You're picking *me* up?'

'Yes. This is my call.'

'OK, whatever you say, boss.'

'Seven o'clock your flat?' she suggested.. 'I hope you won't think it rude of me if I ask you not to dress too casually.'

'For dinner with my PR director? I wouldn't dream of it.'

'Right. See you at seven.'

At seven o'clock that evening, Jason's doorbell rang. Jason, dressed in a crisp white shirt, dark grey worsted suit and a restrained Hermès tie with a stirrups motif, opened his front door to find a uniformed chauffeur standing on the step. Beyond him, parked in the street with its engine running, was a limousine. Eva was sitting in the back.

'Wow, this is a bit of a magical mystery tour,' he said to her, stepping into the car.

'That's what it's meant to be.' Eva looked stunning. She was very plainly but exquisitely dressed in a simple black silk cocktail dress, relieved only by a slender diamond necklace at her throat, with a black pashmina wrap to keep the winter chill at bay. Her golden hair was swept up in a simple chignon and her lightly tanned skin glowed.

The chauffeur closed the door soundlessly behind him.

They drove around Berkeley Square, along Mount Street, into Park Lane and towards Victoria before turning left on to Parliament Square, passing Big Ben and cruising along the Embankment. Jay had no idea where they might be going, and doubtless whichever of Benny's boys was tailing him tonight would be similarly bemused. The limousine turned left and Jay now found himself travelling down The Strand back towards Trafalgar Square. *She's taking me to Simpson's,* he thought. But the car turned left into the forecourt of The Savoy. The door opened and the doorman said, 'Good evening Miss Botha, how nice to see you. Good evening, Sir.' As they entered the lobby Eva was greeted by a grey-haired gentleman in late middle age. 'Miss Botha, how lovely to see you. Everything is ready for you. Please follow me.' He led them into a lift. At the appointed floor the doors opened and they followed the man along a maze of corridors until he stopped in front of a double door. Opening them, he ushered Eva and Jay into a fabulous suite overlooking the river. A dining table was already laid for two, next to it stood an ice bucket containing a bottle of champagne.

Jason was quite speechless.

'The first course will be ready when it suits you, Miss Botha,' said the grey-haired man.

'In half an hour, I think,' said Eva. The man inclined his head in acknowledgement and withdrew, closing the doors behind him.

Jay raised one eyebrow and gave her a quizzical look. 'I take it you've been here before?'

'Many, many times. With my father. He used to always take this suite when he stayed in London, so I thought it would be an appropriate venue for my surprise dinner. I've also taken the liberty of choosing the menu. You're probably going to kill me for ruining your special diet, but I hope that a seafood platter followed by a chateaubriand steak will be acceptable? You will then have a choice of a selection of sorbets or cheese. Why don't we kick off with a glass of champagne?'

The conversation over dinner was constant and lively.

Eva's excitement about the project was growing daily as she immersed herself in the practicalities, which gave her more and more ideas about fleshing out her role. After the food was cleared away, a Monte Cristo No.3 appeared, as if by magic, together with a bottle of Calvados. Sipping his digestif, for once in his life Jay was at a loss as to what his next move should be. This was Eva's night, and she was in the driving seat, which was all very well in theory, but it wasn't a situation he was used to, and it disconcerted him. He wasn't at all sure what was expected of him.

As if she sensed this, Eva excused herself, reappearing five minutes later in a thick, white terry-towelling robe. She smiled coyly at Jay. 'I thought you might like to stay the night,' she said softly. 'It's a long way to Berkeley Square.'

Jay looked into her green eyes without speaking. Then he stood up and, to her evident alarm and confusion, walked purposefully towards the door of the suite. Oh God, what had she done? To her profound relief, Eva realized he was not leaving. He was simply hanging the 'Do not disturb' sign on the outside of the door. He strode back across the room, gathered her up in his arms and carried her into the bedroom, where he laid her gently on the bed. Tearing off his clothes, he was there beside her almost before she had got her breath back, untying the belt of the robe and urgently drawing her warm, smooth body to his own.

When Jay awoke the next morning, for a split second he genuinely didn't know where he was. Remembering, he turned to reach for Eva but the bed was empty. He sat up to see her standing in the bedroom doorway, holding two glasses of ice-cold Buck's Fizz.

She handed one to him. 'I'm almost embarrassed about last night,' she said. 'It's the first time I've ever deliberately set out to seduce a man.'

'Well, it was a wonderful experience, I can assure you,' Jay smiled. His face became serious. 'I think you know how I've felt ever since the night at the White Elephant,' he said. 'But I just didn't want to rush anything. And with us working together...'

'I know,' she said. 'But I decided a couple of days ago it was silly for us to waste any more time. You only have one life, after all, and I don't want to spend any of mine looking back at what might have been. I hope you feel it was all worthwhile.'

Reaching up he took her hand and kissed it gently. 'Of course I do,' he said. 'More than worthwhile.'

She put down her glass and climbed back into bed and into his arms.

It was nearly midday before Jay eventually got up, which was almost unheard of for him. He kissed the drowsy Eva, promised to ring her later in the day and left the hotel as if he were walking on air.

The change in the relationship between Jason and Eva seemed to be gradually absorbed by their partners without anything much ever really needing to be said, to the amusement of the fledgling couple. Jay guessed that Howard and Victor had seen it coming and that it had therefore not been much of a surprise to either of them. Even Fiona refrained from teasing him too much. She was obviously delighted by this development and was wisely giving him and Eva room to breathe, although Jay suspected that he was probably often the subject of girlie chats between her and Eva.

Something that did need to be aired with the new business partnership was the question of threats to Jay's life up until now known only to Howard. Jason didn't want to cause alarm, but it was only fair, not to say practical, that Victor and Eva were in possession of all the facts that could have a bearing on their enterprise. And on a personal level, now that he was spending so much time with Eva, she needed to know about Benny and his boys. She was worried, of course, but took it all in her stride. Coming from such a wealthy family, awareness of danger and the need for increased security from time to time was simply a fact of life to her.

The morning of the licensing committee meeting dawned and Jason, with all the details of his financial backing, the plans of County View and the number of horses he would be training, arrived at the Jockey Club's headquarters at 42 Portman Square.

He was ushered in and was well known to all the members of the committee. Jason showed them the plans and gave them all the other details of the proposed training establishment at County View. After a few searching but friendly questions, he was asked to withdraw whilst his application was considered. Fifteen minutes later he was invited to rejoin them, and with smiles all round, he was informed that his licence had been granted and he was wished every possible good luck in his future as a trainer.

'Well,' said the Chairman of the Committee. 'If you are anything like as successful in your new venture as you have been as an amateur jockey, I'm sure you'll be a frequent visitor to the winner's enclosures.'

Getting into a taxi, Jason phoned all three of his colleagues to say that all had gone well, and that another hurdle had been cleared.

Jay and Eva were invited by Fiona to spend Christmas at Midwood Park. Howard and Bubbles asked them to join them at The Laurels and – to Jay's astonishment – Victor also invited them to his home in Holland Park.

They opted to accept Fiona's invitation as it made riding out much easier for Jay. On Christmas morning Eva also had the opportunity to meet a few new racing faces among the friends who came for drinks. As they chatted in the drawing room Jay looked out of the window to see Benny's trusty BMW coming slowly up the drive. He went to open the door for him.

'Merry Christmas, boss,' beamed Benny.

'And the compliments of the season to you, too' said Jay. 'What on earth are you doing here today?'

'We've been keeping an eye on you from just down the road since you arrived. You don't escape us that easily. But I'm here running an errand for Howard. Can you give me a hand?' Benny opened the creaking boot. Inside was a hamper so enormous that they struggled to manoeuvre it into Fiona's hall. With it was a card which read: 'Here's to a great new venture together.' It was signed by Howard and Victor. Inside the basket was the most amazing array of delicacies, plus three magnums of vintage Krug – clearly Victor's idea. Fiona gazed at it in amazement. 'Well, you and I will do well on this Eva, while Jay keeps to his orange juice and dry toast,' she declared.

'At least I can wash them down with the champagne,' said Jay.

Benny refused their invitation to come in and have a drink. 'Not a good idea on the old anonymity front if you have company,' he reminded them. 'Anyway I need to get back for a family knees-up. I've a couple of associates keeping an eye on the house who'd rather earn an extra few quid than be falling asleep in front of the television. We'll be back tomorrow when you go to Kempton Park.'

Very early on Boxing Day morning Jay got up and went for a brisk run before riding one lot up the gallops. See You Sometime was boxed up shortly afterwards and on his way to Kempton where he was entered in the Three-Mile Handicap Chase. This was above his normal level but as a result he had a low weight. The Boxing Day meeting at Kempton is always one of enormous excitement and expectation, attended by a huge crowd eager to get out in the fresh air after a day of over-indulgence. The King George steeplechase, one of the top races of the National Hunt season, has been won by many famous racehorses, including Arkle, The Fellow and Desert Orchid. The course is one of the flattest on the National Hunt circuit and the fences are not huge, but it is challenging nonetheless, and speed is a major factor.

In the parade ring Jay was talking to Fiona and the Dallings, See You Sometime's owners, while Eva took in everything attentively. Jay who know both the course and his mount very well, had already agreed with Fiona that he would have the gelding handy but he hoped to be able to use his fast finishing speed over the last two fences. There were nineteen fences to be jumped and, surprisingly for a race valued at over £25,000, there were only eight runners.

See You Sometime was third favourite with Mary's Present, having won three on the trot, the even-money first choice. Jay was happy that the favourite liked to make the running, as did another horse, Jack of Trumps, with two consecutive wins behind him. This would ensure a strong pace and Jay was aiming to settle his horse in behind and come with a run at the end.

The two front runners immediately asserted themselves. The first circuit was uneventful but going to the fence on the bend after the winning post the leaders were definitely taking each other on. It was probably the fact that they were concentrating a little more on each other than on the fence itself that resulted in both horses taking off half a stride too soon. Both hit the fence and the favourite slewed right into his upsides companion. Their jockeys did brilliantly to stay on board but lost so much momentum that the third horse, and then Jay, sitting in fourth place, swept past them. By the time Mary's Present and Jack of Trumps had got going again Jay was tucked comfortably behind the new leader a good eight or nine lengths in front. From Jay's point of view things could not have gone better. The leader continued to make a strong pace and jumped beautifully, while See You Sometime travelled easily and jumped with the same precision he showed at home.

With four fences to go, Jay was beginning to feel confident. He glanced over his shoulder to see the two previous leaders struggling and nothing behind them was making any real progress. Steadily he crept up until, jumping the last, he was side by side with the leader. See You Sometime responded to a quick slap down the shoulder and within a few strides he had opened up a length lead. Using only hands and heels, Jay urged his mount on with his voice as they streamed past the winning post with nearly two lengths to spare.

Fiona, her face wreathed in smiles, met him before he had left the track to walk alongside her horse, passed the famous Philip Blacker statue of Desert Orchid, to the winner's enclosure. Don and Joan were waiting for them in the number one spot and, after much backslapping and many photographs, Jay escaped to the peace of the weighing room and the warm congratulations of his fellow jockeys. As he came back from the shower he heard his mobile phone ringing. He picked it up.

'Hello?'

'Don't forget my warning if you want to stay healthy and win more races,' said a menacing Irish voice.

Jay disconnected the line and looked round to see if anyone could have overheard, but there was so much noise it was hardly likely. He speed-dialled Benny. 'Another call,' he said in a low voice.

'Don't fret guv,' said Benny. 'We're all here. And don't bother to try to check the number, it'll be a public phone at the course.'

'The next two and a half months are going to be fun if this carries on,' sighed Jay.

'You have nothing to worry about,' said Benny firmly. 'They won't know what's hit them if they try anything.'

Back at Midwood Park, Jay, Eva and Fiona had a light supper of the Christmas Day leftovers and settled for an early night. They were all tired and Jay and The Conker were competing in the Welsh Grand National the next day. In the morning Jay rode out early again before getting ready to drive down to Chepstow. The Conker was his only ride at the meeting and in normal circumstances they would have expected him to have a very good chance of winning. The big fences and long trip were very much in his favour, but the race was a handicap and his was the third top weight with 11 stones 7. Jay had a feeling that the horse was also slightly short of work and, not having raced for some time, he was not convinced that The Conker was at peak fitness to carry such a weight over more than three and a half miles and twenty-two fences. Jay walked the course: the going was soft, which would not usually have worried him too much, but the combination of his doubts over the horse's fitness, the weight and what would obviously be testing going put a question mark over The Conker's chances.

He joined Fiona and Eva in the restaurant where they were sitting with Howard and Bubbles who were in a state of high excitement. They had already seen Jed, who had done his best to slightly modify Howard's normal enthusiasm, but to little effect. Jason's efforts were no more successful. Ordering a plate of smoked salmon and a glass of sparkling mineral water, he sat back and listened to the animated conversation. He was pleased to see that Eva was beginning to join in, and already bringing a fair degree of knowledge to the party.

After changing in the weighing room, he strode out to the paddock to be legged up on to Howard's pride and joy. As always, they had agreed that The Conker would be in the leading group, even though he was carrying a heavy weight. He was an out-and-out stayer and his magnificent jumping always put pressure on the competition. The going was very much as Jay had expected – soft but not too sticky – and he felt that the conditions would be safe, if rather testing.

The favourite in the field of fourteen was a horse called Action Plan, ridden by Jay's old friend and adversary Freddie Kelly. He was carrying 10lb less than The Conker, and this was clearly going to be a factor in the outcome. The two horses met fence after fence side by side, and from time to time the jockeys exchanged the odd barbed but good-humoured comment. Leaving the back straight for the last time, they were lying second and third respectively as they made their way round the long bend before facing up to the five fences that stood between them and the winning post. The leader was beginning to show some signs of tiring as his rider urged him on and gave him a couple of slaps behind the saddle. There was no change in order as they jumped the fifth last, but Action Plan and The Conker were making steady progress.

'It looks like it's going to be between us!' shouted Freddie as they approached the open ditch four from home. Again they met it stride for stride, but The Conker slightly out-jumped Action Plan. They were fast closing on the leader, and by the time they reached the third last they passed an obviously flagging horse. The Conker was still going surprisingly well, and Jay just sat on him as Freddie brought his horse up alongside to clear the third from home. Again The Conker took half a length off the other horse and continued up the steep hill still with no hesitation in his stride. At the second last, The Conker again out-jumped Action Plan and strode on towards the last. Now, however, Jay sensed there was not quite the same rhythm as had been evident over the previous three fences. Although The Conker was by no means in trouble, he could feel the weight and the lack of peak fitness just beginning to tell. But The Conker was nothing if not brave and, hurling himself at the last, he again out-jumped Freddie's horse. There was now just the uphill run between the final fence and the winning post. Urging his mount on, Jay felt him trying as hard as he could, but as Freddie came upsides he knew he was beaten. Without even hitting his horse, Freddie gained a couple of lengths and sat there steadily as they approached and passed the winning post. But The Conker had delivered an excellent performance to come second, and probably a rather better one than Jay could have hoped for.

As always Howard was cheerful in defeat and, although he had lost £500 because of his stubborn refusal to back the horse each way, he was still celebrating the fact that his baby had run so well and had come back safely. To Howard this was far more important than the £8,000 prize money for the runner-up.

Jay weighed in, changed and rejoined his friends in the dining room. Champagne was again on the table and Howard's ebullience was undiminished. 'How about the Grand National?' he asked Jed.

'I don't think so yet. What do you think, Jay?'

'I agree,' said Jay. 'But why not go for the Midland Grand National at Uttoxeter in March, after Cheltenham? It's a valuable race, a real test of stamina and jumping, and I think The Conker deserves at least another season before taking on the Aintree obstacles. But I still feel the four-mile amateur race at the Festival is made for him. I think we could win that.' Howard beamed broadly at the thought of a runner at Cheltenham and for the rest of the day he talked of little else.

He insisted on taking them all out to dinner at one of his favourite restaurants just outside Lambourn. It was a high-spirited evening, and after an abstemious Christmas Jay was at last able to let his hair down a little. After a splendid meal, with a final handshake and clap on the back for Jay, and kisses for Fiona and Eva, Howard and Bubbles took their leave, full of hopes and dreams for the New Year.

Chapter Ten

The first weeks of the New Year flew by in a whirl – raceriding, schooling, working at the office with Hal, and developing County View. Over a quiet supper at his flat one evening, Jay said to Eva; 'I have a suggestion to make. The next few months are going to be absolutely frantic, and I think it would be good for both of us to have a break. I wondered if you would like to spend a week in the Caribbean with me?'

'That's a wonderful idea. I need to go back to South Africa soon, but the trip can wait a couple of weeks,' she said.

The following morning Jay got a call from his lawyer to say that everything was tied up. He phoned Hal and said 'As far as we're concerned the deal is done. Why don't we meet for lunch, sign the papers and get the whole thing buttoned up? You must be almost as bored with the way this has dragged on as I am. You know I am really anxious to get on with the new project.'

They met at the Mirabelle, signed the papers and Hal's PA took them away.

'You must be ready for a break,' said Hal over a celebratory glass of champagne.

'I certainly am,' said Jay. 'Eva and I are planning to go to Tobago for a few days to get some sunshine. Then she has to go to South Africa to tie up some loose ends, and you know what will be on my agenda.'

'I think that's a great idea,' said Hal. 'Come on, let's have a really good lunch and stop worrying about the business.'

Within four days Jay and Eva were on their way to the Kariwak Village Hotel in Tobago, which Jay knew well. They were warmly welcomed by Cynthia, the owner, a petite

Canadian with a dry sense of humour. She greeted Jay like a long-lost friend and made Eva feel as if she had known her for years, too. 'You must be a brave girl, taking this on,' she remarked to Eva. 'But we all make mistakes don't we?'

Eva grinned back. 'I think I can cope, but maybe I'm kidding myself.'

The hotel was famed for its glorious gardens and wonderful, simple food, growing most of its own herbs and vegetables in plots and greenhouses. It was a real haven of tranquillity. Little guest bungalows were set in the luxurious grounds, which boasted a huge outdoor Jacuzzi and a wooden gazebo where morning yoga classes were on offer. 'It's enchanting,' said Eva, delighted.

The trip was exactly what they needed. They spent their days on the beach at Pigeon Point, sunbathing, reading and swimming or snorkelling off the coral reef. The only reminders of real life were the strenuous exercise programme Jason kept up early every morning and the daily phone calls he insisted on making to Howard or Victor to check up on things, only to be told he was not being missed at all. It was more than a much-needed opportunity to recharge their batteries. Relaxing alone together twenty-four hours a day, thousands of miles away from their hectic routine, gave them valuable time to consolidate their relationship and take stock of their feelings for one another. When they landed back at Heathrow, they felt like two totally new people. They were met at the airport by Benny's brother, Harry, who drove them into London. Not wishing to plunge themselves back into the fray too suddenly, they went to the Dorchester for a light lunch. In the restaurant, Jay reached across the table and took Eva's hand. 'I don't know how you feel,' he said, 'but these nine days have been extremely significant for me. I realise that you mean a huge amount to me, and I think we'd make a good long-term partnership.'

Eva gave him a long and thoughtful look and then, with a warm smile, she took his other hand. 'I agree,' she said. 'But let's pick the right time. You've got so much to do in the next few months, and I have things to sort out in South Africa. I have no doubt that it will work, and when I'm back here for good I'd like to become your partner in every way.'

Jay leaned over and kissed her gently on the lips. 'I am happy to wait till whenever you are ready. You've made me a very happy man,' he said.

'And you've made me a very happy woman.'

'We're going to have a terrific amount of fun, a lot of excitement and, let's face it, plenty of hard work.'

The next day Jay drove Eva back to the airport. They both looked as if they had had very little sleep, which was no more than they deserved. She was flying to Switzerland to meet the manager of the bank where her father had set up his special fund. From there she was going on to South Africa, on the first of what would probably be a couple of trips to settle her affairs there. She promised she to be back well in time for Cheltenham, now only three weeks away, and with a lingering kiss, and a big hug, they parted.

In her absence, Jay worked like a man possessed, speeding between Jed's yard in Sussex and Midwood Park, and galloping or schooling every single horse he was due to ride at the Festival. One morning he took an early flight to Dublin, to ride work and school Oak Tree Mile, the horse that had been set up for him by Freddie Kelly. He was deeply impressed and, although the horse was as strong as an ox, he had no difficulty in holding him and getting him settled on a nice long rein. Oak Tree Mile was a brilliant jumper and, if he was not perhaps quite as clever as The Conker, he made up for it with the sheer ease with which he cleared the highest fences.

Almost before he knew it, Eva was on her way home from the airport, bursting with news from Switzerland and South Africa. There had been even more money in the Swiss account than she'd anticipated, and in South Africa she had managed to complete the sale of the family business to a competitor who had always been friendly with her father in spite of their commercial rivalry. She knew he would take care of it as her father would have wished. She had also decided to put the family house on the market, but would keep a chalet her father had bought in one of the more exclusive safari parks plus a small apartment in Cape Town. 'You never know when I might want to get away from you,' she said with a smile.

'Frequently, if you have any sense,' he advised her cheerfully.

By the Thursday before Cheltenham Jay knew what his rides would be. Oak Tree Mile was to run in the Kim Muir Challenge Cup Amateur Handicap Three Mile Chase and The Conker in the National Hunt Challenge Cup Amateur Chase, which meant Jay taking part in two of the three amateur races, giving the hunter chase a miss. He had two other rides, one for Fiona – her very useful juvenile, Hopeful Return, in the Triumph Hurdle – and Pewter Queen for Howard and Jed. Pat O'Hara had offered Jay another ride apart from Oak Tree Mile, but Jay had to say no, as he was already had a ride in the Triumph Hurdle. So no Champion Hurdle or the Gold Cup Chase for him this year, but he took comfort from the thought that, if all went to plan, he would be saddling runners in both races next Cheltenham.

On the Sunday night before the Festival he set off to meet Eva, who had been spending the afternoon with an old schoolfriend from South Africa, for an early supper at Claridge's. Closing his front door, he turned to walk down towards Berkeley Square. A few yards down the road he stepped to one side of the pavement to allow two joggers running towards him to go by, but as they approached they separated and slowed down. Immediately he sensed danger. Without hesitating he turned and ran for his door. The two men accelerated and closed in on him. In the lamplight he saw a flash of metal and realised they were wearing knuckle-dusters.

Suddenly he was blinded by a flash of light. A spotlight had been switched on from a van parked just down the mews. Already tumbling out of it were three men, all dressed in black with black balaclava hoods. God, reinforcements, thought Jay. But the two tracksuited thugs were as surprised as he was, and he realised in a wave of relief that the men in black were on his side. Two more men, similarly dressed, appeared from the back of a battered minibus parked on the other side of the mews. Showing more bravado than sense, one of the joggers tried to grab Jay who, confident now of escape, was far too quick for him, and in an instant the five men surrounded them. The fight was brief and brutal. The crack of wood on arms and shoulders was accompanied by screams. Both joggers went down and heavy boots thudded into them. Within seconds handcuffs had appeared and, with their arms pinioned behind their backs, the two assailants were bundled into the back of the first van which sped off smartly followed by the minibus. It was all over so fast that Jason, standing alone in the now empty street, could barely believe it had happened. Not a word had been spoken to him, but he was in no doubt as to the identity of one of the black-clad avengers. Unhurt but somewhat shaken Jason continued on his way to Claridge's. He found Eva already sitting at the table. One look at his face and she knew straightaway something was wrong. 'Sit down,' she said, jumping up and taking his arm. 'Are you OK?'

'Shaken, but not stirred,' he replied wryly.

'Let's forget dinner here,' said Eva. 'I'll make us an omelette at your place. I think we'd both feel safer at home tonight. You can tell me what happened when we get back.' As an additional precaution they took a taxi the few hundred yards to the flat and gave the driver a very fat tip to make up for losing him his pole position outside the hotel.

As they opened the door, Jason's mobile rang. 'We've taken care of your little local problem,' said Benny. 'Are you OK? Where are you?'

'Back at home. I hope you haven't done anything too extreme,' he said. He was starting to become concerned about things getting out of hand.

'No, but we've learned a lot from the geezers who were so keen to make your acquaintance, and we're keeping them here for a while. Is it all right if I come round and talk to you?'

'Absolutely.'

'I'll be with you in forty-five minutes.'

'Are you going to tell me what's going on?' called Eva from the kitchen, where she was assembling the ingredients for their omelettes.

Jay wandered in and poured a glass of wine for her and a mineral water for himself. No more alcohol for him until after Cheltenham.

'A couple of thugs tried to jump me outside the flat.'

She looked at him in alarm.

'It's OK, Benny's boys were there in seconds. That was him on the phone. I think he's got some information out of them – he's on his way over anyway. Let's have something to eat before he arrives.

They had just finished Eva's delicious fluffy omelettes and were about to embark on a seriously strong farmhouse cheddar when the doorbell rang. Checking through his spyhole that the caller was Benny, Jason let him in and led the way up the stairs to the kitchen-diner. Eva offered to make Benny an omelette. He declined but seeing the cheddar on the table, said that bread and some cheese and a glass of red wine would be very acceptable.

They all sat down and Jason and Eva waited patiently while Benny painstakingly constructed a doorstep cheese sandwich and fortified himself with a generous glass of rich burgundy.

'Right', he said at last. 'Those two villains have told us pretty well everything. The horse they're terrified of is Oak Tree Mile. Evidently their boss has accepted an enormous bet on him, and also a double with the favourite for the Gold Cup. What's more, the bets are with some very tough members of

112

the Dublin underworld, and if he doesn't pay up he'll be lucky to survive. So he's hell-bent on stopping your horse from winning. He knows the security round the Gold Cup favourite will be watertight and so you and Oak Tree Mile are the softer target. It would be much harder to go for the horse, and as they don't think there is another available amateur jockey who could win with it, they've opted to stop you.'

'We're going to keep these two locked up in a warehouse we've got down in the East End until after Cheltenham. We'll let them sweat, and see if they remember anything else of interest. But I don't think their boss will sit back and forget it when he realises that tonight hasn't worked out. In fact I'm sure there'll be more of his goons out there already. So it would be great if you could disappear till Tuesday – as long as I know where you are, of course.'

'I can't do that, but I can probably put them off the track for at least a day. We're supposed to be driving down to Midwood Park tomorrow and staying there for Cheltenham. But I could to go Jed's instead – tonight if necessary.'

'I can get Fiona to put the word around Lambourn that I haven't turned up and she's worried.' He stood up and paced around the kitchen as he thought things through. 'I'm due to ride at Newton Abbot tomorrow afternoon, but I can scrub that. It will make Fiona's apparent concern more plausible. I'll phone the Jockey Club's security people and tell them what's happened, so that there isn't any trouble about a change of jockey after the overnight declaration time. They ought to know what's going on anyway. Obviously I won't tell them how I found out.'

'What shall I do?' asked Eva.

'Unfortunately, I think you will have to go to Fiona's on your own and look suitably troubled. You can let Howard and Victor know what's going on and I'll get a message to Hal.'

'That all sounds good,' said Benny approvingly.

There was a buzz of activity as the two men began a round of telephone calls.

Jay rang Jed and asked if he could come down later that night, warning him not to mention this to any one. Then he phoned Fiona and told her that Eva would be coming down by herself and would explain all. Benny arranged for two drivers to come over to take Eva and Jay to their separate destinations. He then had another idea.

'Why don't I have your Jaguar taken to one of the private car parks at Heathrow? We could make sure that the *Racing Post* knows you haven't turned up at Midwood Park and also that your Jaguar has been seen at the airport. That might confuse our Irish friends for a while!'

Within half an hour a rather forlorn-looking Eva was on her way to Fiona's and Jason was sitting in the back of an ancient-looking Jaguar bound for Sussex at considerable speed.

As soon as he arrived Jay brought Jed up to speed and they hatched a plan. Jed would send out all his stable staff on a long road-work first lot while he, Jay and Jed's head lad, who he trusted with his life, went go down to the gallops for a relatively short canter and schooling session. They would all be back well before the stable staff so Jay could keep out of sight. During the breakfast break, when all the staff would be in their room behind the tack room, Jed would smuggle Jason out to a quiet part of the downs where he could have a vigorous run, and they'd come back while the second lot were out at the gallops. Only Jed's wife and the head man would be party to what was going on.

On the Monday morning the revised schedule went like clockwork. After lunch Fiona rang to say that Jay's disappearance was all round Lambourn and that the *Racing Post* had already been on the telephone to her to see if she knew where he was. After a decent interval, Jed called the *Racing Post*, asking whether they had heard anything about Jay and claiming to be worried about who would ride his horses at the Festival.

Jason was forced to hide away for the afternoon, reading. At any other time he might have been glad of a few free hours, but it seemed a strange thing to be doing the day before Cheltenham. He took the opportunity to have a long chat with Sean when the Irishman made his regular call to update him on some promising horses he had seen. 'By the way,' Jay said when they'd finished their conversation, 'don't believe what you read in the papers tomorrow.'

The next morning Jed went down to the village to collect his newspapers. Jason's 'disappearance' was front-page news. All sorts of weird and wonderful explanations were offered but none of them seemed at all likely.

Two cars and four bodyguards, brought down to Sussex by Benny, appeared at the yard. When the Jason himself calmly walked out to ride the first lot the stable staff's jaws hit the ground. Neither he nor Jed made any comment on his presence. After two strong gallops, carefully watched over by Benny and his colleagues, Jason got into the back of the old Jaguar for the drive to Cheltenham. His stomach lurched when his mobile rang but happily the Irish voice on the end of the line was Sean's. 'Hey, are you all right?' he asked anxiously.

'Sure. What about our code?'

'Sorry. With all this going on I'm a bit distracted. What the hell happened?'

'I went to ground. There was a bit of trouble so I'm keeping out of the way.'

'Thank God for that,' Sean sighed with relief. 'I heard the bookie was convinced his men had got you, and that he's jubilant. I also heard there is really big money on Oak Tree Mile. My friends tell me that the trainer frankly just doesn't know who he can get at the last minute.'

'How well do you know him?' asked Jay.

'Not that well.'

'Is there the remotest chance he'd recognise your voice?'

'Not at all.'

'Then do me a favour, ring him and leave an anonymous message. Just tell him, "Jay said relax," and leave it at that.

Both the horse and I have some heavy-duty protection, so you can relax, too.'

'That's grand,' said Sean. 'I'll be keeping an eye open for you at the races – on the TV, unfortunately.'

'You and a small army!' chuckled Jay. 'I'll be seeing you.' He switched the telephone off.

Jay's arrival in the Cheltenham weighing room was met by astonishment first, and then a mixture of relief and somewhat ribald amusement. The speculation as to where he had been and what he had been up to was largely unrepeatable and indicated a more vivid imagination in some of his riding colleagues than you would have given then credit for. The barracking died down when the head of security, Giles Sinclair, came in and asked Jay for a quiet word.

Sitting in the racecourse manager's office, Jay told Sinclair how he had been attacked on Sunday night, missing out the rescue by Benny's heavies. Instead he said he'd been very lucky that a large group of passersby had frightened off the assailants. The security officer's raised eyebrows suggested that he found this version of events unlikely but was not prepared to question them. The matter of the bets and the connection with criminal elements concerned him much more. He assured Jay that both horses would be under the tightest of guards, and that he would assign two of his men to his personal protection. Jay thought it wiser not to reveal that he was already catered for in this department, so he just thanked Sinclair warmly. He made a mental note to update Benny in this development on his way back to the weighing room.

Jason was not riding until the fifth race, but it seemed wise to stay in the safety of the weighing room and watch the first four on the closed-circuit television. It was a shame to have to miss out on the unique atmosphere of the Festival, but he had to be sensible.

Before his first race, Freddie Kelly came in. He noticed Jason immediately and made a beeline for him, the surprise on his face melting into relief. 'What the hell's been going on?' he said.

'Long day,' said Jay.

'Can I have a word?' said Freddie. They walked over to the little canteen that served the jockeys with hot drinks, breakfasts and snacks and sat down at a table in the far corner. Freddie leaned across, his voice low. 'I've heard there's a big bet riding on your horse *not* winning. Be very careful.'

'So have I,' said Jay. 'It doesn't seem to be much of a secret.'

'Pat O'Hara rang me when you disappeared. He's frantic and thinks it's his fault. I tell you, he's as straight as a die, and certainly not a gambling man.'

'Don't worry,' said Jay. 'There have already been two attempts to get at me, and both the horse and I are now under very heavy protection.'

They went back into the changing room, where three security officers had joined the jockeys. Giles Sinclair, came over. 'Nobody's got near the horse, I can assure you, and you'll be surrounded like the prime minister when you go out. We'll have police and security guards each side of you and the horse on the way to the course. Short of someone shooting one of you, you'll be safe.'

'I hope they're not that desperate,' said Jason, but a nagging doubt crept into his mind. 'What about someone with an airgun or air-pistol?' he asked. 'If they fired even a plain dart it could be a disaster. What extra precautions can we take?'

Giles thought about this. 'If the horse was brought straight to the parade ring and saddled there, instead of in the saddling boxes, that would put their calculations out. And we could seek permission to walk him round the middle of the ring rather than on the outside tarmac. That would make their aiming anything at him really difficult, especially if there were security men outside him.'

'Perhaps we could get agreement to go down to the start early,' suggested Jay.

'We could also keep the paddock sheet on top of the saddle until I'm on the course.'

The security man sucked in his cheeks. 'I'll go and see the chief steward.' He turned on his heel and strode out.

Fifteen minutes later, he was back. 'He's agreed,' he said. 'It was the fact that two attempts have been made on you and that I could confirm there were strong rumours about the betting that swung it. As you can imagine, they're not happy about breaking with normal procedure, but as long as you walk once round the ring, none of the rules will be broken.'

As Jason sat down to watch the first race he heard the doorman who checked authorisations at the entrance to the weighing room asking for him. He stood up again to talk to him. 'Pat O'Hara, the trainer, is outside looking very worried. He wants to see you,' the doorman said. Jay went to the door. Oak Tree Mile's trainer looked like a man with the cares of the world on his shoulders. Jason gave him a broad smile and shook his hand. 'Everything's all right,' he said.

'I heard you'd been attacked. I promise you, it's nothing to do with me. I don't understand what's going on.'

'Don't worry, about it,' said Jason soothingly. 'It's all under control now. The security people have made some slight changes to our schedule, just as a precaution. Giles Sinclair will come and tell you what's happening just before the race. He'll have men guarding the horse all the way from the stables, so try to relax and enjoy yourself until it's time for our race.'

'Just go out and defeat the bastards!' Pat growled.

'The more I think about it, the more I think we've got a wonderful chance. We must have, if somebody's going to such desperate lengths.'

Chapter Eleven

Just after four o'clock, Jason made his final preparations. He pulled on his back protector, his racing colours and his skin-tight racing boots, and walked over to his valet. He put on his skullcap while Johnny fitted the silk cap on top of the helmet. Picking up his whip and slinging his saddle over his arm, he strolled into the area where the clerk of the scales sat checking the weight of every rider before he went out and the first four upon their return. Occasionally there would be an extra spot check requiring all riders to weigh in after their race.

Looking out into the parade ring, he saw Oak Tree Mile arriving in solitary splendour. Jay scrutinised him as objectively as he could. He was not a handsome horse, more of a big bruiser with just a touch of arrogance that suggested that he was not a horse to be easily beaten.

Pat O'Hara came up the steps into the weighing room. Jay handed him the saddle and flashed him an encouraging smile. 'OK, guv'nor?' With a slightly half-hearted grin the trainer nodded and walked back down the steps and into the middle of the parade ring. The paddock sheet keeping the horse warm was removed and Oak Tree Mile stood stock still while the saddle was put on and the sheet and number cloth replaced. He was then led round well away from the outside of the parade ring, accompanied by three security guards. Jay could see six other security men standing with their backs to the inside of the ring, watching the crowd carefully.

A few of the spectators were murmuring to each other. The experienced race goers and professionals in the crowd would be aware of the departure from the usual routine. Doubtless some of them were concluding that this could be an unruly horse and that the stewards must have given special permission for him to be kept away from the rest. As he had been trained in Ireland, little was known about his idiosyncrasies. Others might well have been wondering whether all this could have something to do with the well-publicised disappearance of the jockey. If they were, there was no accounting for what explanations they were coming up with.

When the other eleven runners started to enter the ring, Giles Sinclair appeared next to Jay. 'Tell me when you're ready,' he said. Jay looked at his watch. There were a little over ten minutes to the start. 'This'll do,' he said. The security officer led the way out on to the steps, where eight burly men were waiting. They flanked Jay, four on each side, as he walked down the steps and over to the horse.

The trainer signalled for Oak Tree Mile to be brought into the middle and stood still. He took the paddock sheet off, pulled down the stirrups and legged Jay up. 'Put the paddock sheet back on him,' said Jay. 'I'll sit on it. It'll give him a little extra protection if anyone tries anything silly.'

Jay was led straight across the ring and out into the now cordoned-off footway down to the chute, which took the horses past the grandstand on to the course proper. By now Oak Tree Mile was really on his toes, and the trainer, lad and security men were almost trotting to keep up with him. As soon as he turned right to pass in front of the stand, Jay said to Pat: 'Pull the sheet off now. Looking down at the lad, he instructed: 'Release him as soon as possible.' The leading rein was already off the bridle and the horse was being led by his rein. The lad stood to one side and let go. With a little plunge, Oak Tree Mile burst into life and cantered down the chute on to the course. Jay went a good stride or two faster than normal. He wanted to take as few chances as possible.

Passing the stand, keeping well to the middle of the course, he slowed his horse down, turned him round and then made his way towards the start as the racecourse announcer informed race goers: 'Number seven, Oak Tree Mile, has been given special permission by the stewards to go to the start early.'

Milling around at the start were various policemen and security types. The chief security officer's Land Rover arrived and he got out. 'All seems to be well so far,' he commented, looking across to where Jay was having his girths checked by the starter's assistant.

'Let's keep our fingers crossed it stays that way,' said Jay.

He was grateful that it wasn't long before he was joined at the start by the other eleven runners and some semblance of normality was restored. Apart from the two other contestants from Ireland, he knew all the riders, including one of the leading French amateurs, the son of one of that country's best-known trainers. Although they were tense there was plenty of good-natured banter and one or two questions about why Jay had come down so early. 'He's a bit of a character,' lied Jay. 'But he seems to be on his best behaviour today.'

They lined up and walked in steadily to the start. As expected, Oak Tree Mile was straining to be away. 'My horse pulls like hell,' said Jay to the company at large, 'so I'll be up there.' It is common practice for jockeys who are likely to 'make it' to let the others know, although just occasionally this might be used as a double bluff. Then the tapes were up and they were off. True to form, Oak Tree Mile was anxious to get on with it and, rather than strangle him, Jay let him bowl along to the first fence.

Having enough experience of him to know the horse was capable of making extravagant jumps, Jay kept him under moderate restraint going into the first. A huge leap took him clear into the lead, but very rapidly one of the other Irish entries was up alongside. It was plain that the other jockey was having some trouble restraining his horse. Jason took a slightly firmer hold on his own mount and let the other horse go ahead. To his great relief, rather than fight to get back in the lead, Oak Tree Mile settled in behind the first horse at a strong but still sensible gallop. Jumping the second and third with equal ease, Jay was going well down the hill and by this time the favourite was upsides him. This was ridden by Jimmy Carruthers, a jockey who would almost certainly become the leading amateur when Jay retired.

On the final circuit, the first two fences in the home straight were taken well. By this time Jay's horse was totally settled and going beautifully. Heading down the hill towards the first down the back straight there was no change in the order. Approaching the water jump the leader made a mistake and dropped his back legs in it. Jay's and Jimmy's horses were foot perfect again, and found themselves jointly in the lead, stride for stride, as they approached the open ditch. Again there was nothing between them, and from the noise behind it was obvious that most of the rest of the field were in close contention.

The next two fences were again taken stride for stride and the leaders started to climb the hill towards the crown of the final bend. As they approached it another horse ranged into view alongside Jimmy and they all took it abreast. Going down the hill Jay was still cruising and a quick look back showed that the three of them had drawn well clear of the fourth horse, with the others strung out in Indian file behind. But the strong gallop had already taken its toll on the favourite. As he turned for home, Jimmy raised his whip and gave his horse a couple of cracks. Although it responded and rejoined the other two as they jumped the third last, it was certain that, barring accidents, the first two places would be taken by Jay and the recent arrival. Jay glanced sideways and recognised the other rider's famous colours. They belonged to one of the Jockey Club's stewards. He knew the horse was being ridden by Harvey Molineux, an extremely competent and experienced amateur, but one who was a little too fond of using the whip, in Jay's opinion. If it came to a close finish he would have a real race on his hands. The second last was jumped upsides, but this time he saw his opponent's whip rise and fall three times in quick succession. 'Come on my fellow,' he whispered to Oak Tree Mile. 'We're not going to need any of that, are we?' Slowly but surely, his horse inched away and was a good length clear as they went into the last. 'Steady fellow, steady,' crooned Jason and, as if he understood what Jay was saying, the horse shortened his stride, met the fence perfectly and soared over it and away in one glorious movement. It was a long climb from the last to the finishing post, and Jay wanted to make sure nothing was coming out of the pack with a surprisingly fast finish. He checked behind him to see that he was a good five lengths clear, and that the second horse was even further ahead of the third. Urging Oak Tree Mile on with hands and heels, he strode up the finishing straight and passed the winning post with that very special feeling of exaltation that comes with riding a winning horse that has given everything and run like a true professional.

The other jockeys gathered around, calling their congratulations or leaning over to shake his hand. He turned and trotted past the grandstand, where he saw the lad, and an exuberant Pat O'Hara rushing towards him. They were both absolutely ecstatic. 'Well,' said Jason, looking down at the trainer, 'in spite of everything, we managed to do it. This is a great horse you've got here, and he's going to be a Grand National proposition one day.' To the cheers and whoops of the vast Irish contingent Jay was led into the paddock and across into the winner's enclosure where photographers and press men swarmed around him.

'Where's the owner?' Jay asked Pat.

'The owner is my wife,' he replied. 'She broke her leg hunting so she can't be here, but she'll have watched every stride on the television, I promise you!'

With the saddle off and under his arm, Jason headed up the steps to the weighing room. He was interrupted by the television crews. Questions came at him from all sides. Had there been any bad moments? How good was the horse? What was it like to win at Cheltenham? Where had he been for the last two days? All these save the last he answered briefly but goodnaturedly. 'Anything else you'd like to say?' asked the BBC interviewer.

'Yes,' said Jay. 'I'd like to thank Mrs O'Hara for giving me the ride, and hope that her leg mends soon enough for her to be able to give this fella a nice quiet ride round her farm, and to let him have the fun and rest he deserves after an effort like today's.' With a smile and a wave, he threaded his way up to the weighing room, where he was met by Giles Sinclair. 'Well, it was all worth it, I guess,' he said, 'There was never a sign of trouble.'

'I know,' said Jay, 'but perhaps that was because of our precautions. Who can tell?'

'If I hear anything I'll let you know.' said Sinclair. He shook Jay's hand warmly and scurried off to fulfil other equally important but rather less exciting duties.

A friendly cheer went up as he weighed in, but there was no time yet to relive the race with his colleagues. An official was shepherding him out again for the presentations. A fine trophy was given to the trainer on behalf of his absent wife, and there were bottles of champagne and mementos for Pat and for Jay. Then came more questions from the press, to which he responded cheerfully but for the most part noncommittally. The matter of his apparent disappearance seemed to have been shelved in the heat of the victory, at least by the specialist racing journalists. There was a muffled inquiry from the back which it was easy to pretend he hadn't heard. Happily, the ratpack reporters were not accredited for the winner's enclosure. He hoped the fuss would die down and they wouldn't bother to pursue him later.

The interviews over, he was climbing the steps back to the weighing room when he felt a hand on his arm. He turned to see a radiant Eva, accompanied by a delighted Hal. She reached up and gave him a big kiss, full on the lips. 'I don't think I've ever been more excited in my life!' she declared. Hal pumped his hand up and down until Jay thought it might fall off. 'Well done, young man! Well done, young man!' he said, over and over again.

'I'll see you later,' Jay called.

'Box twenty-seven,' said Hal. 'Don't forget!'

On his way to Hal's box, Jay checked his voicemail on his mobile phone. Running through the messages of congratulations, he heard Benny's voice among them. 'I've got some really interesting news for you. Call me when you have a moment. It's not urgent.'

In the box the syndicate, including Hal, Bart and Len, were still celebrating, knocking back the champagne (or Scotch in Victor's case) and watching a rerun of the Kim Muir Handicap Chase on the closed-circuit television, cheering Oak Tree Mile as if they were seeing the race for the first time.

Jay accepted one glass of champagne as he talked them through it, and then he and Eva took their leave. He needed to be in good shape for the next two days' racing. As they walked towards the car park, he fished his phone out of his bag and called Benny. 'Eva and I are on our way' he said, 'What's this interesting news?'

'I'll see you along the road in front of the stables,' said Benny. 'I've got a lot to tell you.'

He appeared, flanked by a couple of his mates, from the gathering gloom of the March evening as Jason and Eva reached the stable block.

'There you are guv'nor. Well, we picked up three more of those low-life, he told them gleefully. One turned out to be just a driver who didn't know what was going on. The other two were hired muscle. We got word of where they would be and we caught them on the way out. They didn't give us any trouble.'

'Where are they now?' asked Jason.

'In London with the other two,' replied Benny. 'None of them are very happy, and there's been a lot of aggravation and accusations flying around between the two different factions. I think they are all terrified of going back to Dublin.'

'What you might be interested to know is that we found two air pistols on them, loaded with those sharp, pointed darts. There weren't any drugs or anything. They were going to stand on the rails where you went on to the racecourse and put two darts into the horse's rear. They reckoned that would be enough for the horse to gallop loose long enough to spoil his chances, or just to gallop off and be withdrawn. But the security men and all the other precautions put them off. We've got the guns if they're any use to you, and with their fingerprints on them too.'

'That's great – they could be a terrific help. Keep them safe.'

'What do you think will happen now?' asked Benny.

'I think it's probably all over, but I'd be grateful if you'd keep an eye on me for the next couple of days while the dust settles, just in case.'

'What about the Irishmen?'

'I suppose they should stay where they are till after the race meeting,' said Jay. 'Then it might be easiest all round if some rough sorts are found tied up in the back of a van that can't be traced to you.'

'Just my thinking,' said Benny.

'They are all right aren't they?' inquired Jay slightly nervously.

'Oh, there's been no need to bring ourselves down to their level and resort to physical violence,' Benny assured him airily. 'It's amazing what no food or drink and being tied up to your waist in water in a tidal boathouse will do. They were chattering like monkeys by the time it got up to their armpits.'

'I don't think I want to know anything more,' said Jay faintly. Eva's eyes were already like saucers.

'You're going back to Midwood Park tonight, are you?' asked Benny, obligingly changing the subject.

'Yes. I think I can safely join Eva there now.'

'Good. Harry picked up your Jag from the airport this morning and took it there for you. What car are you in now?'

Eva gave him the registration number of the Range Rover Fiona had lent her that morning.

'I'll have the old BMW with you.' He raised an arm in farewell and disappeared into the shadow of the stable block.

In the car park, Jason went to the driver's seat of the Range Rover.

'No you don't – you've done quite enough for today. I'll drive,' said Eva firmly. 'I know it's been a thrilling day, but I haven't been trying to keep up with our partners in the champagne-quaffing stakes.'

The next morning Jason was up at his usual time and had a frugal breakfast with Fiona, leaving Eva fast asleep, and went out and rode the first lot up the gallops twice.

He and Eva were back at Cheltenham before midday, and by the time Jay had come out to mount The Conker the adrenaline was flowing. He was on a real high, too, at being able to properly savour the exhilaration of riding at the Festival after all the tensions of the previous day. He really thought that he had a great chance in the 'amateur riders' Grand National,' and he knew The Conker had never been on better form.

His own mood was in marked contrast to that of the owner. He had never seen Howard so nervous, and even Jed seemed to be letting the occasion get to him. The bell rang and Jay was helped on to the chestnut's back. 'Come back safely, both of you,' implored Howard.

After two circuits of the ring, The Conker was being led down the chute on to the course. The Four Mile Chase starts down the back straight, with twenty-four fences to jump. There is always a big field, and this year there were twenty-one runners. Although this was an amateur riders' race, all the jockeys were experienced, as were their horses, and they set off at a sensible pace. Jay had The Conker in the middle of the field and soon they had cleared all the fences down the back straight and were climbing the hill for the first of three ascents. As always, The Conker was bold and fluent. By the time they passed the grandstand for the first time the whole field was still standing and well bunched.

Going down the back straight, one of the horses in front of Jay slipped on landing and lost his jockey, interfering in the process with another horse whose jockey was also shot out of the saddle. Two less to reckon with, thought Jay as they went up the hill for the second time. There was little change in the order but, checking behind him after they jumped the fence at the top of the hill, Jay saw that a number of the horses were beginning to lose ground. He was seventh, moving easily. All the remaining horses jumped the fences in the home straight and soon they were going up the hill away from the stand before swooping down into the back straight. They all cleared the water jump, and by the time they reached the next open ditch the pace had quickened.

Jay made sure he didn't lose any ground and moved The Conker to the outside of the fence as he approached it. He wanted him to have a good, unimpeded view. It was just as well, because the leader hit the top and took a crashing fall, and in so doing brought down two other horses. Suddenly, Jay found himself in fourth place. The Conker was still moving sweetly and crept up to within three lengths of the leader. Turning for home, with four fences to jump, Jay felt the excitement. The Conker had never felt better under him, and two of the horses in front of him were already being hard ridden. The third horse passed them with two more to jump and Jay just tracked it. Taking the second last, the leader did his best to shake off Jay by injecting a little extra pace. The Conker responded smoothly and easily. As they came to the last, Jay moved upsides and well to the leader's right to ensure that if a mishap occurred he would be clear. The Conker saw the stride beautifully and soared over the fence, leaving his opponent two lengths behind. It was still a good hard climb to the winning post, and for once Jay gave The Conker a slap on his rump just to make sure he did not slacken now that he was in the lead. The Conker got the message and surged past the winning post a good twelve lengths in the clear. If Jay was over the moon Howard and Bubbles were in another galaxy. Jed was grinning from ear to ear. 'You did it my boy!' chortled Howard, and Bubbles, dressed more appropriately for Ladies' Day at Ascot than for a chilly March day at Cheltenham, gave him a smacking great kiss which left a huge scarlet smear on his cheek. Jay turned to Jed. 'I've never had a better ride in my life.' To Howard and Bubbles he said: 'This fellow will be a Grand National horse within a couple of years. He just doesn't know how to give up.'

When they all met again for the presentations, Howard, still euphoric, slapped him on the back rather too heartily.

'Steady Howard,' said Jed. 'Remember he's still got another ride for us this afternoon. We don't want him bruised!'

Bubbles was almost bursting with pride when Howard insisted she receive the trophy. He put his arms round Jason. 'You've done me proud, Jay, I'll never forget this day as long as I live.'

'It's not over yet,' said Jay.

Eva, who had been keeping quietly in the background to give the owners their well-deserved moment in the spotlight, kissed him briefly on the cheek and promised 'I'll do better later.' He walked back to the weighing room as if he were walking on air. He felt so privileged already he hardly dared contemplate the possibility of another place on Pewter Queen. He sat down with a cup of hot, sweet tea, watched the thrilling Mildmay of Fleet Handicap Chase on television and tried to bring himself back down to earth.

The Champion National Hunt Flat Race brings down the curtain on the second day of the Festival. This year there were twenty-five runners, which meant it would inevitably be a bit of a scrummage and would be run at a breakneck pace. He had already discussed the race with Jed and Howard and they were all quite relaxed about the fact that it would be fast. They had every confidence in Pewter Queen. Her previous runs had indicated that, as long as she was reasonably close over the last furlong, her finishing speed would pay dividends. And being a mare, she would get a 5lb weight allowance from the colts and geldings in the race.

Although the runners were all relatively inexperienced, having had a maximum of three races before getting to Cheltenham, they were surprisingly well behaved, with the exception of one colt that was a little excited and starting to sweat up. Girths were checked and very soon the starter had them walking in a line. The tapes went up and, with just over two miles ahead of them, the field was soon streaming up past the grandstand.

Over the previous few years the Irish had dominated this race and once again there were two horses from across the water, the favourite and second favourite, along with one runner from France. Freddie Kelly was on the second favourite. 'Let's see which of us comes out in front today,' he said to Jason, as they started down the back straight alongside each other. 'I think your mare will run really well, but this fellow I've got here has a pretty good motor, too.'

Both Freddie and Jay were in the middle of the pack leaving the back straight, and as they started up the hill and round the bend they advanced to fifth and sixth respectively, and stayed in that position as they swung down the hill before turning for home up the long and always demanding straight. Freddie's horse started to edge forward from fifth to fourth, and Jay kept just half a length behind him. With a furlong to go they both moved up smoothly to second and third, surprised to see that a complete outsider was still in front of them. It continued to run on very strongly and Jay began to wonder if either he or Freddie would be able to pass it. With half a furlong to go, the jockey on the leading horse started to ride really hard and to use his whip rather over-vigorously. Freddie's horse followed him and was soon a length ahead. Pewter Queen doggedly stayed the half length down. With a hundred yards to go Jay gave her two slaps down the neck and urged her on with hands and heels. She responded so quickly that she was past Freddie in just a few strides and the winning post with a neck to spare. 'You've done it again, you old bastard,' Freddie said as they pulled up. 'That's a really decent mare you've got.'

'I know,' said Jay. 'She might be something really special if she jumps as well as she runs.'

First The Conker, and now this. Bubbles thought all their birthdays had come at once. Jay was delighted just to see them both so happy. 'Champagne by the bucket!' yelled Howard as Jay got off. 'That's what we're going to have tonight. Champagne by the bucket!'

So it was a very high-spirited bunch who met shortly in the hospitality tent that Howard, along with his sons Andy and son-in-law Peter, had hired to entertain their biggest clients. Hal had his own clients to look after but Jay, Eva, Jed, Howard and Victor were all there, all talking at once, and all congratulating each other on a highly successful and wonderful day. They were still on cloud nine when Eva drove Jay, Howard, Bubbles and Victor back to Midwood Park. Even Jay who usually had no trouble keeping his feet on the ground, had difficulty believing he had won three races at the Festival. But in the end the ceaseless congratulations got too much for him. 'Let's remember it was Jed who trained the horses,' he said. 'I just steered them round.' Everyone agreed and there began a round of expressions of regret that Jed had insisted on going home. At a quarter to ten Jay left them to their celebrations in Fiona's drawing room and went to bed. When Eva joined him twenty minutes later she snuggled up to him and whispered, 'You're an absolute star.' Jason had a smile on his face, but he was fast asleep.

Chapter Twelve

The final day of the Cheltenham Festival, Gold Cup Day, dawned bright but cold. By half past eleven the course was already buzzing with excitement and seething with a huge crowd. Jason, arriving in the jockeys' car park with Eva and Fiona, was almost mobbed by well-wishers. The weighing room entrance had already been staked out by journalists eager to quiz him about the previous day's rides and his hopes for the Triumph Hurdle. The Racing Channel also sought his comments. After a while he politely excused himself and moved into the weighing room where Johnny Hampshire bustled around him. At least today he did not have to sit around for long: he was riding in the first race, and after that he would be able to relax until the last in which he was piloting a 20-1 outsider for Pat O'Hara.

The Triumph Hurdle is one of the most hotly contested races of the Cheltenham Festival. It is also a race that always attracts a very large entry and is run at a breakneck pace. The twenty or so young horses competing have perhaps raced only three or four times over hurdles before which means it is seldom short of incident and often throws up a surprise winner. Jay was riding Fiona's Hopeful Return which, like most of his opponents, had run with considerable credit on the Flat. He had been rather a backward baby and consequently had not run as a two-year-old. This, in Jay's view, gave him a great advantage. He always felt that racing immature horses, very often on firm ground, did nothing for their long-term future. What was more, Fiona had nursed this horse along carefully, and he had not only won two three-year-old races over a mile and a half but had gone on to win two hurdle races quite easily in good if not spectacular company. The first of these had been at Worcester, a relatively uncomplicated flat track, and the second at Towcester, which has a finishing straight every bit as testing as the one at Cheltenham. The fact that Hopeful Return had come from the middle of the field to win quite effortlessly that day had given Jay enough confidence in him to tell Fiona that he certainly should run in the Triumph.

Hopeful Return had been bred by Paul Campbell, one of Fiona's original owners, who had owned the dam. She had been bought when the owner returned from a long period of working in Africa. Named Return to Blighty, she had been consistently successful in both France and England without ever being quite good enough to run in a Classic. Paul became so fond of her that he decided to keep her and breed from her and, although a number of her previous foals had been successful, this was the first that showed outstanding talent.

The adrenaline was already pumping through Jay's body as he walked into the parade ring. There was something so special about this meeting. He knew he was going to really miss riding in it the following year. Involvement as a trainer would not bring the same surge of excitement that welled up inside him the moment he descended the steps from the weighing room into the paddock.

As always on Gold Cup Day, the crowd was enormous and, after a chilly start, it had turned into a glorious day, more like the end of May than the middle of March. Jay touched his cap and shook hands with Paul Campbell. 'Well, there's not much to say now, apart from good luck, is there?' he said with a smile.

'I'll certainly need that,' said Jay. 'But I think he'll run well for you.'

The bell rang and there was a scurry as trainers and jockeys ran forward to find their mounts, take off their paddock sheets and leg up each horse's pilot. Hopeful Return was a big chestnut horse with a white blaze and four white socks, which made him very easy to pick out. He was 12-1 in the betting, which meant he was considered to be in with a chance. The favourite was 3-1 and there were four other horses 10-1 or less, which left Jason more or less in the middle.

The favourite was an Irish-trained horse that was an almost white-grey, very unusual in a young horse. Appropriately named Rugged Snowman, he was easy to spot and Jay understood why the bookmakers had made him favourite. His form in Ireland had been impressive on the Flat and over hurdles. Jason followed the Irish horse on to the course where, as was customary, the runners trotted up in front of the stand before turning to go back to the start to give the crowd an opportunity to make their final assessments of each horse's appearance, the way it was moving over the ground and whether it looked relaxed or unduly excited. This was all part of the pageant and, like most jockeys, Jay was at his most nervous. They all wanted the tapes to be up and to get away.

At the start at last, they heard two cries of 'Wait, wait!' coming from the starter's rostrum to allow a couple of the runners at the back to be turned round and pointed in the right direction. 'Right, jockeys!' he yelled. The tape flashed across the track and they were away.

As Jason had anticipated the speed to the first hurdle was furious. He took a firm hold on Hopeful Return, heading him out towards the side of the track to avoid any interference, from which vantage point he could see the first hurdle well before he reached it. There were bangs and crashes as the horses flew over, some clipping it with their front legs and others with their hinds, but all were still standing as they approached the second. By now the field was beginning to sort itself out and one of the outsiders was making an extremely hot race of it. Going at that speed, Jason calculated it was likely to run out of steam up the final hill.

Climbing away from the stand he found himself in the middle of the field, on the outside, but not so far wide that he was losing too much ground. The favourite was just two horses in front of him. As they went down the back straight they met a hurdle very fast and one of the horses ahead of him stumbled badly, shooting his jockey out of the saddle. As far as Jay could tell the rest of the field was still intact. Now the gallop had settled to a very strong but much more sensible pace and the early leader was rapidly losing ground. Hopeful Return had overtaken him before they reached the next hurdle.

Return was now eighth, Rugged Snowman sixth, and both were flying. Jumping the last down the back straight, the field was unchanged. Jay had a strong feeling that his horse was going to run a very good race. The Irish favourite, too, was going ominously well. Then a small, dark bay moved up alongside, ridden by Charlie Forbes, a very talented young amateur who would undoubtedly turn professional the next season. 'How's your horse going?' Jay called to him.

'Got a double handful!' came the reply. 'Whether or not he'll last the hill remains to be seen.'

Jumping the next hurdle on the top of the hill Jay had dropped back to ninth and the young amateur had moved past him and was now up to fifth. Hopeful Return was still moving easily, and he felt it was far too soon to ask for any additional effort. He glanced over his shoulder. Although there was one horse behind him who was still a contender, the rest were beginning to struggle. It looked as if the first ten would be the ones that counted. As he raced down the hill and into the home straight with two hurdles to go he knew he was going really well. His horse jumped the penultimate hurdle brilliantly and hit the ground running. He was fourth now, with an outsider he did not recognise and Charlie in front of him as well as the favourite, the leader. Into the last the four of them were in line. The outsider and the amateur matched another good leap by Return; the favourite stumbled and lost half a length.

But he was not finished, and soon he was upside Jay again. The two of them moved away from the outsider and Charlie's horse, which seemed to have shot its bolt. With a hundred yards to go, Jay saw something coming up on his outside and realised that he had not one but two horses to contend with. The grey steadily inched away from Jay, and as hard as he tried, Hopeful Return could make no impression. On the other side, Charlie's horse had found a second wind and was travelling even more easily with some enthusiastic if not particularly elegant urging, and managed to draw a length and a half away from Jay and the grey. Jay just could not make any more progress and crossed the line third, a length and a half behind the winner and half a length behind the favourite. Another amateur had won.

From the exultant expression on the stable lad's face, you would have thought Hopeful Return was the winner. The excitement of the race and the knowledge that he was going to be in the winner's enclosure, never mind in which spot, was enough to overcome his disappointment that his horse had been beaten, particularly as no one had expected the horse to win. Back in the parade ring, a delighted Fiona and an ecstatic Paul Campbell rushed over to greet him. 'Well, he did everything you could possibly have asked,' said Jay. 'Give him another year to mature, and you'll have a real staying hurdler here.'

'I'm absolutely thrilled,' said Paul. 'This is the first time I've ever been in the winner's enclosure at Cheltenham, and it's a moment I will savour for ever! Please join me in my box at the end of the afternoon for a little celebration.'

'I'd love to,' said Jay. 'I'll be with you as soon as I can.'

Jay watched the Stayers' Hurdle, the race before the Gold Cup, in the weighing room. After the horses jumped the hurdle on the top of the hill, he saw Freddie Kelly's mount stumble on landing and go down. The runner immediately behind him swerved violently to try to avoid the faller and was hit by the horse behind him. In the twinkling of an eye, five horses were on the floor as, one after another, two more tripped over the three prostrate horses. There was a gasp from the commentator. All five horses struggled to their feet and galloped off, without their riders, seemingly none the worse for their experience, but of the five jockeys, only one was on his feet. Within seconds the ambulance was there and two other riders were up and dusting themselves down, apparently only winded. But it was clear from the activity that all was far from well with the two men still lying on the ground. Another ambulance came careering across the inside of the track towards the scene of the incident. Each jockey was stretchered into one of the ambulances.

A hush fell in the weighing room; the kind of hush permeated by the dread that always comes with the realisation that colleagues have been hurt, perhaps seriously. All eyes were glued to the screen as the TV cameras followed the ambulances up the track and off the course to the medical room.

Proceedings in the winner's enclosure were overshadowed by the concern of the officials and crowd over what had obviously been a very nasty accident. The stewards' secretary came in. 'They're all relatively OK,' he announced. 'Connor O'Leary may have a broken leg, and Freddie Kelly looks as if he has broken his wrist. The other two are concussed. None of them will ride again today, so some replacement jockeys will be needed for the Gold Cup. I'll let you know the situation as soon as I can.' At that moment one of the attendants came in and called Jay's name. He went out to find Jack Symes, the trainer of Splendid Warrior, the favourite for the Gold Cup, standing by the door. 'Freddie isn't going to be able to ride and he's recommended you. Do you feel up to it after the Triumph?'

'Absolutely,' said Jay. 'How is he?'

'He'll be right as rain in a few weeks. He said to go and talk to the horse while he's being saddled. It'll pay dividends. The other thing he asked me to tell you is not to worry that he won't travel down the hill very well. Just keep him in contention, and once you've jumped the second last, go for it.'

Jason went back into the weighing room and sat down, stunned. His anxiety about Freddie had been such that he had answered Jack's question almost on autopilot, but now the enormity of what he'd been asked to do began to sink in. To ride the favourite in the Gold Cup was not only something beyond his wildest expectations but an awesome responsibility. He heard the announcement of the change of jockeys for all four horses being made and here was Johnny, fussing, scurrying over with the new colours, his saddle and a weight cloth. 'Wow!' he said. 'This is quite something for you. I know you'll give him a great ride.'

Even for a jockey as experienced as Jay, the preparations seemed like a dream sequence. Almost as soon as he was ready they were called to weigh out and, as instructed by Freddie, Jay went with the trainer to meet his mount. Although the horse had run many times Jay had never been this close to him before. He was evidently over sixteen hands but, unlike the more heavily built steeplechasers such as The Conker and Oak Tree Mile, he was fine-boned, with a greyhound look that bore witness to his Flat racing pedigree.

He certainly lived up to his name: he was every inch an aristocrat. Splendid Warrior looked at Jason with interest as the jockey spoke to him, patted him on the neck and fondled his ears. Jason carried on talking to him quietly for as long as time permitted, making sure the horse knew his voice and, as far as possible, recognised him as a friend. All too soon the horse was being led into the parade ring. On his way back to the weighing room, Jason was waylaid by reporters and television crews asking him how he felt, what his plans were and countless other obvious questions. For once Jay was curt. 'I haven't had time to think,' he said. 'I'm trying to concentrate on the job in hand.'

When the jockeys were called out Jay made a point of keeping in the middle and as far away from the spotlight as possible. His weighing room colleagues treated him to a mixture of encouragement and gamesmanship as they filed on to the perfect green turf of the parade ring. 'Lucky devil', he heard in one ear, 'Don't let it get to you!' in the other. Jack Symes and the horse's owner were standing near the centre and Jay walked straight across to them. 'Well,' said the owner, 'A surprise for all of us, isn't it?'

'It certainly is,' acknowledged Jay. 'Thank you very much for the ride.'

'Don't thank me,' said the owner. 'Freddie was adamant you were the right man for the job.'

'You know what to do, Jay,' said Jack. 'This horse needs to be kept in contention but not make the running. As Freddie mentioned, he won't go down hill all that well, but if you're thereabouts jumping the second last, there's nothing that can come back better.'

'It's the Derby blood,' explained the owner with a smile.

The bell rang. 'Will jockeys please mount,' instructed the speakers, and in a flash Jay was on the back of the most valuable horse he had ever sat on. The blood was positively coursing through his veins. On the way down to the course through the crowd he could hear the almost routine cries of 'Good luck,' and 'Don't let us down,' from the horse's supporters, many of whom had backed him as early as three months before.

Almost in a trance, Jason found himself at the start going through the regular routine of having his girths checked and then circling round waiting for the clock to click round to the appointed time. As is normal for the Gold Cup, the field was not a large one, and every one of the fourteen runners was a class horse which had won big races to prove itself worthy of what is undisputedly the most important race in the National Hunt calendar.

Jay knew that one of the Irish entrants would make the running and, as soon as the tape was away, it duly strode into the lead. It was not a stupid gallop, and Jay was very happy to settle his horse in fifth position.

Not having ridden Splendid Warrior before, Jason decided that it was probably best to leave him to his own devices over the jumps. After all, by this stage of his career, the horse probably knew enough about what he was doing to manage perfectly well without any help from him. So Jay sat very quietly approaching the first three fences all of which his mount cleared accurately but economically. Coming to the first open ditch Jay realised that the horse in front was hesitating and that Splendid Warrior sensed it. In two strides, he put himself right, met the fence fluently and took off, landing at the same speed. 'You're a class act,' said Jay admiringly to Splendid Warrior, giving him a quick pat on the neck.

With the first circuit completed, they again made their way down the back straight. The leading Irish horse injected a little extra pace into the race and all but one of them in front stayed with him. Splendid Warrior had no problem matching it. At the top of the hill he cleared the fence with another perfect jump. He was fourth and perfectly placed for going down the hill less than three lengths off the leader. As predicted, at this accelerated speed, Jay's horse slightly lost his stride and another horse passed him, relegating him to fifth place. But he was still no more than five lengths off the leader as they swept round out of the bend and faced the long uphill finishing straight. Almost as if he was finding another gear, Splendid Warrior changed pace beneath him as he met the rising ground. Jay could feel the power behind the saddle. At the third last, he cruised past the horse that had overtaken him. By this time the early leader was tiring, but the other two contenders were full of running and still three lengths in front of Jason. As he jumped the second last, Splendid Warrior came upside the early leader and into third position.

One of the two in front was the main Irish hope. As soon as Jason passed the second horse the Irish one accelerated. Even above the thundering hooves, Jay could hear the cheers starting in the grandstand. Now he was up beside the leader but both horses had plenty left in the tank. Jay's mount took the last fence economically, but one stride past he stumbled. Jason suspected he had put his foot into an earlier hoof print, and for two strides he was terrified the horse had hurt himself but no, he was back in full gallop, thank God. However, it was enough for the leader to poach another length and a half and now Jay was four lengths behind.

'Come on, fella!' he hissed, administering a slap on the neck, and immediately he could feel the surge of power. Picking up the bit, Splendid Warrior hurled himself in full pursuit of the only rival in front of him like a greyhound after its quarry. With fifty yards to go Jason was half a length down but still closing. Ears pricked, as if he could see the winning post, Warrior found yet another gear and edged into the lead. The stands erupted as they crossed the finishing line a length and a half up on the Irish horse. For once the normally phlegmatic Jason allowed himself the indulgence of raising his stick to the crowd in an exuberant show of triumph. He simply could not believe what they had achieved.

Two lads rushed out to lead him in. One of them looked up at Jason and said, 'He's a star, isn't he?'

'He's amazing,' breathed Jason. 'In a class of his own. Best I've ever sat on.' They entered the winner's enclosure to a rapturous reception. Jason touched his cap as he rode through the crowd towards the owner and trainer standing in the number one spot. 'Well done, Jason,' said the owner.

'You gave him a great ride,' added Jack.

'I didn't,' said Jay. 'I just sat on him and steered. He is magic. It was a privilege to ride him at all, let alone in the Gold Cup! I've ridden a lot of good horses in my time, but never anything like this. He's truly majestic. You've given me the ride of my life!'

The press and television cameras deluged him. 'How did it go?' 'How was the horse?' 'Were there any bad moments?' 'What will you remember most about the race?'

'There's no doubt about that,' said Jason in response to the last question. 'The fact that Freddie recommended me, and it was he who told me how to ride the race. All I did was follow his instructions. He is the true champion, and it's a tragedy for him that he didn't get the chance to ride what must be one of the greatest steeplechasers of all time.'

His answer prompted a spontaneous outbreak of applause from the other journalists and those members of the public who had heard it. This final touching accolade was too much for Jason. Choking with emotion, he fled into the weighing room and on to the scales, tears of pure joy running down his cheeks.

He went through the presentation in a trance, and back in the changing room he could hardly remember what had been said. Nor was he given much chance for reflection here: he was surrounded by jockeys shaking his hand and patting his back – it was complete bedlam. Eventually the riders were called for the next race and some semblance of order was restored. Jason went into the little canteen and sat in a corner. 'Tea for me,' he said, as Johnny came in and sat down opposite him.

'Well, what a day – and still another ride to come!' exclaimed the valet. 'It'll be a bit of an anticlimax after that, won't it?'

For the first time Jay was able to draw breath and focus on the race. 'No,' he said, looking his valet straight in the eye. 'We've been friends for a long while, Johnny, so I know I can rely on you not to tell anyone. This will be my last race at Cheltenham.'

Johnny leaned across, grasped Jason's hand and held it firmly. 'Seriously?' he said. 'Your last race altogether?'

'Not quite altogether. I've promised to ride at Aintree for Jed, though not in the National. He's got a real chance with one of his horses and I'd hate to let him down.' Johnny spent some twenty minutes getting Jay organised for the race, performing each task very deliberately as if the occasion demanded some ceremony.

The last race at the Cheltenham Festival is the County Hurdle, a two-mile handicap for which the field is always large and competitive. Jay was riding Pat O'Hara's Ivan's Paddy. A horse that had won some good handicaps in Ireland and was approximately halfway down the handicap. The morning paper had shown it at 14-1, so evidently the pundits thought it had at least a chance of finishing in the first four. Although he had never ridden this horse before, Jay had studied its form and two videotapes of its runs in Ireland to familiarise himself with it as much as he could. The horse had always finished well but had never run on such a stiff course as Cheltenham, so it had been agreed that Jay would keep him near the back of the field and hope that his relatively light weight and good finishing speed would prove effective going up the hill.

The twenty-three runners, having streamed towards the first hurdle, were still pretty well bunched-up as they passed the grandstand and made their way round to the back of the racecourse. Jay was lying fifteenth or sixteenth and his horse was travelling nicely. Going down the back straight, he moved to the outside of the pack and gradually left one or two tiring horses behind him. Ivan's Paddy was jumping beautifully and was either gaining, or at least not losing any ground, as he overcame each obstacle. By the time they got to the bottom of the hill leaving the back straight, they were eighth and cruising very easily. Clearing the hurdle on the hill, they were in sixth place and Jason was beginning to feel quietly confident as they ran down and turned into the home straight. As they approached the next hurdle, he suddenly became aware that something was wrong. The horse had abruptly slowed down and for a horrible moment Jay thought he had injured a leg. Looking down, he saw blood on his left boot. He knew instantly what had happened. Ivan's Paddy had broken a blood vessel and was now inhaling blood into his lungs. Nothing else stops a horse so quickly. Jay immediately pulled him round the wing of the approaching hurdle and leaped off him. Although Ivan's Paddy was bleeding quite copiously, he didn't appear to be in distress, so Jay began to lead him gently up the hill. Within minutes the vet was there and Ivan's Paddy was loaded into the horse ambulance. The vet drove Jay back to the grandstand in his Land Rover. 'Well,' he said. 'Today has certainly been a day of mixed fortunes for you, hasn't it?'

'You can say that again. I'm terribly sorry about Ivan's Paddy and for his connections, but I have to admit that nothing could take the icing off the cake for me. It's been a truly memorable day and a truly memorable meeting.'

In the weighing room Johnny soon had his boots and breeches off and began to remove the now drying blood. Jason gracefully accepted the commiserations of the other jockeys but, in spite of the sad end to the day and the Festival, what he had said to the vet was absolutely true. Having wondered three days earlier whether he would even survive to ride at Cheltenham at all, he had finished his career as the Gold Cup winner. He could hang up his boots knowing that there was nothing more he could have achieved, and it was the best feeling in the world.

Chapter Thirteen

Jason sat quietly in the passenger seat of his car letting the events of the day wash over him. Outside Cirencester Eva suddenly turned off the main road and, without comment but obviously deliberately, headed off down a country lane. Jay glanced at the rear-view mirror and saw their escort following on behind apparently unconcerned at this deviation. 'Where are we going?' he asked.

'It's a surprise.'

A few minutes later they turned through some gateposts, drove up a gravel drive and stopped in front of a small but beautiful Georgian house which Hal had rented for the three day Festival. The door opened and there was Hal beaming from ear to ear. 'Welcome to the hero!' he yelled. Inside, to Jay's bewilderment, were all the owners and trainers involved in his Cheltenham rides, even Jack Symes and the owner of Splendid Warrior, and Jed. Jay was stunned.

'We'd planned this party anyway,' Hal told him, 'but as soon as we realised what a special three days it was going to be for you we hurried round and got this crowd together. Some of them can only stay for a drink or two, but we all wanted to let you know what these three days have meant to us, as well as to you.'

As the champagne flowed, the stress and worry of the preceding weeks melted away, and Jay had a real ball reliving his races with people he cared for and who really understood what it all meant.

Eighteen of the party eventually sat down to dinner. Hal had put Fiona on one side of Jason and Pat O'Hara on the other. Pat was soon asking him when he could ride for him again and would he go over and ride some of the big races in Ireland next year. 'We'll see about that,' hedged Jay. 'But I tell you now, Oak Tree Mile could be a real contender for the Grand National next year or the year after.'

The time seemed to flash by, and all too soon the guests started to leave. 'I think it's time we were on our way, don't you?' he said to Eva.

She put her arm around him. 'Oh, but we're not going anywhere tonight.'

Hal smiled at the couple. 'Everyone who's still here is staying. Your bags have already been put into your room upstairs.'

By now Jason was beginning to feel the effects of the day. Tiredness was sweeping over him in waves. Wishing everyone goodnight he went upstairs to the room Hal showed him. Throwing off his clothes, he went into his bathroom and had a shower before clambering into bed. In seconds he was fast asleep.

He awoke with a start when somebody sat down on the bed next to him. 'Sh!' said Eva. 'Just relax.' She bent over and gently brushed his face with her lips and then moved up and caressed each of his eyes. He reached out for her. 'Lie still,' she whispered. 'I'm going to massage those aching shoulders and them I'm going to make love to the winner of the Gold Cup. If that's what he'd like, of course?'

'The perfect end to a perfect day.'

She began to soothe the tension out of this shoulders and back, and then her fingertips caressed his face, gently tracing the outline of his eyes, nose and mouth. Little shivers went through his body. Her hands moved from his face to touch and caress every part of him. The tiredness vanished and every nerve seemed alive as she slowly moved on top of him and her softness engulfed him. Her movements were slow and rhythmic, she increased the tempo of her hips until he was lost in his own sensations and controlled by her. He abandoned himself to an ecstasy of intensity he had never

146

experienced before until, exhausted, they drifted into sleep, their bodies still entwined.

The next morning Jay woke to find the bed empty. With a sigh he swung his feet to the floor, showered and shaved. Pulling on a pair of jeans which had already been laid out for him and a matching denim shirt, he slipped into a pair of casual loafers and headed downstairs.

Hal and the other guests were already having breakfast with Eva. 'How does the conquering hero feel today?' she asked.

'Damn good!' came the reply. 'Although I'm not certain it all really happened.'

'It did,' she assured him mischievously.

After a glass of orange juice and a cup of coffee, Jason rang Cheltenham Hospital. He was told that Mr Kelly was fine and could take a telephone call. Within a few minutes a familiar cheery Irish voice was on the line. 'Bloody wonderful! You're a credit to me!'

'Freddie, I'm so sorry,' said Jason. 'You missed such a fantastic ride.'

'Don't worry me boy. There'll be other chances for me. I just hope you haven't stolen all my rides on that horse.'

'Not a chance,' said Jay. 'I know who the real champion is. Are you all right?'

'Fit as a fiddle. They're letting me out this morning. Its only a crack and will be just fine in few days.'

'Would you like me to come and pick you up?'

'That'd be grand.'

On the way to the hospital Jay and Eva stopped for the newspapers, all of which were plastered with Jason's triumphs. The consensus was that the previous day had been the greatest day an amateur had ever had at Cheltenham.

At the hospital, Jay helped Freddie into the car, introduced him to Eva and set off for Lambourn. Freddie was desperate to hear how everything had gone after his dramatic exit from the racecourse, and listened eagerly to Jay's Gold Cup commentary without a hint of bitterness.

As they drew up outside Freddie's house, Jason handed him an envelope. 'What's this now?' he asked.

When Jason didn't reply, he opened it. Inside was a cheque for £20,000. 'I can't take this,' he said.

'Yes you can,' insisted Jason. 'It's not a gift. I'm buying your future services, and you'll earn every penny of it.'

'What are you talking about? Has that ride addled your brain?

'I'll tell you in a few days,' said Jay. 'But I mean it. You'll earn every penny.' He got out of the car to give Freddie a hand. At the front door of the house, he put his hands on Freddie's shoulders and looked straight into his eyes. 'It was probably the greatest day of my life, thanks to you. And I'll never forget it.'

Freddie looked embarrassed. 'Ah, think nothing of it,' he said, opening the front door. 'Thanks for everything. I'll be seeing you soon.'

'Maybe sooner than you think,' said Jay. He went back to the car and got into the driver's seat.

'Your mobile has been going mad,' said Eva. Jay picked it up. His voicemail told him to call Benny.

'I think we should let these goons go now,' said Benny. 'Have you said anything more to the Jockey Club security people?'

'Not yet,' said Jason, 'but I think it's a good idea.'

'OK, wait to hear from me again, and by then we should have a little surprise for them,' said Benny. 'I'll talk to you later today.'

Jay and Eva drove over to Midwood Park to collect the rest of their belongings before driving back to London. Eva spent the journey reading out snippets about Jay from the newspapers. 'You're not going to be able to keep your plans hidden for much longer,' she remarked to Jay. 'After yesterday, a lot of people are going to be wanting a piece of you.'

'I know,' said Jay. 'I think we ought to have dinner with Howard and Victor tomorrow, and maybe Hal as well, to catch up. But let's keep tonight for ourselves.'

A few hours later, Benny called him at the flat. 'Well, we put them in the back of an old van, with hoods over their heads and their arms handcuffed behind their backs. Then we drove them into the middle of Epping Forest, took off the cuffs and made them lie on the floor. They were told that the key was in the ignition, but if they knew what was good for them, they should stay on the floor until they heard a car hoot its horn three times. Then they could go. If they were ever seen in England again there would be real trouble for them. We drove off, stopped at a callbox and told the police that an old van loaded with drugs was on its way to London via Epping Forest. I wouldn't be surprised if they were picked up before they'd even gone anywhere. It probably took those idiots a while to work out there wasn't going to be a car horn.'

Jason laughed.

'We'd planted enough gear under the spare tyre to give the police something to think about,' Benny went on. 'We also said there was an air pistol and some darts wrapped in an old cloth under the back seat, which the head of security for the Jockey Club would be interested to see. But I'll leave that side of it to you.'

'Well, thanks for everything you've done, Benny,' Jay said. 'I think it's safe to call off your troops now. We'll settle up in a day or two. But I might have some more work for you soon. In Ireland.'

'I've always enjoyed a drop of the draught Guinness' was the instant reply.

As soon as Benny had rung off Jason called the head of security at the Jockey Club and gave him an edited version of what had happened. 'Don't ask me how I know this,' he said, 'it was an anonymous telephone call.' There was a pause at the other end, followed by an extremely sceptical laugh.

'Well, I suppose I'll have to accept that, won't I?' Giles Sinclair said. 'I'm sure I'll be hearing from the police soon. I assume there's no further action you want to take on your own account?'

'I just want to forget it happened. Not Cheltenham, obviously – just all the hassle at the start.'

'At least nothing went wrong,' said Giles with feeling.

'I have you to thank for that. I haven't really had the chance till now to tell you how much I appreciate what you and all your people did.'

'Don't mention it. That's what we're there for. If we can make life more difficult for these bastards, we will. I doubt if we'll see them around any English racetracks again, and we'll make sure our Irish colleagues know all about them too. Goodnight, Mr Jessop. And well done, again.'

By the next day, life was starting to shape itself into some semblance of normality. The weeks of being shadowed by bodyguards and even the thrill of Cheltenham were already beginning to recede. Jay had given himself a few days off from riding out, but his body clock was used to early mornings.

In his little kitchen he poured himself an orange juice and made some coffee. Hearing a footfall in the hall he turned to see Eva standing in the doorway, wearing one of his shirts. It looked like a cross between a pyjama jacket and a dressing gown on her ample-bosomed but slender figure. She walked over, put her arms around his neck and gave him a long, gentle kiss. 'Let's plan the day,' she said. He smiled to himself. It was as if they had known each other for a lifetime rather than just a few incredibly intense weeks. He poured himself a second orange juice and handed one to her. Soon they were sitting companionably at the table with steaming cups of freshly ground Blue Mountain coffee.

I think I need a day in the office after being away all week,' said Jason. Now that his company was sold, Victor had kindly lent him a room at his Aldwych offices to work in until he moved down to County View. As it was a Saturday, it would be quiet there. 'I'll call the other partners from there and try to set up a dinner tonight. I'll go to the gym for an hour on my way home this afternoon.'

Eva needed to finalise her travel plans for another trip to South Africa. Before the family house was sold she would have to dispose of its contents, deciding what to sell, what to store for shipment later to the UK and what to move to her apartment there.

'I thought I'd try to get a flight tomorrow,' she said.

Jay agreed that it made sense. 'At least the sooner you go, the sooner you will be back.'

'With a bit of luck, I should be able to wrap everything up on this visit. So when that's done, maybe it would be a good moment for us to start our new life together. After all, as I said to you once before, it seems silly to waste any more time. What do you say to me moving in here with you till we have County View up and running?'

Jason didn't need to say anything. It was crystal clear from the joyful expression on his face what he thought of her suggestion. Instead he flung his arms around her and hugged her.

At 8.45 Jason was at his desk. He rang Victor, Howard and Hal at home. Victor insisted on entertaining them at Holland Park to ensure confidentiality. 'No problem, I'll be in London this afternoon anyway,' Howard told Jay. 'I'm taking Bubbles shopping,' he added gloomily. 'But I'll have someone drive her home.'

Hal said he'd be delighted to join them. 'So Jay, with Cheltenham over, what's next on your agenda?' he asked, evidently in a chatty mood.

'I need to get over to Ireland to start looking for horses,' said Jason. 'I've already started to put out some feelers around one or two of the bloodstock agents I'm friendly with over there. And I'm going to take a few rides between now and Aintree, just enough to keep myself fit – and I'll be keeping away from novice chasers. To be honest, if I hadn't promised Jed I'd ride his horse at Aintree I would have hung up my boots as soon as Cheltenham was over. But I suppose that's easy to say now I've won the Gold Cup. That is something nobody could have predicted, least of all me.'

After finishing all his calls, Jay went round the corner to his gym to have a good workout.

By eight o'clock, they were all gathered around Victor's dining table and Jay was somewhat clumsily announcing that when Eva got back from South Africa she was going to move in with him. Highly amused by this touching shyness from someone usually so urbane and self-assured, Howard and Victor declared that Eva was mad and that the gods were clearly smiling on Jay this week. Victor, of course, immediately called for champagne for a toast but was persuaded to defer this until the business in hand had been dealt with.

Victor gave a little cough before he began. 'Jason,' he said, looking sideways at Howard. 'Howard and I have been talking about the implications of your Cheltenham performances. They seem to bring some new dimensions to our plans.'

Jay looked slightly puzzled.

'Aren't you going to have a lot of people offering you horses when it's announced that you're going to start training?'

'I don't know about a lot of people, but you're right, there are bound to be some, and it's going to be difficult.'

'Well,' said Hal, 'If anything comes up you really want let me know. We could always take one or two extra partners into our Big Apple syndicate. Although inevitably some of the owners would want sole control of their horses.'

'That's a pretty interesting thought,' said Jay. 'I'll certainly bear it in mind.'

'I think we should give some serious consideration to outside owners,' said Victor. 'If you get the opportunity to train some really top-class horses we would be crazy to turn it down out of hand. We both know your main objective, and we totally agree with it, otherwise we wouldn't have come in, but I think we've got to keep our options open.'

'The immediate problem is that everybody is going to want to know what you are going to do next. You're not going to be able to keep your plans secret for much longer. Your profile is too high. Selling your company will be public knowledge any time now. If we don't make an announcement pretty soon someone is going to find out about County View and we don't want the thing going off half-cocked.'

'I don't think there should be too much of a problem,' said Jay. 'As you know Eva is going to South Africa for a couple of weeks and I'm going to take off for Ireland to start looking for horses. I suggest we plan a press conference for, say, four weeks' time.'

Turning to Victor he asked 'Do you think we can have the new facilities looking at least interesting by that stage? How far along will the all-weather gallops be, and can we have the grass gallops at least mown and distance markers put up? That will make them look like something approaching what we want them to be.'

'No problem at all,' said Victor. 'We're prioritising the gallops and the stable blocks on the basis that, if we run short of time, the stable staff can always be put up in caravans or other temporary accommodation. So by then I'd hope to have quite a lot of work done on the stable blocks as well as the gallops. As we agreed, we'll put half-doors down the outside so that the horses can have their heads out during the day, but access will be from the inside, and in really bad weather we can close the outside doors. Otherwise I know you're a great believer in as much fresh air as possible.'

'The feed store and hay barns will be very easy to crack on with. Those old out-buildings are in very good condition and essentially they just need cleaning out on the inside and painting on the outside. Jack Rosebury has said he'll spend the next two weeks up there and the contractors are moving in on Monday to start the all-weather gallop. I'm quite convinced we'll have one, if not both, ready by the time of the press conference.'

'That sounds absolutely fine,' said Jay. 'I suggest we go for a Sunday when there is no racing, or at least no more than a couple of meetings. As long as we announce what we are going to do, we can leave the open day for a few weeks. What do you think Eva?'

'That's fine. I have a PR company in mind to help me. I'll call them from South Africa on Monday and have them sort out the catering and other practicalities, and then I can concentrate on overseeing the invitations, press packs and so on when I get back. I suppose we ought to give the press a buffet lunch?'

'There's a splendid idea!' agreed Victor. 'Let's get this off in style!'

'Do you think we'll have any horses there by then?' asked Eva.

'Well, that'll largely depend on how I get on in Ireland and also on how quickly the first set of stables is ready.'

'Now, what about outside horses?' asked Hal, returning to Victor's other point.

'I really can see what you're getting at,' said Jason. 'It's going to be difficult to turn down really good, proven young horses. But do we want to change the basic rules?'

'What we thought,' said Victor, 'is that anyone who wants to send a horse to us will have to join on the terms Eva, Howard and Hal and his syndicate have agreed. In other words, you'll have complete control and the only difference will be that in their case the horse or horses will run in their colours. By the way, we don't imagine this involving many horses, but it seems a shame to turn down one or two stars if you get the opportunity.'

'I agree in principle,' said Jason. 'But I think the personality and style of the owner must be equally important as the calibre of the horse.'

Everybody round the table nodded their support.

After one glass of champagne from the bottle Victor now opened to drink their health, Jay and Eva excused themselves on the grounds of Eva's flight the next day and the start of Jason's tough training for Aintree.

Chapter Fourteen

At the airport that Sunday Eva promised Jay that she would be back as soon as possible. 'I don't want to miss any of the excitement of seeing County View come to life,' she said.

'And there was I thinking you were going to be missing me.'

She gave him a playful punch in the ribs.

Jay found her a porter, and gave her a big hug, a kiss and a cheerful wave.

Halfway back to London his mobile rang. Pressing the hands-free button, he heard a familiar voice that made his heart sing. 'Love you, going to miss you a lot, take great care.'

'The same to you, too,' said Jay. 'I'll be thinking of you.'

At the flat he got himself ready for his trip to Ireland. That evening Jay rang Benny and asked him if he would pick him up the next morning and drive him to the airport, so that they could talk privately on the way down. At 7.30am that Monday, Jay was in the passenger seat of the old battered BMW, his bag, including his riding gear, on the back seat.

Jay expanded on the vague suggestion he had already made to Benny that he might have some more work for him and his boys in Dublin. He told Benny a little of what had happened to Sean Maguire, without of course revealing Sean's identity or the nature of his own relationship with the Irishman. 'So we could need some of your troops to come over and bring some pretty heavy pressure to bear on this so-called Friend.

Benny smiled. 'That'll be no problem guv'nor. It'll be a pleasure to continue doing business with you.'

At the Aer Lingus desk Jay was recognised by the girl checking him in. His Cheltenham exploits had made him almost a household name among the racing-mad Irish population. Emerging through the green customs exit after landing in Dublin, he spotted Sean waiting for him in the arrivals hall. But before he could reach him, Jay suddenly found himself surrounded by reporters and even a TV cameraman. The young lady at Heathrow had clearly been talking to friends in Dublin. After answering the standard questions about his experiences at Cheltenham, he was asked what had brought him to Ireland. 'I'm here for a short break. I'm going to keep myself fit by riding out for one or two of my trainer friends here, and then I'll be back to ride at the Aintree meeting,' he smiled.

Eventually they wished him luck and left him alone, by which time Sean had, quite sensibly, disappeared. Jay called him on his mobile. Sean told him to go outside to the front of the taxi rank, where he would pick him up in a couple of moments. On their way out of Dublin, to what Sean assured him was a small and discreet hotel between Naas and the Curragh, he brought Jay up to date with a total of sixteen more horses he had inspected. He had seen all of them canter and over half of them schooled. None of them was cheap and, with very few exceptions, they would be entered for top bloodstock sales later in the year. This meant that the vendors would be looking for something near the top price; otherwise, they would risk waiting until the sales.

Sean hadn't dare ride any of the horses himself for fear that somebody just might recognise his style, but he had arranged for Jason to ride anything he wanted.

'There's one in particular I think you'll like. He's a dead ringer for The Conker. In fact I thought I was looking at him when I first saw this horse.' He handed Jason a list he'd prepared of the horses, as yet unnamed except for those which had run in point-to-points. They were all bred in the Irish tradition of 'store' horses, specifically bred with National Hunt racing in mind, and most of them, although carefully fed, had spent much of their first three years in a field. A majority of Flat horses would already be racing by the time they were two years old.

Pocketing the list to study later, Jay asked Sean what news there was of the bookmaker who had set out to nobble him.

'He hasn't paid and he's disappeared. The word is there's a contract out on him, so I wouldn't like to be in his shoes.'

'What about the Friend?'

'Still up to his old tricks' said Sean. 'He's just been too clever and too careful for anything to be pinned on him. Even when any of his street dealers have been caught they've been too terrified to talk. I think he always makes sure their families don't starve, so he's got them with the carrot as well as the stick.'

An effusive welcome awaited them at the small hotel Sean had booked. Jay settled into his unfussy but comfortable room and got down to business. His first call was to Jim Newman, a trainer on the Curragh, to arrange to ride out next morning. Jay also asked the trainer to keep it quiet as he did not want his visit disrupted by the press and hangers-on. The last thing he needed in Ireland was publicity.

That evening Jay met Sean in the cosy hotel bar, to the excitement of their host who wanted to hear all about Cheltenham. Fortunately, his good manners and hospitality soon overcame his curiosity and it was not long before they were presented with two large steaks and a surprisingly good bottle of red wine. The latter, it was insisted, was on the house, but could Jay send them a signed photograph that they could frame and put on the wall? 'I'd be delighted,' said Jay warmly, 'but I'm afraid I'm getting by far the better end of the deal.'

As Danny Derkin had ridden so often for Jim Newman, Sean had dealt with him over the phone and did not go with Jay. Sitting in the trainer's kitchen just after seven the next morning Jay casually asked if there was anything for sale.

'The second one you're riding might be, but the owner would be a man who'd know his value,' said Jim cautiously.

158

Jason followed him into the yard where eighteen horses were already mounted and walking round. Jason was legged up on to the nineteenth to a hubbub of recognition. The head man rode up alongside him and told him how thrilled they all were to see him and that, in spite of having beaten a couple of the Irish great hopes, he was still welcome in the yard. 'Although you've cost a lot of the lads a week or two's wages, I can assure you!' he grinned.

They set off to the gallops at a brisk trot. After a ten-minute walk they were sorted out and cantering alongside each other in pairs, with a good twenty lengths between each pair. Jay had already learned that his mount, Peter's Pal, was a very fair young handicapper and would be running in two days in a good race at Leopardstown. If that went well he would probably be sent over to Aintree where it was expected he would compete in the John Hughes Handicap Chase, approximately two and threequarter miles over the Grand National fences. Jay was very impressed with the horse and disappointed that he wasn't for sale.

After they had cantered a second time he walked with Connor, the head lad, back to the start where two other horses were being walked round in a large circle. Both men jumped off and were legged up on to the two fresh horses by the trainer, while the two that had been exercised were sent off to join the rest of the string heading back to the yard to cool off. They were asked to go a steady canter first time, and then to go back and work at racing speed upsides for a mile and a half.

'Tell me about my horse,' said Jason as they made their way down to the start.

'Ah, he's still a bit of a big baby. He's only four years old and hasn't raced yet. You tell me what you think of him after you've ridden him.'

Jay and the head lad went up the gallop at a nice pace and the horse moved smoothly and strongly, taking a keen hold but not fighting. Jay gave an approving nod as they pulled up.

They hacked gently back to the start again. 'I'll jump off four or five lengths in the lead,' said the head lad. 'You join me when you can.'

They jumped off under the watchful eye of Jim Newman who was driving alongside in his Land Rover. As soon as Jay asked his mount to quicken there was an immediate response, and within a few yards he was sure this was the sort of horse he was looking for. By the time he had gone half a mile both horses were fairly flying and the mile and a half was over in a flash.

As they pulled up the head lad gave Jay a questioning look.

'How good's your horse?' asked Jason.

'Good enough to win three bumpers this year. How good do you think yours is?'

'Good enough to beat yours!'

'I told you he was pretty useful,' said the head lad, 'and there's more to come from him yet.' They walked over to where the trainer was waiting in his Land Rover. 'Well?' he inquired. 'Are you interested?'

'Has he ever jumped?' asked Jay.

'Sure. The fella's got a fair leap in him. Do you want to try him over a couple of hurdles?'

'I'd love to.'

'Right,' said Jim. 'Connor, you give him a lead, and he can go over the full-size hurdles.' A short hack-canter took them to the schooling grounds, where four hurdles were set up in a line. The two horses were trotted over to have a look so that they knew what was expected of them. Then they were hack-cantered half a furlong away and turned in towards the hurdle. Both were on their toes.

'Are you ready?' asked Connor.

'Sure.' The other horse was away. Jason gave him fifteen to twenty lengths' start and took off at about threequarters speed. Both horses flew all four hurdles, and Jason knew he was sitting on a natural athlete. They trotted back to Jim.

'Do you want to try it upside?' he offered.

'No, thanks,' said Jason, 'I've seen all I need to see. What's the asking price?'

'I'm not certain. Give me a call tonight and I'll let you know.'

Back at the hotel, Sean had already settled the bill and, to warm farewells and entreaties to return soon, they drove off on their day's work. Sitting in the passenger seat, Jay made extensive notes on the horses he had just ridden and took another look at the breeding and other details of the horses they were due to see that day. Two more yards and one stud were on the agenda. By the end of the day they had seen ten more horses. Jay had ridden most of those in training and made copious notes about the ones which were still unbroken. He realised how much hard work Sean had done and everything he saw confirmed that he had chosen a first-rate scout.

They checked into another small hotel for the night, and over a mercifully quiet and uninterrupted dinner they went over the horses they had seen in some detail. By the end of the evening they had all been marked out of twenty. The lowest score was fifteen, and two of them – the first horse Jason had ridden – and an unbroken gelding by the previous season's top Irish National Hunt stallion – had scored twenty.

Peter's Pal would have scored top marks, too, if he had been for sale.

With the feeling of a good day's work done, Jay telephoned Jim Newman to ask the price of his early-morning ride.

'Fifty thousand,' said the trainer.

'You told me your owner drove a hard bargain,' said Jay, 'but you didn't show me the other two horses.'

There was a chuckle at the other end. Some more good-humoured banter ensued before Jay offered thirty thousand. 'I don't think he'll take it,' said the trainer.

'Ah well, it's his horse,' said Jay, 'and his decision.'

'Will you call me tomorrow?'

'No, you call me. I'll give you my mobile telephone number. But that's my offer. Whatever happens, I thoroughly enjoyed the ride this morning. Thank you for being so kind.'

'It was a pleasure. I hope you'll do the business.'

Jay gave him his phone number and rang off.

'What will you really go to?' asked Sean, who had been following the conversation.

'Not a penny more,' declared Jay. 'But I'll offer him an extra five thousand if the horse wins before the end of next season.'

'There's a man after my own heart!' smiled Sean.

They were back in the car just before seven the next morning, with three more yards to visit, including the one where Sean had seen the dead ringer of The Conker. 'Let's stop and pick up some papers and check yesterday's racing results and tomorrow's Leopardstown card,' suggested Jason. 'If we've got time, I wouldn't mind going there and seeing how that chaser I rode yesterday gets on.'

Sean pulled up outside a general store in the next village they came to, bought the papers and handed them to Jason as he got back into the driver's seat. They drove off again and Jason opened the first paper on the pile. 'Bloody hell!' he shouted suddenly. Sean instinctively hit the brakes.

'What's up?'

Jay read the headline to him. ''Bookmaker found dead in hunting lodge.''

'Bloody hell,' echoed Sean.

Jay read on aloud. 'The body of Paddy O'Flynn, the well-known bookmaker, has been found in a burned-out fishing lodge. The police have not ruled out foul play and are awaiting the results of a post mortem to be held today.'

'Well, they didn't waste much time, did they?' said Sean. 'You can see why he was so desperate. You winning the Gold Cup as well must have been the final nail in his coffin.'

They drove on in shocked silence.

'We've got one more yard to see after the three places today. Is there any chance we could cram in a fourth?'

'Not and do it properly.'

'I really would like to go to Leopardstown tomorrow,' said Jason. 'I've had a thought. Do you think the Friend will be there?'

'It's odds-on. There's no reason why we shouldn't see the horses early in the morning and still be at Leopardstown in time for the first race. Three hours should be plenty of time to take a look at the four horses I've got marked for you there.'

'Right, that's what we'll do.'

'I'd just as soon not be seen at the course with you,' said Sean. 'I've developed my own modus operandi at the races, and I don't want anyone associating us at this stage.'

'Very sensible,' agreed Jay. 'But I do want you to be close enough to help me recognise the Friend if he should show up. We might be able to kill two birds with one stone.' He took out his mobile phone and called Benny in London.

'Benny, can you come over tomorrow with one of your brothers? Good. Meet me at Leopardstown races.' He turned to Sean. 'What's a convenient spot?'

'Why not by the parade ring before the first race?' suggested Sean.

'Did you hear that, Benny? Good. One more thing: don't have your brother with you when we meet. I'll explain why later. See you tomorrow.'

He put the phone on the dashboard.

'I'll arrange for Benny's brother to meet you exactly where I've met Benny, but after the second race, and you can show him the Friend if he's there,' he said to Sean. 'Then he'll find Benny and point out our man to him, and Benny can point him out to me. That way the chances of anybody realising that you've figured out the Friend are as remote as they could possibly be.'

'That sounds grand,' said Sean.

Jay picked up the papers again and turned to the racing pages, looking up the English results to see whether Fiona and Jed had had any winners the day before (they hadn't.)

Turning to the entries for Leopardstown, Jay saw that there were twenty-two and that the horse he'd ridden, Peter's Pal, was due to carry 10st 12lb. This was a pretty useful weight if the horse ran up to its top form which seemed likely on the evidence of his work the day before.

At their first yard of the day Jay looked at a couple of first-season winning point-to-pointers, a winning novice hurdler and two backed but unraced four-year-old geldings. They were all in the fifteen to twenty thousand bracket, and nice. Jay took further notes on one point-to-pointer, the winning hurdler and one really fine four-year-old gelding.

The next port of call was a stud where there were two three-year-old geldings and a three-year-old filly. For the first time Jay disagreed with one of Sean's choices. One gelding, although sharp and flashy, did not have enough substance for his liking. 'He might make a good hurdler, but I don't see him growing into a chaser,' was Jason's comment.

'You're probably right,' said Sean. 'Perhaps I was getting less picky by the time I got here.'

The filly, however, Jay liked enormously and scored her eighteen – the second top mark he had given to any unraced horse. He gave the other gelding fifteen, making him a definite possibility.

The last yard was owned by Marcus Fitzgerald, a top jockey in his day. Here there were only two horses to be seen, a bumper-winning five-year-old gelding whose win first time out had been followed by a hard-fought but very close second in a highly competitive race at Naas, and the unraced four-year-old that reminded Sean so strongly of The Conker. Jay did not react when it was led out, but he could hardly believe his eyes. This really was a ringer: same size, same colour, same markings – even the same carriage of the head. He asked to see both horses canter, but declined the offer to ride either.

Remaining very noncommittal about the unraced double, he enthused to the trainer about the first horse and thanked

Marcus for his time. 'I'll call you tonight,' Jay called as he got into the car.

'Well, what do you think?' asked Sean as soon as they were on their way.

'I've got to have the four-year-old,' said Jay. 'There's a very special reason. I'll tell you if we get him.'

That night he and Sean went through all the horses that they had seen and reassessed them, taking into account the different order and circumstances in which they had been viewed. Of those horses they had seen so far, Jay decided that he wanted twelve, provided, of course, that the prices were right.

Before turning in Jay telephoned Victor and Howard to bring them up to date on his progress and to check if the story about the bookmaker had hit the English press. Apparently it was not in the national newspapers but it had been reported in the *Racing Post*. He wondered whether to call the head of security at the Jockey Club, but decided he was bound to have picked up the news himself. And the less Jason was connected with the whole affair, the better.

Chapter Fifteen

The two horses to be seen the next day had both been placed in a point-to-point. These had been their only runs. Although one had come second and the other third, Sean felt both of them had a lot of scope to develop as they had fine, strong frames. The differing rules in Ireland and England meant that they could both run in National Hunt Flat races the following year before starting a hurdling campaign or going straight into novice chases. Jay would make offers for both of them if he liked their looks and action.

By seven they were sitting in the kitchen at a small but very neat yard. They politely declined the offer of a full breakfast but did accept a second cup of the delicious coffee percolating on the stove.

Lanky Murphy had earned his nickname as the tallest, and thinnest, Irish National Hunt jockey of his time. 'I've got a third horse you might be interested in,' he said. 'Since Sean was here, unhappily the owner has died, and the widow has asked me to get rid of the horse as quickly as possible. She doesn't want the training fees.'

'Tell us about it.'

'He's a five-year-old; came second in a bumper. He was very green in his first hurdle race, made a lot of mistakes, but managed to come fifth. Next time he ran he came second in a pretty good novice hurdle at Clonmel. The way he's developing, I'm quite convinced he will get two and a half miles, if not three, and he's getting stronger every day. Anyway, have a look at him.'

As soon as they had finished their coffee they went into the yard. Twelve horses were ready, including the new contender.

Three were brought into the middle. Jay gave them all an appraising look, felt their legs and, finding no sign of any problem, he nodded for them to be mounted. He and Sean followed them to the gallops in Lanky's Land Rover. At the start of the gallops was a sand circle which the string were trotted round a few times and then circled at a very slow hack-canter. All were settled apart from the novice hurdler, My Final Fling, which was bucking and squealing.

'He's really ready for a run,' said Lanky. 'Since the owner took ill, I haven't been able to take the risk of him being injured in case they decided to sell him.'

At a signal from the trainer the horses moved across to the seven-furlong uphill gallop and set off in single file. They travelled at no more than half pace. Reaching the top, most of them walked off home, but four of them, including those Jay was interested in, stayed back.

'I'm going to work that hurdler with Silver Prince. He's won two novice chases and he's no slouch. The other two can go up at threequarter pace, unless you want them to go faster?'

'Suits me fine,' said Jay.

On the nod from Lanky the horses turned away and cantered down to the start.

The two leading horses strode out upsides at racing pace. My Final Fling, nearest to Jay, stayed with Silver Prince until the last furlong and as the gallop quickened he was still with the mature horse. The other two went past well within themselves but both were moving with an elegant stride that convinced Jay they had real potential.

'How much does the widow want for the hurdler?' he asked.

'Her name is Kate Harty. She's asking twenty sterling, but I'm sure she'll take a little less for a quick sale.'

'I'll want him vetted, and that can be done within the next two or three days – Jack O'Hanlan's my vet over here and he'll do it.'

'Ah, I know Jack well,' Lanky replied.

'You'll get the money the day after the horse passes,' said Jay.

'How can I get hold of you?' asked Lanky. Jay took out a business card and wrote his mobile number on the back.

'How long are you in Ireland?'

'Until tomorrow.'

'You're welcome to ride out here in the morning, if it suits.'

'That would be great – thanks very much,' said Jason.

Back in the kitchen they were given another cup of the coffee that seemed to be constantly brewing by Lanky's cheerful wife who was as rotund as he was thin. Jay shook Lanky's hand. 'I'll be in touch about the other two within two or three days.' Both horses were owned by Lanky himself, so Jay was sure he could get a good deal for the pair. 'If Mrs Harty agrees the price after the vetting I'll have your two vetted at the same time.' He paused, then decided to strike while the iron was hot. 'I'll give you 25,000 for the two – and I won't be asking for any "luck money,"' he added amiably. This traditional Irish 'discount' could take as much negotiating as the original price.

Sean drove, as usual, as they headed for Leopardstown. But a mile from the racecourse he pulled over and got out of the car. He was going to complete the journey under his own steam and meet up with Jason after the races at a café they had passed en route, well away from the course.

Jason slid over into the driver's seat. 'Remember,' he said through the window, 'if you don't find the Friend straight away, just keep looking and meet Benny's brother Harry after each race at a different place until the end of the afternoon. Good luck.'

Arriving at the racecourse alone, Jason showed his jockey's identity to the gatekeeper at the owners, trainers and jockeys entrance and was ushered into the car park as if he were a film star. He was given the same treatment when he presented himself at the window for admittance to the grandstand area. Irish racing friends and acquaintances all greeted him like a conquering hero. Since his name was not among the riders that afternoon, they wanted to know what he was doing at Leopardstown. 'Just enjoying myself at one of the great Irish National Hunt courses. A bit of a busman's holiday,' he told everyone. A couple of trainers assured him earnestly that if he wanted rides they could certainly fix him up within the next day or two, and that if he didn't he was most welcome to go and ride out for them if he wanted some exercise.

As soon as the first race was over he made his way to the parade ring. He was suddenly aware that Benny was standing beside him, apparently having materialised from nowhere. 'Harry,' said the East Ender, out of the corner of his mouth, 'was watching them discreetly.' They wandered away non-chalantly and watched the second race, a handicap hurdle which resulted in a close, hard-ridden finish between two of the Irish jockeys against whom Jason had ridden only a few days earlier at Cheltenham.

After a drink they picked a spot overlooking the parade ring and waited. It was not long before Sean arrived, a folded copy of the *Racing Post* in his left hand. Almost immediately Harry appeared and shook hands with Sean whilst thumping him on his back as if he had known him all his life. Together they cast a professional-looking eye over the runners in the next race before moving off to place what Jay knew would be very modest bets with the bookmakers in front of the stands.

This was the race in which the steeplechaser was running. The entry of fourteen horses had been whittled down to nine by the overnight declaration stage and Peter's Pal was still carrying 10st 12lbs with four horses weighted above him. Wandering down to the bookmakers, Jason saw that the horse was the third favourite at $5\frac{1}{2}$ – 1. He put £200 each way on it – an unusually big bet by his standards. By this time the horses were circling at the start and the last-minute procedures being completed. When the tape was released the horses set off in a tight group at a pace that was certain to test their stamina over the two and a half miles ahead of them. At the end of the first mile they were all still closely bunched and all had been jumping with the fluency to be expected of good handicappers.

With half a mile to go the pace was beginning to tell on the two top weights, and Peter's Pal and three others were starting to move steadily away from the other five runners. It was at this stage that the first mistake occurred. The leading jockey asked his horse to stand off and make a really big jump. At the last moment the horse decided to put in a short stride and got too close to the fence. Hitting it, he stumbled on landing and, although the jockey did well to stay seated, by the time horse and rider had collected themselves the other three had gained a valuable three to four lengths. As they approached the last three fences the jockey on one of the remaining first three horses had his whip out. His mount was beginning to show some signs of distress as the pace increased rather than slackening. The other two jumped the fence economically, the third was somewhat careful and came out a good length behind the leaders. It was clear to Jay that it was now a two-horse race. Both jockeys were still riding with hands and heels as they approached the second last, and both cleared it stride for stride. The winning post was in sight as whips were raised coming up to the last and again they were in the air together. This time, however, Peter's Pal quickened significantly under the strong driving of his rider and passed the post two lengths clear. Jason, turned to Benny, his face flushed with triumph. 'Well, that'll pay for my trip anyway,' he announced.

While Jay went to collect his winnings, Benny went to meet Harry. He returned to the bar to tell Jay that the Friend was indeed on the course, and that he was now joining Harry to have him pointed out.

'Evidently he isn't too hard to spot,' grinned Benny. 'He's wearing a yellow waistcoat and a black-spotted yellow tie. By the way, he seems to have something in common with you.'

'And what's that?'

'He chain-smokes cigars.'

'I hardly chain-smoke them!' retorted Jay indignantly.

'I've seen you when there wouldn't be many minutes between one and another.' Benny winked and disappeared into the crowd.

Tut tutting to himself, Jay stalked off to the unsaddling enclosure to congratulate Jim Newman, who introduced him to Peter's Pal's owner, Frank Donovan.

'It's just possible I'll run this horse in the amateur race at Aintree instead of the John Hughes,' Frank told him. 'Would you consider riding him in either?'

'Most certainly. Let's talk nearer the day.'

Frank handed him a glass of champagne. 'I'm going to be spending quite a lot of time in England next season,' the owner went on. 'I wonder if you could recommend a trainer who would look after Peter's Pal if I moved him there? Obviously I'd be very happy for you to have the rides on him.'

'Oh I'm sure I could do that,' said Jay. He would be very keen to add this horse to his string if Frank Donovan agreed. 'Give me about a week and I'll come back to you. I'll definitely let you know what I would suggest by the time we meet at Aintree, if you decide to run him there.'

After a decent interval, he excused himself, shook hands with Jim and Frank and went off in search of Benny.

It was a good ten minutes before Benny reappeared. 'Well, I've seen your man all right,' he said. 'And a nastier bit of work you'd have to go a long way to find. He's in the bar behind us.' He jerked his head backwards almost imperceptibly.

Jay resisted the temptation to look in the direction of the bar. 'Good work,' he said. 'All I wanted from today was to make sure that you and Harry had a good long look at him so that you can recognise him. You might need to identify him in the dark. Now I'd like you to go back to London and organise a team to come over here in a few days' time. I want you to come separately, and I want one person with a convincing American accent.'

'No problem there. I can get you the real thing. My mate Vince is over from Chicago for a while, and they don't come much more American than him.'

You'll need to find an empty warehouse, as isolated as possible with easy access day or night, and room to keep a van and at least three cars in it. I want you to get a tent set up inside it and to provision it for four or five men to be able to live there for up to five days without drawing any attention to themselves.'

Benny gave him a hard look. 'This sounds like a kidnapping job to me,' he commented.

'It is, but it shouldn't take that long. I'll tell you all when we get back to London. Keep me posted on how things are going, but don't say anything too explicit on the phone.'

'Understood. Anything else?'

'That's it for now. Can you pick me up at Heathrow at two o'clock tomorrow? We can talk then.'

They parted without any telltale gestures of farewell and Jason strolled casually into the bar where Benny had seen the Friend. As Benny had remarked, he certainly was an unpleasant-looking character, and his flamboyant dress sense was hardly the mark of a man who liked to keep a low profile. Jay smiled to himself. It was a trait that, if all went according to plan, would prove his undoing.

Leaving the car park before the last race, Jay drove to the roadside cafe earmarked for his rendezvous with Sean and ordered himself a mug of extremely strong tea. Sean arrived some time later in a cab, nodded briefly to Jason through the window and went straight to the car. Jason folded up the newspaper he had been reading and went to join him.

Sean took the wheel once more and they drove off towards Naas, where they were going to spend the final night of Jay's trip in the small, friendly hotel they'd stayed in when he arrived. Their conversation about the events of the day was interrupted by a phone call from Lanky Murphy. To his surprise, he said, Kate Harty had accepted Jason's offer, on one condition. The horse must run in her late husband's colours, which she realised meant transferring them to Jay. Jason considered the implications, in particular the fact that it had already been agreed that Eva's diamonds would be the stable's main colours. 'It's possible we can do that,' he told Lanky. 'But Mrs Harty must understand that they would be second colours, and that other horses might also run in them from time to time.' He reminded Lanky that he would have to get clearance from the colours department at Weatherbys which controls entries, colours, horses' names and so on for the Jockey Club and the British Horseracing Board. The trainer said he would explain all this to the widow.

The more Jay thought about it, the less he saw it as a problem, particularly as the partners had already recognised that there would be a few horses running in individual owners' colours if the right horses were offered. He made a note to call Weatherbys first thing the next day. He then rang Jack O'Hanlan and told the vet he'd like him to examine approximately twenty horses at a number of different locations as soon as possible. He promised to fax over the details as soon as he got back to London, by which time he would have agreed prices with most of the owners – or not as the case may be.

At the Naas hotel, Jason and Sean were once again welcomed with open arms. In the bar Jason asked for a bottle of champagne. They both deserved it, he told Sean, and anyway he felt a modest celebration was in order after his winning bet that afternoon. The bar was fairly busy, but not noisy, so they sat down with their bottle of champagne against the pleasant background hum of conversation punctuated by the voice of a newsreader coming from the television in the corner.

At the edge of his consciousness he became aware that the newsreader was talking about the discovery of the body of the bookmaker, Paddy O'Flynn. He looked up at the television to see pictures of a burned-out building on the edge of a lake.

'A post mortem has revealed that a considerable level of alcohol and an unspecified illegal drug were present in the body,' an on-the-spot reporter was saying. 'Although foul play has not been completely ruled out, all reports so far point to an unfortunate accident.'

Sean gave Jay a sceptical look but they said nothing, quietly returning their attention to their list.

The next morning Jay went off to ride out at Lanky's, leaving Sean to check them out and arrange for the use of a small meeting room in the hotel. Sean had already arranged that they could make telephone calls later. He rode just one lot and then sat down to do business with Lanky. Over a cup of the ever-present coffee and with surprisingly little haggling it was agreed he would purchase all three horses, provided, of course, that they passed the vet. Protesting that surely Jay could stay a little longer and ride a few winners for him, the trainer saw him to his car and waved him off.

Back at the hotel Jay agreed offer prices with their trainers on all the horses except for two, which Jay rejected out of hand when he was told that their owners wanted significantly more than he was prepared to put on the table. This left only the first day's unraced horse whose owner still had not telephoned.

Jay deliberately did not mention this horse in his conversation with Jim Newman. Eventually the trainer raised the subject and asked Jay if he had any further thoughts. Jay reminded him that he had left the ball in the owner's court and said that he had no intention of chasing after him. He had made what he thought was a perfectly fair offer and that was as far as he would go. He hesitated, as if a thought had suddenly struck him. 'I tell you what,' he said. 'Say to him that I'll give him an extra five thousand if the horse wins within twelve months of being owned by me. But that really is my last offer.'

174

There was a chuckle at the other end of the line. 'That might just clinch it. One of us will let you know before the day's out.'

Jay's last call was to Marcus Fitzgerald, the trainer and owner of Conker's double. He agreed a price for the horse and then said something that astonished Sean. 'Marcus, this deal is strictly between us. I don't want anyone to know that I have bought the horse, and I want you to continue training it, but I don't want it to run. You and I will talk weekly as to its progress. I will of course pay you full training fees.'

There was a flabbergasted silence from Marcus. 'Well, Jay, your wish is my command,' he said eventually. 'That sounds like an extremely good deal: money in the bank for me and training fees on top. I can certainly keep my mouth shut for a deal like that!'

'Try to register it under the name Surprise Packet if you can,' Jay requested.

When he put down the phone Sean appeared to be still in shock.

'One of these days I'll tell you the whole story,' said Jay. 'I think that horse looks so like The Conker that it might give us the opportunity to have a big gamble one day.'

Sean's expression changed from shock to disbelief.

'No, Sean,' Jay laughed. 'I'm not going to start running ringers. But if a horse that looked like The Conker ran a not particularly good gallop after racing at a major track, as long as no one said anything we just might see Conker's odds improve.'

'Jesus,' replied Sean. 'And there was me thinking you were as innocent as the day is long.'

'I am,' said Jay, a twinkle in his eye. 'But someone's got a big debt to collect, and I'm going to help him.' He looked at his watch. 'Right. We had better get going – I've a plane to catch.'

On the way to Dublin Airport, Jay outlined to Sean his plans for the new syndicate. 'When you reappeared as Sean I told you I might have a long-term job for you. Well, I'd like you to come and be my head man or chief work rider.'

Sean looked thrilled, but then a shadow crossed his face. 'Isn't that tempting providence? I might be recognised.'

'I've thought about that. For a start, I think that within the next two to three weeks the Friend will cease to be a problem.' He held up his hand before Sean had a chance to speak. 'Don't ask any questions. Just leave everything to me. I just need his address and a list of the places you know he frequents. Names of his cronies would be a help too. You can give that information to Benny when he comes back to Dublin in a couple of days' time. Secondly, in the early days I wouldn't expect you to go to the races, at least not with me. We'll get a really good deputy head man or assistant trainer, and you can keep behind the scenes.'

At the airport they continued their conversation in low voices at a corner table in the noisy restaurant. Sean had immediately accepted the salary Jay had suggested to him and he was full of excited questions about the new operation. Jay told him he hoped to have first claim on Freddie Kelly when Jack Symes retired at the end of the season. He wanted a very good young stable jockey, too, and he had in mind Paul Jenkins who had beaten him at Plumpton. Since then the lad had been going from strength to strength. Jay ordered a half bottle of champagne and they clinked glasses to clinch the deal. Earnestly, but with a little embarrassment, Sean leaned across the table and took both Jay's hands. 'I'll never forget your kindness, and you know you can always rely on me,' he whispered.

'Of course. That's why I want you next to me. Who was it who came to England at great risk to himself to warn me that bookie was out to get me? That's something I won't forget. Once you're the other side of the Irish Sea we'll have no secrets and we'll be a great team.'

Chapter Sixteen

Benny was waiting for Jason at Heathrow. As they sped into London Jay filled him in, without blowing Sean' cover, on the nefarious activities of the man identified for him at Leopardstown. 'And if that wasn't enough, I'm almost certain that he is responsible for the death of the bookie whose body was found while I was in Ireland. There are any number of reasons to put this crook safely behind bars.' He outlined what he wanted Benny to do. Benny listened with rapt attention, and for the second time that day Jay found he had taken by surprise a man who knew him pretty well. 'I'm a bad bloke to cross,' he said, by way of explanation. 'And that goes for people who cross my friends, too.'

Jay changed the subject. There was something else he needed to clear up with Benny before they reached the flat. 'Now, I know Howard took care of the money side over the Cheltenham business, but I must owe you a fair bit for everything you've done since then, so I'll need to square you up before you go to Ireland again.'

'You don't owe us a penny,' said Benny. 'It's all been taken care of by Howard. He's paying me a regular retainer plus expenses for organising his security services.'

There was no point, Jason knew, in protesting to Benny. He would have to take it up with his partner. Howard was generous to a fault, but there was no question of him footing the bill for all this. But first he needed to discuss the Conker situation with him. He phoned Howard.

'Let's have breakfast tomorrow with Victor, if you're both free, so that I can bring you up to date,' he suggested. 'But I'd like to see you on your own first. Shall we say a quarter to eight at Simpson's?'

Benny dropped Jay off at his front door. 'There's a fair bit of organisation ahead of me,' he said with a wry smile.

'Best to say as little as possible to anyone until you've got the team there, and then only two or three of you need be involved with the final stages,' advised Jay.

'Right you are, guv'nor.' With a cheery wave, he disappeared around the corner.

Although Eva's presence in the flat was so recent, already the place seemed empty without her. Jason smiled ruefully to himself at the thought of how quickly she had transformed his life. She had been phoning regularly from South Africa – indeed, there was a new fond message on the answerphone now. He was staggered by how much he missed her. As the flat was so quiet he decided to work there for the rest of the afternoon. He telephoned Weatherbys and checked that the late Mr Harty's colours could be transferred to him, which, as long as the executors agreed, would be no problem. Payment for the registration of colours had already been made for the rest of the season, and so there was no question of anyone else having the opportunity of getting them. He made notes for his breakfast meeting with Victor and Howard.

In the evening he took a break and walked into Soho where he enjoyed a large plate of antipasto followed by spaghetti alle vongole at the Capanina restaurant in Romilly Street, a genuine Italian restaurant with a family atmosphere and food that would be hard to beat in its owner's native country. To hell with my diet, he thought.

Returning to his flat at 9.30, he telephoned Fiona and arranged to go and see her in a couple of days' time, probably on his way back from checking how work was progressing at County View. He turned his attention to the cash flow projections Victor and Howard had prepared for him. He was deep in concentration when the phone rang and was rather slow getting the handset to his ear. 'Is that you Jay?' asked a familiar voice. It was Jed.

'It is. Sorry – I had my nose in some figures. How are you?'

'Well, to be honest that's why I'm phoning. I've had a bit of a shock. I haven't been feeling too well for the last week or two, so I went to see the doctor. It seems I have a bit of heart problem. It's nothing very serious and can easily be controlled with drugs, but I've been told I've got to take things easier. In particular I've got to stop driving round the country like a maniac.'

'I'm really sorry to hear that,' said Jay, slightly alarmed.

'Well, it could be a lot worse,' Jed told him cheerfully, 'although I've been told I've got to cut my smoking down too.'

'That might not be quite so easy,' Jay sympathised.

'Anyway,' Jed went on. 'Cathy and I have been having a long chat, and we've decided that the time has come for me to give up this place.' He gave a slightly embarrassed cough. 'I know it's probably something that you wouldn't even consider, but I've always thought you'd be a good trainer. A damn good trainer in fact. And I just wondered if you'd consider taking over this yard. I'd be very willing to help as long as I could cut things down.'

'Hell,' breathed Jay. 'This is a bit of a bolt from the blue.' He paused. 'Look, Jed, as luck would have it, I've been working on something which just might fit in with this, but then again it might not. I need to get my head around it. Could you give me a couple of days to think about it?'

'Of course. I hardly expected you to say yes on the spur of the moment, but Cathy and I both felt, having got to know you so well, that you were the person we'd like to talk to first.'

'I'm flattered. I really am, Jed. And I promise you I'll come back to you very soon.'

'No problem.'

'I could come down and have a chat with you the day after tomorrow. I tell you what, why don't we make it the evening? If you don't mind putting me up for the night, we could have our talk then and I could ride out the next morning. We could discuss this Aintree race as well.'

'That's bloody marvellous. I'll look forward to seeing you, and I won't mention this to anyone else.'

'My own plans mean I'll have to talk to two other people, but we can trust them implicitly, I guarantee. Are you happy with that?'

'Sure. It's going to come out fairly soon anyway.'

'All right, old friend, just look after yourself. And take the doctor's advice.'

'Oh, I'll do that all right – Cathy will make sure of it.'

When Jay put the phone down, he went and poured himself a cup of coffee from the nearby percolator and thought hard. The agenda for his breakfast meeting was getting longer by the hour.

The next morning Jason was sitting in Simpson's shortly after 7.30. Promptly at 7.45 the ever-ebullient Howard bounced up to his table, grinning from ear to ear and wearing an expectant look. They asked for orange juice but told the attentive Peter they would wait for Victor before ordering breakfast.

'So,' said Howard. 'What was it you wanted to talk to me about?'

Jason told him about The Conker lookalike in Ireland. 'I've agreed to buy him, but I'm going to leave him there. Nobody except Sean and the trainer knows about him. When we have The Conker running in a race we're sure he can win, I'll bring the Irish horse over and work him with two good horses at a racecourse beforehand. It's highly unlikely that a young horse like that could possibly live with them at a real racecourse gallop. I'll make sure that the form-watchers know that the workout is taking place. All you have to do is place a substantial bet with Frankie Johnson at inflated odds. My worry is whether he'll try and lay it off.'

'The chances are he won't,' Howard calculated. 'He's so damned greedy. But just in case, the minute I'm ready to make the bet, I'll phone Harry Boston and tell him to spread the word that if Frankie tries to lay off a bet, nobody should accept it.' Looking up, he saw a familiar figure bearing down on them. 'Good morning Victor,' he said.

Victor raised one eyebrow. 'Well, I hope it wasn't our figures that prompted this meeting to be called at such short notice,' he said to Jay.

'Oh no,' said Jay, 'they look fine. We all knew that expenditure would far outrun income for the first few months. To be honest, it's not as bad as I thought it might be.'

Victor sat down. 'I think there's every chance that once the press conference has been called, we'll have sponsors of various sorts queuing up,' Victor told him. 'And they can make a hell of a difference, even to those figures, which, as you say, are far from discouraging already.'

'Victor's right,' agreed Howard. 'Believe it or not, my son Andy has even said he'd like his company to be involved in some way. He might well want to sponsor the horseboxes.'

'So what's the main item?' asked Victor, once Peter had taken their breakfast order.

'I just wanted to update you on the horses, but in fact something more pressing has arisen since we arranged this meeting,' said Jay. 'I had a rather interesting telephone conversation last night...'

When they heard about Jed's call, Howard and Victor both looked at him with some surprise. 'Surely, after all we've done, you wouldn't think of buying Jed's yard?' said Victor incredulously.

'Strangely enough, it might not be a bad idea, in one sense. It could be a place where we could put young, injured and resting horses. But that's not what I'm really concerned with.'

'You both know, and you in particular Howard, that I've always had a very high regard for Jed's abilities. He has just never had owners, other than you, who could afford to buy him the sort of horses that can win really big races. But when you look at the way he's placed his horses, and always managed to come out on top in a few decent handicaps, the man really does know what he's doing.'

'So?' queried Victor.

'What about if I brought him in as my assistant? He'd be there most of the time. He could go to other meetings if we've got runners at two places on the same day, he's brilliant with stable staff and he's got a few horses that I'd be happy to have in the yard. Though we'd have to be brutal and explain to him and his owners that many of them are just not what we're looking for.'

The two older men sat back and thought while Jay handed round the toast Peter had brought.

'You know I've always thought the guy's an ace,' said Howard. 'He's as honest as the day is long and he's always done well by me.'

'I don't know him as well as you two,' admitted Victor, 'but I've always heard good things of him, and if you can work with him, Jay, it seems like a hell of a good idea. How many of his horses do you think you'd want?'

'The owners might not want to move, of course, especially as they're going to have to pay our fees, but I was thinking in terms of six or seven, including all of yours, Howard – that is if we decide to keep them all. I know you've already said that Pewter Queen would come to me, and I've always felt a bit guilty about that as she and The Conker are undoubtedly the best horses that Jed would have trained next year.'

'Well,' said Howard, 'it sounds to me like the best of all possible worlds. What about accommodation for Jed and Cathy?'

'I don't think that would be too much of a problem,' said Victor. 'I've been looking at the building that was the administration block. It seems a shame to turn it into storage. It could be made into a very nice three-bedroomed house with a large kitchen/dining room and a decent-sized living room, if you think that would suit him. What's more, at this stage, he could be involved in it being designed more or less as he wanted, within reason.'

'I think he'd jump at it,' said Jay. 'He's never been one for luxury, and I'm sure Cathy would love the idea of having something a bit easier to run than that ramshackle place they live in at the moment.'

Howard nodded in agreement, but he looked pensive. 'I think that's all fine, but I'm not at all sure about having a second yard, Jay. 'It's not the money. I can see it just being too much of a drain on your time, which in the early stages I just don't think will be viable. In my view it would be better if Jed could sell it. That would give him some capital. If he can't or doesn't want to, why don't we try to lease it for him, with an option to buy in a couple of years' time when we've got the new establishment really bedded down and we have more idea about where we want to go next?'

Jay pondered this. 'You're probably right,' he said. 'Are you both happy for me to go and talk to Jed along those lines tomorrow night?'

'Absolutely,' said Howard. Victor nodded.

With that out of the way, they concentrated on their smoked salmon and scrambled eggs and talked about the Irish horses Jason had bought. 'There's something else I wanted to discuss,' he said when that subject had been dealt with. 'I've also got a head man in mind. But what I'm going to tell you is strictly between ourselves.' As he related the full Danny Derkin saga, including the death in highly suspicious circumstances of the bookmaker, Paddy O'Flynn, their jaws dropped. Even Victor was too astounded to touch his Danish pastries.

'How the hell are you going to handle that?' asked Victor, horrified. 'It's all very well him hiding in the way he has up until now, but if he's going to be part of one of the highest-profile racing operations in the UK somebody's going to spot him, or start asking difficult questions.'

'I know,' said Jay, 'but I think the problem is going to be solved.'

'And how exactly do you propose to solve it?' Howard was equally unnerved by this development.

Jay hesitated. 'I don't think you need to know too much about it. Suffice it to say that Howard's friend Benny and I are working on the matter. Perhaps that will reassure you a little. I'd be very surprised if we're not able to announce who Sean really is by the time we have the press conference.'

'Well, that should give the hacks something to think about,' said Victor with feeling. 'I can see why you might want to reveal his identity then, but what about holding it off until a little later?' reasoned Howard. The opening of our yard is going to get an enormous amount of coverage, and if Jed is going to join us as well, that's going to be another huge story. Wouldn't it be better to wait a month or two to announce the Danny thing? Otherwise we'll be dropping all our bombshells at once, whereas if we stagger them it'll keep us in the racing headlines for a good long while.'

'That makes sense to me,' said Victor, 'but we're getting ahead of ourselves. Besides, as a PR matter, this is Eva's pigeon. First we need to be sure it's safe to unmask Danny, and when it is we'll need to take Eva's guidance as to the hows and whens.'

'She doesn't know any of this yet, obviously,' conceded Jay. 'We'll have to put our heads together when she gets back and see what she advises.'

'And in the meantime, you're not going to tell us any more about your plans for this Friend?' asked Howard, intrigued.

'No,' said Jason firmly. 'And don't give Benny a hard time about it. I know he's your pal, and I am very grateful indeed that you introduced me to him, but on this occasion I want both of you out of it. If anything goes wrong, let me carry the can.' With some reluctance they both agreed to leave him to it.

By this time Victor was running late for his next meeting, so they collected their coats and said their goodbyes. Outside, on the Strand, Howard and Jason watched his retreating figure hurrying in the direction of the Aldwych. Howard patted Jay on the shoulder. 'God, you're a dark horse,' he said admiringly as he turned to go down the street and into his waiting car.

Jay took out his mobile phone and called Benny. 'I need to spend an hour in a gym later. Is there one that you use regularly we could use to meet?'

Jason's taxi pulled up outside the shabby-looking gym in the East End. Not knowing the area, he had thought it wise to leave his car at home. According to Benny, the place was used mainly by young boxers. The owner was a friend of his, so they would be able to have a private chat after Jason's workout rather than trying to talk while exercising.

Jason swung his holdall out of the back seat and paid the driver. In the lobby of the gym he was greeted by a man in his fifties whose face told the story of his earlier profession. Despite his years, he was clearly still in shape. 'I've been expecting you, but we won't be using names, will we?' he said, tapping his fearsome nose with a finger. He led Jay to a small changing room and, with a cheery smile, invited him to use whatever he wanted, when he wanted. 'Benny's already here and working up a fair old head of steam,' he added.

Jay opted first for the rowing machine, to strengthen and tone up the muscles he used in raceriding, varying his routine with other pieces of apparatus that would achieve the same effect. After forty-five minutes of non-stop exercise, he went for a shower, standing first under almost scalding and then ice-cold jets. By the time he had changed his host had appeared. He beckoned Jay to follow him down a small corridor. At the end was a small but extremely tidy office with walls covered in pictures of boxers and other sporting celebrities. Benny was sitting in a huge brown leather chair with a bottle of Lucozade in his hand. 'Will you join me?' he asked, walking over to the refrigerator in the corner.

'Plain mineral water would suit me better if there is some.'

'Of course.'

Jay settled himself in a second, equally voluminous chair. Benny nodded to their host. 'You won't be disturbed,' said the older man, leaving them to it and closing the door firmly after him.

'Right,' said Benny, getting down to business. 'I know you want to see this geezer in jail. How do we get from kidnapping him to putting him behind bars?'

'The perfect justice would be if he went down for drug-dealing, but we'd have to pin it on him. It seems highly unlikely we'd be able to get him to confess, however much we frighten him. And I don't want to go further than frightening him.'

'So you're saying you want us to frame him?'

'That's my idea,' said Jay. 'But it means getting hold of some drugs, and you know I'm not into that.'

'I might be able to help you there. One of my friends discovered one of his cross-Channel lorry drivers was smuggling in all kinds of stuff, including drugs. He's got rid of him, but he's not quite sure what to do with the contraband – particularly the drugs. If he hands them in to the police he's worried he'll get dragged into it.'

'Can we get them into Ireland?' asked Jay.

'I'm sure I can,' said Benny, 'but leave that to me. The less you know about it, the better.'

'I suggest you all go over tomorrow and buy the second-hand cars and vans you need.' Jason produced a wad of Euros from his holdall. 'It's a biggish expense, so here's some cash to help you with that. Take enough clothes to be able to change your basic appearance. One police uniform would be handy.'

They discussed where Benny's team should stay, agreed an alias for him and finalised a few other details. 'I'll get Sean to meet you at your motel tomorrow evening,' Jay told him. 'He'll have some information for you on this guy's haunts and associates. Good luck.'

'They shook hands and Jason left Benny in the office. On his way out he stopped to ask the ex-boxer how much he owed him. 'Ah, if you're a friend of Benny's, the answer's nothing,' he said. 'He's done me many a good turn.'

Back at flat he called Sean and told him where to meet Benny who would be checking in as Mr Franklin. Sean was to brief Benny as fully as he could on the Friend's usual movements and then the next day perhaps he could take Benny and a couple of his brothers for a gentle drive round the relevant areas so that they could get their bearings.

His second job was to fax Jack O'Hanlan the details of all the horses he wanted vetted in Ireland. There was one horse missing from the list: Surprise Packet. Once the fax was dispatched, Jason phoned an English vet he knew very well and arranged for him to go over and check this horse which, he told the vet, a friend of his was thinking of buying.

When he put down the phone his head was buzzing. He poured himself a large gin and tonic and stretched out on the sofa.

Chapter Seventeen

The morning brought the welcome news in a telephone call from Eva that she would be back at the weekend.

In high spirits as he prepared to leave for County View, on the spur of the moment Jay rang Hal to see whether he'd like to go with him to have a look at how the work was coming on. There was a pause while Hal flipped the pages of his appointments book. 'There's nothing I can't change. When do you want to go?'

'In a couple of hours? We could stop on the way for a pub lunch.'

'Sounds great,' said Hal. 'I love your English pubs. Shall I phone Bart and Len and see if they're free?'

'If they can make it at this short notice, they'd be very welcome,' said Jay.

So it was that, a little after one, the three Americans were gliding down the M4 in Hal's chauffeur-driven Bentley, following Jason's E-Type Jaguar. At Lambourn they pulled in at the Pheasant, one of the favourite watering holes of the Lambourn racing community, for a quick beer and a sandwich before piling back into their cars and driving on to County View.

The transformation was apparent almost as soon as they'd gone through the entrance. Howard and Victor really had set about putting the place to rights. The grass gallops had been mowed and already little white markers were showing the furlong distances. The main all-weather gallop had been excavated and the drainage stone base laid, and it was now in the process of being levelled ready for the drainage membrane. The addition of a top surface of fibre-sand would be relatively simple and quick.

They parked outside the buildings and walked into the main section which would soon be the stable block. Windows had been cut into the outside wall so that half-doors could be fitted and the inside partitions were already in place. All that remained here was for the stable doors, already piled up in one corner of the old hangar, to be fitted.

Murmuring their approval to one another, the four of them strolled over to the accommodation area. A young and enthusiastic man in jeans and a denim shirt came striding across to them. 'Good morning, Mr Jessop. Good morning gentlemen – my name's Henderson and I'm Mr Victor's building foreman here.'

'This is Mr Bancroft, Mr Eastington and Mr Lavinger,' Jay said to the foreman, who shook everyone's hand.

'You're doing a fine job young man,' said Hal.

'Thank you,' said Henderson.

'I expect you'd like to see how the accommodation's coming along?' He was already leading the way.

'Everyone calls him "Hurry",' explained Jay.

What was to be Jay's house and office was well advanced as little of the general structure had had to be significantly changed. A conservatory-type extension had been added. It had a view of the yard and would be the office. It was clear why Victor had chosen this man. It was an impressively professional job.

'We'll have this finished in two to three weeks,' said Hurry. 'And if you want fitted carpets and things like that, there's no reason why you shouldn't have people down here by the end of next week.'

'That's fantastic,' said Jay. 'Now, what about the staff quarters?'

'I've made arrangements for that block over there to be converted into temporary lavatories and washrooms and I thought we could put the mobile homes over there. I understand you want about fifteen people to start with?'

'That's right,' confirmed Jay. 'And we're going to need accommodation for up to twenty-five when we get going, of course.'

'We're planning on four units with a bedroom, sitting room, bathroom and kitchen, and the rest would be bed-sits with a bathroom for every three.'

'That sounds fine,' said Jay. 'Let's go and have a look at them.' Little had been done yet to the old buildings but the plans pinned on a blackboard inside gave them all a good idea of how they would look.

'How's the perimeter fence coming along?' asked Jay.

'It's all OK. I just didn't think there was any point in putting in any electronic equipment until there was somebody here full time.'

'My suggestion is that you put the control room a reasonable distance from the entrance gates so that if anyone really wants to cause trouble they've got some way to go before they can get to whoever is in charge.'

Hurry had taken that on board and was already heading for the storerooms by the time Jason had finished speaking. The feed room was now ready, as was the area for the hay barn. The tack room, adjacent to the stable block, needed racks for the saddles and bridles, cupboards for various other items of equipment and chests for blankets and sweat sheets, but most of the materials were already on the floor ready for installation. The laundry room had been completed, and two huge industrial washing machines plus a giant tumble-drier were standing waiting to be connected.

'Where do you want the medical supplies kept?' asked Hurry.

'I'd like those to be in a locked cupboard in my office,' said Jay. 'You can't be too careful. We'll also need a fridge in there for certain antibiotics and other medications that need to be kept cool.' With a last and thoroughly satisfied look round, he and Hal joined Len and Bart who had walked over to look at the gallops.

Thrilled to see their dream taking physical shape, Hal, Len and Bart climbed into the Bentley to return to London. As he and Hurry waved them off, Jason gave the foreman a congratulatory squeeze of the shoulder. 'Well done, Hurry, he said. 'I'm really pleased with the progress here.' He got into his own car and headed for Midwood Park where Fiona had offered him a bed for the night and a ride out in the morning.

He found her bubbling with plans for her trip at the end of the season and he had plenty to tell her about County View. They discussed which of her horses might go there now that it had been agreed that the partnership would train for one or two outside owners.

'I know one owner I don't want,' said Jay, sipping a welcome cup of tea.

'I can't imagine who,' said Fiona tartly. 'I'm sure you'll be disappointed to know that Harry Clough has already said he is intending to move his horses to Jed's at the end of the season.'

'Has he told Jed that yet?' asked Jay.

'I don't think so. I think he's keeping it as a bit of a surprise for the next time they meet at the races.'

'In that case, he might get a bit of a surprise himself,' said Jay with a smile.

Fiona raised her eyebrows but did not press him further. He could be maddeningly cryptic sometimes, but she knew he wouldn't tell her what it was he found so amusing until he was ready.

The following morning, after cantering two horses and schooling the hurdler that Fiona was considering running at Aintree, Jason was putting his gear into the boot of his car. 'You know you can ride him at Aintree if you want,' said Fiona, standing in the drive.

'I don't want to play hard to get, Fiona,' he said, 'but can I keep my options open till a little nearer the day?'

'Of course you can.' She gave him an affectionate hug and sent him on his way.

Back at his temporary office in the Aldwych he made a few telephone calls and then touched base with Benny in Dublin. 'The one person I don't want to speak in the Friend's presence is your American pal,' said Jay. 'We're going to need him for some telephone work later on.'

'Understood,' said Benny. 'I'll see you in Dublin tomorrow.'

Jason had already spoken to both Howard and Victor to warn them that he would be in Dublin for two or three days. They had both wished him a somewhat cautious good luck, but it was clear that from the little they knew about it they had strong reservations about his Irish enterprise.

It was hardly surprising. Not only were they justifiably worried, as his friends, for him and his safety, but as businessmen it was only natural that they should be concerned about all the hard work and money that would go completely to waste if anything happened to Jay as a result of his determination to sort out this man Liam whose surname they didn't even know.

At half-past four Jay drove down to Jed's yard, for once in no hurry and drinking in the beautiful countryside as he crossed from Surrey into Sussex. Evening stables had just finished when he arrived, but the head lad insisted on taking him round his charges with the pride of a mother showing off her talented offspring, paying particular attention to Pewter Queen, The Conker and the other horses with which Jay was personally involved. Every one of them looked in tremendous condition – a great tribute to Jed and his team as the long hard season was approached its end.

'If you don't mind me saying, Mr Jessop,' said the head man, 'I really think Pewter Queen would have a cracking chance at Aintree. I know it's probably a bit short of her eventual distance, but with a five-pound allowance and so many of the top bumper horses having had hard seasons, I reckon she could do really well. I'm sure she's improved ten or fifteen lengths since her run at Cheltenham, and there's no denying she's real class.'

'I'll talk to Jed and Howard about it,' Jay promised him. Jed could not have failed to see Jason's car but he hadn't come out to greet him. Jason knew he was keeping out of the way so that he didn't steal the head man's thunder. It was a manifestation of the unexpected sensitivity and tact that made for such a happy team at his yard. Jason left the head man now to go and find the trainer in the house. He had half-expected to be faced with a changed man, but Jed seemed his normal self, a cigarette hanging out of the corner of his mouth as usual.

'I thought you were cutting down on those,' Jay remarked.

'Oh, I am. I'm down from sixty to forty a day, and I promised Cathy that within four weeks I'll be down to twenty.'

'Is that going to be enough of a help?'

'Well, the doctor's not wild about it, but he recognises that the chances of me giving up overnight are pretty remote. I will get there in the end. In fact, I'm wondering whether to follow your example and switch to cigars.'

'Do that and I'll buy you your first month's supply – as long as you don't smoke more than three a day,' pledged Jay.

'You're on!' They shook hands on it and Jed led Jay into the kitchen where he was given a big hug and kiss on the cheek from Cathy and the customary offer of a cup of tea.

'That would be great.'

'I know that you two have got some business to talk, so I'll bring it through to the front room for you,' she said as she filled the kettle.

Settling themselves down, Jed and Jason talked a little about Jed's horses and the possibility of running Pewter Queen at Aintree. Jed admitted that the idea had its appeal and phoned Howard to get his reaction. As always Howard's response was 'Of course I'd love to have a runner at Aintree, but you and Jay are the experts. I'll go along with whatever you think.' They agreed that Jed would make the entry and they would make their final decision nearer the day when the going could be assessed and they had a more accurate idea of the likely opponents.

'Now then, Jed,' said Jay. 'You've told me what your plans are; let me tell you mine.'

Jed listened quietly to what Jason had to say, though it was clear that this time it was his turn to receive a bolt from the blue. 'I know it's a bit of a nerve to ask you to be my assistant when I'm just starting and you've been going for so long,' Jay continued. 'It just seemed to me that it might take a lot of the pressure off you, and yet keep you involved. You would be working with some really great horses and excellent conditions.'

Jed whistled. 'My, oh my,' he said at last. 'I think Cathy had better hear this.'

He called his wife, who put her head around the door, thinking he needed something.

'Come in and sit down, lass,' said Jed.

Jason ran through his proposition again for Cathy's benefit. 'I think it would make life easier for you, too, Cathy. The house won't be palatial, but it will be comfortable. And if you should want any part-time work there will be plenty of options – helping with the cooking for the stable staff, or something of that order.'

Cathy positively beamed. 'I think it would be wonderful,' she said. 'He'd die if he didn't have a real involvement in racing, and this would take so much of the stress out of the job. You two have always got on well together. Jed respects you as a man as well as a jockey. And Howard has always been a great friend and supporter, and it would be lovely to keep in touch with him and his horses.'

'Don't make up your minds tonight,' said Jay. Drive over and have a look at the place, and if you're still interested we'll sort out the details. But we won't make any announcements for a while yet. Cathy can sit down with Hurry Henderson and talk about how she'd like the house designed.'

Cathy stood up, went across to Jay and gave him another big kiss. 'It's more than I could have dreamed of,' she said. 'I'm sure it will be ideal for both of us. Now, I think it's time we all ate. Come on through.'

Over dinner and a brandy they covered a lot of ground, notably which of Jed's horses were likely to come with him, assuming their owners were happy to move them to a yard whose training fees were going to be significantly higher than Jed's. There were a couple of quite good horses belonging to syndicates that just wouldn't be able to afford the extra cost, and one or two local owners who would probably want to keep their horses trained in the Sussex area, but otherwise there was quite a lot of scope for adding to County View's stable.

Jay told Jed what Fiona had said about Harry Clough's intention to send him his horses. Jed burst out laughing. 'Well, that's ironic,' he said. 'More often than not he's hardly had the time of day for me. Ah well, that's how it goes. What shall I say if he asks me before this is all decided?'

'There's no point in burning your bridges or starting off any rumours before we're ready to go public. I'd suggest you tell him your doctor has said you've got to take things easy, and can he give you a week or two to think about it while you sort out what you're going to do. But one thing I can tell you, Jed, is that even if you did ask me, there's no way I'd handle that man's horses.'

The following morning Jason found that The Conker's performance matched his excellent condition and agreed with the head lad that Pewter Queen had certainly not gone backwards, indeed had probably made progress since he had ridden her at Cheltenham. She certainly enjoyed her work and seemed stronger each time he sat on her. At the same time there was a controlled competitiveness about her as she responded to his signals. She didn't run too freely in the early stages of the work, but got down to it in earnest when he asked her over the last quarter of a mile. As he and Jed walked back over the downs, the early-morning dew still glistening on the grass, and he was glad to be alive. He was struck by a powerful awareness of how lucky he was. 'Jed, I think we probably ought to run her,' he said suddenly. 'She really is getting better all the time.'

Jed gave a nod of acknowledgement. He cast a nostalgic look around him. 'I want to come and work with you, Jay, but I guess I'm going to miss this place,' he admitted.

'Of course you are,' said Jay. 'It's been your life's work, and a damned good life's work at that, but I'll make sure you'll enjoy what you're going to do with me.'

'I know,' smiled Jed. He threw a half-smoked cigarette away. 'I think I'll start on those cigars next week.'

The same afternoon, Jason was on board an Aer Lingus plane bumping gently through the clouds on its descent into Dublin. A pair of dark glasses and a cap that covered his telltale crop of hair, ensured that for once he emerged from the airport unrecognised and, hiring a car at the desk in the arrivals hall, drove to his hotel, where he checked in and made for his room as quickly as possible. Stretching out on the bed, fully clothed, to ease his back after the flight, he reached for his mobile to find out what was happening with Sean and Benny.

Chapter Eighteen

Smoking a cigar in his hired saloon, parked in a dimly lit car park on the edge of Dublin, Jason noticed a rather dented Volvo station wagon drawing up into a nearby bay. He glanced around casually, got out of his own car, walked over to the station wagon and slipped into the back seat.

'Evening, boss,' said Benny quietly. He was sitting in the front with Angel. 'Good flight?'

'Fine, thanks. So, what's the story?'

'We've got all the vehicles we need. Two cheap vans, which we've adapted for our purposes by blacking out the windows, except for one little gap to look out of – we've got one of those monitoring this bloke's front door, and we'll swap it with the other one tomorrow night. Plus a couple of old motors, as well as this one, with a bit of poke. We probably won't need them all but it's as well to be prepared. And the premises are sorted. I've rented an empty warehouse on the outskirts of town for cash. It's on an old industrial estate that's due for demolition and redevelopment, so it's nice and deserted. There are only about three businesses still active there, and they're nowhere near our place. I went over and fitted new padlocks this morning and I didn't see a soul.'

'Have you been able to get a sense of the Friend's movements?'

'Oh, yes. Luckily for us, the Friend – or Liam Ahearne, to give him his real name – seems to go out every evening around seven-thirty or eight, regular as clockwork. So we reckon we should have no bother springing him tomorrow night. What we'll do is have Angel park the van there, make out he's locking it and go off. But one of the boys will stay in

197

the back as a lookout. He'll let us know when the target appears. I'll be in this station wagon at the other end of the street with my Yank mate Vince driving, along with the other van. We'll all be tooled up with coshes and baseball bats. This Liam might take a bit of persuading to come with us.'

Benny could see Jason wincing through the rear-view mirror. He laughed softly. 'Don't worry. My trusty can of mace should do the trick on its own – the other stuff is more of a display of firepower than anything else, just to show him we're dead serious. You don't think he's going to just jump in the car and meekly hold up his wrists to be cuffed, do you?'

There was nothing to be done till the next evening so they all went back to their hotels. Jay had supper in his room and lay on his bed half watching the television, channel-hopping in a vain attempt to find a programme that was even remotely interesting – anything to keep his mind off his worries. He slept fitfully, his dreams a jumble of baseball bats and unknown, terrified faces. In the morning he ordered a rather more substantial breakfast than he normally ate, mainly to pass the time. It felt strange to him to be at such a loose end, especially in Ireland, where there were any number of trainers he could ride out for or friends he could visit, but he had to keep his head down. After breakfast he drove out into the countryside and took a long walk trying, without success, to think about something other than the evening ahead. Reluctantly he returned to his hotel room and read the papers. As the evening approached his anxiety, mixed with a little excitement, grew. At five o'clock he phoned Benny to check that everything was ready. Jay was to park half a mile or so away from the Friend's street and keep his mobile on, but he would not get involved himself unless he was required for some urgent reason.

Concerned that something might go wrong and he might be late, Jason was in position far earlier than he needed to be, which only increased the time he had to wait. By 7.15 Angel had left the van fifty yards up the road from the Friend's front door, with the keys in the ignition and Robbie in the back, watching the house. As soon as Angel was out of sight round a corner he increased his pace and, turning right covered three sides of a square to bring him to where the Volvo station wagon and the other van were parked. Benny was sitting in the back of the Volvo, dressed in a garda's uniform, with Vince at the wheel. Benny watched Angel getting into the drivers seat of the van and called Jason to tell him that the first phase had been completed.

The next fifteen minutes ticked by so slowly that it seemed to them all that time was almost standing still. They kept looking at their watches and then at the clock on the dashboard. Jason, out on a limb, resisted the temptation to call Benny back. Another eight long minutes passed before Benny's phone rang. 'A Merc's just drawn up,' Robbie told him. 'Driver getting out and walking towards the front door.' Vince started the Volvo and drove up the street.

Benny, wearing dark-rimmed glasses, got out and walked slowly down towards the stationary Mercedes. He could see there was no one else in it. He paused and looked in a shop window. He could hear the engine of the Volvo ticking over behind him. Moments later the front door of the house opened and the thickset driver, the Friend and another heavy came out to get into their car.

Benny approached them briskly but apparently unhurriedly. As the doors of the Mercedes were closed behind them he moved past the car and waved to them. The driver was clearly disconcerted by the sight of his uniform. Benny knocked on the passenger window. The other heavy opened it. 'There's been an accident just down the road,' he said. 'Drive slowly, there might be a bit of a block while the ambulance takes the injured away.' Then, in a flash, just as they all looked up at him simultaneously, he whipped out his can of mace and sprayed it into the Mercedes.

As he did so the Volvo roared into life, the second van appeared from down the road and a bunch of men in balaclavas burst out of the back. Before the three occupants of the car knew what had happened, they were dragged out, gasping for breath and rubbing their eyes furiously. The Friend was hustled into the back of the Volvo. He could feel something cold and tubular being held behind his ear as he was pushed to the floor. 'Stay there if you want to live,' a voice hissed. A bag was pulled down over his head and handcuffs clamped on his wrists. In the back of the van, his two sidekicks were receiving similar treatment.

With his quarry secured, Benny leaped out of the Volvo while Terry, one of the men in balaclavas, jumped in to take his place and the station wagon sped away with only a moderate screech of tyres as the van headed off.

While all this had been going on Robbie, the lookout, had got into the front of his van, leaving the rear doors open, and driven it up behind the abandoned Mercedes. Benny flung himself into the back and closed the doors. The whole operation had taken less than three minutes, and as far as any of them could tell it had gone unnoticed in the quiet Dublin street.

Benny quickly wriggled out of the garda's uniform and into the ordinary clothes that had been left in the van for him. Then he called Jason. 'Operation successful,' he said. At the other end Jason heaved a sigh of relief and the knot in his stomach began to ease for the first time in several hours.

When they were at a safe distance, Robbie pulled over to let Benny get out of the back of the van and into the passenger seat. They continued their journey unhurriedly.

The van carrying Liam Ahearne's protectors travelled rapidly, but not so fast as to attract attention. Within fifteen minutes it was bouncing it's way down a quiet rural lane. Angel pulled into the gateway of a field and the men guarding the captives dragged them out of the back and dumped them on the cold earth. Angel bent down and whispered in the Mercedes driver's ear: 'This time we haven't hurt you. Go home and say nothing, or next time we won't be so gentle.' He gave the man a kick in the ribs to reinforce his point and crouched on his haunches to unlock the handcuffs while one of his colleagues did the same for the other gorilla. Their socks and shoes had been removed and the sacks around their heads were tied with multiple knots, so it would take them a while to sort themselves out. For good measure Angel poured half a bottle of cheap whiskey over their clothes so that they would not be welcome in any passing cars. Giving the second heavy an equally hard kick, he jumped back into the van with the others and headed sedately towards Dublin. Half a mile or so along the road he threw the confiscated socks and shoes out of the window.

At a large and anonymous car park near the airport they carefully transferred all their equipment from the van to a car they'd left there earlier, and removed all traces of their occupation of the vehicle. They had observed Benny's strict instructions not to so much as sit in the van without gloves on from the moment they had taken possession of it. There was no danger of any fingerprints being found even if the gardai were ever called upon to search for them, which seemed unlikely. Angel put in a call to Benny. 'Mission accomplished.'

In the Volvo not a word had been spoken. The captive remained very still. The pressure of the cold steel behind his ear was making him co-operative. The fact that it was actually a piece of piping was not apparent to him through the sacking that covered his head and shoulders. As the station wagon came slowly to a halt outside the warehouse, Vince could see the headlights of Robbie's van arriving just after them. Benny got out and opened the gates, the two vehicles backed in and the gates were closed behind them. Liam was hauled out and manhandled into the building.

'What the hell's going on?' protested the Friend, in muffled tones.

'Shut up,' growled Benny in his most menacing voice. The Friend was thrown to the floor, and someone was tying his ankles together. The lights and a transistor radio went on. To the outside world – if anybody was out there to notice, which was highly improbable – it would have seemed as if some evening workers had just come in for their shift. Terry whistled along as Aretha Franklin sang 'I say a little prayer for you,' which seemed rather appropriate in the circumstances. Robbie asked Benny in a stage whisper: 'What's going to happen to him?'

'I think he's going for a one-way swim to the bottom of the Irish Sea – the boss really doesn't like this guy.'

The reaction from the bundle on the floor was immediate. He struggled violently and got a kick in his ribs for his trouble.

'I don't think he likes the idea,' laughed Benny. 'I told you once, now shut up!' He gave him another kick.

'Let's have some tea,' he said to the others. A Thermos flask was opened and cups were rattled ostentatiously as they enjoyed their well-earned cuppas. This pleasant ritual did nothing for the state of mind of the trussed man, who once again tried pleading, only to be treated to another hefty though not too vicious kick.

When they had all finished their tea Benny gave Vince a nod. As the others chatted idly he crept outside with the mobile phone and sat in the Volvo. Benny's phone rang.

'Yes, boss. What now?' Benny sounded somewhat surprised. 'OK. Give us two or three minutes to get him organised.' He rang off. 'Turn all the lights off,' he said to his colleagues. 'And someone give me some tape.' To the bundle he said: 'We're going to take your hood off and we're going to blindfold you with tape. You're going to be given a chance to talk to our boss. You'd better listen to what he says, because it could make the difference between you having a future or not.'

As soon as the lights were off, the Friend's hood was removed and his head held very firmly from behind while thick black masking tape was wound across his eyes and his forehead. They left one ear free. 'Now,' said Benny, 'I'm going to hold the phone to your ear. You listen to what the boss says.'

He spoke into the phone. 'He's ready for you boss.' Then he put the phone against the Friend's available ear.

'Well, Mr Friend,' came Vince's husky American accent. 'Or should I say Mr Liam Ahearne? I think you can see that I have an organisation. It's an organisation that's gonna take over your territory in Dublin. In fact, it's gonna take over the whole of the business in Ireland. Listen to me very carefully. You have a choice. You either work with me or against me. And if you work against me, what has happened tonight will only be a dress rehearsal. Next time it will be the final curtain for you. Do you understand?'

'Yes,' said the Friend shakily.

'OK,' said Vince. 'You'll be taken back to your apartment now. You'll be blindfolded, but otherwise you won't be hurt. Go in and stay there tonight. And no phone calls. Put your answering machine on and leave it on. Tomorrow morning a cab will pick you up at 7.30. You're going on a little trip. Don't worry about packing anything. As its such short notice I'll provide everything you'll need for a few days away. When you get home you'll find in your pocket a key for a locker at the airport. Number 305. In that locker you'll find a bag. Inside there will be some changes of clothes and other essentials, together with a return ticket to Heathrow and an envelope containing $3,000.'

'At Heathrow, check into the Crest Hotel, where a reservation has been made in your name. You'll have a call there to give you the details of a club class to New York which will be booked for you, and a second bag will be delivered to your room. That bag goes with you to the US of A. The key will be left for you separately in an envelope at reception, just so you can check it and satisfy yourself there is nothing in it to give you the heebie-jeebies before you leave for New York.'

'Play ball with me and there's $75,000 in it for you, as well as a round trip to the Big Apple, just to show that in return for your co-operation I am prepared to make you a real partner. You'll be better off on my side, believe me. When you arrive I'll tell you about my plans for Ireland and how I want you to fit into my operation. Is that understood?'

'Yes,' mumbled Liam.

'Let me make it crystal clear that if you don't carry out what I've said exactly, you're in serious trouble.'

'Yes, yes, I understand, and I'll do it. You'll have no problem with me,' jabbered Liam.

'Be sure you do. I'll see you in New York in a couple of days, now I want to speak to my man.'

The Friend nodded to Benny. He took the phone and walked away, listening intently to imaginary instructions with Vince.

'OK,' he said finally. 'We'll put the key in his pocket just before we throw him out. OK, boss.'

He put down the phone. 'Right, everybody get moving.'

The lights were switched off and Liam was told to lie on the floor. The tape was removed and the hood put back over his head. The handcuffs were taken off and his feet untied. Once he had been put back into the Volvo with Benny, Terry and Robbie went off ahead in the van.

'Right,' said Benny to Liam. 'We're going to take you home. When we let you out, keep the hood on over your head until you've counted to a hundred. If you don't, we'll know, and we'll take that as an indication that you're not co-operating with the boss. Somebody will be watching you, and if you don't follow your instructions to the letter, it's goodnight Vienna.'

As the Volvo turned into Liam's street, Benny put the locker key into his pocket. 'Just pick up the bag in the morning, go to Heathrow and do as you're told. Keep your nose clean and you'll have the easiest payday you've seen in a long while. Just remember, not only is our boss not a man to cross, but he's not just some little local operator. His tentacles go everywhere. So if you're tempted to try any tricks when you've left Dublin, forget it. You'll be monitored all the way.'

The car stopped and Liam was pushed out, none too gently. The Volvo swept off around a corner. Terry and Robbie were already parked up the road in the van, looking out through the darkened rear windows. After a decent interval the Friend took off the hood and rubbed his eyes and face. Slowly he got his bearings and, once he'd figured out where he was, he scuttled towards his front door a few yards up the street. Terry and Robbie took it in turns to keep watch all night, but no one came or went.

At 7.30 the next morning a licensed cab drew up and the Friend came out and got into the back seat. He looked none the worse for his experience, though the nervous glances he cast up and down the street betrayed his anxiety. 'He's off,' said Terry, on his mobile to Benny. Robbie, ready in the driving seat, started up the van and followed the taxi at a discreet distance.

In the airport terminal Benny, extremely smartly dressed in a suit and tie, was sitting with an attaché case balanced on his knee, pretending to read the *Financial Times*. When he received word that the Friend's cab was outside, he rang Vince who was positioned close to the left-luggage lockers. It wasn't long before Liam was walking briskly towards the bank of lockers. His eyes scanned the numbers. Finding 305, he took the key from his pocket, opened it up and pulled out a Louis Vuitton holdall. He sat down and examined the contents. He seemed reassured by what he discovered: some neatly folded shirts, underwear and socks, and a pair of trousers; a capacious toilet bag, containing razor and shaving cream, toothpaste and so on; a couple of paperbacks and a wooden cigar box labelled 'Upmanns', the brand he'd been seen smoking at Leopardstown. He undid the box and unscrewed one of the tubes, evidently pleased to find that it indeed held what was advertised on the outside.

There was also an envelope addressed to 'The Friend'. Inside was a plain sheet of paper on which was typed: 'So far, so good. You are being watched. Your ticket, in your own name, is waiting to be collected.' There was also a wad of cash: the promised $3,000 in used notes. This brought a smile to his face and, looking rather more confident, he strode across to the ticket desk, gave his name and was presented with a first-class return ticket to London.

Benny and his colleagues, strategically placed round the airport to ensure that nothing untoward occurred, noted that the Friend did not attempt to use a mobile, or indeed any other telephone. He checked in, tailed by Benny, also in possession of a first class ticket. The Louis Vuitton holdall went straight through the X-ray camera without incident.

The Friend waited calmly in the first-class lounge. The flight was called on schedule, the journey smooth and uneventful. The first-class passengers disembarked in front of the others and both Benny and Liam with hand luggage only, were among the first to enter the terminal. Benny saw the Friend, unconcerned, walking through the green 'Nothing to Declare' channel. Almost immediately two customs officers approached him and asked him if he was sure he had nothing to declare. He shook his head, but seemed slightly less self-assured. Very politely they invited him to accompany them to a small room out of sight of the other passengers. Benny smiled to himself and passed through the green channel behind him and out of the airport.

'Please open your bag,' said the first customs officer to Liam. With a growing sense of foreboding, he complied and as requested proceeded to take everything out. The junior customs officer opened the toilet bag and produced the large aerosol tin of shaving foam, an apparently unopened carton of aftershave, a new plastic soap container wrapped in cellophane, an aerosol deodorant, a toothbrush, a tube of toothpaste and a jar of hair gel. He set about removing packaging and unscrewing lids to examine each item thoroughly.

As the jar of hair gel was opened, the colour drained from Liam's face. Instead of gel, it seemed to be full of a fine, white powder. So was the soap container. His jaw dropped as false bottoms were discovered in the two aerosols and the aftershave carton. All three were crammed with more of the same.

The other customs officer was investigating the cigars. Although the top layer of tubes held his favourite Havanas, those underneath were packed with yet more white powder. Even the bottom of the holdall itself proved to be false, offering plenty of space for whole plastic bags of the stuff.

'I know nothing about this,' Liam eventually stammered. 'It can't be my bag.'

'Whose is it then?' came the sharp question.

'I picked it up at the airport.'

'Who from?'

'I don't know.'

'You mean to say you picked up somebody else's bag?'

'No, I, um... I got it out of a left-luggage locker.'

'How did you come to get it?'

'Somebody gave me the key.'

'Who?'

'I don't know,' said Liam lamely. By this time he realised he was gibbering. If he said anything more he was likely to incriminate himself even further. 'It's all a mistake! It must be!' he cried, raising his arms in a gesture of utter bafflement.

Chapter Nineteen

As soon as Jay heard the news from Benny he made a call to a journalist he trusted. The rest had followed as surely as night follows day. The later editions of the *Evening Standard* carried a story headed: 'Irish Businessman Arrested for Drugs.' Carefully avoiding any comments that could be potentially libellous or might prejudice any subsequent trial, the *Standard* reporter filled in the Friend's somewhat colourful background. Reading between the lines, anybody with a rudimentary knowledge of journalism might well have deduced that not only had the police been tipped off but that a very well-informed source had supplied much of this background, along with details of Liam Ahearne's known association with some of the more dubious members of Dublin society. As an apparently unconnected afterthought, the recent mysterious death of the bookmaker was also mentioned.

Jay, who had returned home on the first flight that morning, read the *Standard* with considerable satisfaction before ringing Sean. 'We'll have to wait for a little while to see what happens as far as the trial is concerned, but I don't think there is much doubt he'll be sent away for long enough to keep him out of your hair.'

A little while later he had a chortling Howard on the telephone. 'I don't know how you did it – I don't even want to know how you did it – but well done. I think you deserve a bottle of champagne tonight.' They agreed to meet later that evening, along with Victor, at Annabel's.

Earlier that afternoon, Jed had accepted Jason's offer to join him at County View as assistant trainer. Jay told him to go down and discuss with Hurry any changes he felt would be useful and to ensure that Cathy was happy with the house.

No sooner had Jay got into the shower than Eva was on the phone with the welcome news that she was leaving South Africa that night. Jay promised to have a car at Heathrow to meet her. Feeling that the last few days had been spent extremely effectively, he got back into the shower, then dressed and wandered round to Annabel's to meet Howard and Victor. After a drink there they walked round the corner to the quieter surroundings of the Greenhouse restaurant where they ate simply and got down to business.

Howard was happy to sort out Jed's contract and also to put his property on the market. They agreed that all Jed's good horses would join the new yard and the moderate horses would be sold. He was greatly relieved that he would not be letting Jed down. As they drank their coffee Victor looked at his watch and gave Howard a playful nudge. 'I think we had better let this young swain have an early night if Eva's coming back tomorrow!'

The next morning Jay jogged down Mount Street and into Hyde Park where he went for a brisk run round the Serpentine. He slowed down as he went past the barracks to watch the cavalry on their early-morning exercise round Rotten Row. Although they were very different from the horses he rode, Jay could still appreciate the fine condition of these strong animals and the total harmony between horse and rider. Pausing for long enough to do fifty press-ups and some simple stretching and suppling exercises, he was soon back in his flat taking his customary scalding shower followed by a cold one. Fortifying himself with orange juice, freshly ground coffee and two bananas, he changed into a pair of slacks and a casual shirt and got out his blazer ready for later in the day. He felt on top of the world: not only would Eva be home in a few hours, but the arrest of the Friend had lifted a great weight off his shoulders.

He sauntered out again, just as far as the newsagents off Berkeley Square, where he bought a pile of national newspapers. Both broadsheets and tabloids had picked up the story of Liam Ahearne's fall from grace. He learned in a phone call from Sean that the coverage in the Irish papers had been even more prominent and even more humiliating. If Jay was elated to have dealt with the Friend, Sean was almost incoherent with joy. He had his life back.

Jay tried to settle down to some paperwork but was finding it difficult to concentrate. He telephoned the airport to check that Eva's flight was on time. It was. He kept looking at his watch until at last the phone rang. 'Hi, I'm home,' said the familiar voice.

He was touched that, without thinking about it, she was calling England home.

'I can't wait to see you,' he breathed.

'Me too,' she whispered. 'Ah, there comes my luggage'. He pictured her standing by the conveyor belt in the arrivals hall. 'See you soon.'

It seemed an age before he heard the door bell and the driver was bringing up her bags. As soon as they were alone she looked at him with a mischievous smile. 'Well, aren't you going to welcome me properly?' He took her into his arms and kissed her. 'Sit down,' he said eventually, disappearing into the kitchen. He returned with two glasses and a bottle of Krug. He popped the cork and the glasses turned misty as he gently filled them with the sparkling champagne.

'Welcome home, my darling.'

'I've missed you so much,' she replied.

They sipped the delicious Krug and then she took the glass from his hand and led the way into the bedroom. He picked up the bottle and followed her. Feverish with anticipation, they fumbled with each others' clothes and tumbled on to the bed, desperate to repossess one another.

'Well,' he said, not very much later. 'That was more like a sprint than a stayers' steeplechase.'

They both laughed.

'We've got all day,' she reminded him. She stroked his face with her finger. 'And there's no reason why we shouldn't enjoy a mixed card, is there?'

'Not at all,' he agreed, reaching over to refill their glasses.

At half-past one they strolled down to the Dorchester bar, where they were enthusiastically greeted by Giuliano, the head barman. Over a light lunch and a bottle of Chablis, Jay brought Eva up to date with everything that had happened on both sides of the Irish Sea. His concise but nonetheless graphic account of the downfall of Liam Ahearne left her wide-eyed.

'My God!' she said. 'I knew you were a determined man, but I didn't realise you were quite that ruthless.'

He grinned. 'Only if I'm crossed. So be warned!'

'I'm really burning to get on with County View,' she told him. 'With the press launch scheduled for a week on Sunday, there's a hell of a lot to do.'

'If you're up to it, we could make an early start tomorrow and go down there. You can see how it's all coming along and we can review the situation with Hurry. Then we could come back and have dinner with Victor and Howard and draw up a timetable for unleashing the whole thing on the world.'

Eva put down her fork. 'We've got an awful lot of interesting stories all wrapped up in one,' she said. 'Don't you think we ought to release them bit by bit? That way we stand a chance of grabbing the front page of the *Racing Post* on more than one occasion.'

'Yes, I do,' he said. 'But obviously it's your call.' He smiled. 'Victor has been particularly insistent about that.'

'Good old Victor. I knew I'd have at least one gentleman in my corner.'

That afternoon Jason phoned Jed to invite him and Cathy down to County View the next day so that they could have a good look at the place and talk to Hurry about their new house. It would also be a good opportunity for Eva to get to know them properly.

After calling to arrange a meeting with the PR company who were handling the practical details of the launch of County View, Eva got on with her unpacking. She sang to herself as she wandered around finding homes for her clothes, shoes and other belongings. The knowledge that she was beginning to install herself permanently in this life gave Jay a warm glow. Relaxed and content at last, he was able to focus on the paperwork from which he had been so distracted that morning.

'Where shall we go for dinner?' he asked her later.

'Nowhere. Let's eat in. What have you got in the fridge?'

While Eva prepared and grilled a couple of fillets of salmon, Jay made a salad with his own very lemony French dressing. As they ate they watched the television news.

The fickle media machine had already moved on from the shaming of the Friend to fresh scandals, and no further mention was made of his arrest. But the press would be back to pick over his carcass when the case went to trial.

'Have you got any ice cream?' Eva inquired.

Jay opened the freezer door and produced a choice of three flavours.

'What are you going to have?' she asked, helping herself to a generous portion of each.

'Nothing,' he replied. 'Just some fruit. I've still got to watch my weight until after Aintree.'

'Sorry,' she smiled. 'I'm going to have to get use to your eating habits, aren't I? With so much else to think about, I must confess I'd forgotten all about Aintree. What are you going to ride there?'

'I'm not absolutely certain yet, but almost definitely Pewter Queen and The Conker. Then there's the Irish horse, Peter's Pal. And Fiona has another one I might ride.'

'That should keep you busy for three days. What about the big one, the National?'

'I haven't been offered a ride for that,' he admitted, 'and frankly, it's unlikely I'll be given the opportunity on anything with a real chance.'

'I thought everything in the National had a real chance.'

'Not these days. It's a much higher-class race than it used to be. It certainly isn't the sort of lottery it was when Johnny Buckingham won on Foinavon.'

'When was that?'

'Oh, that was a long time ago – 1967.' Jay told her the story of how a horse had fallen at a fence before the Canal Turn, bringing down a whole host of runners and causing mayhem. Johnny Buckingham, on Foinavon, a 100 – 1 outsider, managed to avoid the carnage and got such a big lead that nothing could get near him. It was truly one of the great surprises of the many extraordinary Grand Nationals in the long and often controversial history of the race. That fence was now named after the unlikely winner of 1967.

They went to bed early and this time they made love slowly and tenderly before falling into a deep and contented sleep.

Eva, as Jason told her, looked radiant the next morning, showing no signs of suffering any after-effects from her long flight. Pulling on a pair of jeans and a blouse, and slipping a sweater round her shoulders, she followed him out of the flat and waited while he extracted his beloved Jaguar from the garage.

As they cruised down the M4 Eva recounted all that had happened in South Africa. Much as she had enjoyed it there, she was even more enthusiastic about being back in England, being with Jay and being a part of all the excitement of the new venture. She felt she had really found her niche. As they climbed the hill up to the stables, Jay slowed down to give her a chance to survey the countryside. 'I can see how it earned its name,' she almost whispered. 'It's absolutely sensational.'

'You can see that the hills will make it much easier for us to get these horses fit than trying to do it in a flat area.'

At the perimeter fence Jay was pleased to see that the electronic barrier was already in place, although raised to allow the site traffic in and out. There was a security man in the solidly built control point a few yards inside the gates. Jay slowed down to identify himself but was immediately recognised and waved on. The all-weather gallops were finished and tidied up; the buildings ahead of them were a hive of activity. Quite a few of the workmen recognised Jay's car and nodded or waved. He parked the Jaguar in front of the house that would be both his office and their living accommodation. Hurry had found some old Cotswold stone to match that used in the existing building and, although the surrounding area needed cleaning up and planting, it already looked enchanting.

Eva was like a little girl, rushing from room to room in excitement, looking at the views from the windows. 'It's fantastic!' she said.

'Do you think you could live here?' he said.

'You try to keep me away!' Coming back out of the front door they were met by Hurry who wanted to know what they thought of the place.

'You're a miracle man,' declared Jay.

The stables were complete apart from some painting. The storage barns were ready, with the huge feed bins waiting to be put in wherever Jay wanted them. 'Someone else is joining me today; I'd like his input,' Jay told Hurry. He wanted to make sure that Jed felt he was part of the final preparations. Besides, Jed had a lifetime's experience whereas Jay's only knowledge came more from watching what other people did rather than from the deep understanding that comes from caring for horses every day of the year. He was wise enough to recognise his limitations. It was Jed and his head man who would be crucial to the smooth day-to-day running of County View.

The stable lads' accommodation was well on its way; 'Two to three weeks would do it,' Hurry said. The mobile homes

Hurry had arranged as an interim measure were now neatly parked in a row. Electricity had been installed and the toilet and shower facilities were already in one end of the permanent buildings.

'It's great that we're all set for the staff,' commented Eva, 'but have we actually got any staff to come yet?'

Jay laughed. 'A good point. Initially, we're only going to need a few, and I have people lined up to come at short notice if necessary to settle in the first horses when they arrive. I imagine Jed will be bringing one or two of his staff who will come with his horses. I've a couple in mind at Midwood Park with whom I've always got on well, and I am sure Fiona would be relieved to see them given the opportunity to come here now that she's beginning to run down her yard. And I'd be amazed if Sean doesn't have some candidates in Ireland who'd jump at the chance. So I think we'll be able to pick and choose. In fact it's probably going to be more of a question of having to disappoint a lot of people rather than trying to fill the jobs. But you're right, we should start talking to some of them soon.'

'When do you think we could start bringing horses here?' Eva asked.

'I would want to ask Jed, but I would have thought within a week. We'll want at least some of them here for the press launch.' Behind the mobile homes he pointed to what looked rather like a bombsite.

'What's that?' asked Eva.

'Over there will be two horse walkers, both of them covered so that Jay will be able to have eight walking at a time,' explained Hurry. 'Next to them is a water treadmill.'

'A what?'

'A treadmill that works underneath two or three feet of water. Wading through water gives the horses harder work than an ordinary treadmill. It's also good for horses who have had bad legs or are getting over jarring.'

'Wow!' exclaimed Eva. 'This really is sophisticated. What's that big hole over there?'

'That's something that's going to take a little bit longer,' said Hurry. 'That's the equine swimming pool.'

'It's going to be a circular pool, covered in and it'll have thermostatically controlled water so that in the winter you're not going to freeze the poor animals when they get into it.

Turning to Jay, he said, 'Most of this will be completed in a week, but the swimming pool's going to be at least another three to four.'

'That's fine,' said Jay. 'We're hardly likely to use it in the early part of the season anyway.'

'Thank goodness for that. I thought you might give me a hard time and tell me that was the most important thing of all,' said Hurry, the perfectionist.

Jay punched him on the shoulder. 'You must be joking. You're achieving the impossible as it is. Talking of which, is everything on course for the press launch a week on Sunday?'

'Yup. We should be shipshape by then, and Howard has organised the marquee.'

'Great. Obviously, as long as everything is ready for the horses, if a few things behind the scenes aren't done it won't be the end of the world. The important thing is making a good impression – making sure the gallops are freshly mowed and so on.'

'And since the gardens won't be finished, masses of potted plants to put in front of the main house wouldn't go amiss,' added Eva.

'Right you are,' said Hurry. 'As it happens, I have a mate who runs a nursery, so that's no sooner said than done.'

They looked up at the sound of a car engine and saw Jed's elderly Mercedes coming up the tarmac drive in stately fashion. Jed and Cathy got out, gazing around them with an air of mild bewilderment.

Jay went over to welcome them, shaking Jed's hand and kissing Cathy on the cheek. 'Well, I see you found the place,' he said. He introduced Hurry, who was only a couple of steps behind him. 'And Cathy, this is Eva – I don't think you two have met yet.' Eva greeted Jed's wife warmly. 'Right. Before you go round the houses, let's have a quick tour in Hurry's Land Rover,' Jay suggested.

Hurry was already starting the engine as they all piled in. As they drove round the property, Jay pointed out to Jed the grass and all-weather gallops, the sites he proposed for the schooling hurdles and fences. Jed was, in his quiet way, enthusiastic about everything, contributing, as Jay had hoped, his own wisdom, recommending slight alterations to the angle of the hurdles and fences so to avoid schooling straight into the light early in the morning in winter when the sun would be low.

As they headed back to the stable block, Jason said he would leave Jed and Cathy to look over their new house on their own with Hurry. You just tell Hurry what you want and it'll be done, he promised. 'Remember, this is your home, not ours. He saw the anxious expression on Cathy's face. 'Don't worry, Hurry won't let you break the bank. I've told him he can't spend more than £150', he teased her conspiratorially.

While the new inhabitants inspected their house, Jason and Eva sat on a low stone wall, enjoying the warm sun and the spectacular views.

'I think they're both great,' said Eva. 'They'll be a huge asset to the place. I'm very impressed by Cathy. I think she will run her side of things like a firm but extremely caring and efficient school matron.'

'Got it in one!' smiled Jay. 'That's just what she's like.'

Cathy and Jed emerged from the house looking delighted. 'It's fantastic!' enthused Cathy. 'As long as you're happy with it, of course,' she added hastily. 'And everything is sorted out with Hurry.' The anxious expression returned.

'It'll cost you a fortune, boss,' warned Hurry with a mock sigh.

'Oh well, she's worth it,' shrugged Jay. 'Even if he isn't.'

'A fine way to talk about your assistant trainer,' grumbled Jed contentedly.

'Come on, let's go and have some lunch,' laughed Jay.

They repaired to The Shepherd's Rest where they went over the adjustments to the design of the house and Jed and Jay finalised which horses and which of Jed's staff would make the move.

'We can't say anything to them for a week, I'm afraid,' said Jason. 'We can't risk anything leaking out before the launch.'

'I understand that,' said Jed. He looked at his watch. 'Well Jason, thank you very much indeed for showing us around, and for a lovely lunch – it was extremely generous of you to take us out. But I think we'd better get on the road now. Duty calls.'

As they left the pub Jay was treated to an even bigger hug than usual from Cathy, and Eva got one too.

'I think she likes you,' commented Jay as they waved off the Mercedes and climbed into the Jaguar.

'The feeling is mutual.'

Driving back to London they firmed up plans for the launch ahead of Eva's meeting with the PR company the following day. They were expecting to issue about 180 invitations and to have about 150 guests turn up. 'I'll sort out the wording tomorrow and get the invitations printed,' Eva told Jay. 'I'd normally allow for a higher percentage of no-shows, but somehow, given the extraordinary nature of the enterprise, not to mention the surprise factor, I think most of the people we ask will be there. They'll be far too curious to stay away.'

'Can we be ready to send out the invitations on Saturday by courier? If they hit the journalists' doormats on Sunday, we should get good initial coverage on Monday. It'll mean we'll miss the Sundays, but the dailies are more important.'

'Sure.' Eva flipped over a page of the notebook on her lap and looked at her notes. So, just to recap on the information we've decided to release at the launch, before we finalise it with Howard and Victor. First, you've bought this training establishment, backed by Howard and Victor, with additional support from Hal's trio, and we're looking to train the crème de la crème. I'd prefer to leave my own financial involvement out of it for the time being and just establish myself with the press as the PR director. I don't want to be dealing with questions about me rather than about County View. Second, we announce Jed's appointment.'

'Fine,' said Jason. 'We can mention some of the horses, including Pewter Queen and The Conker and maybe Splendid Warrior. At this stage I think we should avoid going into detail about quite how exclusive we're going to be. You never know, we might be offered something really impossible to turn down.'

'Hope springs eternal,' said Eva.

'Nothing ventured, nothing gained,' countered Jason. 'Well, he continued, 'I've heard a whisper that if I start training, Splendid Warrior would come to me.'

'Wonderful.'

'So Freddie assures me.'

'Could we get him down for the opening? Eva asked.

'It's certainly worth a try. I don't see why not. Now I know why I want you as a partner – you certainly saw the opportunity this would give us.'

At an adrenaline-fuelled reunion at Holland Park that evening the four partners worked over dinner on the time-table for the countdown to the launch. The excitement in the air was palpable. Now that it was only a matter of days before the project they had so carefully nurtured would be unveiled, it began to take on a new reality for them all.

Chapter Twenty

Eva dressed carefully in a pale blue suit, chic but businesslike, and cream silk shirt for her meeting at the PR company. She had of course already given them some indication of the nature of the project, swearing them to secrecy, but only now did she have the green light to be specific but there was a lot of ground to be covered. Jason had left early to ride out at Midwood Park where he would no doubt by now be drinking coffee in the kitchen, giving Fiona chapter and verse on County View and Jed's agreement to join them. He'd left details on the kitchen table of the horses whose arrival they had agreed to publicise. She needed this information to get nameplates made for their boxes and to write copy for the press leaflets she wanted to sort out today. Picking up Jason's notes, she hurried out in search of a taxi.

Jay arrived back at the flat shortly after she had left. He could smell her perfume lingering on the air in the hall. They were going to be passing like ships in the night until the launch as they criss-crossed between County View and London. They had booked a couple of rooms at The Shepherd's Rest for the duration. One was for Sean – Jay wanted him over from Ireland as soon as possible – and the other for himself and Eva, so that they could stay overnight when necessary. With a bit of luck, he thought to himself, they might manage to be there at the same time. Eva would remain down in the country for the last few days before the big event to be on hand to supervise the erection of the marquee, the flowers and the thousand and one little details.

Before heading out again for the Aldwych, he took advantage of the privacy of his flat to call Sean. They discussed arrangements for Sean's arrival and the timing for turning him back into Danny again. For the moment he would work with Hurry to get everything finished but otherwise keep a low profile. As Jason predicted, Sean confirmed that he had five staff who were ready to move to England as soon as they got the nod, including one couple who were both excellent work riders.

In his borrowed office, Jason settled down to the lengthy and complex phone calls required to organise transport for the Irish horses, all now vetted and given the thumbs-up, to County View. Just before lunchtime, Victor's face appeared around the door. 'Can I have a word?' he whispered. Jason, still on the phone, motioned him to sit down while he finished his call.

'I've been on that thing so long it's made my ear sore,' complained Jason as he put down the phone. 'What can I do for you, Victor?'

'Howard and I were talking after you two left last night. We still haven't sorted out a financial package for either you or Eva.'

'Victor, we don't need—'

Victor raised his hand to silence Jay's impending objection.

'That's not the point. This has got to be run as a proper business, and everybody involved has got to take out appropriate salaries or it will be sloppy and we won't know whether we're coming or going. We all want success, but it has to be a commercially viable proposition as well. We all expect to lose money, of course, but we need to know how much we are losing.'

'This is all very embarrassing,' said Jay.

'No, it's not,' insisted Victor. 'I've just come in to tell you that Howard and I will be putting our heads together and will coming up with proposals for both you and Eva, and then there won't be any embarrassment at all. We'll let you know what we've decided in the next couple of days. We'll leave Jed and the stable staff to you of course. Talking of which, I think perhaps we had better start putting a proper budget together. I know we've discussed some pretty good ball-park figures but now we've really got to get things buttoned up.'

Jay agreed, and assured him he had already done a lot of the calculations.

Victor stood up to leave. 'Lunch now, I think. I'm due to meet a business contact in ten minutes. Are you going out?'

Jay pulled a face and, by way of a reply, held up the prepacked sandwich he had picked up on his way in.

After he had eaten it and got himself a cup of tea he was back on the phone.

'Hi, boss,' said Benny. 'So what have you got in mind for me next, after all that excitement?'

'Something much less exciting and much easier, you'll be relieved to hear.' He told Benny about the press reception and said he would like one or two of the boys down there, just to watch over things. 'I'm not expecting any trouble, but quite apart from anything else it would be a good opportunity for you to get to know your way round before we have any seriously expensive residents to worry about. There may be times in the future when we'll really need your special help down there.'

'Fine,' said Benny. 'Will four of us be enough?'

'Ample. I'll have ordinary security people on the gate, but I'd like you to familiarise yourself with the electronic devices as well as the general layout.'

'As good as done, guv,' came Benny's reply, as breezy as ever.

The days zoomed by as if on fast-forward. Jason prepared the detailed budget he'd promised Victor, and concentrated on getting to the yard all the horses he wanted, together with the necessary complement of staff to look after them. The young, unraced, unnamed horses from Ireland would, he felt, add to the aura of mystery surrounding the venture, which was being stoked by some speculation in the press that indicated the launch invitations had been received. With

Aintree approaching almost as fast as the launch, he was also driving every morning to Lamborn to ride out.

Eva had taken the Range Rover down to County View where, in between organising the press reception, she was having carpets fitted and curtains hung in Jed and Cathy's house and, while she was at it, in their new home as well. She was also trying to equip their place at least with the basics, though most of the fixtures and fittings would have to wait until they had time to draw breath.

On the day before the horses from Ireland were due, Sean arrived at The Shepherd's Rest. Jason drove straight to County View after riding out to show him round. Even after hearing so much about it, he was clearly amazed and delighted by the facilities.

Just before lunch they got the telephone call they all had been waiting for; the horsebox carrying the first load of horses was one hour away. Although everything was ready for them, their instinctive reaction was to rush around madly to make sure.

One huge horsebox arrived just after lunch and before long ten of the boxes were filled. Later that afternoon the rest of the Irish contingent arrived and evening stables was both frantic and exhilarating as everybody went from horse to horse familiarising himself with each animal. Eva had already produced the name plates for those that had names, and plates giving the age and breeding for those that hadn't. These were slipped into the little plastic-fronted frames beside each door.

That evening Jed phoned Jay with a suggestion. 'As you're going to announce at the weekend that I'm joining you, why don't we send The Conker and Pewter Queen up for two or three days? They'll add to the excitement on Sunday and there's no reason why it should interrupt their training for Aintree. Though obviously they'll have to come back to me as they're running under my name until the end of the season.'

'That's a brilliant idea,' said Jay. 'It's great of you to have thought of it.'

'I'm not just a pretty face,' said Jed jocularly. He was clearly getting caught up in the heady atmosphere. 'I'll come with them on Saturday.'

By Saturday morning not only was everything looking superb but the weather was beautiful. Howard, Victor and Hal had all come down for the weekend and they walked round and round the yard as if they couldn't quite believe it was real. There were already over twenty horses in their boxes, all now groomed and sparkling after their long walk in the surrounding countryside that morning. These handsome animals, sporting matching grey saddle pads embroidered in scarlet with Jay's initials, had caused quite a stir among the locals.

When Jed arrived, Jay took him to one side for a few minutes. Sean would be joining them all for lunch and it would be ridiculous if Jed was the only person there who knew Danny Derkin but didn't know he was talking to him, so Jason was keen to let him in on the secret. Jed was the last man who would break a confidence, and besides he was one of the team now.

The whole sorry story would have to wait until there was more time, but Jed was in any case too flabbergasted to ask any searching questions. Although, after hearing this incredible news, he had had a quiet work with Sean and had told him how pleased he was to see him again and know that he was OK, all through lunch he could be seen constantly shooting surreptitious glances at the young Irishman, much to the amusement of everyone except Hal, who wasn't acquainted with the saga. In truth it wouldn't have meant much to him anyway since he didn't know Danny Derkin from Adam. The expression of disbelief on Jed's face said it all. He just couldn't take it in.

After a simple lunch – bread, cheese, salad and soup, warmed on the newly installed cooker – in Jason and Eva's half finished dining room, temporarily equipped with a trestle table borrowed from the builders and some of the chairs hired for the reception, Jason offered Jed a cigar, which was gratefully accepted. Having noted that his assistant trainer had not succumbed to one cigarette so far, in spite of the shock he had had, he felt Jed deserved it.

Then Jason took Hal outside to show him the small replica parade ring he had installed on Jed's advice. This would serve the dual purpose of enabling them to show owners their horses and getting the animals used to one of the otherwise unfamiliar routines they would face when they went to the races for the first time. The next morning Jason planned to have the horses led around the ring in three separate lots to give the press and other guests a good look at them. Most of the horses featured in the leaflet Eva had produced for each guest, together with their racing records where relevant, and their breeding. Jay had kept one card up his sleeve. Just after lunch a beautiful horsebox arrived and out of it stepped Splendid Warrior. The whole staff were stunned. 'This will be our star,' said Jay, then paused. 'One of our many stars.'

Later that afternoon Benny and his brothers arrived and were installed in a couple of the mobile homes. They all had supper together in The Shepherd's Rest before retiring for an early night in readiness for the next day.

On the Sunday morning Jed was in the yard before six o'clock to oversee the feeding of the horses. It was another beautiful day, thank goodness. At 7.30 half of the string were saddled up and taken off for some gentle exercise. The riders returned for a quick breakfast before taking out the second lot. None were cantered even though some of them were already three quarters fit. Jed advised keeping them reasonably cool to simplify grooming them for later in the day.

Shortly after midday the first guests started to arrive. They were shown into the marquee, where they were served with a glass of champagne and invited to help themselves from the buffet.

The catering company, recommended to Eva by Howard, had done an excellent job with the bar and buffet, managed by a team of smartly turned-out staff, in crisp, white shirts and black skirts or trousers, under the supervision of Jenny, who worked for the PR company assisting Eva and to whom she had taken an instant shine. Jenny's presence allowed Eva to concentrate on the announcements that would be made later in the afternoon without worrying about whether the flowers might be wilting or the plates were being cleared fast enough. Not that there was much to worry about. The light, airy marquee with its arrangements of fresh spring blooms and pristine white tablecloths, wouldn't have disgraced a wedding. By one o'clock the television cameramen from Channel 4 and the BBC were circulating, and the marquee was humming with excited chatter and an atmosphere of keen anticipation.

When everyone had eaten lunch, Jason, Howard, Victor, Hal and Eva made their way to a table on a raised platform to one side and sat down behind their microphones as Jenny organised the distribution of the press packs. Jason called for hush and introduced everyone in turn, announcing as they had agreed that this new partnership was one between himself, Howard, Victor and Hal. Eva he presented simply as their PR director, describing a little of her background and her father's longstanding love of National Hunt racing. After he had outlined the new venture he invited questions from the floor and was inundated with inquiries about which horses would be coming.

In response to a query about the horses Howard had with Jed, he revealed that Jed would be joining him as assistant trainer and that a number of Jed's horses would be joining the new establishment, including Howard's. As regards some of the others, discussions would be had with the owners concerned. This news sent a ripple of excitement around the room. The professionals were clearly of the opinion that Jay had done extremely well to persuade Jed to come to County View.

There were searching questions, too, on the financial aspects of the organisation. These were answered by Howard and Victor deftly and with charm. Eventually Eva took the microphone to announce the parade, promising that all the directors would be available to answer any further questions from individuals throughout the afternoon. Jason was pleased that they had been able to neatly sidestep the question of who would be the stable jockey, but at the same time make it plain that at the end of the current season he would be hanging up his own boots. In consultation with Jed, Howard and Victor, he had privately agreed retainers with Freddie Kelly and Paul Jenkins to ride for them the following season, but he could not make this public until the end of this one.

As everyone left the marquee for the parade ring Jay felt a tug at his elbow. 'There's a guy taking a lot of photographs of the stables and facilities,' Benny whispered anxiously, 'and I'm not sure whether he's an official press bloke or not.'

'Where is he? I'd better come and have a look,' said Jay. They slipped away quietly and Benny pointed out the photographer, still snapping away.

'His name is Jimmy James,' Jason told Benny. 'He is a bona fide freelance racecourse photographer, but I can't think why he's taking photographs here. Keep an eye on him will you? I've got to go back and introduce the horses.'

Back at the parade ring, there were a lot of approving nods as the horses were led round, gleaming with well-being, every one looking every inch an aristocrat. Over the PA system, Jason described each animal's breeding and state of readiness. The Conker and Pewter Queen had been joined by Peter's Pal who had just arrived from Ireland to be looked after by Jay in the run-up to Aintree. He was still listed under the Irish trainer's name and had his own lad with him. When Splendid Warrior, who had moved in two days earlier, was led in, he was greeted with spontaneous applause.

Jay was soon surrounded by journalists asking questions, most of which he was prepared for, though he was taken by surprise when one of the tabloid reporters asked him if he had any big gamblers among his owners. 'They all are,' he replied with a broad smile. 'Otherwise they wouldn't be backing an entirely unproven trainer like myself.' This prompted a hearty chuckle among the guests, but the reporter was not put off.

'No, I mean people who will lay down big bets.'

'I'm afraid you'll have to ask them that,' said Jay. 'But one thing I can tell you is that I'm not a big gambler myself, and I don't think any of my owners are naïve enough to think that anyone can make money out of gambling on National Hunt horses.' There was a murmur of agreement from the crowd.

Seeing that Eva was signalling to him, Jason excused himself and headed off for some prearranged interviews with the television companies. Eventually they began to pack up their gear, encouraged by Eva's promise that any of them who wanted to could come back to film the horses working in the morning.

Jay couldn't believe it was five o'clock already. He began to politely shepherd his guests in the direction of their cars. Most of them had been sensible enough to bring drivers, and a sizeable contingent of journalists had wisely taken advantage of a bus laid on for them by Eva. As everyone got the general idea that the event was over and the yard began to clear, Jason sought out Benny. 'I'd like Jimmy James, that photographer, checked out,' he said.

'No problem, guv'nor.'

Once the clearing-up operation was underway, Jason and Eva returned to The Shepherd's Rest where they were joined for a well-earned dinner by Howard and Bubbles, Victor, Hal, Bart, Len and Fiona. Jed and Cathy had had enough for one day, and Sean had made himself scarce for the day. Though they were all tired there was a general feeling of exhilaration that at last the operation was really up and running.

At six the next morning, after giving a sleeping Eva a gentle kiss, Jay quietly closed the door of their room in The Shepherd's Rest and set off for County View and his first day in his new job. It would not be long before she was up, too. Her priority now was to get the house ready to move into as soon as possible – but after the rigours of the previous days, he thought she deserved another hour's peace.

When he arrived Jason was pleased to find that the security man was alert and he was not allowed in until recognised. As he parked, he was surprised to see a light in his office. Jed was already sitting there, with a cup of steaming coffee, looking down the list of horses. 'Well,' he said, happy as a sandboy, 'we'd better start work!' They divided the horses into various groups according to their age and experience, deciding that in principle the most advanced horses would normally be first lot, and that both Jed and Jay would always supervise them if they were both there. The second and third lots would normally be taken care of by Jay, while the youngsters who had been broken in or just started would be Jed's responsibility. It was also agreed that Sean would take charge of the first lot, as main work rider, working alongside Jed's head man who had arrived with The Conker and Pewter Queen and had already moved into one of the mobile homes.

'How are we off for staff?' Jay asked.

'We've certainly got enough to cover the first two lots, but we're going be struggling with the younger horses to start with. What I suggest is that the really young ones are put on the horse-walker for an hour every morning and then turned out in the small paddocks until we have enough people to get on with them properly.'

'I want you responsible for taking on staff,' Jay said. 'But before we actually hire anyone new, I want their references to be taken up. If we've any doubts, a friend of mine will do a private security check on them.'

After a cup of coffee, Jay was astride a horse and leading the first string up the gallops with Sean alongside him, both of them grinning from ear to ear with anticipation. 'It's certainly all happened in a short time, hasn't it?' said Jay.

'It certainly has guv'nor. We're really going to make this work, you know.'

'I don't doubt it for a second.'

'I'm glad Jed knows about me. I like him so much that I wouldn't have been happy keeping any secrets from him. I think I should tell him the whole story over breakfast.'

Jay gave him a meaningful look. 'Fine, but I think perhaps we should leave out our involvement in the Friend's downfall.'

Sean laughed delightedly at the thought of the Friend sitting in that office at the airport. 'Well perhaps not quite the whole story, then. But it's only fair he knows the truth about me.'

By now they were at the start of the all-weather gallops and, casting a quick look behind him to make sure all was well, Sean took off in front while Jay waited at the back to watch each horse as it went past him.

By the time they got to the top, the steam was rising from the entire string. As they started on their way back Jay was pleasantly surprised to see Howard, Victor and Hal, all of whom had stayed overnight in The Shepherd's Rest, standing in front of a Land Rover threequarters of the way up the gallops. From this vantage point they had been watching the horses through their binoculars. He trotted over to them. 'Good morning!' he called. 'Well, what do you think?'

'It's fantastic!' breathed Howard. 'You can see every yard of the way as they come, and you can see just how hard they have to work to get up there.'

Jason patted his mount. 'That's going to do this lot for today. I don't want to rush them. Let's all go back and have some breakfast.'

'Good idea,' said Howard. 'I've got all the newspapers for you in the car. You're going to be very pleased with the coverage we've got!'

Jason rejoined the string and returned to the yard where one of the lads took his horse. He had a word with each of the riders to find out how their horses had gone. Everything, it seemed, was satisfactory.

In her kitchen Cathy already had the breakfast underway. Huge pots of coffee and tea were keeping warm on the Aga. Everyone pored over the racing pages of the dailies. They were headline racing news in every paper and, as they had anticipated, had made the front pages of the *Racing Post*. There were photographs of the facilities, of some of the horses, and several of the eminent racing people at the opening party whose presence had got them into one or two gossip columns, too. There could be little doubt that this was the most significant development in training circles for many a year and, although judgement was reserved as to Jay's ability as a trainer, no such caution whatsoever was expressed about his talents as a rider. As one journalist put it: 'It's a huge responsibility to have a string of horses of such high potential in the knowledge that from now on you'll never be out of the racing spotlight.'

Amid the lively conversation they all agreed that on the whole the coverage was full and fair. Sean quietly slid the *Sun* to Jay. 'Look at page five,' he whispered. There the headline screamed out 'IRISH DRUG DEALER WANTED FOR MURDER'. The Irish police, said the *Sun*, wanted to question Liam Ahearne, currently in custody in the UK charged with smuggling quantities of cocaine into Heathrow, about the murder of a bookmaker who had died in a fire in what they now believed to have been an arson attack. They had already arrested a well-known minor drug-dealer who had confessed to setting fire to the bookmaker's home, insisting that a man known only as the Friend had paid him to do so.

'Well, well,' said Jay. 'One way or another, I think we can be sure that that gentleman is going to spend a pretty long time behind bars, whichever side of the water he ends up on.'

After breakfast Howard, Victor and Hal left to return to London together. Waving them goodbye, Jay told Jed that he and Sean would like a word.

They went into Jed's office and closed the door. 'Jed, you know who Sean is, but he doesn't want to have any secrets from you,' said Jay. 'You two will be key factors in the success we hope for, so I agree with him that it's only right you should know exactly what it is he's had to deal with since his accident. He made one silly mistake and it almost cost him his life. But he's learned from it and emerged a much stronger man.'

'Fire away, Danny – I mean, Sean. I'm listening,' said Jed quietly.

Sean settled himself in a chair and honestly recounted everything that had happened to him in Ireland and America, just as he had to Jay, explaining how he had met up again with Jason when he came over to warn him he was in danger over his ride at Cheltenham. '.... and now that this man had been caught,' he concluded, making no mention of his new boss's role in nailing Ahearne, 'I have my life back. And I am truly grateful for that.'

'You've been through a lot and I think you have been very courageous,' said Jed at last. 'I've always thought you were one of the best riders who ever crossed the Irish Sea, and if you're a friend of Jay's, you're a friend of mine.' He shook Sean by the hand. 'It will be a pleasure to work with you.' He toyed with his coffee cup, thinking. 'I must say, though, I'll be happier when your identity is out in the open. Now that this crook is no longer to be feared, what is there to stop you coming clean about who you are?'

'Nothing,' interjected Jay. 'We just didn't want to dilute the impact of our announcement about the new venture by giving the press too many big stories in one go. But as soon as they have finished chewing that over, and after Aintree, we can toss them this new bone. I've given it some thought, and my feeling is we need to say no more than that, after Danny was injured, he want to the States for a while and unfortunately he had more bad luck there – another accident, a car crash maybe, as a result of which he needed plastic surgery, and it took him a long time to get fully fit before he came home and met up with me.'

'I can't see anything wrong with that,' said Jed.

'Me neither,' agreed Sean.

'OK. I'll clear it with Howard, Victor and Eva before we go any further, but I'm sure it's the right way to go. I am glad we have this dealt with. I think it's important that we avoid having too many secrets. It's inevitable that as things develop here, there will be times when we'll want to play our cards close to our chests – about how some of our horses are doing, for example – but let's try to be as open as possible. It will make life much easier in the long term.'

Chapter Twenty-one

The big plans Jason and Sean had for the yard had to be put on hold for a few days while they dealt with the Grand National meeting, which was due to begin that Thursday. Every morning they examined The Conker, Pewter Queen and Peter's Pal thoroughly, checking the horses' legs for heat or any other sign of a problem that would prevent them running. Jason had agreed to ride Hopeful Return for Fiona and twice popped over to Midwood Park to school him.

The Aintree party travelled up to Liverpool on the Wednesday night. The Conker was running in the Handicap Chase on the Thursday, and that morning Jay walked the course before giving The Conker a brief, steady canter before they both had their breakfasts. Joining Eva, Howard, Victor and Jed in the restaurant at the Holiday Inn, he reported that the going was a little on the soft side of good, which would suit their horse.

Looking around the paddock that afternoon, Jay had to admit that The Conker, a really workmanlike horse, didn't have the same aristocratic looks as some of his rivals. But nothing was more muscled up, and he looked as well in his coat as Jay had ever seen him. Whatever he lacked in the beauty stakes The Conker more than made up for with courage and his ability to jump fences. After a lot of discussion it had been decided to run The Conker in the three-mile-plus Martell Chase, run over the Mildmay rather than the Grand National fences. The Mildmay is a separate course whose fences, although testing, are not quite as awesome as Becher's Brook or The Chair, the feared obstacles that are synonymous with the history and challenge of the

National. But it is still a real measure of stamina and jumping ability. It was not that The Conker would have any trouble with the National course, but the John Hughes Handicap was only two and threequarter miles, and they all felt this would be a little short for him and would not make full use of his stamina. Some of the horses that run in the Martell go on to compete in the Grand National, but for others the extra mile plus proves just too far. Not every 5,000 metre athlete is equally good over 10,000 metres!

Howard was more than usually nervous about his 'baby'. The Conker had become even more precious to him after Cheltenham. 'I'll look after him,' soothed Jay, 'and what's just as important, he'll look after me.' Howard laughed in spite of himself. Jed legged Jay up and after two circuits of the parade ring he and The Conker were on their way to the start.

As always, he let The Conker bowl along at his own pace. He jumped the first with ease, lying ninth of the fifteen runners, and Jason was very happy with this. The first five fences were cleared without mishap and soon the field was approaching a big, open ditch. The Conker soared over it. Jay immediately let the reins slip through his hands and sat back as they descended. As sure as a cat, The Conker landed and was on his way with hardly a break in his stride. Round the turn towards the home straight, Jay realised there must have been some grief behind him when a riderless horse came up alongside. Fortunately it soon veered away from them and didn't interfere as they jumped the next fence. Turning up the home straight for the first time, they had moved up into eighth place without the need for any change in The Conker's own pace. Soon they were approaching the water jump in front of the stands. The Conker saw the stride and glided over it, passing two horses that had not jumped as fluently. There was no change in the order down the long run round the bend to the back straight but, as the horses started to tire, Jay expected more falls here. Sure enough, over the first fence down the back straight, one horse got too close, and hit it.

Although it managed to stay on its feet, it ejected the jockey out of the saddle. At the big, open ditch another horse made a mistake and, striking the top of the fence, failed to keep its footing on the landing side. Jay was now sixth.

The Conker approached the seventh with the same confidence he had shown on the first circuit. There were five horses bunched together on the inside and Jay decided to give them a reasonably wide berth. He aimed The Conker at the middle of the fence which proved a very fortunate decision. One of the five runners jumped at almost forty-five degrees to the right over the fence and gave the horse beside him no chance. They collided in mid-air and both fell. Happily neither the horses nor their jockeys were seriously hurt. Jay was now third, and could detect no sign of fatigue in The Conker. They took the next fence with no trouble and the places remained unchanged.

Facing the final obstacles in the home straight, Jay decided it was the time to call upon The Conker's stamina. Asking for a little extra effort, he moved from third to second, a position he maintained over the last. The run from the elbow to the finishing line is infamously long and hard. Jason looked properly at the horse beside him for the first time and realised it was the favourite, which was giving The Conker 5lbs. Jay asked The Conker to move away. This he did readily, but there was an instant response from the other horse. Neck and neck, they fought their way up the steady incline. Jay could hear the crowd roaring and for a moment he thought the other horse was going to win but somehow The Conker's famous courage and stamina came to the fore. With an almost imperceptible increase in effort the chestnut gradually drew away, inch by inch, from his hard-ridden and gallant opponent to cross the line half a length in front. Both horse and jockey were as tired as they had ever been after a race, and as they were led in by The Conker's elated lass they were greeted by a huge cheer from the sporting crowd which loved to see a really game horse.

Jed and Howard were in seventh heaven. Howard was literally dancing with joy, and the granite-faced Jed actually had a tear in his eye as he shook Jay's hand and patted the horse. They were immediately surrounded by flashing cameras recording this moment for posterity, but it was a moment that none of them would ever forget even without a commemorative photograph. After a high-spirited evening with Howard and his friends Jay went to bed early in readiness for his ride on Hopeful Return in the long-distance novice hurdle on the Friday.

Before the race Paul Campbell, Hopeful Return's owner, stood with Fiona and Eva in the parade ring watching his horse walk round with the appreciative eye of a man who knew what he was looking at but also with the affection that all good owners develop for their horses. He had bred this horse himself and it was a proud day for him. Jay touched his cap to Paul and shook his hand, smiling at Fiona. 'Good luck, both of you,' said Paul. 'This is her last race, Jay, and whatever happens, I'm going to breed from her. With Fiona retiring I might concentrate on just breeding now.'

Fiona gave him a puckish look. 'I wouldn't make your mind up about that yet,' she said. 'This new trainer might give you as much fun as I have.'

'But is she good enough for you?' Paul asked Jay. 'I've been reading that you are going to be really choosy.'

'Let's wait till after the race,' replied Jay.

As the mounting bell rang he gave Paul a wide grin, walked up to the mare and was popped into the saddle.

Jay knew Hopeful Return well, having ridden her many times, including in the Triumph Hurdle at Cheltenham. He liked the filly. She was strong and she galloped and galloped. She wasn't particularly fast at the end of a race, so she always had to be up there, but he knew she'd stay on up the hill in the same way as she had at Sandown and Cheltenham.

Jay managed to get on the inside of the starting line so he could have the rail. He was also determined to be in a position to make the pace a hot one. The tapes went back and they were off. No one seemed particularly interested in making the pace so Jay took his horse into the lead and set a good, strong gallop.

Jay continued to let the mare bowl along. Going into each hurdle he tried to steady her slightly. She was a very confident jumper but could be a little careless and had fallen on a number of occasions in her earlier races. Halfway down the back straight on the second circuit, he reined her in slightly to give her a breather, which allowed a small group of three horses to close up on him, one alongside and two hot on his heels. But they all seemed content to carry on at the pace Jay was dictating and he maintained the same even gallop right the way round the bend and into the finishing straight. As soon as they straightened for home, he urged Hopeful Return on, reasserting a lead of a length or two. A grey horse was still tracking him confidently, but the other two were beginning to struggle and the rest of the field was several lengths behind. Not allowing himself to become overconfident, he made his mount look carefully at the second last which she cleared efficiently and economically. He urged her on a little more and she kept the lead but Jay knew that the grey was still in close contention and that his chances of winning in a sprint over the last hundred yards were poor. So, at the last hurdle, he asked her for a big jump. She almost got it right but hit the top of the hurdle hard, stumbled on landing and Jay found himself up her neck. For a moment he feared he'd let go but she quickly recovered her balance and he was soon back in the saddle. However, the momentum had gone and the grey horse had gone past them and gained two lengths. Slowly but surely, Jay inched up towards him. Fifty yards from the line he knew it was all over. A glance over his shoulder assured him that he was in no danger of being beaten for second so, using hands and heels, he rode the mare out without asking her to do what he knew was impossible.

Jumping off in the winner's enclosure, he turned to Fiona and the owner. 'I'm sorry,' he said. 'I shouldn't have asked for that big one at the last.'

'Not at all,' said Paul. 'You did the only thing you could, and we're absolutely thrilled. To come second in a race like this will add substantially to the value of any foals she has, and we couldn't be more pleased with the way you rode her.' He took Fiona's hand. 'Thank you for looking after her so well. It's been a delight to have you train for us for so many years, and we wish you every success in whatever you decide to do in the future.'

They allowed themselves to be shepherded round the horse's head for the mandatory photograph before, with another pat on the back for Jay, they let him return to the scales to weigh-in. He was chatting to some of the other jockeys when one of the weighing room officials came over. 'Mr Campbell would like a word with you.'

'Jay,' Paul said outside the weighing room. 'I think I might like to keep at least one good horse in training. Would you be interested?'

'Of course!' replied Jay with enthusiasm. 'If you decide to retire her, why don't you come and look at some horses I've brought over from Ireland?'

'That's a great idea. I'll call you next week.'

The last day of the three-day Aintree meeting is always one of huge excitement and enormous press coverage. Media people from around the world descend on the course to cover the Grand National, perhaps the most famous race in the world and certainly the most famous steeplechase. Over the years it has been the subject of drama and heartbreak, immense bravery and almost fairytale endings like that of 1981, when Bob Champion, then recovering from cancer, rode to victory on Aldaniti, a horse that had had so many leg problems that it had been doubtful that he would ever race again, let alone win this ultimate test of jumping stamina and courage.

Jay walked through the crowds to the weighing room, soaking up the atmosphere, occasionally stopping to talk to people he knew, many of whom were still congratulating him on Cheltenham and his successes on the other days' Aintree races. His two rides were in the last two races of the day. The first of these was the Amateur Hunter Chase, run immediately after the Grand National over three miles and one furlong on the Mildmay course, in which he was to partner Peter's Pal. As soon as that was over he'd be dashing to change his colours and weigh out again to ride Pewter Queen in the Champion National Hunt Flat Race. Earlier that morning he'd gone down to the course and taken first Peter's Pal and then Pewter Queen for a gentle hack canter around the area specifically marked out for the early-morning exercise. Now all he could do was sit and wait.

Although he was not himself competing in the National it was impossible to be immune to the growing excitement and tension of the build-up to the great race. As always, when the forty runners finally streamed away from the start there were a few early falls, but none resulted in injuries to either horses or jockeys. By the time they had cleared Becher's Brook for the last time there was still seven in with a chance. One of them was a big Irish horse being ridden by his old friend Freddie Kelly. Turning for home there were only three horses left with a real chance and Freddie's horse was going particularly well. They jumped the last and came to the famous elbow with its very long run in to the winning post. Freddie got into the lead as Jay, leaping up and down in the weighing room, screamed encouragement. To his absolute delight his friend cruised past the winning post to win his first Grand National.

Both horse and jockey were mobbed as they headed for the winner's enclosure. Jay barely had time to fight his way through the jostling fans and press men to congratulate Freddie, before weighing out, make his way to the relatively deserted paddock to talk to the owner, Frank Donovan, mount Peter's Pal and go down to the start.

Frank had told him earlier in the day that he definitely wanted Peter's Pal to stay in England, and had asked whether Jay would train him if everything went well in this race. And went well it did. If ever Jay was given an armchair ride, it was now. In the first stages the race went at a furious gallop, led by one or two of the less experienced amateurs who were probably still feeling the effects of the adrenaline rush created by merely watching the great Grand National. Jay was much more sensible, settling Peter's Pal almost at the back and biding his time. Going down the back straight for the last time, he crept up gently and, turning for home, started to pick off the seven horses in front of him, one by one. As he jumped the second last, he knew that unless something extraordinary happened he was going to win. The horse in front of him was labouring and Peter's Pal was cruising. At the elbow he asked for just a little more effort, got an instant response and a few seconds later he was pulling up past the winning post. His senses assaulted by the noise of the crowd and the pure joy on the face of the young Irish lad out there ready to lead in Peter's Pal made it a heady moment for Jay, in spite of all his experience. Trainer Jim Newman and Frank Donovan met him with the enthusiastic elation that somehow seems special to National Hunt racing. These horses are so much more than mere racing machines to most of those involved with them.

Frank was now desperate to have a long talk with Jay. The jockey reminded him that he was riding in the next race, but promised to have a drink with him at the end of the afternoon and tore into the weighing room where he was passed by the clerk of the scales, then into the changing room. Johnny Hampshire had his new colours ready and quickly adjusted the lead in the weight cloth to ensure that he was the correct weight for his last ride.

Although he was still savouring the thrill of winning his second race at Aintree, the prospect of riding this lovely mare for two of his great friends was enough to make him slightly nervous as he walked into the paddock to join Howard and Jed and the exuberant Bubbles.

Typically, the two men congratulated him warmly on his last ride before turning to the business of his next. But it was clear he wasn't the only one who was nervous. There was a lot at stake. If Pewter Queen won this race it would establish her indisputably as the leading National Hunt Flat horse of the season, and perhaps the most successful National Hunt Flat mare of all time.

The last time he had worked Pewter Queen, on Wednesday morning, she had lived up to his every hope that she would improve steadily after her first run at Sandown and then her triumph at Cheltenham. Perhaps his judgement was clouded by the recent victory, but he had a good feeling about this race. The sun was shining and, looking at the mare, he saw a thoroughbred at her very best. 'How will you ride her?' asked Jed, much more for Howard's benefit than his own as he and Jay had discussed tactics many times already.

'They normally go a good gallop here, but the long run in often catches them out' replied Jason. 'I'm sure the two Irish horses will be set on making it a true test of stamina. I won't let them gallop me off my feet. I'd like to stay about fifth or sixth, but she always starts well, so I shan't lose any ground there. If I'm in the first two or three after the first furlong, I'll just let her settle, so if a few go past me I won't worry. As you know, she always quickens, so I'll try to be second or third with a furlong or two to go and make for the line in the last hundred yards or so.'

Howard and Jed nodded their agreement.

The bell rang and suddenly he was in the saddle. On the way down to the start he noted this was the quickest going he had ridden Pewter Queen on, and she was clearly enjoying the 'top of the ground'. At the start the twenty-one runners circled, the jockeys chatting to one another as the starter's assistant checked the girths and the starter consulted his watch to make sure the race was off on time but not a second too early. All these relatively inexperienced horses behaved extremely well, the line was formed efficiently and, on the cry from the starter, the tapes went up.

To begin with, everything went almost exactly as Jay had predicted. Pewter Queen got away quickly and was soon in a leading bunch of four. By the time they reached the winning post, with a circuit to go, she had been relegated to eighth position as a number of horses went flying past her, some of them pulling far too strongly for their own good. She was settled beautifully on a long rein and was obviously having the time of her life. From Jay's point of view it was another armchair ride. All of a sudden, on the crown of the bend, the third horse in the leading group slipped and went down. For a moment there was pandemonium as the other runners swerved to avoid horse and jockey. The rider in front of Jay cut across him to navigate round the faller and Jay had to pull hard to prevent a collision. Pewter Queen responded perfectly but they had lost a good ten lengths. They were now in tenth or eleventh position and some fifteen or sixteen lengths behind the leaders rather than the seven or eight that had separated them before the incident. But the mare was still going so easily that he was not unduly worried. Keeping her settled, he let her go down the back straight at the same pace. Nothing got further away from them, though neither did he make any significant progress. As he turned out of the back straight the pattern of the race started to change. Some of the early leaders, particularly those that had pulled hard, started to drop back and Jay edged slowly up. Hugging the rails, he saved every inch of ground he could, and by the time they straightened for home they lay fifth. Pewter Queen was still going like an angel. He clicked his tongue at her and, giving her a slight squeeze with his heels, moved her up from fifth to fourth.

By this time he could see that two of the horses in front of him were already being ridden hard, though the Irish favourite was still going well. With a furlong and a half to go he asked the mare for a little more effort and she powered past the second and third horses. They were now only a length behind the favourite. Jay saw the Irish jockey glance over his shoulder and register the grey head of Jay's mount gaining on him. He picked up his whip and drove hell for leather to the finishing line, less than a furlong away. Jay kept his cool. He gradually sneaked up until Pewter Queen was neck and neck with the big bay horse. With a hundred yards to go he gave her a slap on the shoulder and hissed at her. She reacted instantly and, with a change of pace which surprised even Jay, swept into the lead, passing the finishing post with six lengths to spare.

Jay was ecstatic. He had known this was a really good mare; now he was convinced that she was without question the best he'd ever sat on. With any luck she would make one of the stars of his new training establishment. To his amazement, the normally reticent Jed was already halfway down the walkway leading to the winner's enclosure, his arms in the air, fists clenched in triumph. 'She's a real champion isn't she, lad?' he cried.

'She certainly is,' said Jay. Within seconds Howard was jumping up and down beside them, alternately beating Jay's boot and wildly patting Pewter Queen's neck. 'She's the best I've ever had,' he crowed. 'Absolutely the best!'

'I think you might be right,' smiled Jay. 'But let's not sell The Conker short. He's going to be a special horse for you, too.'

After celebrating with the connections, an exhausted Jason climbed into the passenger seat of his Jaguar. Eva, at the wheel, was chattering away happily when she became aware that he was very quiet. 'My darling, what's the problem?' she asked, concerned.

He looked at her solemnly. 'I can hardly believe it,' he said. 'To ride three winners and a second was just beyond my wildest dreams. It's a fantastic way to finish. But it's just starting to hit me how much I'm going to miss it.'

'Well, why don't you carry on riding just our horses? None of the owners could possibly object.'

He smiled wearily. 'You're terrific, but it's going to be hard enough to do my job properly as a trainer without trying to ride as well.'

'Just remember that when one door closes, another one opens,' she replied

'I know.' He squeezed her hand.

The Sunday newspapers were full of Jay's Aintree exploits and some of them speculated whether he would continue to ride, even though he had made it quite clear in all his answers to the questions put to him in the post-race interviews that he would not. Although it is an accepted truth that it is best to quit while you are ahead, nobody, it seemed, could quite believe that he could stop riding after such a marvellous success.

He was pleased to see that his comments about the victories really being the work of Jed and Fiona were widely quoted. It was great to see Jed winning two really big races and proving at last that, given the ammunition, he was as good a trainer as any other in the country.

Howard was soon on the phone, still high as a kite. He admitted that he had a £500 each-way double on his two horses which had netted him a little under £20,000. Add to that his prize money, Aintree had given him and a really handsome profit on the purchase of The Conker and Pewter Queen.

'As you know, Jay,' he said. 'I'm not in it for the money – what am I talking about? Who on earth is in National Hunt racing for the money? But it really is nice when you get some of your investment back.'

Chapter Twenty-two

With Aintree over, Jason, Eva, Jed and Sean were able to turn their full attention to putting down roots at County View. Hurry had put the finishing touches to the stables and started in earnest on the stable lads' living accommodation. The training hurdles and steeplechase fences were erected and a steady stream of applicants for stable jobs were interviewed, shortlisted, checked out and hired. Four weeks after the open day, County View was a going concern in every sense and the routine of a busy racing yard was firmly established. Jed's horses were all moved out of Sussex to their new homes, and he and Cathy settled into theirs. As Fiona wound down her own yard, she popped over from time to time and Jason was enormously grateful for her support and calm, sound, no-nonsense advice. Jason and Jed, and often Sean, too, sat down every night and planned the next day's work, splitting their charges into different lots to bring the young ones on steadily and increase the workload for the more mature horses week by week.

Eva arranged for the BBC and Channel 4 to film features at the yard, including footage of the facilities, interviews with Jason and one highly entertaining one with Howard and Victor. In between she got the house organised and they were able to move out of The Shepherd's Rest. Though it was hardly grand, it benefited greatly from her style and imagination, and what had originally been planned as a basic, functional place for a busy bachelor trainer to lay his head at night, turned into a comfortable, welcoming home as she trawled the local antique shops for furniture and other bits and pieces to add to some possessions of her own that were on their way over from South Africa.

All the publicity they received from the launch, Jason's personal success at Aintree and the television features, kept them permanently in the news for weeks and, to everyone's gratification, the phone soon started to ring with owners wanting to come and talk about Jay training for them.

In order not to waste anybody's time, such inquiries were met with courtesy but their policy was made clear over the phone. Those owners who still wanted to come and see the facilities and talk to Jason were welcomed, but in the end only two horses were accepted in the early days. One was Big Angus, a six-year-old which had won all five of the point-to-points he had run in the previous year – his first year of training. He was a strapping great gelding and Jay saw him as a likely top class hunter-chaser who would perhaps go on to even greater things in two or three years' time. The other, The Zircon, was a complete surprise. He was a three-year-old who had come fourth in the St Ledger, the stayers' Classic, and had real potential as a hurdler. 'He could easily be a Triumph Hurdle horse,' Jay remarked to Jed on their way back from looking him over in Newmarket, where The Zircon had been trained for the Flat.

The press coverage was, it seemed, self-perpetuating, but eventually the papers began to run out of meaningful things to say about Jason and County View and Danny Derkin was, at last, allowed to 'come out'. The whole circus then began again, with reporters and television cameras turning up at the yard. Though they had all steeled themselves for such an onslaught, nothing could have prepared them, especially Danny himself, for quite how intrusive and persistent it would be. The tabloid news reporters were a different breed altogether from the racing journalists, and a far less pleasant one. Eva was kept extremely busy parrying all the requests for exclusive interviews. One journalist even wanted to write

Danny's life story for a book, which led to a lot of mickey-taking around the yard.

Aware that he would be left alone sooner or later if he agreed to talk to somebody, and in order to discourage the newshounds from digging too deeply into Danny's missing time, Eva arranged one or two interviews with hand-picked members of the racing press, on the condition that the main focus was his work at County View. He did speak about the long road to recovery after his second 'accident', but the circumstances of the 'accident' itself were kept vague. The official line was that his memory of it, and of the immediate aftermath, was extremely sketchy.

It was a very stressful period for Danny. Perhaps one day he would be able to tell the whole story, but if that was ever possible, it wouldn't be for a long, long while. Although Liam Ahearne and his associates could have no way of connecting his arrest with Danny, there was no point in taking any risks and Danny didn't want his head to be above the parapet for too long. Eventually the fuss died down, and once he was finally left alone, the relief of shedding the burden of his double life was immense.

They were all grateful for the short summer break in the National Hunt calendar, although some courses kept going by watering their turf. Jason had decided to miss this to give everyone a much-needed breathing space to prepare for the next season. They all agreed it was sensible not to be tempted to rush out any runner too soon and Jason felt they should wait until September when, with a bit of luck, the ground would be good enough not to jar up any of their horses.

In June Howard gave Jed the good news that he had found a buyer for his Sussex yard. The sale went through smoothly to Jed's evident relief.

'Well, that's it, you're stuck here now whether you like it or not,' Jason joked to him.

'I wouldn't go back now for any amount of money,' Jed declared. And it was clear he meant it. He was in his element at County View, doing the work he loved without the heavy financial worries that had come with running his own yard. He had weaned himself off cigarettes altogether and was looking happier and healthier than he had for a long time before his heart scare.

A week of widespread thunderstorms at the end of August, followed by a couple of days of steady rain in early September, did wonders for the ground as Jason prepared to make his public debut as a trainer. He had chosen Stratford-upon-Avon as the venue, a relatively flat course just over an hour's drive from County View. The whole stable was buzzing with anticipation and, to Jay's surprise, the normally unflappable Eva seemed in a real tizzy. Only Jed was his normal pragmatic self. As Jason supervised the loading of the horses and watched the horsebox depart, Jed said to him: 'Well, you'd better be off. I'll see you when you get back.'

'What do you mean?' Jay asked incredulously. 'Aren't you coming?'

'No. This is your day, not mine.'

In spite of Jay's entreaties, he remained adamant that he would stay behind and look after the yard. Defeated, Jason went upstairs and changed into a tweed suit. This was an entirely new experience. No longer would he be wandering into the weighing room dressed as casually as he liked. He was a trainer now and on show.

Arriving at the racecourse with Eva, he was taken aback by the presence of so many racing journalists, not to mention two television channels, for such a run-of-the-mill meeting. The clerk of the course came up as he was checking that the horses had been correctly declared. 'You can come here any time you like if you bring this much publicity for us,' he joked. 'Seriously, Jay, the stewards would like you and Eva to join us for lunch – if you've got time, that is.'

Jay smiled ruefully. 'To be honest, I don't think I could do justice to a proper lunch. Perhaps we could join you for a drink at the end of the afternoon when my butterflies have subsided?'

'Of course. We'd be delighted. And I hope it'll be more than one.'

Jason had three runners on the card, all of them horses he had picked in Ireland. It Pays to Wait was a two-mile novice steeplechaser with several point-to-points under his belt, as yet unraced over fences. Buck's Fizz was here for his first outing as a hurdler, having won a bumper in Ireland. The third was My Final Fling, the horse sold to Jay by Kate Harty, which would be running in her late husband's colours. All three horses were to be ridden by Freddie Kelly.

As he saddled It Pays To Wait, Jay felt the tension building. It was incredible; by the time he'd got to the parade ring, he was far more nervous than he had been for any race he'd ever ridden in. 'You look like an expectant father waiting for his first child to be born,' said Freddie gleefully.

'I don't know how that feels,' said Jay, 'but I can tell you this is much more nerve-wracking then riding, even against tough buggers like you.' As the bell rang Jay legged him up and, patting the horse's neck and Freddie's boot, he wished them both good luck.

Standing beside him on the steps of the new grandstand, Eva was a nervous wreck. 'I can hardly bear to watch,' she admitted.

'Me neither.'

She squeezed his hand.

As the race got underway, Jay's horse showed his point-to-point experience as he cleared fence after fence cleanly and smoothly. Turning for home with three to jump, It Pays To Wait was lying third, and he and the two in front soon drew away from the rest. Jumping the second last, they were all upsides, and remained that way until the last. On the run-in, however, the other two drew away quickly and Jay's horse came in third, beaten by about eight lengths.

Jay went off to meet Freddie. 'We don't need to worry about that,' said the jockey. 'This fellow's grand but he needs another half, probably another mile. You've got a really useful young horse here and you'll win at least a few races with him.'

Howard and Victor were waiting for him in the winner's enclosure. 'Not a bad start at all!' said Victor encouragingly.

'No, it isn't,' said Jay. 'It would have been nice to kick off with a winner, but this is pretty satisfactory.' They went off for a cup of coffee in the owners' and trainers' bar above the restaurant until it was time for him to saddle Buck's Fizz, the novice hurdler. Jason knew he was a decent horse, not only on his bumper form but also from the sort of work he had been doing at home. But several of his opponents were unknown quantities, too, so he really couldn't guess what the outcome was likely to be.

'I know he stays,' he told Freddie in the paddock, 'so I think you can stay fairly handy in this race with two miles six and a half furlongs to go.' Stamina would be the key factor.

On that day's fast ground at Stratford, two or three horses set off at a breakneck gallop. Freddie let them go on, aware that the chances of them staying were remote, and settled Jay's horse in fifth.

With a circuit to go, Buck's Fizz was still lying in the same position and had been jumping extremely well for a young horse having its first run over hurdles. Going down the back straight, he gradually passed three of the four in front of him, but the leader was still going as strongly as ever. Turning for home, he was still three lengths down and apparently not making any progress. But the picture changed dramatically at the second last. Suddenly the lead horse tired and Jay's horse was hauling him in hand over fist as they approached the last. Only half a length down, it looked odds-on that Jay would be celebrating his first win, but then Buck's Fizz's inexperience showed. The horse took off a full stride before Freddie asked him, he hit the top of the hurdle and sent the Irishman flying out of the saddle.

Eva was almost in tears, but collected herself when she saw the horse clambering to its feet and galloping past the finishing line, clearly none the worse for its mishap. Happily, Freddie, too, was climbing to his feet and walking back towards the weighing room before the ambulance picked him up and gave him a lift the rest of the way.

Jay rushed over to the weighing room door to make sure that Freddie was all right. 'I'm so sorry about that,' said the jockey mournfully. 'We would have won for sure, but his enthusiasm let him down. He'd been jumping so well that it was probably my fault not keeping a bit of a firmer hold on him as we approached the last. I think he was looking at the horse in front of him rather than the obstacle.'

'That's racing,' said Jay. 'You'll both live to fight another day. Right, we'd better talk about the next one, if you're OK.'

He wanted to warn Freddie that, although My Final Fling was a horse with a fast finish, in a two-mile handicap hurdle he couldn't afford to be too far away. It was the last race of the afternoon so at least the jockey had a chance to get his breath back. He went into the weighing room for the mandatory once-over by the doctor, but he'd suffered no damage from his tumble and there was no question that he would certainly be fit to ride Jay's last runner.

Sadly, Kate Harty had not been able to come over from Ireland for the race. In the parade ring Jay could see that Eva was a bit depressed by their lack of luck in the previous race, but the sympathy shown by the racing journalists, with many of whom she had already developed a good rapport, bucked her up. She handled their questions with her customary aplomb while Jay concentrated on his own duties.

My Final Fling was second favourite, but the odds-on favourite was a course specialist at Stratford having won here four times. As the race began there was a faller at the first which resulted in a number of horses having to swerve. Fortunately, My Final Fling was not one of them. Freddie settled the horse fourth out of fifteen, carefully tracking the leaders with the favourite a length and a half behind. There were no more errors from the experienced field as they crossed the fence on the bend before turning to face the three fences in the finishing straight.

By now Jay's horse had moved smoothly into the lead but was still under threat from the favourite. This was the moment when Freddie's class as a jockey proved a decisive factor. Coming off the bend, he gave his horse a kick and slightly increased the tempo. As he went into the second-last, he gave My Final Fling a quick slap down the shoulder and asked for the horse to put in a big jump. His mount responded magnificently and gained a good length over the favourite whose jockey was slightly taken by surprise at the manoeuvre. Using his speed My Final Fling accelerated towards the last fence. This time Freddie was a little more conservative in what he asked for and the response was excellent. Their one-and-a-half-length advantage was held, in spite of the best efforts of the pursuing favourite. The extra 6lbs he was carrying as a result of an excellent record over similar races was just too much, and the very short run from the last to the winning post at Stratford gave him no time to make up the ground.

All Jay was aware of was his own voice cheering Freddie and My Final Fling and Eva screaming her head off beside him. Then Howard and Victor appeared, and were jubilantly slapping him on the back. They all trooped into the winner's enclosure where the photographers and TV cameras elbowed each other to get pictures of jockey and trainer before Freddie went to weigh-in. Through the din Freddie tried to tell Jay that this horse was a hell of a good buy and would win him a lot more handicaps; in fact he might even be a lot better than that. The horse would have no problem going to Ascot or Newbury, and even the Cheltenham Festival might be a possibility, he thought.

Eventually the media were satisfied and the clerk of the course came and escorted Jay, Eva, Howard and Victor into the restaurant where the stewards had their own room.

Champagne corks popped and Jay was heartily congratulated. He had always been a popular jockey and people were genuinely pleased that he should have had a winner on his first day as a trainer, quite apart from the satisfaction the locals felt that it had been at Stratford. One of the stable lads drove Eva and Jason home. 'You've had to be very abstemious in toasting our first winner,' Jason acknowledged. 'I'll make it up to you when we get back. There'll be a bottle of champagne for you.'

'That's very decent of you, guv'nor,' he replied, 'but we've all done well today. We all backed him. We had the other two as well, but we saved our money on It Pays To Wait, and we made a nice few quid on My Final Fling.'

They arrived home well after evening stables had finished, so Jay was astonished to find that the entire staff were still there. A huge cheer went up as he got out of the car. Jed was the first to pump his hand. 'Well, this calls for a bit of a celebration, I think. How about I take you all down to The Shepherd's Rest?' Eva gave him the number of the local coach company she used. They agreed to send down a couple of minibuses, and whatever other transport they had to spare. He telephoned Steve, the landlord, to arrange for sausages and bubble and squeak for everybody.

Before they left he went into his office and rang Kate Harty. 'It's a grand thing to have a winner,' she told him, 'but to provide you with your first is a real thrill. It must be fantastic for you, and everyone associated with your yard. I know this will be the first of many, but whatever My Final Fling does, this will always be special to me. Thank you so much, Jay. My husband would have been over the moon.'

Then Howard and Victor appeared. Victor's chauffeur was prevailed upon to help with the transport. At The Shepherd's Rest, dishes of sizzling sausages stood ready for them, along with huge bowls of bubble and squeak and thick slices of homemade wholemeal bread.

The champagne corks had been popped and the food was already being passed round when the door opened and in came Hal, Bart and Len.

Jason couldn't believe it. 'What on earth are you guys doing here? How marvellous!'

'We couldn't let this day go by without marking it, could we?' said Hal. Looking at the plates, he added: 'And I guess we could all manage some of that. Whatever it is.' The evening really went with a swing. Perhaps everyone enjoyed it all the more because it had been arranged on the spur of the moment. Whatever the case, it was obviously exactly the right note to have hit with the staff, and morale was sky high. At 10.30 Jay marshalled the minibuses and Hal, Bart and Len left for London. Victor's chauffeur dropped Eva and Jay back at County View before taking Howard and his boss home. Jay felt drained, more emotionally than physically. He and Eva almost fell into bed.

After first lot the next morning Jay poured himself a cup of coffee, sat down to look at the newspapers to see how his red-letter day had been reported. It soon became apparent that plenty of others were doing the same as he took one call after another from owners offering him their horses – and in some cases, it would be no exaggeration to say, practically begging him to take them on. Politely but firmly, he explained that, for the time being, he did not want to expand his string.

As the phone rang yet again, he braced himself to deliver his standard line, but this time it was Benny. 'Hi boss. I thought you'd like to know that Jimmy James, that photographer, has been seeing a lot of Howard's old friend Frankie Johnson the bookmaker. I'm keeping an eye on them, but they seem to be as thick as thieves.'

This was an interesting development. That same afternoon, Jimmy James himself rang. 'Hello, Jay.' His tone was unpleasantly ingratiating. 'I wonder if I could come down and take some photographs tomorrow?'

Jay thought for a moment, trying to decide whether he should keep the photographer at arm's length or let him come and try to work out what he was up to. 'Of course,' he said, opting for the latter course of action. 'What time were you thinking of?'

'If I could come down for first lot, that would be great,' Jimmy said. 'I'd like to spend the morning with you, if that's possible.'

'Sure,' said Jay. 'If you want to stay somewhere nearby tonight, I'd suggest The Shepherd's Rest. Would you like me to phone the landlord for you?'

Jimmy sounded very keen on this idea.

Jason booked him in at the pub, and asked Steve to keep tabs on him. 'I'm a bit worried about what it is he might be after, so it would be a help to know if he meets anybody or anything like that,' he explained.

'Sure, Jay.'

At 10.30 that evening, just as Jay and Eva were thinking about bed, he had a call from Steve. 'Your friend's been in the bar since just after seven. One or two of your lads have come in and he's made a beeline for them, buying them drinks and asking them a lot of questions. What sort of answers he got I don't know, but I thought you'd like to know.'

'Do you know which of my lads were talking to him?'

Steve named two or three. 'There were a couple of others, but I don't know them by name.'

Jason had a pretty good idea who they'd be and decided to have a word with the staff in question once Jimmy was out of the way the following day.

Promptly at 6.50 the next morning security buzzed to say that Jimmy James was at the gate. Jay gave the all clear and watched an old Japanese 4WD lumbering up the drive. Jimmy jumped out, unloaded his camera gear and offered a treacly smile and an outstretched hand. Jay was polite but not overly warm. He pointed to Jed who was waiting by the Range Rover. 'Jed will take you to see the first lot working.'

Jimmy was also keen to take some photographs around the stables.

'Fine. I'll get one of the stable lads to meet you when you get back from the gallops and show you round.'

When Jimmy had gone, Jay asked Billy, a lad who had come up from Sussex with Jed's team, and who was totally discreet, to take charge of the photographer personally.

'I'm not sure he's on the level,' Jay warned the lad. 'So, I don't want him wandering around on his own or talking to the other staff out of your earshot. OK?'

'Understood, guv'nor.'

In the stables Jimmy snapped picture after picture, carefully checking the names of all the horses he had photographed both on the gallops and in their boxes. He had to get his information right for his captions, of course, to ensure that he didn't send prints of the wrong horse out to his clients, but even so it seemed to Jay that his approach was unusually forensic. The trainer got the distinct impression that this rather seedy character was compiling a catalogue of his horses rather than simply collection images for future news items

When at last Jimmy had everything he wanted in the can he left the yard, Jay called in the three lads he knew had been talking to the photographer the night before. They openly acknowledged that he had probed them about a number of the horses – how close they were to running, how good the lads thought they were. They had answered him truthfully insofar as they were able, but the fact was they couldn't tell him much simply because they didn't know the information he was after. Nothing they could have said to him gave Jay particular cause for alarm, but warning bells were beginning to ring more loudly about Mr James. The same pattern had emerged at the yard. According to Billy, he had stopped every lad or lass he could to find out as much as he possible about each horse, writing everything down in his little notebook. Perhaps he was just showing a highly professional interest, but his reportedly close relationship with Frankie Johnson posed a big question-mark in Jason's mind. He phoned Benny to tell him what had happened, asking him to keep monitoring the pair of them, and alerted Howard to what was going on. For the moment, there was little else he could do.

Chapter Twenty-three

Over the next three weeks Jay sent out a total of twenty-one runners. Only three were serious disappointments. With the other eighteen he managed four wins and five places, a thoroughly satisfactory strike-rate for any trainer, and especially for such a new recruit. After all the initial excitement he began to relax, find his rhythm and enjoy the work. To his surprise he did not miss raceriding as much as he had expected. He discovered the deep pleasure and satisfaction to be gained from planning each horse's routine and placing it in suitable races. He still rode at least one canter every day and schooled when he could.

Just before lunch one day he had a telephone call from Harvey Molineaux, an amateur jockey with whom he always got on well, even if Jay had reservations about Harvey's rather zealous use of the whip. 'I'm moving down to work at Cirencester Agricultural College,' he told Jason, 'and I wondered if there would be an opportunity for me to ride out with you?'

'You'd be most welcome,' said Jay.

'I know you've got Freddie and Paul Jenkins working for you, and you couldn't ask for two better jockeys, but I also wondered if there might be any chance of some amateur rides?'

Jay hesitated, fiddling with a paperclip on his desk. 'I'll be honest with you, Harvey,' he said. 'I think you're a really good jockey and horseman, but I do think you hit your horses too hard and too often, and I wouldn't tolerate that.' There was a pause at the other end of the phone. 'I've got to be honest with you, too. My father said exactly the same to me. And I'm going to try very hard to be a bit more restrained. It's not because I enjoy hitting the horses, you know. It's just that I get overenthusiastic and overexcited.'

'What you've got to remember is you must give a horse a chance to respond to one smack. Besides, I believe that with most horses hands and heels and a slap down the neck is just as effective. If you look at the records of people like Francome and Dunwoody, they were seldom in front of the stewards for overuse of the whip, and riders don't come any better than those two.'

'Point taken. So can I come? When would you like me to start riding out?'

'When are you going to be down here?'

'Next Sunday night.'

'In that case,' said Jay. 'I'll see you on Monday morning. We pull out at 7.15 so be here at seven sharp. I look forward to you working with us.'

He strolled over to the yard and told Jed and Danny the news.

'Ah,' said Danny. 'I know what you mean about the stick. But he is a bloody good rider, and sometimes there are easy amateur races to pick up. Lots of the top trainers aren't keen on putting amateurs on good horses, even if the prize money's OK.'

A fortnight later Britain found itself in the grip of Arctic conditions and there was scarcely any racing for ten whole days. Jay, Eva and Jed spent hours planning where and when they would run their horses as soon as the big freeze was over, aware that they would probably have to have runners at two, if not three meetings a day. This meant they would have to split the outings between them. They decided that Jed would go with some horses, Jay with others, and that Eva and Danny would look after the rest. Eva was becoming increasingly important to the running of the yard, quite apart from her PR role. She had quietly taken over the majority of the routine administration, including making the entries and declarations produced by Jed, Danny and Jay.

The team was running like a well-oiled machine. The stable staff were hardworking and got on well together. Jed, Cathy, Danny, Eva and Jay had built up a great deal of mutual affection as each came to appreciate more deeply the others' strengths.

It was just as the thaw came that Jay received another call from Jimmy James. This time he put him off, explaining that because of the backlog created by the bad weather, he was very sorry but he really couldn't afford the time for any diversions. In a wheedling tone, Jimmy tried to talk him round. But he was adamant.

Four days after speaking to Jimmy, the security man buzzed him. 'Guv'nor, I think you ought to know that there's somebody perched up in a tree not very far from our perimeter fence and he seems to have some sort of optical equipment. I haven't gone close enough to disturb him, but I thought you ought to know.' Jay found his binoculars and rounded up Danny. They went into the garage, where Jay got into the back of the Range Rover, and lay down. Danny threw a blanket over him and drove out through the security gate, in the direction of the village. But once out of sight of the copse where the spy was lurking, he did a U-0turn and pulled up behind a ruined barn a few hundred yards away.

As they got out of the car they saw a familiar old Japanese off-road vehicle parked some way into the copse. Jason crept in for a closer look. Leaning against a tree, stabilised by the front wheel of the 4WD, was a ladder. At the top of the ladder, sitting on a bough with a pair of binoculars and a tape-recorder was Jimmy James, absorbed in watching the second string working on the gallops under Jed's supervision.

Jason crept back to the Range Rover, motioning Danny to get back in, and they drove away.

'Don't you want us to get him down?' asked a puzzled Danny in the car.

'No, I think I'll throw him some bait and see if we catch anything with it.' He pondered for a moment. It didn't take Sherlock Holmes to work out where Jimmy James would probably end up early that evening. 'Danny, I think you should pop into The Shepherd's Rest for a well-earned pint with some of the lads at the end of the day.'

'What a grand idea, guv'nor.'

'If Mr James should happen to be in the bar, I'd like you to be friendly to him.'

Danny was rather taken aback when Jason told him how friendly. He wanted Danny to mention how he had overheard a conversation between Jed and himself in which they had agreed that two particular horses due to run in a couple of weeks' time would win, and that both trainer and assistant trainer intended to have a decent bet on them.

'Leave it at that,' said Jay. 'If he asks any more questions, just say you don't know anything else. Then inquire casually whether this sort of information might be worth anything to him. If he offers you money, take it, but bring it straight back to the yard and give it to me, and I'll give you a receipt for it.'

Just before eleven that night Danny knocked on Jason's door. He was wearing a triumphant grin. 'I've been given fifty quid for the information and told that there'll be another £100 for each if they win.'

Jay took a piece of paper from his desk and recorded the details. He signed the note, asked Danny to do the same and put it into the safe with the money.

'What's going on boss?' Danny wanted to know.

Jay told him about Howard's bad experience. 'I've been waiting for the opportunity to set up this Frankie Johnson, and I have a feeling this might be it. According to Benny, he and Jimmy James seem to be great chums all of a sudden. That's why I was so keen to buy Surprise Packet in Ireland when I saw his resemblance to The Conker was as strong as you had told me it was.

'Well, well, well,' said Danny, as all the pieces of this jigsaw began to drop into place.

'If I'm right about Jimmy James's connection with Frankie Johnson, we need to convince him that he is getting reliable information from somebody who knows what's what here.'

'After all you've done for me, I consider it a privilege to help you do the same for another of our friends,' declared Danny. 'Besides, anything I can do to hurt a cheat like him will be my pleasure.'

The day came when the two tipped horses were due to run at Worcester. The first was competing in the novice hurdle, the first race on the card that afternoon. It had already been placed third that season but, with two previous winners in the field, the betting opened at 7-1 and varied between 6's and 10's as the off approached.

The reason for the confidence Jay and Jed had in the horse, apart from the fact they knew the previous run would have brought him on in fitness, was that they had upped the distance by half a mile, which they knew that would suit him extremely well. Howard, who knew about Jay's 'sting', had decided to come along to the meeting, to see how it went. 'Somebody's taken the bait,' he whispered to Jay as the horses were circling. 'The horse is down to 7-2 second favourite. That would have taken a substantial bet.'

Freddie was riding the horse. With a furlong to go it was lying fifth of the field of fifteen. Entering the back straight, the two in front started to increase the pace and the fourth horse rapidly came under pressure. The third was still tracking the two leaders a length and a half behind, and Freddie brought Jay's horse up alongside. Turning out of the back straight, the second horse started to crack and Freddie edged up into second position. At this stage the front runner showed no signs of feeling the pressure and approached the third last still two lengths to the good. Freddie sat patiently, creeping up with no special effort as they approached the second last. Again both of them jumped it well. There was no change in the order, but the difference was now a mere length. At this stage the Irish Champion Jockey asked his horse for an effort and its stamina came into play. Quickening his pace almost imperceptibly he passed the leader as they approached the last, jumped it beautifully, and was soon pulling clear to win by a comfortable three lengths.

As Jay made his way to the winner's enclosure, one of the rails bookmakers who knew him well commented, 'You had a few bob on that one, Jay.'

'No, I didn't,' he replied.

'Then somebody off-course put a bomb on him.'

'Not me,' insisted Jay, looking him straight in the eye.

Freddie was warm in his praise for the horse he had just ridden. 'Give him another year and this'll be a really good three-miler,' he said. 'The way he jumped those hurdles you'd be thinking about putting him over fences, perhaps even next season.'

'We'll think about it,' said Jay. 'The horse you've got to ride in the two-mile chase is a totally different proposition. He barely gets two miles, which is why this flat course at Worcester suits him. But he has a hell of a high cruising speed, so I want you up there the whole time. If you can be two or three lengths clear jumping the last, you should just about hold out.'

'Right, guv,' said Freddie, and went in to weigh-in.

Howard and Jay had a cup of coffee while the next two races took place and then Jay went out to saddle the horse. 'I think I'll have a few bob on this one,' said Howard. 'What sort of price will he be?'

On his way across to the grandstand Jay glanced at the prices to see that this horse, one of Jed's the previous year, was second favourite at 9-2. These were probably fair but not overgenerous odds. As he watched the horses canter down to the start, Howard nudged him. 'I've just had £500 to win. The horse is now 2-1.'

'Wow!' said Jay. 'Someone else must have had another real punt on it.'

The tape was released and the runners approached the first fence in full flight. Freddie had Jay's horse on the inside, and already it was disputing the lead with two others. By the time it had passed the winning post for the first time, having jumped two more fences, it was in the lead, going a very strong gallop heading down the back straight. The field was virtually in single file. Freddie was three to four lengths ahead taking the last down the back straight and suddenly injected extra pace and stole a valuable few lengths. He was leading by a good ten as they entered the home straight with four fences to jump. The field remained relatively strung out but two horses started to make steady progress, cutting Freddie's advantage to only five lengths as they leaped the second last.

Freddie rode his horse hard at the last, steadied it two or three strides from the fence and, getting a beautiful clean jump, they landed running with almost no break in rhythm. With a hundred yards to go the gap was down to two lengths with the favourite closing rapidly. Freddie gave his horse two slaps down the shoulder and rode as hard as he could. The winning post was in sight but the favourite was gaining on them with every stride.

Crouching low over the horse's neck, Freddie rode as hard as he could with hands and heels as the winning post came. 'Photograph. Photograph.' called the commentator. Jay and Howard hurried to the winner's enclosure as the horses pulled up and cantered slowly back past the stands to come off the racecourse and into the paddock. He drew alongside Freddie and gave him a questioning look. 'I just held on, I think, guv'nor.' Almost immediately his gut feeling was confirmed by the loudspeaker. There was a great cheer from Howard.

'Now, that's what I call a very satisfactory afternoon,' observed Jay. 'Let's go and have a drink.'

'What a good idea,' agreed Howard. 'And this one's on me. I made a bit over a grand.'

Down by the rails the same bookie raised an eyebrow at Jay. 'I suppose you didn't back that one, either?'

'No,' grinned Jay. 'But Howard here did.'

'So did somebody else. There was big money off course. I'd love to know whose it was.'

Jason merely smiled to himself.

In the bar Jay took a call from Danny on his mobile. 'I've had a very happy Jimmy on the phone. He says there'll be a present for me in the post tomorrow.'

Christmas was now only eight weeks away and there were some big meetings in prospect. Jay had already pencilled in Splendid Warrior, the previous year's Gold Cup winner, for the King George VI at Kempton. He was also hoping to run Hot Toddy, one of the Irish horses, in the four-year-old novice hurdle at the same meeting. The Conker would be aimed at the Welsh National at Chepstow, but. in addition to this role, he had to take into account the fact that the horse was going to be the major player in settling Howard's outstanding score with Frankie Johnson.

The day after Worcester he telephoned Marcus Fitzgerald in Ireland to see how Surprise Packet, was coming on. 'He looks a picture,' Marcus reported. 'But to be honest, I think he's going to need another year to grow into his full strength.'

'What sort of distance do you think he's going to require?'

'He's pretty quick. At the moment he doesn't stay on too well at the end, but I suspect he's going to be a two-miler or a two-and-a-half-miler.'

'I'd like to come over and have a look at him in a couple of days' time, if that's all right with you?'

'Of course it is,' said Marcus.

That afternoon, Jason drove over to The Laurels for a discreet lunch with Howard. Bubbles had laid a table for the two of them in the conservatory, adjacent to his enormous indoor swimming pool. 'I know the two of you want to talk business,' she said, 'so I'll leave you to it.' Plates of smoked salmon and a superb game pie awaited them, along with some sparkling mineral water and a bottle of Chablis.

'I think we're close to being ready to implement our little plan,' said Jason, sipping his Chablis. 'I'm hoping to bring Surprise Packet over from Ireland in two weeks' time, a few days before the Newbury meeting. Danny will make up a box for him at Fiona's yard, which is deserted now, and stay there with him for a couple of days. I'm going to ask permission to work some of my horses after racing at Newbury. I've spoken to Victor, and arranged for Jed to take The Conker, along with two of our other horses, to his country house just outside Newnham Common. Danny will meet Jed there with Surprise Packet, and we'll switch him with The Conker before going to Newbury.'

'So it will be Surprise Packet that works at Newbury rather than The Conker?'

'You've got it.

'There's just over a week between Newbury and The Conker's race at Towcester. He's bound to be favourite or second favourite. After the races we'll switch the horses again and Surprise Packet will go back to Fiona's until after Towcester. Then he can come to County View.'

Howard chortled. 'I'm going to enjoy this.'

'We must make sure we get it right,' said Jay sternly. 'It's going to be bloody expensive for you if we don't.'

That evening he sat down with Jed and Danny to go through this complicated strategy. It was important that this smoke-and-mirrors subterfuge didn't actually break any of the rules of racing and obviously he needed to be sure the logistics worked. When all the details had been dealt with, Jay turned to Danny.

'Right. The first thing is for you to telephone your friend Jimmy James. Tell him you've got some information for him but that after Peter's Pal, you don't want to talk over the phone. Meet him somewhere and tell him that a piece of work is being done after racing at Newbury Saturday week and that you know Howard is planning a big bet on The Conker, who's been working brilliantly at home. Leave him to make any connection he chooses. Also tell him that Peter's Pal is in tremendous form and should win next Monday at Uttoxeter. As long as Peter's Pal runs as well as we expect him to, it will increase the credibility of what you're saying about The Conker.'

He looked from one to the other. 'OK, guys? I think we're all set.'

Chapter Twenty-four

In the coming days, Jay produced four winners and two seconds and found himself in third place in the trainers' table. In fact, in terms of number of wins, he was second but prize money was the criterion, and as he had won fewer big races than his nearest rival he had earned slightly less. What gave Jay as much satisfaction as his own growing reputation was that young Paul Jenkins was now regularly riding winners and placed horses for him, and getting good rides from other trainers, too.

Between race meetings he squeezed in a flying visit to Ireland to see Surprise Packet for himself and make arrangements with Marcus Fitzgerald to have him brought over to England. He didn't feel comfortable keeping all this from Eva but his desire not to have her involved in the Frankie Johnson business if at all possible outweighed this discomfort. As they usually discussed everything he knew she would immediately pick up on any evasiveness on his part and worry about it, so he sat her down and told her that if it seemed to her that something was going on behind her back, it was because he was trying to resolve a delicate matter for Howard, who had been swindled by somebody a long time ago. 'I'm not doing anything illegal, I promise you, and it's nothing to do with County View itself so you've no need to be concerned about it on that score. It's just that having the yard puts me in a position to be able to help him sort this out. But, as I say, it's Howard's business rather than mine. Besides, I really feel that it's better for you, both personally and professionally, if you genuinely don't know the details for now, so I just want you to trust me on this one.'

She was hardly overjoyed about this but, reasoning that Jay was trying to do the right thing by both Howard and herself, she accepted it at least for the time being.

At lunchtime on the day after Jay had briefed him, Danny had phoned Jimmy James from a callbox in the village. They had arranged to meet at a rather anonymous pub just outside Swindon. Jimmy was clearly highly excited at the prospect of getting another good piece of information and Danny duly passed him the tips they'd agreed.

'There'll be another present for you if this comes off,' Jimmy assured him.

'Where's the money coming from?' inquired Danny innocently.

'Ah, that I can't tell you. ' Jimmy put his finger to his nose.

'I think what I'm giving you is worth a bit more than I've been getting. If I don't get £500 this time I won't be giving you any further information.'

Jimmy gave him a hard look. 'Well, that's not my decision,' he said. 'But I'll tell my boss.'

'Tell him I mean it,' said Danny.

They finished their drinks and left the pub.

Twenty minutes later, as Danny was driving home, his mobile phone rang.

'The five hundred quid is yours,' said Jimmy.

'That's more like it,' said Danny. 'I'll keep the information flowing.'

That Monday Peter's Pal had duly won rather easily at 5-1, and everything was set up for the Newbury switch. That morning Pewter Queen and The Conker were loaded with another young horse. Although Danny was absent, the staff were slightly surprised to see Jed driving the box, though he did do this from time to time. He just told them he just wanted to be at Newbury to see how the horses worked. As two of them had originally been his, a certain sentimental attachment was understood.

When they arrived at Victor's country home they found him pottering around his garden. Surprise Packet was already in residence. Victor was in high spirits: any suggestion of a delicious conspiracy excited him. The Conker seemed slightly bemused at being led out of the horsebox and straight back into a quiet stable, but he was soon settled and munching happily away at his hay.

After the racing at Newbury, Freddie Kelly on Pewter Queen, Paul Jenkins aboard the promising novice chaser and Danny on Surprise Packet went out to canter two furlongs steadily and then work at racing pace for a mile and a half. A few race goers had stayed behind on the rails or in the grandstand to watch Jay's horses, and were tracking them through their binoculars with great interest. Jay spotted Jimmy James standing next to an older man, short, fat and very flashily dressed. This had to be Frankie Johnson.

Just then, the head of Jockey Club security walked by.

'Good afternoon to you,' Giles Sinclair stopped and shook hands with Jason. Haven't you got a bodyguard today?' he asked wryly.

'Those days are over, thank goodness. I was just wondering who that man is over there, standing next to Jimmy James, the photographer.'

Giles followed his gaze. 'Ah, Mr Johnson,' he said. 'One of our more interesting bookmakers. Frankie Johnson. Why do you ask?'

'Just curious. I've seen him around a lot but I didn't realise he was a bookmaker.'

'He thinks he's too important to stand on the rails himself, but he does take some very large bets, I can assure you.'

'Oh, does he?' said Jay casually. 'Well, that's put a name to the face. Thank you.' Smiling apologetically, he changed the subject. 'Well, I had better concentrate on watching these horses of mine work.

'Of course – don't let me distract you. Nice to see you, and I'm glad everything's going so well for you.' Giles raised his arm in farewell and hurried on.

By this time the horses were almost at the mile and a half start. They slowed down and Jay could see the three jockeys talking to each other. Then they were off, going at a very good gallop. Side by side, they glided down the back straight, round the long sweeping bend and then into the home straight, which is just slightly uphill. With two furlongs to go they were still side by side. But through his glasses Jason could tell that Surprise Packet was beginning to struggle a little. A furlong out Danny was having to ride him hard with hands and heels while Freddie and Paul, on the other horses, were sitting tight. By the time they reached the winning post there was a good twenty lengths between them and Surprise Packet.

Instead of walking out on to the track, Jay stayed where he was, letting the horses come in, led by their respective lads. When he eventually met them with Jed he was aware that Jimmy James and another man had appeared behind him. He made a big show of shaking his head. 'Well, what do you think?' he asked Freddie.

'My horse went like a dream. But I shouldn't have left The Conker like that.'

'He just didn't seem to have anything in the tank over the last furlong and a half, guv'nor,' added Paul Jenkins. Danny nodded his head in agreement.

'Oh, well. Take them back and wash them down,' said Jay. Looking pensive, he turned to Jed. 'That was a bit disappointing, wasn't it?'

'I wouldn't be too anxious,' said Jed, with a tersely well-rehearsed response. ' He can have the odd off day, can't he?'

'Yes, but not that bad,' remarked Jay. 'He just didn't look that enthusiastic at the end.'

'I still wouldn't worry too much,' said Jed. 'He's got enough class to win the race, even if he's only ninety per cent.'

'I'm not sure I agree,' said Jay curtly. He walked away, and that was the end of the conversation.

Later that evening, Pewter Queen, the novice chaser and the real Conker were back at County View. Surprise Packet, in Danny's care, was having a well earned rest in Victor's stable. At about 10.30 Danny rang. 'Good news. They've taken the hook. I've had Jimmy on. He was very agitated and wanted to know if The Conker's got something wrong with him. I said we were all disappointed, but perhaps it was just an off day.'

'Phone him back tomorrow and tell him we're all puzzled,' said Jay. 'Say I don't really want to run the horse, but Howard's so convinced he can win, that he's adamant. You can also let it slip that I'm not happy.'

A couple of days later, Howard, Victor, Danny and Jay met up at County View to plot their next move. 'Here's my suggestion for scene two,' Jason began. 'I remain concerned about The Conker's form and think he's probably had enough for this season. We can find nothing wrong with him, but he's just not firing at home. For once Howard and I have had a significant disagreement. Howard is insisting that The Conker runs at Towcester in what is a surprisingly valuable race for that course, arguing that because it's a stamina-testing course, it will suit the horse. He is also dead set on having a big bet. He doesn't want it known that he's behind it, and is therefore asking Victor to shop around for the best odds. Victor can telephone Frankie Johnson and say that he's heard he's a bookmaker who gives slightly better prices and isn't frightened of taking on a sizable bet. He ought to take the bait. The one thing Victor must do is make sure that he gets a voucher confirming the bet.'

'On the day of the race, Victor phones up and has a double with The Conker and one of our other runners we're pretty confident about. It may be we just make it an each-way double. How much do you want to go for, Howard?' They all looked at Howard.

'Fifty grand.'

'Make it fifty each way and I'll take half of it with you, Howard,' suggested Victor. 'It halves your risk, and as long as you get 5-1 or better, we're not going to lose money. It doesn't particularly bother you who gets the money as long as it hurts the bookmaker, correct?'

'Too right,' agreed Howard.

'Fine,' said Jay. 'That's up to you. Now, Danny, you have a face-to-face meeting with Jimmy, tell him the situation and let's see what happens.'

With conspiratorial smiles all round, they finished their coffee and went out to watch the second lot of horses working. Far from being out of sorts, The Conker was feeling great and jumping out of his skin. Danny hopped on board and, after a mile and a quarter's fast piece of work, he popped him over four fences. As always The Conker took them in his stride with a mixture of authority and *joie de vivre*.

Danny met Jimmy in a pub opposite Swindon railway station to nurture the seeds already sown.

'The boss said there's a grand in it for you this time if you're right,' said Jimmy.

'Great.'

'How confident are you?'

'He was as flat as a pancake today. I rode him myself and I've never known him so lethargic. We've had him blood-tested, and there's nothing wrong with him; I think he's just had enough this season. He has had some very hard races, and remember, he's been up against top opposition carrying substantial weights and over very long distances. I think the guv'nor's right and that Howard is mad, but he's got the bit between his teeth and he's going to get someone to lay a really big bet for him.'

'Do you think you might be able to put it our way?' asked Jimmy in his wheedling tone.

'Who is we?' questioned Danny quietly. 'All I know is you've asked me for information, I've given it you, and you've paid me. But I've heard there have been some big bets on

274

some of our horses, and Jay's intrigued. The one thing I can tell you is the last thing he suspects is that I'm giving information. But I can't put anything anybody's way unless you tell me whose way you want it put.'

Jimmy was silent for a moment. 'I'll have to go and make a phone call,' he said at last. He went outside on to the forecourt of the station, where Danny could see him pacing up and down, talking earnestly into his mobile.

'I've been told I can tell you,' he said when he came back. 'But heaven help you if it gets out.'

'Are you kidding me? If it gets out, not only do I lose my job, but I'll probably be banned from all racecourses as well.'

'I see you point,' said Jimmy. God, the man was terminally dim, thought Danny. 'All right. I'm paid by Frankie Johnson, the bookie. It seems he and Howard know each other from way back, so Howard might well go for it. If you can swing that, Frankie says we'd be really grateful. There could be as much as five grand coming your way.'

'I'd have to be careful not to be too obvious,' Danny reasoned. 'But I guess I could just mention in certain quarters that Frankie is well known for giving slightly better odds and never shy of taking a big bet.'

They had one more drink while Jimmy tried to squeeze more out of Danny. Danny told him there was no further really good information to be had at that stage. He wasn't going to spoil his record by giving tips that might turn out to be wrong. 'Remember,' added Danny, as he got up to leave, 'it won't be Howard who makes the bet.'

Jimmy was out of the pub door like a startled rabbit, his mobile phone already at his ear.

Talking to Victor that evening, Jason suggested he waited until the morning of the race to place the bet, just in case anything went wrong with The Conker. And phone one or two other bookmakers to get a price before asking Frankie what his best price is. He'll almost certainly want to ring you back, so he can check out other bookmakers, and with a bit of luck the word will have got around that you're looking to place a big one. That should ensure he'll take it from you. On the morning of the race, you can then place your single bet, but ensure your bet has been accepted and confirmed by fax, Howard can call him and put a double on as we agreed.'

'That sounds damn good thinking to me,' said Victor.

Danny, Jed and Jay were on tenterhooks. The Conker still had to do his full work, and every evening and morning they felt his legs, dreading they might find a sign of heat. Each time they were reassured as they felt like cold bars of steel.

Two nights before the race Danny got a call from Jimmy. 'How are things?' he asked.

'Just the same, if not worse,' Danny told him. 'I think the horse is seriously bored with the whole game. I heard Jay and Howard on the phone having the nearest thing to a row I've ever heard them have. Jay really doesn't want to run the horse but Howard won't give in.'

'That's good to know,' said Jimmy. 'Perhaps we shouldn't talk again between now and the race.'

'I'll call you if I think you need to know anything,' said Danny, 'but otherwise that's probably best.'

At last the morning of the race came. Jay had three runners. Besides The Conker, there was the novice chaser who had worked at Newbury and an unraced mare in the mares-only National Hunt Flat race. Both had excellent chances but the mare was the better each-way bet as the chaser was in a field of only seven runners. The Conker had nine to beat. Howard placed his £5,000 each-way double with Frankie. The bookie knew this was not a particularly huge wager for Howard, but with the mare at 7-1, and The Conker at $5\frac{1}{2}$, odds of $38\frac{1}{2}$-1 would still see Howard winning over £200,000 on this bet alone if they came in. Victor then phoned Frankie and placed £50,000 each way on The Conker in his own name and managed to get 6-1. The bet was acknowledged and accepted by fax.

Jay and Howard had agreed in advance to behave in a slightly strained way at the races. This shouldn't have been difficult, considering the sums at stake, but Howard was hugely enjoying all this skulduggery. Jason was obliged to give him the occasional warning glance to rein in his tendency to overact. Danny, who was looking after The Conker that day, had deliberately not groomed him particularly well. For good measure, he sponged down the horse's neck before it left its box, so that by the time it got to the parade ring, it appeared as if it had been sweating. Yet nothing could have been further from the truth.

As Jay legged Freddie up, he said to the jockey quietly, 'This, Freddie, is the most important race this horse has ever run.' Freddie stopped adjusting his stirrups and looked searchingly at Jay.

'Do I take it the money's down on him today?'

'Yes,' replied Jay. 'In a big, big way.'

'Enough said,' smiled Freddie. 'It this horse doesn't win today, I'm a Frenchman.' He left the ring, full of confidence.

Jay walked back past the bookmakers, deliberately subduing his usual springy step. He saw that most of them were laying 4 or $4\frac{1}{2}$ -1 on The Conker with 5s in some places. For once Frankie was on his stand and taking bets himself. He was offering $5\frac{1}{2}$-1, and a lot of the small course punters were piling in on him. He was even accepting bets from other bookmakers. If The Conker won, this was going to be a very painful day for Mr. Johnson.

Jay stepped up on to the grandstand. He deliberately did not go and stand with Howard or Victor, who had now arrived. As the start time loomed all three of them were becoming genuinely nervous. Even Howard had tired of the novelty of play-acting: his furrowed brow was not put on. The race was three miles one furlong, but Towcester is probably the most demanding course in England. It has big fences and it boasts the steepest climb from the bottom of the final bend to the finishing post of any racecourse – even more severe than the one at Cheltenham. It is a course that gives the real stayer his ultimate chance.

And now the race was off. An outsider ridden by a conditional jockey set off at a swinging pace that Jay knew was far too strong to take anything round Towcester, even though the horse was only carrying 10st. Freddie settled The Conker in fourth and the main pack galloped on at a much more sedate and sensible pace. On the first circuit, the favourite, Rainbow's Gold, stumbled slightly at the last fence down the back straight, drawing a gasp from the crowd, but the fright for those supporting it, was fleeting. Soon the field was coming up the home straight and past the stand with a circuit to go. By this time the leading horse was dropping back towards the main pack, and as they passed the winning post it was only five or six lengths ahead. Climbing the hill away from the stand, they were soon faced with a downhill fence. All cleared this safely. Although the second brushed through the top of it, the horse did not lose any significant momentum. Turning down the back straight, The Conker was in third place, but the speed had been increased and Rainbow's Gold came up and joined him.

The four leaders went down the back straight tightly grouped. All jumped efficiently with no change to the order. Wheeling out of the back straight, Rainbow's Gold started to raise the pace and quickly went into the lead. Freddie sat still on The Conker and did not ask him for any effort. He was by now three to four lengths behind Rainbow's Gold but had moved into third position and was swiftly gaining on the horse lying second.

As they neared the bend and the daunting hill, The Conker was now in second place, but still two or three lengths behind Rainbow's Gold. Jumping the next, the placings remained unchanged but Freddie had yet to ask The Conker for more. Rainbow's Gold was also running well within himself. As they approached the second last Jay could see that the hill was beginning to take its toll on the leader. Instinctively Freddie now asked The Conker to make an additional effort. A quick kick and a slap down the shoulder and the horse moved up alongside Rainbow's Gold. As they took the fence side by side, Freddie asked for still more. Showing no sign of fatigue, The Conker stuck his head out and drew steadily away from Rainbow's Gold. Victor, Howard and Eva were all going bananas in the stand. For a moment Jason scarcely dared move a muscle, but as the chestnut passed the winning post, a good eight lengths in front of the favourite, he joined the cheers of the crowd.

The scenes of jubilation in the winner's enclosure were unbelievable. Eva gave Howard a knowing look. 'You'd have thought he'd won the Gold Cup, not a race at Towcester,' she said drily.

'You know me Eva,' replied Howard. 'I've never been one to curb my emotions. Besides, I've always wanted to win a race here, and Victor and I have made a few pounds as well.' Then he was throwing his arms around Freddie, full of praise for the way he had ridden the horse.

Once Freddie had weighed in the result was official and the bookmakers had to pay out. Victor and Howard smirked at each other like naughty schoolboys and they marched off to see Frankie Johnson about their 'few pounds'. By the time they arrived at his stand there was already quite a queue of racecourse punters waiting to collecting from him their winnings on The Conker. Frankie did not look a very happy man. He was also in a foul temper.

Once the queue had subsided Victor and Howard ambled over and stood in front of him. 'When are we going to get paid?' asked Victor.

'Come off it, boys, I don't carry that sort of money round with me,' snarled Frankie.

'That doesn't answer my question.'

'It'll be in the post tomorrow,' muttered Frankie.

'What about my cash bet today?' asked Howard.

Frankie glanced at his cashbox. 'I don't seem to have quite enough to pay you that, either,' he said sarcastically.

'My, my,' said Howard, 'you are having a bad day, aren't you?'

Frankie glared at him. Howard met the glare without flinching. 'Frankie, if we don't get the money within the next three days, you will be in serious trouble, and I mean *serious* trouble.'

Frankie looked decidedly uncomfortable. 'You'll get your money. Damn you!'

Victor and Howard started back towards the owners' and trainers' bar, but evidently Howard decided he hadn't quite finished with Frankie. Abruptly, he turned on his heel, strode back to the stand and planted himself so close to the bookmaker that their faces were almost touching.

'You know, Frankie,' he said in a frighteningly low voice, 'Victor and I must have made nearly as much money today as you did on that amazing double at Doncaster all those years ago. I've waited a long time for this moment, Frankie. And I can tell you that vengeance is very sweet. Very sweet indeed.' His eyes flashing with triumph, he caught up with Victor. 'A glass of champagne now, Victor, don't you think?'

On his way back home Howard had another thought. He remembered that the son of his old East End mate, Kipper Fish, had just started working as a reporter with the *Racing Post*. He called Kipper on his mobile. After a bit of chitchat about The Conker's fortunes, he said, 'Listen, Kipper, I've got something that might be of use to your boy. But it hasn't come from me OK?'

'Understood, mate. I'll just tell him I got it from an unimpeachable source. What is it?'

'The word is that old Frankie Johnson lost a lot of money today. And he hadn't laid any of it off.'

Kipper chuckled. 'Well, well, that is some story. And it couldn't have happened to a more deserving case. Thanks, my old chum. The boy'll be very interested to hear it, I'm sure.'

Jason was amazed when he looked at the front page of the *Racing Post* the following morning to see almost the whole of it devoted to The Conker's win at Towcester and the enormous losses that, it was understood, had been accrued by the bookmaker, Frankie Johnson. He smiled to himself. Howard was clearly reveling in his revenge.

Putting the paper down, he poured himself a cup of coffee. He heard Eva's footsteps in the hall. She came into the kitchen and kissed the top of his head. 'Anything about us in the *Post*?' she asked.

'A bit,' replied Jay. 'A bit on the front page.' He held up the paper. Eva gasped. She took it from him and scanned the story. 'Am I to take it,' she said at last, 'that this ''business'' of Howard's is now resolved?'

Jay laughed. 'My smart girl,' he said. 'A man would have to get up very early in the morning to catch you out.'

Eva folded her arms. 'Well?'

'Now it's all over, I'll tell you the whole terrible tale.'

Eva poured herself a cup of coffee and listened to Jason without interrupting.

'...so you see, Howard didn't want anyone else involved in case it all went horribly wrong. And I certainly didn't want you involved. But nothing did go wrong, so now I've told you everything.'

Eva's face was very serious.

'You do see, don't you, darling?' persisted Jason anxiously.

'Yes I do. But from now on, Jason, no more secrets. It hasn't been much fun knowing that something has been going on behind the scenes, and it's no less worrying not being involved, believe me. More so, probably. I hope nothing like this ever happens again, but if it should, I want to know the worst, OK?' She stood up and stroked his face. 'After all, I'm a big girl now.'

Jason smiled. He felt so relieved that the dual stress of staging 'the sting' and keeping it from Eva was gone. 'It's a promise,' he said fervently.

Chapter Twenty-five

Much of Jason and Eva's first Christmas Day at County View was not very different from any other day, with the big race meeting at Kempton on Boxing Day topmost in everyone's thoughts. They politely declined an invitation from Howard and Bubbles on the basis that with everything that needed to be done in the yard that day there wouldn't be time to go elsewhere. Instead they opened their doors to anyone who wanted to join them. Hal came to stay and rolled up his sleeves to help with everything from the horses to cooking the lunch. There were drinks for the staff after work that morning, the numbers swelled by others dropping in, including Freddie Kelly and Paul Jenkins and locals like Hurry Henderson and, after he had opened for an hour himself, Steve from The Shepherd's Rest and his wife. Howard popped in briefly before his own big family lunch ('If Mohammed won't come to the mountain...,' he beamed as he made his entrance). The phone rang often with callers wishing them a merry Christmas and lots of luck in the New Year, among them Fiona, who was off on her travels, Victor, also away, and some of Eva's friends from South Africa.

In the afternoon, Cathy and Eva laid on turkey with all the trimmings for Jay, Jed, Danny, Hal and one or two of the staff and other stragglers who stayed on. Although it was a day of only partial relaxation for many, with diet and alcohol restrictions for some, everyone thoroughly enjoyed it, and nobody seemed to mind the comings and goings to deal with other matters. In fact, in a lot of ways it was the happiest Christmas Jay and Eva could remember. 'Not a bad family occasion for two orphans, eh?' said Eva sleepily to Jason later.

He held her closer, marvelling again at how readily she had accepted England and County View as her home.

On Boxing Day morning the yard was a hive of activity. Hot Toddy was running in the two-mile novice hurdle, the opening race of the afternoon, and Splendid Warrior in the King George VI Chase. Jay felt they both had excellent chances. Hot Toddy was another of the horses Jay had bought in Ireland. He had already won a nice race at Huntingdon, like Kempton a relatively flat right-handed course, so he had every chance of repeating that form. The papers shared Jay's confidence and had made Hot Toddy the 5-2 second favourite to a horse that had been extremely successful in its native France and had won impressively at Ascot a few weeks earlier.

Seeing the horses safely on their way, Jay had a word with Jed and made his final decisions about how the rest of his charges would be exercised that day. Then he, Danny, Eva and Hal were on their way to Kempton. Even though they arrived a full two hours before the first race, the traffic was already extremely heavy and the racecourse teeming with excited and enthusiastic race goers. Danny went off to the stables and reported back that both horses had travelled quietly and were totally relaxed but interested in their surroundings.

Sticking to orange juice, Jay went with Eva to meet Hal, Howard, Bart and Len in the owners' bar, where they discussed the horses' chances until it was time for him to saddle Hot Toddy. The course is almost a perfect triangle, with two hurdles to jump on each side. The start of the novice hurdle was to the right of the grandstand, so the sixteen runners had two hurdles to clear before they made their way down the side of the course going away from the stand.

Jay joined his party on the stand to watch the horses canter down to the start at the beginning of the home straight. They were quickly off and soon the field was streaming towards the first hurdle and then the second. Turning away from the grandstand on the very sharp bend, the horse on the inside slipped and fell bringing two more down with it. Hot Toddy was still on his feet but seriously hampered. From a handy position in the middle of the pack, he was now last but one and a good twenty-five lengths behind the leader.

Freddie sat quietly on the horse and did not try anything overdramatic. Slowly but surely, he inched through the back of the field towards the four in front and was content to tuck in behind them as they jumped the second of the two hurdles going away from the stands and turned the bend to face the two jumps on the far side of the track. The two leaders now injected some extra pace and started to move away from the other three. Freddie took Hot Toddy to the outside of the third and fourth placed horses and steadily pursued them. Jumping the third last, he was third but still four lengths behind the first and second horses who were racing neck and neck. Turning for home, the grey horse on the inside accelerated again and moved away from its galloping rival. Freddie urged Hot Toddy on and, jumping the second last, moved into second place. Approaching the last he cut down the lead – three lengths, two and then one. Both horses jumped the last well and, with a little over 200 yards to the winning post, went for it hell for leather. But for Freddie the winning post came too soon, and he had to settle for a second place, a neck behind the winner.

It was disappointing that Hot Toddy hadn't quite done it but, as Freddie pointed out if it hadn't been for the mishap that had lost him both distance and momentum, there was no doubt that Hot Toddy would have won. 'He'll like Cheltenham even better,' added Freddie. 'But he might want another year before we put him in at the very top.'

With a breezy wave he went to weigh-in before getting ready for his next race, a novice chase for another trainer in which he recorded a comfortable third. He was not riding again until the big race, so then he – and the Country View team – were able to relax a little.

As the Kempton course is much flatter than Cheltenham not all Gold Cup stars find it to their liking. But considering Splendid Warrior's extraordinary speed at the end of a race Jay saw no reason why he should not be able to cope with the Kempton track. The fences were certainly much easier, for a start. Freddie was equally confident that the horse would justify the 7–2 price tag the bookmakers had given him.

Standing in the paddock talking to his owner, Barry Davey, Jay felt almost the same surge of adrenaline as he used to when riding in a big race. Splendid Warrior looked magnificent. Jay explained to the owner that Freddie would have the horse handy but would not make the pace. If it was not a genuinely fast gallop, this would actually play into Splendid Warrior's hands, as there was nothing else in the race with his finishing speed. But, with such a big prize at stake, it was almost certain that at least one of the other horses would try to make it a true test of stamina.

Freddie joined them. He touched his cap and shook hands with the owner, whom he knew well, and then he was being legged up. Jay went across to the grandstand and waited there for Barry. Although he wasn't betting on his horse, he was interested in seeing what the market looked like. Barry reappeared and reported that from 7-2, the horse was now 3-1, or 100-30. Obviously the bookmakers still considered him to be the main player.

The start of the King George VI Chase is just round the corner from the finishing post, so the field was clearly visible from the grandstand as they approached the first fence. As Jason had suspected, two of the horses, including an Irish challenger, were making it a good gallop and soon all eleven horses had taken the first and were rapidly advancing on the second. These were all seasoned campaigners and their jumping ranged from good to excellent. As always, Splendid Warrior was smooth and effortless in his clearance of the obstacles. It was interesting, thought Jay as he watched this wonderful horse, that his jumping was so economical that it did not look particularly spectacular. Yet there was nothing that moved away from the fences faster, and very few horses that did not actually lose ground to this champion.

Splendid Warrior remained in fourth or fifth position throughout the first circuit and was going really easily. As they passed the winning post for the penultimate time, Jay could see that all the horses were still moving well, as would be expected of such a high-class field. Turning down the back straight, one of the Irish horses suddenly set a dramatic increase in the pace and caught the two horses closest to him by surprise. Soon it had opened up a five-length lead. Freddie moved Splendid Warrior out, and with no apparent effort passed the second and third horses to settle with the Irish horse in his sights. They headed down the side of the track and jumped the open ditch, they leaped two more plain fences before sharply wheeling right to face the last three in the home straight. By now it was really a two-horse race. Freddie sneaked up to within a length of the leader. They both dealt with the third last superbly and the distance between them remained the same. Over the second last, Splendid Warrior outjumped his rival and powered towards the last with a half-length lead. The Irish jockey, riding his horse vigorously, came alongside Freddie and went half a length in front. Freddie sat still and kept that margin. As they approached the last, Freddie allowed his wonderful mount to manage the fence in his own economical way. The two horses landed side by side. This was when Freddie moved. With a kick and a slap down the shoulder, he asked Splendid Warrior to quicken. There was an instantaneous response, and a wall of sound hit them from the stand as the Gold Cup Champion effortlessly added the King George VI to his already impressive list of wins.

Jay rushed down with the owner and was in the chute from the course by the time Splendid Warrior started to pick his way through the applauding crowds. Freddie, his face glowing, reached down and shook both his and Barry Davey's hands, and then acknowledged the cheers of the crowd. Splendid Warrior was breathing heavily, but he certainly didn't look like a horse that was in any distress after his exertions.

In the winner's enclosure he was surrounded by humans all brimming with enthusiasm and excitement.

'What's next, Jay?' the television commentator asked.

'I've got to talk to Mr Davey, of course, but perhaps one race before Cheltenham. No more than that.'

With one last salute to the owner, Freddie went to weigh-in with the air of a man who really enjoyed his work. The same could be said of the demeanor of his trainer as he accepted questions from the press and the congratulations of well-wishers alike with good-natured attentiveness. If anyone could have doubted Jason's total immersion in his new role, they needed only to look at the light that shone in his eyes now.

Chapter Twenty-six

In the New Year there began the countdown to Cheltenham as always – but this time a very different kind of Festival from Jason's perspective. Last year's Gold Cup-winning jockey was now obsessing over which horses he should run.

Having originally entered seven, when the entries were released and he reviewed the going, he decided to reduce this to four. It was a year too early to run either of his best hurdlers in the Champion Hurdle, he thought. Peter's Pal was down for the National Hunt Handicap Chase, a little over three miles and nineteen fences. On the second day My Final Fling would compete in the Coral Handicap Hurdle over two miles five furlongs. On the last day he would run The Zircon in the Triumph Hurdle and Splendid Warrior in the Gold Cup. Freddie was due to ride three of the horses and Paul Jenkins was being given a chance in the Handicap Hurdle.

The preparations reached fever pitch in the week before the Festival. Everyone was on edge and, for the first time, tempers occasionally became a little frayed. After breakfast one morning Eva gently put her arms around Jason. 'Just steady up, darling,' she said. 'You're starting to snap at people. We know how important this is to you, but it's just as important to everybody else.'

Jay smiled apologetically. 'I suppose it's just that I've never been so nervous about anything,' he admitted. 'This is our really big test. We've got four horses running, all with a real chance, and I know I'm going to be judged not only by the racing public at large, but also Victor, Howard and Hal. Although they are hugely supportive, they will also want to see how well we do. Last year will be a hard act to follow, and some of the press will be looking to knock us down.'

As they loaded up the horses on the first day, Danny seemed a bit wistful.

'Everything OK, Chief?' asked Jason.

'Oh, fine. Just a bit of a pang that it won't be me riding today.'

'I know exactly how you feel,' said Jay, slinging an arm round Danny's shoulder.

'I wonder if I could get my licence back?' mused Danny.

'You know you'd have my support, but I don't think it's a good idea. Even if you pass the Jockey Club's medical, do you really want to take a risk again? I know how fit and well you feel, but like me you're not getting any younger, Danny.'

'I guess you're right. I'll just have to enjoy leading them in, won't I?' The moment had passed and he waved cheerfully as he jumped into the horsebox to escort Peter's Pal the twenty-odd miles to Cheltenham.

As Eva and Jay drove off later Eva was chatting animatedly on her mobile to various journalists and passing on messages from Howard, Victor and Hal to Jay. They were all going to be there but wanted him to know they were keeping their fingers crossed for him.

During the preliminaries for the National Hunt Handicap Chase Jay felt the old adrenaline pumping through his veins. He knew Peter's Pal had a really good chance and had probably never been in better form since Jay had first started to look after him. With Freddie on his back, it was quite clear that the horse was going to attract a lot of support.

Time seemed to drag incredibly slowly until the time came for Jay to go and collect Freddie's saddle. With something to do, at last, he strode round to the saddling boxes behind the weighing room and soon had the horse ready to enter the parade ring. Frank Donovan, the Irish owner, was pacing up and down, evidently as nervous as Jay. 'You've done a wonderful job with him, Jay,' he said. 'Wouldn't it be something to win this? What do you think?'

'I honestly think he'll run really well, but any one of six of them could win on the book, and you never know when some horse is going to do something even more extraordinary out of the blue. We've seen lots of 50-1 winners at Cheltenham over the years.'

'I know,' sighed Frank. 'Let's hope we run to our form.'

Freddie joined them, mounted Peter's Pal's and, after two circuits of the paddock, was on his way to the course.

With twenty-one runners in the field, Freddie had decided to keep out of trouble in the early stages, which turned out to be an extremely fortunate decision. Going down the back straight for the first time, coming up to the open ditch, the two leading horses both made mistakes and slid on landing. Their consequent deceleration caused a huge bunch-up behind them and a number of collisions. Happily none of the horses were hurt, but two jockeys hit the deck. One of them lay there for a worryingly long time before it became apparent, to everyone's relief, that he was only winded.

By the time the field had sorted itself out again the pack was running almost in Indian file. Thankfully there were no more incidents, and turning for home Freddie was lying fifth. Peter's Pal was absolutely cruising. Jay could hardly believe what he was seeing through his binoculars. His horse was going to win the race. Approaching the second last, Peter's Pal moved smoothly into the lead and was supported noisily by the crowd as he drew away. With only one fence to go it looked all over bar the shouting. But that fence, like all Cheltenham fences, takes serious jumping, and for once Peter's Pal got too close and gave it an almighty thwack with his front legs. Freddie shot to one side and lost a stirrup. By some miracle he managed to hang on, but Peter's Pal's slewed right at forty-five degrees. By the time Freddie had got his foot back in the stirrup the second and third horses had swept by, and hard as he tried, there was no way he could catch them.

Jay and Eva were shattered. They just couldn't take it in that glory had been snatched from their grasp at the last fence. Putting on a brave face, they went down to greet Freddie, determined not to show their disappointment.

Freddie looked pretty much how they felt. 'I'm so sorry,' he said. 'He just made a mistake.'

'I know,' consoled Jay. 'But its not too bad, is it, to come third at Cheltenham?'

'He's a great horse,' said Freddie. 'You wait till next year.'

They saw Frank Donovan hoving into view. The expression on his face couldn't have been more different. He was beaming with pride. 'I know we didn't win,' he said, as he reached them, 'but just to be in the winner's enclosure at Cheltenham is beyond my wildest dreams and I'm a really happy man. What's more, as far as I can see, the horse looks fine, and I'm sure you'll win more races with him for me.'

'I've no doubt about that,' said Jay.

'And neither have I,' agreed Freddie, already on his way into the weighing room to get ready to ride in the next race, for another trainer. But for Jay, Eva and Frank the afternoon was over in terms of any real involvement. They retired to Hal's box, where the mood was far more upbeat than Jay had expected. Fiona – back from her travels for Cheltenham and looking healthy and relaxed – was quick to stress the achievement rather than the disappointment, and though everyone was upset that Peter's Pal hadn't won, the general feeling was that it was nonetheless a highly satisfactory start to Jay's first Cheltenham Festival as a trainer.

So the drive home was one of mixed emotions for Jay and Eva, but with the dawn of a new day they awoke with high hopes for My Final Fling's run in the Coral Handicap Hurdle. Freddie had been asked to ride the favourite some months before but had been reluctant to let County View down. Jay hadn't hesitated to encourage him to take the other ride. 'It'll be great experience for young Paul to ride at Cheltenham, and the few extra pounds off My Final Fling's back won't do any harm,' he had assured Freddie. Although by now Paul had ridden a significant number of winners, including five that season already for Jay, he was still able to claim 5lbs allowance.

That Wednesday morning, Jay and Eva stopped at the top of Birdlip Hill to collect Kate Harty, My Final Fling's previous owner, who was staying at the excellent pub there. Kate had remained totally committed to the horse and phoned Jay every week for a progress report. On one occasion she had said worriedly, 'I do hope you don't feel I'm interfering. It's just that I feel very attached to him.'

'I totally understand,' Jay had replied. 'It's great that he is progressing as well as he is. You ring whenever you like.'

Kate, an elegant lady in her late fifties, now skipped excitedly into the car. As far as she was concerned the horse was already in the winner's enclosure, and her enthusiasm was infectious.

As Jay pulled up into the trainers' car park she leaned forward and gave him a pat on the shoulder. 'I am sure he's going to run really well,' she said. 'But as long as he comes back safely, that's all I care about. My husband would have been so thrilled to have had a runner at Cheltenham at all, let alone one with a chance of winning. Now, I'm going to get out of your hair, and you won't see me until just before his race.' She kissed them both on the cheek and walked smartly away, evaporating into the crowd.

'What an absolute ace she is,' said Eva. 'I'm so glad we've kept her involved. She obviously gets so much pleasure out of it, and she is just such a nice person to be with.'

'You are right. As so often.' Jay took her arm and they went off to watch the early races before getting ready to saddle My Final Fling.

Paul Jenkins had travelled with Danny and Jed in the horsebox and had been almost beside himself at the prospect of riding at the Festival. A good ten minutes before the jockeys were due to weigh out Jay went up to the weighing room and asked one of the attendants to fetch Paul. He put his hand on the lad's shoulder. 'I know you'll do your best, Paul. Just remember that I wouldn't be giving you the ride unless I thought you'd do me and the horse justice. So just relax, and I'll see you in ten minutes.'

At the appointed time, Paul came out with his saddle, was checked by the clerk of the scales, and handed his saddle and number cloth to Jay.

At Cheltenham, even something as routine as saddling is a little bit special. The saddling area is always thronged with spectators wanting to have a really close look at the aristocrats of National Hunt racing. The activity steadied Jay's nerves, and by the time he met Kate and Eva in the paddock he was beginning to feel almost relaxed. Paul appeared touching his cap to them all and Kate was absolutely enchanting to him. She told him how pleased she was that he was going to ride her horse and she had evidently taken the trouble to brief herself on how many winners he'd ridden the season before, congratulating him on his success.

As the bell rang she wished Paul and her horse a safe journey round. After a couple of circuits of the parade ring they were on their way down the track and everything was out of Jay's hands. This relinquishing of control before a race was, Jay had come to realise, what made him so much more nervous as a trainer than he had been as a jockey. In his riding days he had at least had half the responsibility for the outcome of a race. You couldn't make a bad horse into a good one, of course, but you could, as long as things went well, get the best out of whatever horse you were riding. Although, as he remembered now, in his early days he had often failed to get anything like the optimum out of some of his mounts. Paul, he reassured himself, was a good way further round the learning curve than he had been then.

As the race began, Paul got My Final Fling in the middle of the pack and was soon on the rails, going the shortest distance, as had been agreed with Jay. Heading down the back straight for the first time, three horses at the front suddenly accelerated and within a hundred yards the twenty-four runners were strung out. Jay was delighted to see that My Final Fling was sitting comfortably in seventh place where he stayed until they reached the top of the hill for the last time. As they swung down the hill, My Final Fling was handling it extremely well and, with apparently no extra effort from Paul, had moved up from seventh to third turning for home.

Jumping the second last he was joint leader. 'Steady, steady,' breathed Jay. But the excitement of the moment and the lad's enthusiasm got the better of him. Urging My Final Fling on, he quickly grabbed a two-lengths lead approaching the last and rode at it hell for leather. He jumped the final obstacle beautifully and gave the horse a couple of quick slaps down the neck. My Final Fling responded immediately and gathered pace up the testing hill. But 150 yards from home the effort started to tell. Inch by inch, the second and third horses were gaining on him, and 50 yards from the post they both went past, leaving a despairing Paul driving his horse on as hard as he could, but to no avail.

'Do you think you put the wrong jockey on him?' asked Eva in the stand.

Before he could answer, Kate cut in. 'We didn't win, but I am so happy,' she said earnestly. 'I am sure Paul will know he made a mistake, he'll be suffering enough. Let's not ruin his day at Cheltenham. Come on, let's all be really upbeat. We're in the winner's enclosure, we've won a nice bit of prize money, and I've had an absolutely thrilling day.' Taking them both by their arms, she marched them off to meet the jockey.

Paul did indeed realize he'd made a mistake, and was expecting criticism. He was absolutely amazed when all three of them congratulated him and said what a shame it was that he hadn't been able to last out the extra few yards. 'It was my fault guv'nor,' said Paul. 'I went too soon.'

'We'll never know that for sure,' said Jay. 'It's your first ride at the Cheltenham Festival and you've come third. Think of it another way: if the horse had been carrying an extra five pounds, he might not even have come third. Off you go, weigh-in, and enjoy the moment.'

'You know, I hadn't thought about that five pounds at all. You're right – perhaps he wouldn't have made the first three with that. After all, the fourth and fifth were both less than a length and a half behind him. So we certainly do have something to celebrate. Come on, the champagne's on me.'

On Gold Cup day, the final day of the Festival, after not quite meeting his own high expectations on the first two, Jay could feel the tension building up in him as he drove to Cheltenham. Eva, too, was a little subdued. 'Well, two thirds can't be too bad,' she said, as if reading his thoughts.

'I know,' replied Jay, 'but it's not the same as having a winner, is it?'

Chapter Twenty-seven

The Triumph Hurdle is always a highly competitive race. Twenty-five horses were entered this year and his ex-St Leger horse, The Zircon, was third favourite behind visitors from Ireland and France. Both had won three hurdles against The Zircon's single hurdle run and, like The Zircon, both had shown considerable ability on the Flat in their own countries.

The previous day Freddie Kelly had been more confident of The Zircon's chances than Jay was. 'I think our horse will accelerate more than the other two,' he had said. 'I've watched tapes of all their races, as I know you have, and I thought that the way our horse sprinted up the last furlong at Doncaster showed just how well this course will suit him. Another fifty yards at Doncaster, and he'd have won; another hundred yards and he'd have won by five lengths or more.'

With this in mind, Jay told the owner Kevin Connolly, a small, unassuming man, that they were going to settle the horse in the middle division until the top of the hill. Turning for home, they would then quietly try to move up before hitting the front after the last hurdle and playing 'catch me if you can.'

For once the Triumph Hurdle, although the usual huge scrimmage, saw no problems over the first two or three hurdles. Not until the last hurdle down the back straight did two tired horses made mistakes and although neither fell, both unseated their riders. By the time the field had reached the top of the hill The Zircon was fifth and travelling supremely easily. What was more the two favourites were lying third and fourth. The course commentator expressed the view that The Zircon was travelling particularly easily.

Hardly daring to agree, Jay, his eyes glued on the race through his binoculars, had a strong instinct that his horse was travelling the best of the first five, which by then had pulled away from the rest of the runners. There was no change in the order going down the hill, but turning for home the horse in front started to crack. The second horse, however, showed no sign of weakening. The French horse now moved up to challenge for the lead, but the Irish joint favourite was struggling as The Zircon advanced steadily into third place. Freddie kept him there between the two final hurdles but moved slightly outside the other two approaching the last. Since this horse had run over hurdles only once before, he wanted to make sure he could see it. He also kept the horse firmly in hand to make sure he didn't try to take off too soon. With an economic but not particularly spectacular jump, The Zircon cleared the last half a length down on the French horse, now in first place.

In accordance with their agreed tactics he gave The Zircon a slap down the shoulder and a kick with his heels. The horse did not respond with a massive surge but he went up a gear and, cruised steadily but surely past the French horse to take up a commanding lead of a length. And the further they went up the hill, the wider the gap between them became. To Jay's elation, his first win as a trainer at the Cheltenham Festival was achieved by a good three lengths. In the stands Jason exhaled slowly. It felt as if it was the first time he had breathed out properly in three days. He was overwhelmed by a sense of delight tinged with relief.

In the winner's enclosure the usually placid Kevin Connolly was a man transformed. He was bubbling. 'I can't believe it,' he cried. 'My first runner at Cheltenham, and I've won one of the big races!'

'You sent me a really good horse, and all we've done is ensure that he's produced what we all knew he was capable of,' Jay told him. Freddie, having removed the saddle, came up and stood next to the owner for the obligatory photographs as Kevin thanked the jockey most profusely for the excellent ride he had given The Zircon. 'I won't be ungrateful,' he promised.

'Oh, don't worry about that,' said Freddie. 'To win a race at Cheltenham is its own reward.'

Jason excused himself briefly to go in with his jockey and make sure there were no problems at the weigh-in. Then they were back in the winner's enclosure for the post-race interviews and presentations. As Freddie returned to get ready for his next ride, Kevin said to Jason: 'I just want you to know something, Jay. This is my first National Hunt horse, but it certainly won't be my last. And they'll all come to you.'

'That's wonderful to hear,' said Jay. 'In the meantime, can I make a suggestion about The Zircon?'

'Of course.'

'He's a really nice young horse, but he's had a hard life so far, with a lot of high-class races on the Flat. Today's race is as tough a contest as a young horse can have. I honestly believe he should have a rest now.'

'I'm not going to argue with that,' replied Kevin. 'In fact, I don't think I'd ever argue with you at all. I mean, what owner can argue with a trainer who wins the Triumph Hurdle with his first horse at Cheltenham? Thanks again, and I look forward to seeing you later for a celebratory drink.'

Jason could scarcely believe that a year had gone by since his magical ride on Splendid Warrior. He hadn't had time then to prepare or worry as it had all happened so quickly after Freddie's fall the adrenaline took over. In a sense he had had nothing to lose then. This time the whole racing world was looking on to judge whether he had trained the horse as well as its previous master, Jack Symes.

There were eighteen runners in the Gold Cup, including two from Ireland, one from France and interestingly, one from Czechoslovakia. Not surprisingly, as the previous year's winner and the winner of the King George VI at Kempton, Splendid Warrior was the favourite. The fact that Freddie, the

Irish Champion Jockey, was piloting him was also not only a matter of general interest but was attracting most of the Irish money that was not following their own horses. With a little over three and a quarter miles ahead of them, and twenty two fences, this was the ultimate test of top-class chasers.

Jason had never seen the stands so packed as they were for this race. As the Gold Cup got underway, one of the outsiders made a mistake and unshipped his jockey, but the other seventeen were still up and running as they entered the back straight for the last time. As they approached the open ditch one of the three leaders suddenly went lame and immediately pulled himself up. The horses behind him had to take evasive action and, through no fault of the jockey, there was an almighty mix-up. Many of the horses were completely put off their stride and lost momentum as they approached the big fence, where three fell. Freddie was behind the leading group, but seriously interfered with by a horse that had half gone down but then struggled up, lunging sideways as Splendid Warrior landed. Somehow the champion managed to avoid a collision, but it was touch and go whether he would remain in the saddle. He managed to stay in his seat, but by the time he'd got Splendid Warrior going again he'd dropped down to ninth of the remaining eleven. Refusing to be panicked, he gave his brilliant horse the chance to regain his own composure and jumped the other fences down the back straight beautifully but without trying too hard to make up too much of the lost ground.

Knowing that Splendid Warrior was not at his best going downhill, Freddie applied some pressure going up to claw back as much of the lost ground as he could at that stage without overtaxing the horse before the fence at the top. Having dealt with that, they had succeeded in moving up into seventh, but they were still a good twelve lengths behind the leading pair. Steadying the horse going down the hill Freddie lost another two lengths. So, unlike the previous year, now was the time when Splendid Warrior had to be asked the question. A quick slap down the shoulder saw the horse accelerate into fifth place but he was still a good eight lengths down approaching the second last. He jumped that brilliantly, and Freddie asked for another slight improvement in his pace travelling between the last two. Again Splendid Warrior obliged. By the time they reached the last he was third, but still three lengths down on the two leaders, who were locked in a head-to-head battle.

Slowly but surely, the magnificent horse powered towards the two leaders, one of which was beginning to falter. With a hundred yards to go, Splendid Warrior was second but still a length down. For the first time, Freddie raised his stick. He gave the horse one sharp smack behind the saddle. Galvanised by this affront to his dignity, Splendid Warrior swished his tail briefly and then put his head down and drove himself towards the post. With every yard he was gaining valuable inches until with one final desperate effort, Freddie flung himself and the horse at the finishing line. 'Photograph! Photograph!' he heard over the tannoy above the din.

The bookmakers were far from sure of the outcome but, because Splendid Warrior was carrying so much money, they were offering 2-1 against the other horse winning the race. They had still heard nothing when Jay met Freddie at the exit from the racecourse. It was evidently very tight.

'I really don't know guv'nor,' shrugged Freddie. 'It was damn close. A few yards past the post I was certainly in the lead – I just don't know where I was on the finishing line.' There was a crackle as the loudspeakers sprang into life. 'First number seven, Splendid Warrior.' A roar rumbled in the throats of the trainer, the horse's lass, and a sizeable section of the crowd and was released all at once. It seemed to Jay as if the grandstand itself was shaking.

Almost the first person to greet the victorious crew as they crossed the paddock on their way to the winner's enclosure was Jack Symes. 'Well done, all of you,' he said. 'We made the right decision.'

Barry Davey was clearly in seventh heaven. Shaking Jay's hand warmly he asked: 'How does it feel to train the winner of the Gold Cup after riding it last year?'

'I don't know yet,' admitted Jay, 'but in some ways I think it's probably an even greater thrill.'

Jay escorted Freddie through the crush into the weighing room to thank him for giving the horse such a fabulous ride. As soon as they re-emerged they were reliving their emotions for the television cameras.

'Well, what a wonderful day for you,' commented one of the reporters. 'You could hardly have expected to follow up last year's Cheltenham with the sort of day you've had today, could you?'

'Not really,' said Jay. 'But I've got wonderful horses, very supportive owners and partners, and without a shadow of a doubt the best jockey in the country.'

When he finally managed to extricate himself, Jay swept Eva out of the parade ring and up to Hal's box. The Triumph Hurdle win had been greeted with acclaim but the euphoria in the box now was even more overwhelming. Hardly anybody could hear what anybody else was saying until Hal hammered on a table with a spoon and everybody turned round. 'It may not be my place to say this, but I think we've all witnessed three quite remarkable days. This young man has taken on the best trainers and the best horses in the world and his achievements have been quite remarkable. I think we should all drink to Jay and his further successes.' There was a huge cheer as a forest of glasses were raised.

For once in his life Jay looked slightly bashful. 'Thank you all very much,' he said eventually. 'But can I also add that there's no way this could have been achieved without the team here. Victor and Howard made it all happen; Jed has been absolutely fantastic as my adviser and mentor; Danny has been incredible on the gallops and in the stables; Eva has been a source of support at all times and has ensured that everything with the press, and indeed with everybody else, has run smoothly.

Approving murmurs of 'Hear, hear,' circulated round the box.

'However, in one sense this Cheltenham meeting has failed Eva.'

Eva's jaw dropped in astonishment.

'When Eva first came to the UK and discussed her reasons for wanting to become a partner in County View,' he continued, 'she explained that her great objective was to have a horse that would win a race here in her father's colours. That is the reason why we agreed that the colours would include diamonds. But the winners of the Triumph Hurdle and the Gold Cup today have run in the colours of their owners. So my objective for next year is to have Eva leading in a winner in those special colours.'

There were tears in Eva's eyes. She cleared her throat. 'Well, I just want you to know that if my father were alive today, he would have been so proud of the whole team. And I know that in the last few months I have found not just a passion in my life but a group of friends which I am sure I will retain and value for many, many years to come.'

She was saved from being overtaken by emotion by Freddie, who having ridden without success in the previous race, chose that moment to enter the box. There were more cheers as he joined the party, and a glass of champagne was thrust into his hand. 'I'll only have one,' he said. 'Believe it or not, I've got to ride again tomorrow.'

A knock at the door was scarcely heard amid the hubbub. In came a member of the security staff, with an envelope for Jay. He opened it and scanned the note, bewildered. Everyone was waiting for him to say something. He handed it to Eva. 'As our PR director, I think you'd better read this.'

'The directors and stewards of the Cheltenham Steeplechase Company would like to inform Mr Jason Jessop that he has won the trophy for the leading trainer at this year's

302

Cheltenham Festival,' announced Eva, 'and they would like him to make himself available as soon as possible to receive the award after the last race.' She looked up. 'They hope that Mr Jessop and the other directors and shareholders in County View will then join them for a celebration drink after racing.'

'What?' gasped Jay. 'How did that happen?'

'I haven't had a chance to tell you,' Freddie piped up. 'You rushed off so quickly that you didn't realise there had been a disqualification in the race after the Gold Cup. That means you and Alan Jackson tied with two wins each, but he had only one other placed horse. So, my friend, you have started off your Cheltenham training career in real style!'

After drinks with the Cheltenham directors and stewards, nobody wanted the day to end. Jason was also anxious that all the staff at the yard should enjoy the occasion. He called Steve at The Shepherd's Rest to inquire about the possibility of bringing to County View bacon and eggs, or whatever he could manage, for fifty or sixty people.

'No problem,' said Steve. 'I've been expecting you lot to be down at the pub later since I head the news, but it's even easier to sort you out at County View – this place is packed with race goers already. And don't worry: I've had the champagne stocked up since well before the meeting.

Jay chuckled at his confidence. 'We've got some at the yard ourselves, but we will certainly need reinforcements now.'

As the headlights of the returning convoy were spotted coming past security at County View the whole staff gathered in front of Jay's house to welcome home the conquering heroes and the party was soon in full swing.

At eleven o'clock Jay banged on one of the tables. 'All right everyone,' he said, 'I hate to be a killjoy, but horses don't have parties, and we have runners tomorrow and Saturday. See you in the morning – usual time!'

Howard and Victor sat down with him and Eva for a nightcap before going home themselves. 'This has been quite incredible,' Victor said to Jay. 'Apart from the success, you've brought together a really extraordinary team. We have loved working with you and Eva. I think Howard and I have enjoyed getting to know each other and working together almost as much as all the rewards.'

'It's been amazing,' agreed Howard. 'And beyond any of our wildest dreams.

'It's going to be a hard act to follow,' Victor went on, 'so once all the dust has settled I think we should have a council of war and a good hard think about what we're going to do next year. After all, we don't want this to be a flash in the pan, do we?'

Jay laughed. 'Good old Victor – always ready for the next challenge. It's hard to focus on the future tonight, but you are dead right, as always.'

Howard and Victor got up to leave. At the door Jay said to them: 'The support you two and Eva have given me has made it all a pleasure as well as a success. I couldn't have done it without any of you, and I'm so grateful.' His two good friends gave him a big hug, kissed Eva and went on their way.

Jay and Eva smiled at each other and climbed the stairs to their bedroom.

'I don't think we could follow last year's night after the Gold Cup, do you?' said Eva.

'I don't know. Even though I'm not the winning jockey any more, I'm certainly prepared to give it a try.'

Chapter Twenty-eight

One night, not long after Cheltenham, Jay woke with a start. According to the bedside clock it was 3.30am and he could not think what had woken him. He heard one of the yard dogs barking. Then there was a whimper. He sat bolt upright in bed and listened. Nothing. He glanced at Eva, but she was still fast asleep. He slipped quietly out of bed, pulled on a tracksuit and a pair of trainers, crept downstairs and stood at his front door. He could hear nothing but he wasn't happy. He crept into the yard and looked round. Neither of the two yard dogs made a sound. Then he noticed that one of the stable doors was open. He hurried towards it and looked in. Its occupant was lying down but on its side, which is not the way horses normally sleep. He switched on the light and gasped. Surprise Packet had blood pouring from a ghastly gash in his throat. The horse was struggling but was clearly dying. Horrified, Jay turned to run out and raise the alarm. The next thing he knew, he was felled by a crashing blow to his temple. And then everything went black.

Unbeknown to Jay, his assailant hadn't finished with him. He stood over the unconscious trainer, looked down at him with a sneer and kicked him hard in the ribs. Then he bent over, picked up one of Jay's lifeless legs and placed it on top of the other. Raising the yard shovel with which he had struck Jay, he brought it smashing down on to the top leg, just above the ankle. For good measure, he delivered several more similar blows before loping off silently into the night.

The next morning Danny was up bright and early. None of the horses were racing today but he was keen to get into the yard to check on the previous day's two runners. As he turned the corner of the stables he stopped in his tracks. There was Jay, lying motionless in front of an open box. Danny dashed across and saw the blood on the side of Jay's face. Bending over him, he could hear that he was still breathing, though very shallowly. He looked inside the stable and was aghast to see the body of Surprise Packet in a vast pool of congealing blood. Screaming at the top of his voice he cannoned across the yard. Eva, in the kitchen making coffee, rushed out. He tore past her shouting, 'Something terrible's happened!' He picked up the phone in Eva's kitchen and dialled 999. 'An ambulance first! Police second.' Eva heard him yelling in response to the operator's calm questions.

Eva grabbed him by the shoulders. 'Danny, what on earth's happened?'

'Come quickly,' he said, 'and bring some blankets.' By this time Jed and Cathy, having heard the commotion, were in the yard leaning over Jay. Seeing this gruesome tableau, Eva dropped the blankets and let out a strange keening cry. 'We mustn't move him,' Cathy said, 'but we must keep him warm.'

She picked up the blankets and arranged them over Jay's unmoving form. 'Keep calm, Eva,' she soothed. 'It's probably not as bad as it looks, and the ambulance is coming. Try to keep calm for Jay.'

Jed, too, had seen the carnage in the stable. As the staff began to appear, wondering what was going on, he took control. 'Just carry on with your normal duties, everyone,' he said shepherding them away from the scene. 'We'll tell you exactly what's happened as soon as we know, but in the meantime the horses have got to be looked after. Danny, you organise the exercises. I'll update as soon as possible, I promise.'

'OK, Jed,' said Danny. His voice was shaky, but he had recovered his equilibrium. It would be good to focus on something ordinary. He set about getting the yard back to some kind of normality with his usual thoroughness.

A few moments later the ambulance arrived. The paramedics examined Jay.

'I think we're going to need the air ambulance,' said one of them. 'I don't want to risk moving him by road.' He got on his radio. Within ten minutes a helicopter was landing beside the gallops. Jay had been gently moved onto a stretcher by the paramedics, a neck brace in place and his battered leg immobilised. He was still unconscious and had been given oxygen. Eva was allowed to go with him. She looked absolutely ashen.

The police had arrived while the paramedics were attending to Jay and had remained in the background until he had been taken to hospital. Now they took control and began trying to find out what had happened. They were already a step ahead of everyone else having discovered the guard bound and gagged in his hut on their way in. When they had freed him he told them that in the middle of the night a car had drawn up and a young woman had got out. She had knocked on his window. 'I'm lost,' she'd said as he opened it. He found himself facing a gun, pointed straight at him. She had ordered him to stay where he was. Immediately a man in a balaclava helmet had appeared from the rear of the car and the guard had been forced to open the door of the hut. The man bound and gagged him and pulled out the wires from the telephone. He also turned off the control switch for the cameras around the perimeter fence.

The police now examined the horse and found that its throat had been deliberately cut. Their search of the yard also revealed two dead yard dogs, killed in similar fashion. When the staff and horses returned from their morning exercise the officers interviewed Danny who had discovered Jay and Surprise Packet, and the few people who had been on the scene immediately afterwards. Then they left to sift through their evidence, cordoning off key areas of the stables.

Jed and Danny sat in Jed's kitchen, waiting for news about Jason and for Howard and Victor, whom Jed had phoned straight away, to get there from The Laurels and Holland Park respectively. Cathy produced a large pot of coffee and asked them if they wanted anything to eat. Neither of them did. She left them to it. Jed lit a cigar.

Once they were alone Danny produced a photograph from under a newspaper in front of him. He slid it across the table to Jed. 'Look what I found in Surprise's box.'

It was a large colour print of a horse's head.

'Why would some thug have a photograph of a horse with him?' wondered Jed incredulously.

'Look carefully.

'My God – it's The Conker.'

'Exactly. I don't know what the police think but I don't think it was a random attack, do you? Somebody came here to kill The Conker and got poor old Surprise Packet instead.'

'But their names are on their bloody boxes!' exclaimed Jed. 'Surely if this killer was able to identify the horse in the dark, with a torch or whatever, he could've looked at the door. It would've been a damn sight easier – and he might have got the right horse!'

'I know,' said Danny. 'I don't understand that, either. Maybe he didn't know his name would be on the door.'

'Did you show this to the police?'

'Of course not. They would have taken it away. And I know whose it is. It's one of Jimmy James's. We'll have to talk to Howard about it before we do anything.'

They did not have to wait long before Howard strode into the kitchen. Jed and Danny told him exactly what had happened and showed him the photograph. 'No prizes for guessing who's behind this,' he said grimly. He picked up his mobile. 'Benny? I'm at County View. We've got a bit of an emergency on our hands. How quickly can you get down here?'

Victor arrived shortly after Howard and got straight on the phone to the hospital to see if there was any word. There wasn't. Jay was being given a brain scan and Eva promised to phone as soon as she had any news.

The four of them sat drinking coffee in Jed's kitchen. 'We must think carefully about what we say to the police,' said Howard. 'Obviously we can't do anything illegal, or deliberately hamper their investigation. We're already technically breaking the law by withholding evidence, but I don't think we have much choice. Let's look at what is likely to happen. If the police catch whoever attacked Jay, he'll be done for GBH, or maybe even attempted murder. But what about Frankie Johnson? A good lawyer will make sure he cannot be connected with the attack at all, but even if they do manage to nail him for what he did to Surprise Package, what is he going to get for setting up the killing of a practically unknown racehorse? A whooping great fine, and maybe probation or a suspended sentence. Jay wasn't supposed to be in the stable, so it's impossible to build a case alleging that Johnson hired the guy to attack him.'

'So what do you suggest?' asked Victor.

'Well, I don't think we should tell the police about the photograph, or what we think it signifies. We know what it means, but legally it's a million miles from implicating Frankie Johnson. I think we should let my friend Benny and his team dig around and see what they can find out. The first thing is to try and unearth the man who attacked Jay and then establish that our flashy bookmaker was behind it.'

They all nodded their agreement.

Soon a Jaguar screeched to a halt in front of the house, and out stepped Benny to everyone's surprise. It was an almost new car, quite unlike his usual modes of transport. Angel was with him.

They trooped into Jed's kitchen where Howard explained the situation.

'Ah,' said Benny. 'I presume we all think this is in retaliation for Towcester.'

'Of course it is,' said Howard, 'but how the hell can we prove it?'

'I think that photograph is our best lever. If you're sure it's Jimmy James's we can put some real pressure on him and he's bound to crack.'

'I'm positive it's his,' said Danny. 'It's the one the press have used a couple of times when he's won. It was in the papers the day after Towcester.'

'What do you want done, Howard?' asked Benny.

'Let's think about this. We've got to sort it out, but not get ourselves into trouble in the process. See if you can frighten Jimmy into admitting who he gave the photograph to and giving you any other information he's got. And start trying to find out who the attacker was, plus this female driver.'

'That shouldn't be too difficult,' said Benny. 'There can't be too many hit men in London with a woman driver. Come to think of it, having a driver at all narrows it down. A lot of them prefer to work alone wherever possible. But of course it might be the first time he's used her. I'd like to go and talk to your security guard.'

'That's fine,' said Jed. 'He's a bit shaken up, but he didn't want to go home yet. You'll find him in the canteen. He's called Alan Moss.'

Benny and Angel found Alan, introduced themselves and asked him if there had been anything at all distinctive about the woman who had knocked on his window.

'There was one odd thing. I might be wrong, but I think she was wearing a wig. Her skin was fair, and her eyebrows looked blonde to me, but she had long, black hair and it just didn't look quite right. She was also taller than me, so she must have been nearly six foot.'

It wasn't much to go on, but is was something.

No sooner were Benny and Angel on their way back to London than two senior police officers and two detective inspectors arrived. This was clearly going to be a very high-profile case, and they were going to leave no stone unturned.

Howard and Victor were interviewed, and everybody else was interviewed again. They all agreed that it was a mystery.

At last Eva phoned to say that the brain scan had shown no damage. Jay was still unconscious, but his breathing was improving and he had been downgraded from the critical to the serious list.

'What are you going to do? Howard asked her.

'I'll stay here with him.'

'You can't stay there all the time.'

'Of course I can.'

'In that case,' said Howard. 'I'm going to put you on to Cathy. Give her a list of anything you want and we'll get it over to you.'

'You're a sweetheart, Howard.' Her voice was cracking and she was obviously breaking down.

When she had finished the phone call, Cathy offered to go over to the hospital with the bits and pieces Eva wanted. 'I think it's probably better for her to have another woman there rather than one of you men,' she said. 'Don't worry, I'll be sure to let her know how concerned you all are.' She hurried over to Eva's house to pack an overnight bag for her.

'Right now,' said Howard to Jed, Danny and Victor, 'I don't think we can do much more here. I'm going to go into the hospital and talk to the most senior doctor I can find. I'll let them know that we'll do absolutely anything to help Jay. I think otherwise we should just all try to return to normal as far as we can. Are we racing tomorrow?'

'Just one meeting, at Newbury. We can handle that,' said Jed.

'OK. Victor and I will leave you to get organised.'

As they saw Howard and Victor out, Jed and Danny were already discussing what needed to be done.

'Thank goodness we've got Jed,' Howard said to Victor as they got into their cars. 'We know we can't go far wrong with him here.'

'Absolutely,' said Victor with feeling. 'And as far as the other business was concerned, Danny was sharp as a tack over that photograph. If anybody else had found it we might not have known anything about it until it was too late.'

'I'll let you know the news from the hospital,' called Howard, raising a hand in farewell as he got into his car.

An hour later he was talking to the doctor in charge of Jay's ward. 'The news is good, Mr Barrack, as I've already told Miss Botha. He's regained consciousness and there's certainly no brain damage. To be honest, although he's weak, I'm much more bothered about the leg. It's a really nasty fracture, and going to be quite a while before it mends. I think you can assume he'll be in a wheelchair for a few weeks before he'll be able to walk on it. At least it's below the knee and the ankle hasn't been damaged. That's going to make life a little more comfortable for him. We won't know for a few days when he can go home.'

Howard went to find Eva. She was sitting with Cathy, looking quite cheerful. 'They're going to let me see him later, and Cathy's going to stay with me until we know what the situation is. Then I'll probably go back to County View with her and come back again this evening.'

'You know all you've got to do is pick up the phone and call Victor or myself if there is anything we can do,' said Howard. He gave her a hug. Kissing Cathy on the cheek, he said, 'Look after her. You've got my telephone number if you need it.'

On his way to London he phoned Benny. 'One other suggestion. You know my friend Kipper Fish?'

'Yes.'

'He knows a lot of people in the East End, and some of them, shall I say, are a little dubious. You might ask him if he'd inquire around to see if there are any rumours.'

'Right you are, boss.'

'If you need any extra help, money's no object, you know that.'

'Oh, I think the four of us will be enough,' said Benny. 'I'll keep you posted.'

The five days before Jay was allowed out of hospital went surprisingly smoothly at County View. Eva reported that the patient was getting steadily stronger, although he was clearly in quite a lot of pain from his shattered leg. Yet again Jason had hit the racing headlines – though in this case he fervently wished he hadn't – the telephone rang constantly with sympathetic inquiries and wishes. The moment Jay was able to come home his spirits rose dramatically. Even from a wheelchair he could watch the horses go round his little parade ring in the mornings and discuss their progress and plans for them with Jed and Danny. He was still unable to get up to the gallops as the leg hurt too much for him to get into the Land Rover. One thing that cheered him up was watching the tapes of his recent Cheltenham triumphs which Eva had got from the racecourse and the TV stations, all of who were fulsome in their praise for his training achievements.

Howard gave him a week to get into a routine before returning to County View. He spoke to Jay every day but he felt it would aid his recovery to leave him in relative peace. When he did come down in person, he was horrified at the change in his trainer. He looked really ill and was clearly still suffering.

'If it's not a silly question, how are you feeling?' asked Howard.

'Believe it or not, Howard, I'm actually getting better every day. I still feel rotten and I'm in a lot of pain, but the doctors warned me I would be. On the positive side, I'm feeling stronger. I haven't got a headache any more, and I'm beginning to enjoy my food and the odd glass of wine.'

'Sounds like a step in the right direction,' said Howard. 'Any news from the police?'

'Nothing of any significance. They seem to have drawn a complete blank.'

'Well, at least I have some news for you.' With Kipper's help, Benny had come up with a likely suspect, an illegal immigrant from the Balkans with a reputation for being willing to take on all kinds of dirty work. He did not have a driving licence so never drove for fear of being stopped by the police. He also did not read English. Perhaps this had saved The Conker. Instead his tall, blonde girlfriend drove him around. Benny had found out where they lived and taken photographs of the car they drove and of the woman.

Howard had these with him and was going to show them to Alan Moss when he came on duty to see whether they rang any bells. It was a long shot. He hadn't been able to tell the police what make the car had been as he couldn't see it in the dark, but maybe there would be something about the woman he recognised.

So far Benny had not approached Jimmy James. He wanted to lull the photographer into a false sense of security. If Jimmy thought they'd made no connection between him and the attack he'd be off his guard. 'Benny's set to confront him tomorrow,' Howard said.

'I still can't believe this all happened,' marvelled Jay. 'It's like something out of a Dick Francis novel.'

'Well, it bloody well did,' said Howard. 'And we're going to make sure that whoever's responsible pays for it!'

On his way home Howard showed Benny's pictures to Alan Moss. The car, the security guard confirmed, was the right shape and size, and so was the girl. Benny phoned Howard. 'I want to come and see you. I've got some news.'

Benny came to see Howard a couple of days later. 'We picked up Jimmy James last night and took him down to our warehouse. He was absolutely terrified. We asked him a few questions about what he'd been doing during the Cheltenham Festival and then suddenly lobbed one in about his horse photographs.' Jimmy had assured the boys that he just supplied them to the press when they required them. Then they had produced the photograph that had been found in

314

Surprise Packet's box, and told him where they had got it. 'He went seriously white, Howard,' said Benny earnestly. 'I told the little rat that he was responsible for a major crime and that, apart from anything else, we could make sure he'd never be allowed near a racecourse again.'

Envisaging his career in tatters and intimidated by the threats of physical violence, Jimmy had caved in and admitted that he had also given Frankie Johnson a photograph of The Conker. He insisted he just assumed the bookie liked the picture and thought nothing more of it. 'Strangely enough I do actually believe him,' said Benny. 'I think he is genuinely petrified of both us and the police. I warned him that if he breathed one word of this to Frankie he would be in very, very hot water. I don't think he had any reason to doubt that.'

'So what's the next step?' asked Howard.

'We're going to pick up this thug and his girlfriend. We're just waiting till we can get them separately. We'll take them down to the warehouse and ask them some pretty pointed questions. It'll be interesting to see how tough they are, particularly when they realise we've got evidence. Even if he wore gloves during the actual attack – he'd have to be a complete idiot not to have done that, and from what I hear from County View the police didn't find any fingerprints on the yard shovel he hit Jay with – there's every chance he handled the photograph at home beforehand. Since he must have dropped it in the stable by mistake, he wouldn't have worried about that, so it's very likely that his dabs are on that photograph. And we're certainly going to tell him that they are. I'm going to give him a choice: tell us everything or be turned over to the police. We'll do that anyway if we can be sure there's enough on him to have him sent down, but I know you're more interested in what happens to Frankie.'

'I sure am,' said Howard.

'All right. I'll let you know what happens.'

Chapter Twenty-nine

That evening Benny and his brothers sat in a car and a van on either side of the road outside the block of flats in East London where their suspect lived. They now knew he was known as Balkan Boris, that his girlfriend's name was Magda – and vitally, they knew which flat was theirs. This could be a problem in these large blocks. A little after 7.30 Boris came out of the entrance to the flats and walked down to the pub at the end of the road. He was a big man and obviously fit. 'We'll have to be careful,' said Benny. 'Don't take any chances.' Angel crossed the road and went into the block of flats and up to the first floor. Angel rang the bell outside the front door. He looked so like his name that the young woman inside, having first opened the door just a crack to see who was there, had no hesitation in letting it off the chain to speak to him properly. To her total astonishment she found herself looking into the barrel of a gun. It was only a replica, but she wasn't to know that. 'Come with me,' Angel demanded, grabbing her arm and pulling her briskly down the stairs. The engine of the car outside, with Robbie at the wheel, was already running. Angel pushed Magda into the back, got in next to her and the car sped off to the warehouse.

Magda was going to be one very frightened lady by the time she met Benny. The brothers employed their favourite technique. At the warehouse the captive was yanked out of the car, taken to one of the rooms below the water level, handcuffed to a ring on the wall and left there. All the while not a word had been said.

Back at the flats, once the car had gone, Harry moved the van and parked it outside the entrance where the car had been. He and Benny got out and went up to Boris's flat. Angel had obligingly left the front door open for them so all they had to do was walk in, close the door and wait. While Harry kept an eye out for Boris's return, Benny made use of the time to forage around in search of any incriminating evidence. A couple of hours later they heard footsteps coming up the stairs and stopping outside. Silently they moved to either side of the door. A key turned in the lock and it opened.

Standing in the hall, Boris called out something in an Eastern European language, presumably to announce to Magda that he was home. Simultaneously he felt something hard in his ribs. Harry grabbed his hands and shackled them behind his back. The advantage of surprise had made it much easier than either of them had expected. Boris was really angry. He kicked out and yelled at them in his own language. Benny, with a fearsome look on his face, growled at him to shut up or he'd shut him up permanently. He jammed his replica gun into Boris's mouth. A look of stark fear came into his eyes and he stopped struggling. 'Right,' said Benny. 'Come with us.'

They dragged the confused man down the stairs. Benny opened the back door to the van and had a quick look around to check that there was nobody in sight before bundling Boris into the back, closing the doors and locking them. Harry drove briskly to the warehouse, where Boris was given the same treatment as Magda, but in another part of the building. Benny left him to stew while he went to talk to Magda. By this time she was truly terrified. Benny started by asking her where her black wig was. She shook her head and said, 'I don't know what you're talking about.'

'Oh yes you do. ' He dropped something dark, floppy and hairy, like a small dead animal, in front of her. 'We found this in your bedroom while we were waiting for Boris.'

She seemed to crumple.

'Now tell us where you've been driving Boris in the car in the middle of the night lately. On a Thursday night just over two weeks ago, to be precise.'

'I don't know what you're talking about,' she said again.

'I think you do. Believe me, you could be in very serious trouble. First, a valuable horse was killed, and secondly there's a very well known man in a serious condition in hospital. He might die.' This, of course, was no longer true, but she didn't know that.

Eventually she caved in and confessed that she had driven Boris out into the country, but didn't know what for. He had wanted to go in the middle of the night and had brought a map with him, so he knew exactly where to go, and she just followed his directions. She admitted that she had helped him deceive the security guard, waited for Boris and then driven him back to their flat. There was probably not much more they could get from her, but this was enough.

They left her again and trooped round to the other room to have a go at Boris. He too protested that he didn't know what they were talking about until they showed him Magda's wig and said that she had told them everything. Then they produced the photograph, told him that he had dropped it in the stable and assured him that it had his fingerprints on it.

Benny pulled up a chair and sat down in front of Boris. 'I'm going to be very direct with you,' he said. 'If we hand you over to the police with this information, you'll go to jail for a very long while. Or maybe you'll be sent back to prison in your own country, I don't know. To be honest, we're not really interested in what happens to you. What we are interested in is getting the man who paid you. So we want some information from you. We know it was Frankie Johnson.?'

'Never heard of him,' Boris said, shaking his head vigorously.

'All right,' sighed Benny. 'Let me explain the situation. If you tell us who it was, how much you were paid and everything about it, we'll let you go and if you are quick, you can get out of the country. If you don't, we'll hand you over to the police and you can take your chances with them. But attempted murder – or murder, as the case may be – is a very serious charge.'

'How do I know I can trust you?' Asked Boris quietly.

'You don't,' said Benny. 'But what've you got to lose? If you're scared of Frankie Johnson, let me tell you, he's the least of your worries.'

Boris thought for a moment. 'All right,' he said. He told them that a man he knew vaguely, from the pub, had approached him. He said that somebody wanted a job done. Boris had gone with him to Mr Johnson's office late one night. He was given instructions and a photograph of the horse so that he would be able to identify it. He had been told the name of the horse, and that it would be on a nameplate outside its box. He couldn't read English, so the nameplate wasn't much use to him. He had been paid £10,000 to do the job.

'What about the man you hit?' asked Benny. 'Did he tell you to do that?'

'No. He told me that he really didn't like the man, but I didn't expect to see him. I just thought I might get a bonus if I hurt him.'

'I see. And did you?'

'Yes. I got another £10,000.'

'OK,' said Benny, 'that's all for the moment.'

He turned to Angel. 'Get these people something to eat and drink, but leave them where they are.'

An hour later they were all sitting outside Frankie Johnson's ostentatious home. They waited until they saw the lights go out. It was just after midnight. Strangely, there was no burglar alarm. Angel, dressed as a gasman, had established this that morning, when he had called by and asked the new Mrs Johnson a couple of questions about how happy she was with her gas supplier.

The four of them got out of the newish Jaguar – selected for this assignment as it wouldn't look out of place in Frankie's well-heeled road – and crept up to the house. Harry and Angel stayed by the front door while Benny and Robbie went round the back. Within seconds Benny had expertly picked the lock. They pulled on balaclava masks, climbed the stairs soundlessly and found the master bedroom. Silently they padded in, one standing each side of the bed with replica pistols in their hands. Then Benny, in a low and threatening voice said: 'Frankie, we've come to get you.'

His wife woke first and, seeing the silhouettes of the two armed figures, screamed.

'Scream on lady,' said Benny. 'It won't do you any good.'

'What the f**k...,' said Frankie, sitting up. 'What the hell do you think you're doing?'

'We've come to hurt you Frankie,' said Benny. 'We've come to hurt you a lot.'

His wife was still screaming.

'Stop that now or we'll tie you up and gag you!' said Robbie fiercely. She stopped. 'Get up and go in your bathroom.'

She jumped out of bed and scuttled into the en suite. Robbie followed her and turned on the light to make sure there was no telephone extension there. Satisfied he closed the door.

'Now,' said Benny, 'We're going to have a little chat about Boris and Magda.'

'I don't know what you're talking about,' said Frankie.

It seemed to be the catchphrase of the evening.

'Oh, I think you do. It's very simple. You've got one week to pay £200,000 into the Injured Jockeys' Fund and then leave the country. If you don't, first of all you'll get hurt one dark night. Look how easy it's been to get you tonight. Secondly, we'll tell the police everything.'

Frankie blustered.

Benny cut him short. 'One week. Don't try to phone the police. Just think about it.' They went back down the stairs, left by the back door, collected Harry and Angel, got into the car, removed their masks and drove off.

Hearing this story the next morning, Howard was absolutely delighted.

'Do you think Frankie will go for it?'

'I'm sure he will,' said Benny. 'Particularly when we give him a little added pressure.'

'What do have in mind?' asked Howard.

'For starters we'll call him at midnight tonight and remind him that he only has six days left. And we'll do that every night, counting down. But I'm also having a courier deliver a small package to him which he'll need to sign for. When he opens it he'll find an empty video container. Well, empty except for a note that says "this could have been a bomb, next time it might be."'

Howard laughed and laughed.

For the next four nights Benny did as he'd promised Howard. By the time he made his third call the phone was permanently on the answering machine. Benny put a handkerchief over the mouthpiece and left his message anyway. Frankie wasn't going to go to the police, and even if he did, what could a mystery voice saying 'Five days left' signify? On the fifth day Howard leafed through the *Racing Post* to find a story headlined: ANONYMOUS GIFT OF £200K TO INJURED JOCKEYS' FUND.'

Howard rang Benny. 'I think it's worked.'

'I'm quite sure it has,' said Benny.

Benny kept an eye on Boris and Magda's flat. Within three days there was no sign of anyone living there. 'The birds have flown,' he reported to Howard.

Howard went down to see Jay, who was looking much better. Although he was still in a certain amount of discomfort, the real pain had eased and now he could go up the side of the gallops in the Land Rover. He was also becoming much more involved in the day-to-day racing plans. Soon he hoped to be fit enough to go to a race meeting.

They were having lunch when Benny phoned again. He had heard from Kipper Fish that Frankie had put his house on the market and was planning to leave the country before the end of the week. Howard laughed delightedly and passed on the good news to Jay. Although he was not a vindictive man, Jay was delighted to hear of his enemy's suffering. He added that if he ever met him face to face, Frankie's additional suffering would know no bounds.

A few weeks later, Howard was relaxing at home with Bubbles when he heard again from Benny. 'I've got some interesting information for you, guv. I've just been talking to one of my friends in the south of France.'

Howard never ceased to be amazed at how many friends Benny had on various parts of the continent. They all seemed to be people who had their ear to the somewhat dubious ground, but Howard preferred not to delve too deeply into the origins of either Benny's friends or the information they delivered.

'Well,' said Howard. 'What is it this time?'

'Our friend Frankie Johnson has got himself into serious trouble. He started to play for heavy stakes in the casinos. Maybe he was trying to recoup his losses in the UK. Whatever, he lost heavily. He then made the serious error of joining a poker school run by some tough local gamblers. That young blonde wife of his had had enough and left him. She's back in the UK. So Frankie is alone and under some pressure. He's had to sell his apartment and he's now living in a little bedsit on the outskirts of Marseilles. He's broke. I think you can say your revenge is complete.'

Howard rubbed his hands with glee. When Benny had rung off he phoned everyone involved and retold the story with relish.

Chapter Thirty

As each week passed, Jay was looking fitter and stronger. The leg was still taking a long time to heal but he was now out of his wheelchair and, getting around pretty nimbly with two crutches.

One evening Eva and he were having a quiet supper in their house when she put down her glass of wine. 'Jay, we've got to have a serious conversation,' she said.

'What about?' he asked, startled.

'Do you remember when we talked many moons ago in the Dorchester about spending the rest of our lives together?'

'Of course I do.'

'Well, if I'm not being presumptuous, does that mean that you were thinking about us getting married?'

'Absolutely. That's really what I want I mean, when you're ready, of course...'

'It's what I want, too,' she said, 'but there could be a problem.'

Jay was baffled, and suddenly anxious. What was wrong? Was she married to somebody else already and hadn't told him? He had the unpleasant sensation of a rug being inched out from under his feet.

'And what's that?' he said as evenly as he could.

'It's money.'

'How on earth can be that problem? I'm a wealthy man, we're backed by Howard and Victor, Where's the problem?'

'You don't understand,' she said.

'What don't I understand?'

'I'm worth five million.'

Jay looked at her. 'It's a really nice sum of money. Why should it be a problem? It's background security for you.'

'It's five million a year.'

Jay's jaw dropped. 'Blimey,' he said eventually.

'My father was a very wealthy and shrewd man,' Eva explained. 'As his diamond business grew, he spread his interests into other African states. Initially he had a major investment in copper in Zambia, plus tobacco in Zimbabwe. As the political situation deteriorated he gradually liquidated his assets and moved the funds to Switzerland, where it's been invested cautiously at relatively low returns, but in round terms I suppose I'm worth about £200 million.'

Jay was staggered. He just didn't know what to say. 'Well that's fantastic,' he tried lamely.

'Yes, but what do you think about it?'

'What do you mean? I think it's fantastic for you.'

'But what do you feel about marrying somebody with all that money? Doesn't it worry you?'

'I can't think why it should worry me,' he replied with a grin. 'I would have thought it was an absolute bonus.'

She half-smiled at him. 'I just wondered if you felt so much money would put you at some sort of disadvantage. Change the dynamics of our relationship.'

'Not at all,' said Jay. 'Why, do you think it will?'

'No. Not if you genuinely feel that. I know you are a very straight person, Jay, it's one of the things I love about you.'

Jay chose his words carefully. 'I think,' he said, 'that in a relationship, you always have to remember that both partners are equal. In your personal life, it doesn't matter who earns or has the most money, who works the hardest or at what. And the work part is easy for us in that respect, as we are doing it together.'

'I'm glad you said that. Because, apart from you, County View has been the best thing that's ever happened to me. The point is, I don't want to go mad with the money. I just want to go on working here, without letting Howard or Victor know we have all this cash behind us. To live a proper, sensible, fulfilling life. We've got such a great team here. I don't want to change it in any way.'

Jay picked up her hand across the table and kissed it. 'I only want it to change in one way. I want you to marry me. I really mean that.'

The tears trickled down her cheeks. 'That's exactly what I want, Jay. We have had so much fun and excitement together. And we've only just started.'

'Perhaps a little too much excitement,' he said drily. 'But as long as the money doesn't mean you want us to go and live in Monte Carlo and sit around all day doing nothing, I don't think we have a single problem, Eva. In time I am sure there will be something worthwhile you will want to do with some of it, and what you do will be fine by me. There's only one thing I regret, and that is that you didn't lead in that Cheltenham winner in your father's colours.'

'There's always next year.'

'For sure,' he smiled.

'Now, turning to practicalities – and seeing as I'm in a slightly demanding mood – when are we going to get married?'

'As soon as you like, if you don't mind marrying a cripple.'

They sat there chatting for a while, agreeing on a fairly quiet ceremony. They would ask Howard to give Eva away, and Victor to be Jay's best man, which they knew would delight both their partners. They would then invite all their friends, both racing and personal, to a reception at County View.

'Then what?' he said. 'I suppose we should go on some sort of honeymoon.'

'We're going to go on a very special honeymoon,' she said. 'Why do you think I kept that little place in Cape Town and the chalet in the game park? We'll go down to Cape Town first and get that leg of yours right, and then we'll go up and I'll show you what big game is all about in Africa.'

'That sounds wonderful,' said Jay.

They kept their secret to themselves for the rest of the day, but they were itching to tell everyone and plan the wedding. So the next morning they phoned Howard and Victor with their news. Both were overjoyed at their decision, and flattered and touched to be asked to take part. Victor, judging by the emotion in his voice, was wiping away a quiet tear in Holland Park and as for Howard, he was so over the moon he couldn't wait till he was off the phone to tell Bubbles, yelling out for her with such urgency that, she told them afterwards, she came running in from the garden thinking he had had some kind of accident.

The wedding was fixed for a Saturday four weeks away at Cirencester Church, with the reception at County View on the Sunday.

Jay and Eva's wedding day dawned clear and bright, and the bride, attended by an old schoolfriend and Freddie Kelly's two small daughters, looked absolutely stunning in ivory silk. They managed to keep the service reasonably intimate, with just their immediate circle of friends and County View 'family' in attendance, though a good crowd of well-wishers, press photographers and TV cameras gathered outside the church. Jay refused to allow the fact that he still had one leg in plaster affect any of the proceedings, and made an excellent job of escorting his new wife back up the aisle with only the vaguest hint of a limp.

On the morning of the reception Howard and Victor arrived early having stayed the night in The Shepherd's Rest. Victor asked Jay for a quiet word. He secretly withdrew an envelope from his inside pocket. 'There's something I'd like you to read.' Jay opened the envelope, read it, and hugged Victor. 'I'm not so sure why it was so important to you, but I'm delighted it's happened.'

Victor, slightly bashful, said. 'I'm thrilled too.' The letter was from the secretary of The Turf Club inviting him to become a member.

'I wonder how it happened?' he mused.

'I wonder, too,' said Jay with a smile. 'It shouldn't be a complete surprise. You've been absolutely fantastic in terms of getting this venture off the ground. Everybody knows what an important role you've played in it.'

There were tears in Victor's eyes. 'I thought you might be behind it.'

'Oh, it's not just me,' said Jay. 'You quietly made quite a few friends at the Cheltenham Festival this year. People have noticed that you're not actually all bad.' His face grew serious. 'In fact you're a hell of a good bloke, Victor,' he said in a low voice. Victor patted Jay's shoulder and walked away, not wanting his friend to see the extent of his emotion.

For the reception Jay and Eva had hired a marquee from the same company that had supplied one for the launch of County View, but this time the microphones and press packs gave way to a band and a dance floor and free-flowing champagne. Into this airy space floated friends, stable staff, owners, trainers, jockeys, trusted press friends, former publishing colleagues of Jay's and old and new friends of Eva's. Benny, beautifully turned out in a subtle, expensive-looking suit, was earnestly discussing some building matter with Hurry Henderson, while Angel, similarly attired, coped courteously and discreetly with the attentions of a rather over-refreshed titled lady. Jenny, from the PR company that helped Eva, who had become a firm friend, was trying to teach Danny to waltz, encouraged by Hal, Bart and Len, who were reveling in the company of so many well-known racing people.

Eva skipped over to Jason and Howard, breathless from doing the rounds making sure she spoke to everyone.

'Ah, my wife,' said Jason. 'I was beginning to forget what you looked like.'

Eva put her arm around him and surveyed the scene happily, her face glowing. 'It was worth getting married just to get all these people together in the same place,' she said. 'Isn't it wonderful?'

'It certainly is,' agreed Jay, giving her a squeeze. 'The only person missing is Fiona. It's such a shame she couldn't be here.'

Fiona was again abroad, and they had not been able to track her down in time to give her enough notice to rearrange her plans and fly home. She had sent an effusive telegram, and promised to see them soon.

'A word of advice from the wise,' said Howard. 'This evening will go by in a flash, so take a moment from time to time to stand back and take it all in so you remember as much as possible. I hope you will both be looking back on it for many years to come.' He raised his glass to the new couple.

As the guests left and the party officially ended, Jay and Eva went back to the house with Howard, Bubbles, Victor, Jed and Cathy for a nightcap. No doubt some of the younger guests would be there for a good while longer, but Danny, who wasn't working the following day, was with them and had volunteered to keep and eye on things. The marquee had deliberately been sited well away from the houses and stables and extra security guards were patrolling just in case of any pranks.

'Can you believe what's happened in just over a year?' mused Howard, swishing the brandy round his glass. 'It's almost like a fairy story.'

'It's been a bloody grim fairy story,' punned Jay, quick as a flash.

Everyone giggled.

'We all had our objectives,' Howard went on, 'and we've all achieved them, haven't we?'

'We certainly have,' said Eva, hugging her new husband.

'You two go off and have a great break, come back refreshed, and then we'll all sit down and plan the new campaign. We've got new fields to conquer next year, haven't we?'

'Without a shadow of a doubt,' said Jay firmly. 'This is in my blood, and we're going to be just as successful next year.

By the way, Howard, I forgot to tell you – Harry Clough phoned me last week and said he'd like me to have his horses. I was very polite and said I didn't feel that it was appropriate for a Savile Row tailor's dummy to be training horses for such an important person. He slammed the phone down on me.'

Jed laughed with delight.

'That was a bit mean of you,' said Howard. 'But who am I to criticise somebody for getting his own back on somebody who's upset him?'

'Hear, hear,' said Victor.

The next day Howard arrived in the middle of the morning, insisting on taking Eva and Jay to the airport for their flight to South Africa.

'Howard, that really isn't necessary,' said Jay.

'I know it's not necessary, but I'm still going to do it.'

He scurried off to supervise the loading of their luggage. while Jay and Eva finalised arrangements for the yard with Danny. 'You know it'll all run smoothly, guv'nor,' said Danny, 'so don't fret. As it's the end of the season proper we're not going to have many runners anyway, and we'll have plenty of time to get on with the young horses we want ready for next season.'

'I know, and I've got no problems at all about that,' said Jay, 'but if anything happens, don't hesitate to call me.'

'You phone us while we're away and God help you,' whispered Eva to Danny and Jed as Jay manoeuvred himself out to the drive.

'We wouldn't dream of it,' they chorused. 'Not for one moment.'

Howard was waiting for them by his car. 'You get in the back when you're ready, Jay, so you can put your leg up,' he instructed. 'I'm going to have the pleasure of the company of this charming young lady in the front with me. I'm going to close the partition between the front and back for some privacy and give her my considered advice on how to handle you. Because I know what a difficult bugger you are.'

'That's rich coming form you, Howard,' teased Jay.

'I'm in no position to argue.'

As soon as the aircraft had taken off Jay raised the glass of champagne that was automatically served to first-class passengers. 'Well, here's to you, Mrs Jessop,' he said.

'Here's to you, Mr Jessop. And to the next season at County View.' She kissed him lightly on the cheek and, with a contented sigh, he sat back, closed his eyes and thought, 'I never thought training racehorses was going to be like this.'

Exhausted from the rigours of the previous couple of days, Jay slept for most of the journey. As the plane began its descent, he went to the bathroom to rinse his face and clean his teeth, returning to his seat as the seatbelt signs came on. Eva seemed nervous. 'Do you get worried about landing?' he asked her. He couldn't remember her show any agitation on their flights to and from Tobago.

'Not at all.'

'It's just that you seem rather nervous.'

'Do I? I guess I'm still not used to being a wife, and I'm wondering what you're going to think of my country.'

'I know I'm going to love it. And love being with you. Just relax.'

Having cleared immigration and customs, they moved through to the arrivals hall. Looking around him, Jay was surprised to see a tall, bulky man in a chauffeur's uniform holding up a card reading 'Mr & Mrs Jessop' in large, scarlet letters.

Grinning from ear to ear, the man came over to them. 'Welcome home Miss Eva. Perhaps I should be calling you Mrs Eva, but it doesn't sound quite right.'

'This is my husband, Jason,' said Eva. 'Jay, this is Patrick. He knows everything about me, including lots of things he's promised he'll never tell you.'

Patrick grasped Jay's hand in his giant bear's paw. 'You're a very lucky person, Mr Jessop.'

'I know that,' replied Jay. 'And so is she.'

With a deep, throaty chuckle, Patrick picked up their bags and led them through to a waiting Mercedes. As he drove Eva pointed out various landmarks, including Table Mountain, capped with a layer of cloud known locally as the Tablecloth. Patrick, she explained, had been her father's chauffeur for many years, and had insisted on getting out his uniform to greet them.

The car came to a halt outside some luxurious apartments overlooking the harbour. Patrick stepped out to remove the luggage from the boot with the help of the hall porter while Jay and Eva took the lift to the top floor. 'You'll see all the seals from the balcony,' she told him excitedly.

She stopped outside the door of one of the apartments. 'This is us,' she said. But strangely, rather than producing a set of keys from her handbag, she rang the bell.

'Is there a live-in maid?' Jay asked. He hoped not.

'No,' she said. 'But inside I do have one last surprise waiting for you.'

Just then the door opened. On the threshold, to Jay's utter amazement, stood Fiona. She looked, unusually for her, slightly sheepish; nervous, even.

'Good God!' exclaimed Jay. 'What in the world are you doing here?'

'Well, that's a nice welcome I must say,' she retorted, more like the Fiona he knew and loved.

'Come on, let's go in,' said Eva.

They paused to deal with the bustle of luggage as Patrick and the hall porter appeared with their bags. 'I'll call you later if I need you,' Eva said to Patrick.

'Thank you Patrick,' added Jay. 'I look forward to spending some time with you.'

'Me too,' replied Patrick with a wide, friendly grin as he left the apartment.

Jay turned to see the two women stand there, unmoving, watching him almost apprehensively. Fiona broke away from this odd tableau and busied herself opening a bottle of champagne. She filled three glasses, passing two to the newlyweds.

'Here's to a very happy and long life for you both,' she said.

They raised their glasses and Eva cleared her throat. 'Jay,' she said. 'I'd like to introduce you to your mother-in-law.'

Jay nearly dropped his glass. 'I think I need to sit down,' he said, faintly.

He sank into the big sofa and took such a long swig of his champagne that he realized he had emptied his glass. Fiona refilled it.

'What is all this?' he asked, recovering his composure.

'Well,' said Fiona, standing up and smoothing down her skirt. 'I think you've had a big enough shock for one day. I'll leave you two to recover from the flight. And Jay to recover from the horror of finding out that I'm his mother-in-law'. She kissed them both. 'Don't worry, I'm not going to cramp your style on your honeymoon. I'd love to have dinner with you tomorrow night, when Eva and I will tell you our histories. Then you won't see me until your last few days on safari, if you don't mind me coming along then?'

Jay got to his feet and gave her a hug. 'I can't think of anyone I'd sooner have with us on safari, or more important, as my mother-in-law. I'm a really lucky man to have both of you as my family.'

Fiona's eyes filled with tears. 'I'm so happy,' she said, 'for me and for both of you.'

When Fiona had gone, Jay gave Eva a long look. 'Have you got any more surprises for me?' he asked sternly. 'In the last few weeks, I've found out that you're a multimillionairess and now if turns out one of my longest-standing friends is my mother-in-law. Have you got any children that I don't know about?'

'No,' smiled Eva. 'No more skeletons in the cupboard. Come on, let's get some sleep.'

'Let's go to bed by all means,' said Jay, 'but I'm not at all sure that after all this excitement it's sleep that I need. It is our honeymoon, after all.'

'So it is,' replied Eva. She took hand and led him into a huge bedroom – their bedroom – with a king-sized bed. On the pillow nestled a horseshoe with a little label attached to it. 'Good luck to both of you,' it read. 'This is one of the shoes that Splendid Warrior wore when he won his first Gold Cup. I though it was appropriate to keep it for a special occasion. Love, Fiona.'

THE END